D0430780

IRRESISTIBLE TEMPTATION

Matt turned to go, only to have Jade's words bring him up short. "If there's any repentin' to be done tonight, preacher man, maybe those prayers ought to be yers, 'cause for a minute there ye were starin' at me like I was the only piece o' candy in the whole store."

He offered her a lazy, heart-stopping grin and replied smoothly, "I'm partial to butterscotch and cinnamon, and I suppose, with your coloring, if those two flavors could be combined, they'd add up to you."

"Sugar and spice, and all things nice?" she bantered back coquettishly.

His smile widened. "More like nice and naughty, I'd venture."

Other Avon Books by
Catherine Hart

SPLENDOR
TEMPEST
TEMPTATION

CATHERINE HART

IRRESISTIBLE

AVON BOOKS ◆ NEW YORK

IRRESISTIBLE is an original publication of Avon Books. This work has never before appeared in book form. This work is a novel. Any similarity to actual persons or events is purely coincidental.

AVON BOOKS
A division of
The Hearst Corporation
1350 Avenue of the Americas
New York, New York 10019

Copyright © 1994 by Diane Tidd
Inside cover author photograph by Tamara Coates, courtesy of Olan Mills Studios
Cover art by Assel Studios
Published by arrangement with the author
Library of Congress Catalog Card Number: 93-91669
ISBN: 0-380-76876-3

First Avon Books Printing: February 1994

AVON TRADEMARK REG. U.S. PAT. OFF. AND IN OTHER COUNTRIES, MARCA REGISTRADA. HECHO EN U.S.A.

Printed in the U.S.A.

RA 10 9 8 7 6 5 4 3 2 1

❧ *Chapter 1* ❧

Richmond, Virginia—September 1866

"**J**ust where might ye be sneakin' off to, at this wee hour o' the night, Sean O'Neall?" Jade asked suddenly, her words shattering the silence of the shadowed room like a cannon shot, making the man before her give a startled jump. She'd awakened just in time to find her husband-to-be creeping toward the door, his knapsack packed and slung over his shoulder, one hand reaching toward the lock. "And aren't ye a sight to behold? Tiptoein' about like a thief, with yer shoes in one hand and me purse in t'other?" she chided, though 'twas a wonder she could speak beyond the growing lump in her throat. Belying her brave speech, her emerald eyes begged him to deny what she was witnessing.

He did not. Though his face flamed with guilt at being caught, he announced brusquely, "I'm leavin', Jade. I'll not be comin' back, and I won't be marryin' ye, lass. Ye were a fool t' believe I would."

Pulling herself upright on her pillows, she stared at him with bright, condemning eyes. "Ye set out to deceive me from the start, Sean? Is that what ye're tellin' me now? All the way from Ireland to Richmond, ye ne'er spoke one word o' truth, did ye? Beggin' for me favors, promisin' 'twould be all right t' give meself to ye, 'cause we'd be wed once we set foot ashore in America. Whisperin' sweet lies, while ye stole me virtue. And I believed ye, dunce that I am."

Blinking back hot tears, determined not to give him the satisfaction of seeing her cry or hearing her beg, she tossed a tangled strand of red-gold hair over her shoulder. "Where are ye off to now, boyo? To lay more blarney on another innocent victim?"

"In a manner of speakin'," he agreed, nodding his head as if to doff his cap to her. "Ye're as pretty a lass as ever there was, Jade, and ye turned into quite an eager, pleasin' little bunkmate once ye'd gotten a taste o' lovin'. A lively diversion on a long, dreary sea voyage. I'll miss our bouts betwixt the sheets, luv, but 'tis a rich American wife I'm needin' now. I'll not settle for bein' just another poor Mick on the streets. I want land and horses and handsome clothes on me back, and plenty of coin jinglin' a merry tune in me pocket."

"Speakin' o' which, 'tis me own coin warmin' yer hand this minute, and I'll thank ye to give it back," she hissed, reaching her palm toward him. " 'Tis all I have. I slaved many a month in that vermin-infested tavern o' Uncle Tobias's, dodgin' graspin' hands and lewd offers all the while, to save even that piddlin' sum."

Edging the door open, Sean shook his head and offered a lame, apologetic smile. "Nay, Jade. I'll be needin' the money for my own purpose, darlin'. Ye see, I have to buy some fancy clothes, the better to impress the rich American ladies and their families. Just use yer natural talents and all I've taught ye these past weeks, and ye'll get by fine as a fiddle." He gave a careless shrug and added, "Sorry, luv."

"Ye're sorry a'right," Jade snapped back, crawling from the bed and yanking the sheet after her. She wrapped the bedding about her and started toward him, her eyes narrowed into green slits. "Ye're the sorriest bastard I ever set eyes on. A'top o' that, ye're as dumb as dirt, to abandon a woman who loves ye the way I do. I'm the best ye'll find, and if ye forsake me now, ye don't need to come crawlin' back when yer grand plans don't work out for ye."

She tripped on the hem of her makeshift gown, nearly tumbling to the floor before she regained her balance. As it was, one bare breast popped over the top edge of the sheet. Sean's smile widened into a smirk. "As temptin' as it is to stay and accept all ye're barin' b'fore me, I'll still take me chances elsewhere. Yer charms, sweet as they are, don't hold a candle to the lure of land and money, darlin'."

He slipped into the hallway and pulled the door swiftly shut behind him, just in time to avoid the shoe Jade scooped up from the floor and hurled at his head.

Her enraged shriek followed him down the hall. "Rot in bloody Hell, Sean O'Neall!"

An answering bellow came from the room next to theirs. "Pipe down and save your fight 'til morning, will you? We're trying to get some sleep here!"

Humiliated, distraught, and completely heartbroken, Jade spent the remainder of the night huddled in a sobbing ball on the bed. When some time had passed, and it appeared Sean was not going to relent and return as she'd hoped he might, she arose and locked the door once more. Silently, so as not to further disturb others lodging in the run-down hotel, she ranted and raved, pounding her small fists into the pillows, then hugging them to her aching chest in a vain search for some small measure of comfort. She railed at herself for being such a gullible idiot, and at Sean for being such a black-hearted rascal.

"How could I have been so blind, to fall into his trap so neatly?" she wailed to herself. "Why, 'tis as if I was ripe for the pluckin'!"

Truthfully, she had been just that. For the past four years, since her parents had died and she had gone to live with Uncle Tobias and Aunt Bess, Jade had been little more than an unpaid servant for her father's relatives. She'd waited tables in their Dublin tavern and taken more abuse, both verbally and physically, than anyone should have been asked to tolerate. And all the while, she'd somehow managed to safeguard her virtue in the most trying of circumstances. But for how much longer, she could not guess, for though she was petite, her figure had matured nicely in the past year or so. Even Uncle Tobias had begun casting lecherous glances toward her, and Aunt Bess had become more sour with each passing day.

Then along had come Sean O'Neall, with twinkling gray eyes and a smile that could woo the birds from the trees, and Jadeen Agnes Donovan had tumbled headlong into love for the first time in her sixteen years. Two years older than she, the young man had more charm than a leprechaun—and was ever so much more handsome.

However, even this advantage did not immediately gain Sean all he sought. Jade had been fending off advances for far too long, and though thoroughly besotted with him, she was not about to award her virginity to the first suitor to strike her fancy. Rather, she stuck to her principles, and soon became such a challenge to him that Sean rashly proposed one evening.

This immediately presented another problem. Though Jade's maternal grandmother had been Catholic, the rest of the Donovan clan was of the Protestant persuasion. The O'Nealls were staunch Catholics, and predictably resentful of anyone who wasn't. Particularly Irish Protestants, whom they considered nothing more than turncoats and profiteers, grabbing up property the Catholics had been forced to relinquish years before under British command. While Protestants, even the poor ones, were not restricted from educating their children, gaining government positions, and owning land, Irish Catholics were scarcely holding a place in their own country, and that by a thin thread of dogged determination. Bitterness ran deep on both sides.

"How can we marry?" Jade had asked Sean then. "Uncle Tobias would kill me before he'd see me married to a Catholic, and yer family would likely do the same."

Sean had agreed. "No doubt yer uncle intends to control yer inheritance for many a day to come."

She'd scoffed openly. "What inheritance? 'Twas lost b'fore I was born, when the blight took the potato crops. All that's left is the farmhouse and four measly acres, fit only for raisin' pigs. Who in his right mind would want it?"

"Yer greedy uncle, for one. And he has his eye on yer skirts as well."

A few weeks later, matters came to a head when Tobias trapped Jade in the pantry. Despite her frantic cries for help and her efforts to defend herself against his superior bulk and strength, he quickly maneuvered her into the corner with her skirts about her waist. He was fumbling with the buttons on his britches when Aunt Bess charged into the tiny room. Shrieking like a banshee, the stout woman grabbed a broom and began beating her husband over the head and shoulders, pausing only long enough to aim a few glancing blows at Jade as the frightened girl made good her escape.

Jade sought shelter in her attic bedroom, and was still quivering with reaction when Bess found her there. "Pack yer bags and be off with ye, missy," the older woman ordered nastily. "And don't be walkin' off with nothin' what don't belong to ye or I'll have the law on yer tail b'fore ye can blink twice. Them what wants to switch their skirts about ain't doin' it here, niece or no. Why, yer da's probably rollin' over in 'is grave!"

Momentarily stunned by her aunt's venom, though she'd received much the same in the past, Jade finally found her tongue as anger overrode good sense. "Ye're right, Bess. Da is most likely spinnin' like a top, and Ma b'side him, if he can see how his dear brother and sister-in-law have been lookin' after his only child all this time."

"Well! That's gratitude for ye! After all we done for ye! Takin' ye in when yer folks died. Givin' ye a roof over yer head and food for yer belly, and puttin' clothes on yer back . . ."

"Ha! A straw pallet beneath leaky rafters, patched clothes from the charity bin at the church, and whatever leftover food I could find in the bottom of the kitchen kettle after a long night o' servin' whiskey and suppers to yer drunken pinch-penny customers! Gettin' me bum pinched black and blue at every turn, hidin' under tables durin' brawls, gettin' drenched with ale when some clumsy sot knocks over his tankard. Slavin' day and night, and all without a pence for pay. Aye, Aunt, I've so much to be grateful for!"

"And now ye've got less than that, ye fresh-faced tart," Bess reminded her hatefully. "I want ye gone b'fore nightfall, and good riddance to ye!"

It had taken no time at all to pack her two spare dresses, both stained and tattered beyond redemption, and her extra threadbare petticoat. These, a comb and brush, her flute, and the small cache of tips she'd earned over four years' time and managed to hide from view, were quickly bound into a bundle, along with a pilfered sliver of soap, a washcloth, and a towel. If Bess even missed them, Jade would be surprised, and if she were mean enough to send the law after her for taking them, Jade figured she'd be better off in jail than back with Bess and Tobias.

Jade was three blocks away from the tavern when Sean caught up with her. "Jade! What's goin' on? I stopped by the tavern, and yer aunt all but ripped me ears from me head when I asked where ye were! After callin' ye every sorry name she could think of, she told me she'd tossed ye out for temptin' Tobias with yer wicked wiles."

Jade kept walking. "Aye, that she did. And they'll be missin' me more'n I'll be missin' them, to be sure. 'Specially when Bess has to serve tonight's customers."

Sean pulled her to a stop and asked earnestly, "What are ye goin' to do now? Where will ye go? Where will ye stay?"

"As I've nowhere else to go, I'm headin' back to the farm."

"But, lass, that's two days' walk from here! And what'll ye do when ye get there?"

"I've no idea, but I suppose I'll figure somethin' out sooner or later. That or starve."

"Come to America with me, Jade," Sean blurted suddenly.

Jade's eyes widened in surprise. "America?" she echoed.

"Aye. That's what I was comin' to tell you. I'm sailin' for Richmond, Virginia, in the mornin', workin' my way across on a passenger ship."

"Ye're leavin'? Tomorrow?" Jade was stunned. And hurt that he was telling her now, when he'd professed to love her so.

This should have been her first indication of what an unscrupulous jackal Sean truly was, how untrustworthy, but she'd been through too much this day to think clearly enough to recognize the warning signs. It never occurred to her at that moment to question Sean's odd reluctance to discuss marriage since he'd first proposed to her, or to ask herself whether it might have something to do with the fact that she'd told him how little she would eventually inherit. After all, he'd still come 'round regularly to see her, still sworn his love and passion for her, and still tried to win more than sweet kisses for his time.

Only one thought stood out immediately in her mind. "How could ye ask me to marry ye one month and run off to America the next? And be tellin' me a day b'fore ye sail?"

"I intended to go, secure work and a place to live, and then send for ye, darlin'," he'd lied smoothly. "But now that ye've nowhere to lay yer pretty head, we'll have to make new plans, eh? Or don't ye want to go with me, if we can arrange it on such short notice? Have ye changed yer mind about marryin' me, Jade?"

"No. I love ye, Sean, and I want to go with ye, but . . ."

"Then let's get hoppin', lass. Time's a-wastin', and America, the land of opportunity, awaits." He paused, then added a final note of encouragement. "Once there, we can be married without causin' such a fuss. There, they don't give a care if ye're Protestant or Catholic or wearin' three heads, as long as ye have the cost of the weddin' license."

That had settled it, at least in Jade's mind. She trudged hopefully along beside Sean to the docks. There, he went alone aboard the ship to talk with the captain about obtaining passage for her. When he returned at last, he said, "Now don't be gettin' yer feathers in a ruffle, lass, but I had to tell the captain we were already married, or ye wouldn't be sailin' with me. And we won't be travelin'

in grand style. It took all me powers o' persuasion to get
the man to find quarters for the two o' us, and that but a
wee room behind the galley."

"Galley?"

" 'Tis what they call the kitchen aboard a ship," Sean
explained. " 'Twas that or a space in the hold." At her
befuddled look, he elaborated. "Below decks, in the bow-
els o' the ship, where all the cargo is stored. All dank and
dark, and little better than a dungeon."

Jade grimaced.

"Uh, sweetlin', I really hate to ask, but would ye have
any coin a'tall t' help pay for yer passage? I'm workin'
mine off, but yers is extra, to pay for the blankets and food
and such. Not as much as regular passage and quarters
mind ye, but . . ."

"How much?"

Sean quoted a sum equal to half of her savings. "And a
mite more for extra biscuits and fruit for ourselves, which
I'm told we'll probably need."

Though it pained her to spend that much, Jade handed
the money over to Sean, already dreaming of the day
they would alight in America and become man and wife,
already picturing the house and family they would have
one day in their new home.

As he pocketed her coin, Sean gave her a wide grin and
planted a kiss on her lips, his eyes shining as brightly as
hers. "Don't worry, Jade," he promised. "I'll take care of
everythin'. All the little details. It's smooth sailin' from
here on, lass."

Smooth sailing? Hardly. At least not for Jade. Scarcely had they cleared the harbor when she began to feel
queasy. By the time they'd reached the ocean, she was
huddled over the chamber pot in their quarters, too sick
to care if she lived or died in this "wee room" the size
of a broom closet, which reeked mightily of onions and
cabbage and cooking grease from the adjacent kitchen.
Fully half the voyage was past, and Sean in a surly mood
over her continued malady, before the mal de mer eased
sufficiently for Jade to retain her meals.

Still weak, but much improved, Jade set about straightening their quarters and airing the bedding as best she could. Though it took some wheedling, she talked the cook into giving her sufficient fresh water to wash herself and her hair, reminding him that until now she had not used her allotted measure of food and drink, though she had paid for it.

By the time Sean was relieved of his duties and returned to their room, he was pleasantly surprised at the change. "Lord, lass, 'tis good to see some color in yer face, other than that putrid green hue ye've assumed since castin' off. I was beginnin' t'wonder if ye were ever goin' to recover."

Now that she no longer had her head stuck in a bucket twenty-four hours a day, Sean seemed to make it his mission in life to seduce her as quickly as possible. When she demurred, wanting to consummate their vows after their marriage, he argued, "What difference will a couple of weeks make, Jade? B'sides, after travelin' together and sleepin' side by side all this while, who would believe differently if ye told 'em? Everyone will suppose ye've already given yerself to me. Or is it somethin' else holdin' ye back? Maybe ye've had a change o' heart and decided ye don't love me after all?"

"I *do* love ye, Sean. I do."

"Then prove it, Jade, the way a woman shows a man how much she cares. The only way that truly counts."

So persistent was he, so utterly beguiling, with those sweet smiles, honeyed kisses, enticing caresses, that Jade could no longer resist him. And his reasoning did make sense, after a fashion. From all appearances, they were already wedded and she bedded; only two weeks separated fact from fabrication.

Until this very night, lying heartbroken and bereft in a lonely, shabby Richmond hotel room, Jade had not once regretted her decision to give herself to Sean. Not once in the past fortnight, fourteen joyous days and nights filled with wondrous passion and glorious promise, had she suspected him capable of such deceit. To her, their love, the joining of their hearts and bodies, had been so precious, so everlasting—almost too good to be real.

And now she would pay the price for her naïveté. She was stranded in a strange city with no friends and not a penny to her name. How would she survive? Sean hadn't left her a single coin with which to buy food or to continue to rent their hotel room, and sneaking off as he had, he probably hadn't bothered to settle their account before leaving either. And now she must do the same, or risk being arrested by the management and tossed in jail.

"Damn ye, Sean O'Neall!" she swore softly. "Damn ye for all eternity!"

Swallowing down yet another sob, Jade arose and began to stuff her meager belongings into a pillowcase. A chance glimpse of her image in the cracked mirror over the bureau clearly revealed the ravages of the night just spent. Her face was blotched and tearstained, her eyes swollen nearly shut from crying.

A glance in the opposite direction showed the soft gray light of dawn creeping around the ragged edges of the window shade. Morning was just minutes away, the start of another day—and Jade had no idea how she was going to get through it. This was to have been her wedding day, but with a few curt words, her dreams had turned to ashes—and she from wife to waif.

ঙ্কিকে Chapter 2 কিউকে

Georgetown, Kentucky—September 1866

Reverend Matthew Richards collapsed into the chair in front of the fireplace in his study and dragged a shaking hand over his pale face. Dear Lord, he thought prayerfully, it's a good thing I don't believe in committing suicide, for this certainly would have been the day for it. The sum total of my twenty-six years of trials and tribulations upon this earth.

His head lolled against the back of the chair as he allowed his weary body to claim what rest it might. Unfortunately, he could not do the same for his mind, or his conscience. A heavy, heartfelt sigh rose from within his aching chest. "Why, Cynthia? Why did it have to be this way?"

Matt didn't really expect an answer, nor did he suppose he would have much more time for self-pity. The children would be wanting his attention soon, and he could probably count the few minutes of solitude remaining to him on one hand.

It had been this way since three days past, when he'd first been notified of his young wife's death. From that moment on, he'd been swamped with sympathetic, well-wishing parishioners who seemed to arrive in droves to take charge of his life, while he had been too numb with the shock of Cynthia's death to do so himself. They'd brought dinners and baked goods by the ton and arranged to watch over the children until he could function properly again. They'd fed the animals and cleaned the house to within an inch of its existence. They'd even offered to find another minister to officiate at the funeral, if it would make matters easier for Matt.

On this last, Matt had firmly declined. Cynthia had been his wife, and he would conduct her funeral service. Though he did not say so openly, in his heart he felt he owed her that final homage. So, today he had stood before friends and family and neighbors, over the open grave and flower-bedecked casket, and bid a final farewell to his wife of three short years.

Afterward, amidst the throng of mourners that had invaded his home, he had still found no peace, not a moment to himself in which to properly grieve her passing. He'd said all the right words, shaken hundreds of hands, even tried to ease the sorrow he knew others felt at losing her from their lives. But time for his own personal grieving had not yet been granted, though his heart felt as if it were bound with flame-tipped barbs, and hot, salty tears stung the backs of his eyelids.

Now, finally, the last mourner had departed. Only Matt, his two elderly household servants, and the children remained. For the moment, an odd silence reigned. A rare phenomenon in this bustling household on any day. But Matt knew that Edna and George had shepherded the twelve children into the kitchen for their supper and probably admonished all of them, or those old enough to comprehend the situation, to be quiet for a time. To give him a moment alone at last.

Though he greatly appreciated their kindness, Matt knew that before long, the youngsters would be getting ready for bed, and for prayers, and his presence would be required once more. Not until each little head rested neatly upon its pillow, and twenty-four bright, curious eyes had drifted shut, would he face that long-delayed encounter with his searing soul. For now, there were only a few minutes for brief reflection upon the life he'd led until three days ago.

From the first moment he'd met Cynthia Ann Johnson, she'd been vivacious, demanding, and outrageously spoiled. She was everyone's darling, a blond porcelain doll of such exquisite beauty that it almost hurt to look at her.

He had been twenty-one, fresh out of seminary, and newly employed as resident minister and teacher of Bible studies at the prestigious Daughters College in Harrodsburg, Kentucky, when Miss Johnson had first been enrolled that fall of 1861, five long years ago. Cynthia was but one of many daughters from affluent families sent to Daughters College during the War Between the States in the hope that there they would be safe from the fighting, since Kentucky was making the vain attempt to remain neutral through the conflict.

She'd been sixteen then, and quite put out that the war had disrupted her debut into society and her plans to be the next belle of Lexington. Nor was she at all happy about being shuffled off to a girls' school, where available admirers were as rare as hens' teeth. All in all, she was a poor student, determined to be thoroughly disconsolate and to make everyone else as miserable as she was. Until the day, nearly a year later, when she suddenly and inexplicably set her cap for Matt. Then, quite abruptly, she became the model student, a paragon of feminine arts and graces, a woman any man would cherish.

That day would stand out in Matt's memory forever. It was October 8, 1862, and the Battle of Perryville had been raging throughout the day just a few miles southwest of Harrodsburg. Cannon fire had been booming steadily, and area churches were being set up as temporary hospitals for the wounded soldiers from both sides of the battle. Accounts of tremendous casualties were being reported.

The girls at the college were understandably upset. A number of them had close male relatives fighting in the war—some for the North, some for the South—and a few had family members who were fighting on opposite sides, against each other. Even those whose families were not involved were anxious, fearful that the fighting would make its way closer and put them all in grave danger.

That was when Cynthia, her violet eyes misty, had literally thrown herself into Matt's arms. "Oh, Reverend Richards! I'm so dreadfully frightened!" she'd gasped breathlessly. "Whatever will we do if the soldiers come here? Will you protect me, sir?"

Stunned by her forward behavior, but thoroughly enjoying the unexpected attention of this young woman whose beauty he had admired from afar for so many months, Matt had answered, "If the need arises, I will lay down my own life to save yours, Miss Johnson."

That had been the start of their relationship. By Christmas, they were engaged. Despite the ongoing war, their wedding was held at her family home in Lexington in June of the next year, following Cynthia's graduation from the college. And then, almost before they had consummated their marriage, Matt's perfect wife began to regress into an utter shrew.

First, she badgered Matt ceaselessly to give up his employment at the college and move closer to Lexington so that she might be nearer her family. When an offer came for him to pastor a church in Georgetown, just north of Lexington, he thought she would at last be happy. She was, for approximately a month. Then, not content to live solely on the salary of a preacher and reside in the modest home allotted them, Cynthia complained to her father until the man bought them a grand house on twenty rolling acres and presented it to them as a belated wedding gift.

No pauper himself, though not nearly as well off as the Johnsons, and certainly not as prone to extravagance, Matt was genuinely provoked. He and his bride had many a spat over the property and the subsequent furnishing of their new abode. Though she'd been agreeable enough before the wedding, it now seemed that nothing he did satisfied her. Their thoughts and wishes were never in accord.

When he suggested that they start a family, she did not want to ruin her waistline. She threatened him with divorce when he first introduced the idea of starting a home for children orphaned by the war, but promptly changed her tune when her own father told her he would disinherit her if she dared disgrace the Johnson name with such scandal. When the orphans began arriving, she moved her clothing and personal effects into a spare bedroom and refused to honor her conjugal obligations. From that day until her death, a full year and a half later, Matt did not bed his wife.

Yet, despite all this, Matt did not denounce her to anyone. He kept his personal problems to himself, literally biting his tongue while Cynthia presented a benevolent, gracious attitude to the outside world and acted the harridan behind closed doors. As far as everyone else knew, with the possible exception of her father, Cynthia was the perfect pastor's wife. Polite. Pleasant. Soft-spoken. Compassionate. Giving her time and energy toward the betterment of the homeless children she helped shelter. No one knew how she carped at those poor orphans, how often Matt had to comfort the little ones after Cynthia had screamed at them over some minor or imagined infraction.

No, to outside eyes she seemed exemplary. And everyone was so distressed when her horse threw her, killing her and the child she carried. A child they all mistakenly assumed was Matt's. They'd all turned out to her funeral, to console the bereaved widower, their beloved pastor. The man who now sat consumed, not with grief but with anger. And with guilt.

Only Matt knew that he and his wife had engaged in the most violent argument before she'd stormed out of the house that last day of her life. That she'd admitted her sin proudly before him, flaunting the news that she was carrying another man's baby. Taunting him with the fact that she would gladly bear her lover's child while she denied him one of his own flesh and blood. And Matt would have to claim it as his or give her the divorce she wanted.

Furious, reacting purely on reflex and the intense pain she'd so cruelly inflicted upon him, he'd said he wished she would magically disappear from his life and cease to be such a constant source of anguish to him. His impulsive request had been granted before the day was out.

Her death. The death of an innocent, unborn babe. These would be burdens his soul would bear for all eternity.

Richmond, Virginia—September 1866

The woman cautiously parted the curtains covering the darkened window overlooking her back yard and peered into the inky night, trying to locate the source of the small sound she thought she'd heard just moments before. Something moved in the shadows by the kitchen steps. The tin plate of scraps she'd set out for the cats rattled slightly. For a moment she thought the dim shape hunched over the plate was a large dog. Then it straightened, taking the form of a small human. Too frail to be a man—it was either a woman or a child. Silently, the lady of the house moved away from the window and hurried down to the lower floor.

For more than a week now, Jade had been living on the streets of Richmond, simply striving to exist. During the day she searched for work, but had little success. There were no jobs to be had in Richmond, a city ravaged by the recently ended War Between the States. At night she sought shelter in darkened doorways or under stairs, anywhere that looked safe and dry.

She had quickly learned to hide from the men who roamed the streets and alleyways intent on robbery and rape. And from other homeless women and children who were just as destitute as she, who would steal what few possessions she had left. Already she'd had several frightening encounters, and it was only by the grace of God that she had escaped unharmed thus far.

From these same people, she'd also learned to watch for homes and businesses that discarded their garbage in the evening, putting leftover food into refuse bins or on compost piles. The few gardens she chanced upon had already been harvested of most of their fruits and vegetables and offered little sustenance. Even begging had earned her little more than a regretful shake of the head or a sharp warning to be on her way or rue the consequences.

With each passing day, Jade grew more bedraggled, more hungry, more weary and despondent. Surely, if she had to go on like this much longer, she would either starve or be murdered, as had so many others like her.

She was sorting through the odd pieces of food on the tin plate, trying to identify them and to convince herself that they were still edible, when the rear door of the house abruptly opened. Startled, she dropped the plate and turned to run.

"Wait!" a woman's voice commanded softly. "Come up onto the porch, where I can see you more clearly."

When Jade hesitated, the lady said, "Don't be afraid. I just want to get a better look at you. Then I can decide if you appear harmless enough to invite into the kitchen for a decent meal."

Just the thought of palatable food made Jade's mouth begin to water. Cautiously, she advanced up the steps, into the glow of the light coming from beyond the threshold.

"Oh, my!" the woman crooned. "You're a little thing, aren't you? And as much in need of a good scrubbing as you are of food, it seems." She motioned Jade forward. "Come on in here, and let's see what we can do for you, dearie."

She backed away from the entrance, waiting for Jade to follow, then turned toward a nearby stove and dragged out a heavy skillet. Just inside the door now, Jade waited, not at all sure if the woman meant to cook with the pan or beat her over the head with it. The woman waved her toward a chair, shaking her head in pity as Jade involuntarily flinched at her innocent gesture.

"Sit down, before you faint dead away. Why, from the looks of you, a stiff wind would blow you clean across the state," Opening a cupboard, the woman pulled out half of an apple pie. From a drawer, she brought forth a fork and

set both on the table before Jade. "There you go, sugar.
Dig into that while I see what else the larder holds."

Jade didn't need to be told twice. Grabbing the fork,
she began shoveling the pie into her mouth so fast it was
a wonder she didn't choke on it. "Slow down a bit," her
benefactress warned with a low chuckle. "Let your tongue
have time to taste it. There's more comin'."

Soon, the aroma of eggs and refried potatoes met Jade's
disbelieving nose. Without turning from her task, the woman said, "I'm known as Vera. What's your name, sugar?
And how old are you?"

"Jade," she said, the answer muffled by a mouthful of
pie. "Jade Donovan, ma'am. And I'll turn seventeen the
week after Christmas."

"Married?"

At this, Jade did choke. "I thought to be, but Sean had
other plans. He stole me purse and was off b'fore ye could
say Willy be still."

"Left you stranded, did he?" The woman shook her
head in sympathy. "Men will do that, like as not, contrary
creatures that they are. Better any day to have their coin in
your pocket than promises of undying love. It lasts longer
and spends further."

A plate of eggs, potatoes, and cold chicken, accompanied by a tall glass of cold milk, appeared beneath
Jade's nose. While she ate, more slowly now that the
edge was off her hunger, Vera watched her with assessing
brown eyes. Finally, her shrunken stomach full to bursting, Jade pushed the plate away and sighed contentedly.
"I thank ye, ma'am. That be the first time in weeks I've
had me fill, and I'm only sorry I have no coin to repay
yer kindness."

"Maybe you can sing for your supper," Vera suggested
wryly.

Jade grinned, a smile transforming her face and giving
Vera a hint of the beauty that lay beneath the dirt. "Aye,
that I could. My Da used to say I had a fine voice, though
Aunt Bess was not overimpressed."

"Aunt Bess?" Vera questioned with a raised brow.

Nodding, Jade explained. "After me parents died, I worked for her and Uncle Tobias in their tavern in Dublin, layin' down drinks and such."

"And did you lay down more than that, little Jade?"

"Pardon?"

Vera laughed. "No, I suppose not, or you wouldn't look so confused. Never mind, girl. So you sing, do you? And can you dance, too?"

Jade spared the woman a disbelieving look. "I'm Irish, aren't I?" she replied, as if that said it all. "O'course I can dance. 'Tis born in me blood."

"Have you ever heard of a hurdy-gurdy?" Vera went on. When she received a baffled look, she offered, "A dance hall, perhaps?"

Jade shook her head.

"Ah, what a sheltered lamb you are, for all your misfortunes!" Vera chuckled. "This place," she continued with a wave, indicating the house about them, "is a dance hall, commonly referred to as a hurdy-gurdy house. Here I, and the girls I employ, entertain gentlemen. We offer them music, dancing partners for a price, drinks, and companionship for the evening. Are you starting to get the idea now?"

Utterly flabbergasted, Jade stared at Vera, her mouth agape and her eyes wide. This middle-aged woman, in her nightdress and slippers, her face washed to a rosy glow, looked so normal—so motherly! "Ye run a—a brothel?" she stammered. "Here?"

"Well, we prefer to think of it in kinder terms, but that's what it boils down to, yes," Vera admitted. "I'm prepared to offer you a position with us, if you are so inclined."

Jade stiffened, rising from her chair. "I won't earn me way on me back. I know I'm beholden to ye for feedin' me, but I won't repay ye by sellin' me body."

"Now, Jade, I didn't say you had to. The meal was free, with no strings attached. And if you want a job here, you wouldn't be forced to entertain upstairs, if you didn't want to, dear. You could merely serve drinks, take your turn at dancing, be lovely and congenial, and, if your voice is adequate, perhaps you could entertain our guests with a song or two during the course of the evening."

"That's all?" Jade asked suspiciously. "No sellin' me favors?"

"Not unless you decide otherwise, though the pay is better for those who do. However, you can still earn a considerable amount of money without it. Of course, you would need a good gown or two to start with, as our guests expect to see our girls well dressed. I would be pleased to loan you the necessary funds for your working clothes and take it out of your pay in small increments. Also, there is a modest weekly charge for your room and board, but nothing too burdensome. Think about it, Jade. Food and shelter and pay—or life back on the streets . . . with winter coming."

"Can I stay the night and think about it?" Jade asked hesitantly, almost too weary to stand upright, let alone sort through the turbulent thoughts rioting through her tired brain. All she wanted at this moment was a safe, clean place to lay her head.

Vera smiled. "I'll show you to a room. And tomorrow you can have a hot bath and meet the other ladies in my employ and impress us all with your talents at song and dance."

Chapter 3

𝕵ade woke late the next day, and slowly. The longer she could remain asleep, the longer this impossibly wonderful dream would remain. She was floating on a cushion of clouds, bathed in sunshine. Somewhere, there was coffee brewing, bacon frying, and biscuits baking, and the aroma was heavenly. Almost real. So much so that Jade instinctively lifted her nose from the feather-soft warmth and sniffed in delight. Her brow furrowed in confusion as the smell lingered. Cautiously, lest she chase the illusion away too soon, she eased her eyelids open.

It took her a moment to recognize the strange surroundings and to recall how she had come to be in this small, tidy room with the sun creating lacy patterns through the curtains at the window. Last night, or more accurately this morning, since it had been nearly five A.M. by the time Vera had led her up the stairs and into this snug little haven, Jade had been too tired to appreciate more than the feather bed and fluffy pillows that beckoned her. Now she took note of the armoire in one corner, the chest of drawers, the little dressing table near the door, the cheerful flowers-and-ivy paper on the walls.

She sighed and burrowed farther into the mattress, reluctant to leave the cozy bed but knowing that she must soon relinquish its comforts. She could not remain here. This was a bawdy house, where women sold their favors and performed unspeakable acts with men who paid them! A den of debauchery—though Jade wasn't sure exactly what constituted debauchery, and was just a wee bit curious in some dark corner of her mind. Everyone condemned it, but no one ever explained it, which only made it seem that much more mysterious and evil. No, this was not the place for her, as peaceful and comfortable as it might appear at this moment.

Jade was still attempting to convince herself to get up when the door opened and a young woman with frizzy caramel curls peeked inside, sweeping Jade with an inquisitive hazel-hued glance. "Oh, good! You're awake!" she announced, breezing into the room. "I didn't want to disturb you, but your bath is about to arrive. And breakfast won't stay warm much longer."

No sooner were those words spoken than a giant of a man entered, his muscles bulging as he lugged a big brass tub into the room. Jade shrank beneath the bedcovers as the burly fellow sent her a mildly assessing look and left as quickly as he'd come.

Seeing Jade's stunned expression, the girl laughed. "Oh, don't mind Butch. He looks like an ape, but he's fairly harmless. Vera hired him to keep the customers from gettin' rowdy. I get the notion it drives him a tad crazy that she won't let him touch any of us girls, but he needs the money too badly to go against her rules—and she'd probably shoot him if he did."

Four more ladies entered, each carrying a bucket of warm water, and behind them came Vera with soap and towels. "Good morning, Jade. Did you sleep well?"

"Aye. Thank ye." Jade continued to huddle beneath the sheets.

"Good." Vera motioned toward the others. "I want you to meet my girls. This is Bliss," she said, gesturing toward the first woman who had come in. "Then we have Mavis, Peaches, Lizette and Fancy. The others are still at breakfast. You can meet them a little later. Girls, this is Jade Donovan. I'll leave her in your capable hands."

With that, Vera was gone, shutting the door firmly behind her, and before Jade quite knew what was happening, the "ladies" were taking over. Bliss tugged the sheet from Jade's grip as Mavis and Fancy pulled her to her feet. One of them, Lizette perhaps, whisked Jade's filthy petticoat over her head. Then, clucking and chattering, they led Jade, naked as the day she was born and blushing fit to set her hair aflame, toward the tub of water and helped her into it.

Despite her acute embarrassment, Jade could not contain a sigh of pleasure. The water felt marvelous. And when Peaches, with her sleek mahogany mane and eyes that shone like gold coins, poured in a liberal dose of lilac scent, it smelled like heaven. Jade wanted to wallow in it forever! But her companions had other ideas. Two of them took charge of washing her hair, while another pair concentrated on her body. Much to Jade's concern, she was set upon by four very determined sets of hands, all scrubbing and tugging and giving directions at once.

"Close your eyes, honey, so the suds don't sting."

"Lift your chin a bit, Jade."

"Sit up, sugar, so I can reach your back."

No sooner had she attempted to do so than another of them lifted her leg, and Jade slid backward, her head plunging beneath the soapy water. She bobbed back up, aided by a firm grasp on her dripping hair, and gasped for air. As the water drained from her ears, she heard Peaches exclaim, "Lord A'mighty, Fancy, whatcha tryin' to do, drown her? Ain't she been through enough?"

About this time, just as Jade was praying she might survive this bizarre ordeal, someone grabbed her foot and began washing her sole. "Oh! Oh!" Jade squealed, trying to squirm away. "Don't! It tickles!" By now she was giggling uncontrollably and thrashing about in the tub, splashing soap and water in every direction. When her tormentor finally ceased, Jade gulped in a breath of relief, sluiced the water from her face, and peered about her. The five merry maids were almost as soaked as she was.

"*Cherie*, washing you eez like trying to peel an eel!" Lizette groused, flipping a drenched raven lock from her forehead, where it had drooped over one silver-gray eye.

"Now, that I'd like to see sometime," Bliss declared on a snort of laughter.

"I'll let you watch the next time I remove Lieutenant Danfield's 'protection,' " Mavis stated with droll humor, rolling her dark eyes heavenward. "I swear that man's so finicky it's a wonder he doesn't have someone do his loving for him!"

Jade listened, agape, as the girls continued to comment on the lieutenant's peculiarities, most of which were beyond her comprehension. Meanwhile, the ladies finished washing her, rinsed her hair, pulled her from the tub, and proceeded to dry her with big, fluffy towels.

"There you go, sugar. All squeaky clean. Now, what are you gonna use for clothes while Glenna is washing yours?"

"I've a bag b'neath the bed with me spare things," Jade managed to answer.

Bliss retrieved it, and Jade wanted to die at the looks of pity that came over the girls' faces as they viewed the two tattered dresses and petticoat inside.

Fancy, a perky blond with wide lavender eyes, saved the day by asking "What's this?" She held up Jade's flute.

" 'Tis me flute."

"Can you play it?"

Jade shrugged. "Well enough to suit meself."

"Will you play something for us after you've had something to eat? Please?"

Peaches brought a tray from the kitchen, heaped high with hotcakes swimming in butter and syrup, grits and gravy, biscuits and jam, and a small pot of tea. While Jade ate, the others fussed with her hair, raving over its color and arguing about the best way to arrange her long tresses.

"What made you choose the name Jade?" questioned Mavis, who appeared to be several years older than the other girls.

"Me ma gave it to me. I had no say in it," Jade answered. "Why? Does it sound strange to ye?"

"Not strange, exactly," the tall brunette answered. "Different. Rather fitting, if you decide to stay on with us."

"Beggin' yer pardon?"

"Haven't you ever heard the word *jade* used to describe a . . . how shall I say this . . . a flirtatious girl, a disreputable woman? Or applied to someone who is so accustomed to excitement that it becomes dull to him?"

Jade was speechless. She stared and shook her head. "Truly?" she breathed.

"Oh, I wouldn't give it much mind if I were you," Mavis added. "We just thought you'd chosen the name for yourself, like Fancy did, or Peaches. Fancy's real name is Francine, but she hates for anyone to call her that. And Peaches is from Georgia, and never has revealed her true name to us. And if Lizette here is French, despite that accent she puts on, then we're all nuns and Vera is our mother superior!"

Lizette swatted at her friend, and they all laughed.

"Me full name's Jadeen Agnes Donovan, but no one's ever called me naught but Jade in all o' me sixteen years. I s'pose it don't make much difference what it means, since 'tis the only name I know and answer to."

"It's a lovely name," Bliss told her, putting an arm about Jade's shoulders and giving her a quick, hard hug. "They tease me about mine, too, though I was born with it. Besides, I happen to know that *jade* also refers to a pretty green gemstone which is highly prized in some countries."

The more they talked, the more Jade found herself warming to these ladies. They certainly didn't seem a bad sort, despite the way they earned their livings. They weren't dismal, downtrodden, or hardened by the hand Fate had dealt them. Rather, they were cheerful, attractive, friendly, and gifted with a rare ability to laugh at themselves, to find humor in life and their own situations. And just now they were not dressed much differently from any other woman Jade had seen. Nor, at least at this hour of the day, were their faces garishly painted.

The girls ushered Jade downstairs with them and into the large receiving parlor. Here, at last, Jade noticed a definite difference in decor, colors, and textures, which she assumed, with her limited knowledge of the world, to be unlike the average home. Red was the prominent hue, with vivid splashes of gold and teal and silver. A huge crystal chandelier hung from the center of an ornately painted ceiling. Jade gaped in awe at the erotic scenes depicted high above her and in the gilt-framed pictures on the adjoining walls. There appeared to be an abundance of mirrors in the room, reflecting back the images of fringed lamp shades, tufted settees, and polished tabletops. A piano stood next to a corner bar, where several rows of whiskey and other liquor bottles vied for space with crystal stemware.

"Faith and begorrah!" Jade blurted out softly, twirling slowly about in an effort to take it all in. "I've never seen the likes!"

Vera, entering the room from behind her, gave a husky laugh. "Rather takes your breath away, doesn't it, dearie? It's a bit opulent for most tastes, but it serves its purpose well. Puts our clients in the best mood for loosening their purse strings."

"As well as those to their britches," Fancy added wryly, earning a chuckle from her companions.

"Come on over here and meet Billy," Vera said, taking Jade gently by the arm and steering her toward the piano, where Jade had overlooked the thin, rather homely young man seated on the bench.

With his lanky frame hunched over the keyboard and his stringy brown hair straggling nearly to his eyes, Billy had all but blended into the background. "He might not be as pretty as you girls," Vera commented lightly, "but Billy is the best piano man this side of the Mason-Dixon line, with no dispute. Now, you just tell him what you would like to sing, and he'll provide the accompanying music."

Suddenly Jade felt more self-conscious than she had since she'd arrived in this strange place. "I . . . uh . . . I promised Fancy I'd play me flute," she murmured, putting off the moment when she'd be required to sing.

"Whatever suits you, dear, but I do want to hear you sing, too."

Taking a deep breath to quell the butterflies in her stomach, Jade brought the flute to her lips and closed her eyes. Clear, sweet tones filled the room, dancing in the air and blending to form the familiar strains of "Greensleeves." Billy picked up the melody, and for the next few minutes they entertained the women with a duet. When Jade stopped playing, Billy did not. "Sing it," he urged softly, as his fingers deftly continued the tune.

Those listening could not believe their ears as Jade began to sing the words to the old ballad. It was as if the flute had gained a voice, so perfect, so pure and dulcet were the notes issuing from her throat. The words took on new meaning, fresh and poignant with her lilting Irish intonation. Haunting. Moving. Unbelievably beautiful.

At the end of the piece, Jade's performance was answered with pregnant silence. Then, when Jade thought she could stand it not one minute longer, Vera spoke in a hushed, almost reverent voice. "Girl, you've a voice of pure gold. You're Ireland's answer to Jenny Lind, and just the solution I've been looking for. Forget everything I said last night about serving drinks and dancing. If you will come to work for me, all I'll ask you to do is to sing for our gentlemen clients each evening. I'll provide you with the proper clothes, throw in your room and board for free, and pay you top wages. What do you say, young lady?"

Jade was stunned, as was everyone else, at Vera's generous offer. She glanced from Vera to the others, noting the varied expressions on their faces. Surprise. Admiration. Disbelief. Hope. Envy.

"Do it, honey," Bliss entreated. "If I had a voice like yours, I'd do it in a minute. When word gets around that we've got an angel singin' here, men'll be flockin' in here like flies to molasses, and I'll be double-damned if we aren't all gonna wind up as rich as queen bees on account of it."

Mavis nodded. "We need you, Jade. And you need us—to take care of you. To watch out for you."

Vera whispered in her ear what seemed to Jade a staggering salary.

"Can I keep me same room?" Jade asked wistfully.

"Honey, I'll give you any room in the house. Your choice," Vera promised.

Jade grinned. "Then I guess I'll be stayin'."

Georgetown, Kentucky—December 1866

Christmas was only two weeks away, but the serenity and cheer of the season were eluding Matt. Oh, he'd been delivering all the right messages in his sermons, inspiring his congregation to peace and goodwill, but his inner soul seemed to echo like an empty chamber, throwing his own words back to mock him. Since Cynthia's death, he'd been wandering around in a mental fog, functioning bodily but emotionally crippled.

God help him, but the only genuine feeling he could generate these days was a guilty sense of relief that she was forever gone—though much to his amazement, he also found himself missing her somewhat, even as he celebrated her absence. There was no one constantly haranguing him, berating him, making waves in his life. Though the orphans created the usual noise and disruption, and some crisis or other always seemed to crop up among his parishioners, his days seemed to plod along, one much like the next, with little challenge. At least Cynthia had provided that, in abundance.

In truth, her life and death had afforded Matt much more. She'd forced him to take a long, honest look at himself from the inside out. She'd proven to him how human he was, with all the failings and feelings of any other man. Even as he was striving so hard to be good and kind and godly, she'd humbled him by bringing out the anger and frustration bottled up within him. And for that alone, he supposed he should be grateful to have known her, for it had taught him a hard lesson in life, kept him from thinking too highly of himself or from judging his fellows too harshly. All he had to do was look at his own faults and he could better understand those of others. It prevented him from becoming so heavenly-minded that he was of no earthly good to anyone else.

But for all that, Matt was disturbed by his current lethargy, this sensation of aimless drifting. "What is wrong with me?" he lamented to his friend, Carl Jansen, one day. "I feel as if I'm encased in a glass cage, unable to touch the rest of the world as it revolves around me. Stuck in a rut, with no direction to my life and no goals within sight. Where is the satisfaction I used to get from my work? The energy I brought to it?"

"It takes a while to recover from a blow such as you've had, Matt," Carl commiserated. "Losin' your wife and babe. Havin' your life turned upside down. Give it time."

Matt sighed. "I feel as if I'm running out of time, Carl. Or perhaps as if I'm standing still while everyone else marches forward."

"Then set a new course for yourself," Carl proposed.

"I wouldn't know where to start," Matt admitted wearily.

Carl sighed dramatically and shook his head, a slight smile curving his lips. "Ah, Matthew, what would you do without me? Ask yourself this. If I came to you with a similar problem, what would you advise me to do?"

"Take it to God," Matt answered immediately, "and let Him show the way." Abashed, he grinned. "A dose of my own medicine, Carl?"

"Physician, heal thyself," Carl quoted, reaching for Matt's Bible on a nearby table and handing it to him.

The Book fell open in Matt's hands, and he read aloud the first verse to meet his gaze. " 'And the Lord said unto me, Arise, take thy journey before the people, that they may go in and possess the land, which I sware unto their fathers to give unto them.' " He frowned. "Now, what do you suppose that means, Carl? Am I to go on a journey soon to a new land?" he mused thoughtfully.

"You think on it a spell," Carl suggested. "And while you're doin' that, consider this." He drew a handbill from his pocket and gave it to Matt. It was notice of a wagon train heading for Oregon in the spring, departing from

Independence, Missouri. "That's what I came to tell you, friend. Nell and I have decided to sell out and move west, to greener pastures. The Sandersons are doin' likewise, and Jamie and Lucy Lockhart are ponderin' the notion. We'd sure be glad to have you along, Matt. It might be the answer for all of us."

❧❧❧ *Chapter 4* ❧❧❧

Richmond, Virginia—March 1867

The brisk winds of spring were blowing through the streets of Richmond—fickle, bitter winds, indeed. In this second week of March, with showers beckoning the first brave flowers from the warming earth, a pall had fallen over Vera's hurdy-gurdy hall. The doors were closed, the curtains drawn, the gaiety suspended. A black wreath adorned the front door. Inside, the girls wept, all in various stages of grief and disbelief. Vera was dead.

What had begun as an annoying cold had quickly escalated into pneumonia. In the final dark hours, Vera had heeded her doctor's grim advice. She'd called for her lawyer and then for her girls. Having no living relatives to whom to bequeath her wealth, Vera had divided her estate equally among her dozen "ladies," the cook, the maid, Billy, and Butch, setting aside only enough for her own burial. It was an act of generosity typical of the way she'd lived her life, and it surprised no one who had known her well.

Now, as the girls gathered in the shaded parlor following the funeral of their beloved friend and benefactress, they whispered among themselves.

"What will we do without her? She was like a mother to all of us," Bliss lamented.

"Not many madams are as kindhearted and generous as our Vera, that's for sure," Peaches put in. "If we have to

31

go to work for someone else, we'll all think we've died and gone to Hell, and count Vera the lucky one."

"But why should we have to do that?" Fancy asked. "She's willed us the house and everything in it, as well as all her money, however much that might amount to. We could keep the house running on our own, or maybe even afford to retire if we want."

Mavis shook her head at Fancy's naïveté. "As my dear old mother was fond of saying, 'Don't count your chickens before they hatch.' There are twelve of us girls, and if you think all of us are going to easily come to one accord then you have mush for brains, Fancy. If enough girls want to leave, money in hand, this place will have to be sold in order to split the inheritance evenly. Fact is, I've been considering taking my share and starting up fresh somewhere out west. Oregon, maybe."

"Why there?" Jade questioned, glad to have something other than Vera's sad demise upon which to focus her thoughts.

"One of my customers was talking about it recently. He intended to go to Oregon soon, but his plans fell through. Just last week he was bemoaning the fact that he'd already signed up with a wagon train leaving Independence, Missouri, the first of May and that he'd made partial payment to secure a position in it and a couple of wagons for the trip, and doubted he'd get his money back at this late date. I was thinking of taking his place—if I could convince some of you to go with me. We could start up a new hurdy-gurdy there and most likely turn a tidy profit."

"Has your mind come unhinged?" Bliss asked bluntly. "Mavis, dear, why in bloomin' Hell would we want to go all the way to Oregon to do that?"

"Because zat eez where all zoze sweet, lonely men are, Bliss. Hundreds of zem, practically begging for brides and female companions," Lizette informed her friend. "Zey are even advertising in ze newspapers, pleading for more women to come zere. Zey are hungry leetle rascals, *cherie*, with moneys and lands—but, alas, no ladies and little entertainment."

"I've heard they're so desperate they're not nearly as particular about marrying a woman with a questionable past as the men here are," Fancy put in. "Could be we'd have a choice of being wives or working gals. Maybe both."

"I'd be willing to try it, as long as Jade came along to sing and to draw the crowds into the dance hall like she did here," Peaches said.

Again, Bliss rebuffed the suggestion. "Why would Jade want to go to someplace as unsettled and uncivilized as Oregon when she'd do better to go to San Francisco, or New York, or Charleston? Or to stay in Richmond, for that matter? She has her own career to think of, you know."

"Which is precisely why she should come with us," Mavis told them all. She now directed her comments to Jade. "Think about it. Doesn't it make much more sense to gain some fame for yourself first, among friends, rather than go directly to a larger city, where you are completely unknown and know no one in return? Where you would run the risk of aligning yourself with any number of disreputable characters intent only on taking advantage of your talent while they steal you blind? With us, you would be safe, at least."

Peaches nodded enthusiastically. "And once you've properly made a name for yourself in Oregon and thereabouts, you can go on down to San Francisco and take the town by storm. Make a truly royal entrance, like a queen at her coronation."

"What about it, Jade? Will you come?" Mavis asked. "I've heard folks claim that Oregon is as green and glorious as Ireland, only better. Rich, ripe, and ready—for us."

"I'll go if Bliss will," Jade agreed, slanting a look at the young woman who had become her closest friend.

"Oh, all right!" Bliss grumbled. "With Vera gone, there

sure as spit isn't anything in Richmond worth stayin' for. Count me in."

"I weel go, too," Lizette said. "What of you, Fancy?"

"I suppose so, but I'm not thrilled at the thought of traveling by wagon train. It must take months to get there that way," Fancy pointed out. "With mountains and Indians and God knows what between here and there. If we went, wouldn't it be better to go by ship and get there quickly?"

"Y'all can go by ship if ye want, but for meself I reckon I'd sooner be boiled in oil than step foot on a boat again," Jade told them, her acquired Southern drawl blending oddly with her Irish brogue. "I'd walk to Oregon b'fore sailin' there."

Lizette agreed with a shudder. "Green eez not my color. I vote for ze wagon, or ze train. Why can we not take ze train, or ze stagecoach?"

"I don't think the trains go that far," Mavis said, "and I can't see all of us, with our luggage, piled into a stagecoach. At any rate, we're putting the cart before the horse. First I have to talk with my client and see if we can strike a bargain. Then, if that works out, we'll have to meet with the lawyer concerning Vera's bequest."

"Set up ze time and I weel come with you," Lizette volunteered. "Between ze two of us, I am sure we can find some way to convince your gentleman friend to give us a fair price, and I would wager we can deal just as well with ze lawyer—and leave both of zem with fond memories of our negotiations."

Georgetown, Kentucky—April 1867

Matt loaded another heavy crate into the bed of the wagon and straightened to wipe the sweat from his brow. His gaze swept over the rolling green fields and came to rest on the big white house that he and Cynthia had called home. Just last week, he'd signed the final papers of sale on the property. This past weekend, with little regret, he'd auctioned off most of the furnishings Cyn had spent so much time and money purchasing. Tomorrow he would leave it all behind—the empty echoing rooms, the land-scaped gardens, and the taunting memories that seemed to cling to the very walls of this place.

He was glad to go. To escape, if the truth be known. His friends and parishioners would be shocked to realize how relieved he would be to brush the dust of Georgetown from his heels. There were those who thought they under-stood, who supposed the pain of losing Cynthia was sim-ply too much for him to bear, that staying here where they'd lived together grieved him too greatly.

It was an erroneous conclusion, but one that Matt was loathe to correct. Though he ministered to others for his livelihood, he was himself a very private person, not one to air his troubles readily or unburden himself on his friends. Besides, what purpose would it serve to tell everyone the truth about Cynthia and her baby? Would it lessen his feelings of guilt and humiliation at having failed at his own marriage? Let them, one and all, go on believing that Cynthia had been a sweet and loving wife. What would it hurt? Especially now, when he would be free of their unfounded sympathy, miles from those who repeatedly, though innocently, brought such miser-able memories to mind.

Of course, a few of these same church members were also traveling on the wagon train to Oregon, but Matt imagined they would soon be caught up in their new plans and adventures and less prone to dredging up the past. Then, perhaps, he could begin to forget. The memories would fade. And he could get on with his life. Shake off the shame of his disastrous union with Cynthia and the harsh words they had exchanged the day of her accident. Ease his conscience of the blame he placed on himself for the death of her baby, a child everyone still assumed had been his.

Matt's thoughts turned to yet another Kentucky prop-erty he would soon be leaving behind—the farm outside Frankfort, where his parents had raised him and his broth-er, Jordan. He had not been able to bring himself to part with it altogether, however, and had settled on leasing the land to a neighboring farmer for the time being. His parents were buried there, and to one side of their graves stood a more recent marker, though no body rested in the earth beneath the stone that bore his brother's name.

For nearly three years, Matt had stubbornly refused to admit that Jordan was dead. In all that time, he kept hoping Jordan would miraculously appear, though the War Between the States had been over for two years now and there was still no word, either from his brother or the army. If Jordan had been killed in battle, no one knew how, or precisely where or when. There had been fierce fighting in Georgia at the time Jordan had come up missing. His body had never been found. Most likely, he was buried in some unmarked grave, like so many of his comrades.

For Matt, the worst was not knowing for certain— waiting, praying, and finally, sorrowfully, accepting that he would never see his brother again this side of Heaven's gates. Just last month, with a heavy heart, he'd placed Jordan's gravestone next to those of their parents and said a final farewell. Yet even now he could not bear to sell the land, for somewhere in the recesses of his heart a tiny flame of hope still flickered, refusing to be extinguished.

Youthful laughter intruded on his dreary musing, and Matt looked up to see the children playing happily on the sunlit lawn. There remained only five orphans for whom he had not found good homes, and they would be going with him on the westward trail. A smile crept across his mouth and into his eyes as he watched them tumble over the grass like gamboling puppies. This was what made life worth all the heartache and pain. To see their small faces light up with joy, to witness the hope and love shining from their eyes, was to Matt the greatest reward on earth.

These homeless youngsters, and others like them, were the reason Matt had ultimately decided to give up his church ministry and journey to Oregon. He was going to start an orphanage there, to follow the latest plan God had laid on his heart, and to set down roots in fresh rich soil, where his dreams, and those of the children, could grow and prosper. Together, they would begin a new adventure in a new land.

Richmond, Virginia—April 1867

Jade stood on the boarding platform at the railway station, practically prancing with excitement. In a few minutes, she and her friends would be off on the first leg of their trip to Oregon. Once Vera's house had been sold and the inheritance evenly divided, half of the girls had declined the westward excursion. This left six of them—Jade, Mavis, Fancy, Peaches, Lizette, and Bliss—all bound for Oregon.

They had also convinced Billy to come along, for a number of reasons. Not only did they need him to play piano for them once they reached their destination and set up their new dance hall, and to manage the heavier chores that required a man's strength, but Billy would act as a male chaperon of sorts. According to Mavis's client, women traveling alone were not welcome on the wagon trains. Without exception, they must have a man traveling with them, supposedly for protection, though the ladies much doubted that they could rely on mild-mannered Billy for that role. They would combine their feminine wits and wiles and take care of themselves.

"I reckon it's a good thing we're not sailin' to Oregon," Peaches drawled, bringing Jade's attention to their small mountain of luggage and furnishings now being loaded onto the train they would take as far as Independence. "A ship would likely sink under the weight. Do you suppose we'll get all that into two little wagons?"

Jade shook her head. "Mavis seems to think we can, but it appears to me we overpacked a wee bit. That guidebook she got from Mr. Goodrich warned against bringin' anything but the barest necessities."

"Which is exactly what we did," Fancy put in. "You can't start up a hurdy-gurdy without the proper trappings. Beds, mirrors, liquor, music, not to mention a decent assortment of appropriate apparel."

"Yeah," Bliss agreed, "but don't you think those two chandeliers and the piano are goin' a mite overboard?"

"Billy wouldn't have come without his beloved piano," Mavis pointed out. "Besides, I hear they're as rare as frog's hair out west."

"And where would we put our clothes wizout ze wardrobes and dressers?" Lizette asked.

"I'm sure there must be somewhere in Oregon City to buy furniture or to have it made," Jade said. "But 'tis glad I am we're bringin' that big copper tub. That's one luxury I'd hate to give up."

"I declare, Jade! You're either the dirtiest person I know or the cleanest," Bliss announced on a chuckle. "You'd live in that tub, given half a chance."

Their conversation was interrupted when a well-dressed young man approached them, hat in hand. He'd been a frequent visitor to the hurdy-gurdy house. "My, don't all of you look fine this morning!" he declared, running his eyes over the six of them with obvious male appreciation. "Why, decked out in your traveling suits, you look almost like . . . like . . ." A flush crept up his neck as he floundered for words.

"Like real ladies?" Mavis supplied haughtily. "Why, thank you, Mr. Harrison. How dreadfully kind of you to think so."

"Uh, well, I wouldn't have put it just that way," he stammered.

With a sheepish look, he turned toward Jade. "I came to see you off, Miss Jade. To wish you much success and to tell you how much we're all going to miss your delightful performances. These past months, you've become our ray of sunshine, you know. Our Irish songbird."

" 'Tis been my pleasure, Gerald," Jade informed him, gracing him with a smile.

"Isn't there any way we can persuade you to stay?" he implored, his brown eyes practically melting with supplication. "Why, we've barely begun to know you, and you're leaving us."

Biting back a chuckle, Jade thought to herself that

there were numerous men of her acquaintance who would, indeed, have enjoyed the opportunity to get better acquainted with her—between the sheets. But she had held them all at a distance, taunting them with her elusive allure. The more she'd denied them, the more they'd flocked about her, trying in vain to gain her favor. She'd sung for them, danced with them, even accepted invitations to supper and the theater with a select few, but she had taken none to her bed.

"I'm afraid I must go," she told the young gentleman. "Me bags are packed and me future awaits." Just for good measure, and because she did so adore flirting with her many admirers, she batted her long lashes at him and pretended to blink back a tear from her eye.

Before he could implore further, a dirty-faced boy elbowed his way through the crowd shouting in a shrill voice, "Miss Jade. Message for Miss Jade!"

"Here!" Bliss called out, waving him toward her friend. The lad thrust a note into Jade's hand and stood waiting until she dug a coin from her reticule and gave it to him.

Jade removed the letter from the envelope. Upon reading the message, a derisive smile curved her lips.

"What is it?" Bliss wanted to know. "Who's it from?"

"From a very rich, very married gentleman," Jade answered wryly. "He's wantin' to set me up in a town house of me own if only I'll stay and entertain him—very privately and exclusively, o' course."

"Ya want to write an answer back?" the messenger boy inquired.

Jade shook her head. "Just tell him I'm not for sale— at any price."

"Zat eez quite an offer," Lizette commented lightly. "Are you certain you should refuse it so quickly?"

" 'Tis not the first, nor the best, and probably not the last," Jade answered with just a touch of arrogance. "But I'll not be dependin' on any man for me welfare. If y'all recall, Sean taught me a hard lesson. One I won't soon be forgettin'. As long as me voice holds out, I intend to make me own way in the world. I've grand plans and dreams for meself, and just now they don't include a man to drag me down or hold me back."

Bliss laughed. "You've come a long way from that ragged, hungry waif Vera took in a few months back, Jade. Just look at you now. Confident, proud, bound and determined to prove your independence. If you don't watch out, you're gonna become so damned pompous we won't be able to stand you."

"Now, Bliss, you know that won't happen," Peaches said in Jade's defense. "Jade's just found her feet, that's all. It does a body good to have some self-worth. She's sweet and lovable and generous—and so blasted cheerful it's downright sickenin' at times!"

"And an outrageous flirt into the bargain!" Mavis supplied with a wink.

"Sean might have pricked me pride some, but that doesn't mean I'm set on blamin' all men for his stupidity," Jade informed them. "I'm simply bidin' me time, waitin' for the right fellow to come along. But I want to meet him after I've had me chance at fame and fortune. After I've toured the world singin' for royalty," she added on a wishful note. "In the meanwhile, it doesn't do any harm to practice me charms along the way. A lass has to have some fun, doesn't she?"

Bliss agreed readily. "Sounds fine to me." Just then the train whistle sounded, followed by the boarding call. "And so does that! Oh, sweet music to my ears! C'mon, gals. It's Oregon or bust!"

"Hell, I'll be glad just to make it to Independence," Fancy grumbled. "I hate trains! They're smelly and dirty and crowded."

Jade slanted her an amused look. "Ye think this is bad, just wait 'til we have to crowd into those wee wagons. And live in 'em for months on end. Saints, but this sure is gonna be fun, ain't it?" she added with droll humor.

✤ Chapter 5 ✤

"*O*oow! Get off o' me, ye big dumb ox! Great flamin' balls o' fire! I declare, for as big as ye are, ye got the brains o' a blarsted flea!"

More than the actual content of her words, or the volume behind them, it was the peculiar accent that drew Matt's attention, an odd mix of Deep South and Irish lilt. Intrigued, he left his own wagon and headed toward the one stationed just ahead of his. He really didn't want to become entangled in a marital dispute between this woman and her man, but he was curious about the owner of that unusual intonation.

He rounded the foremost corner of the wagon and stopped short, a chuckle rising in his throat. Before him stood a copper-haired pixie of a girl who was struggling not with a husband but with an actual ox. She looked no bigger than a minute, didn't appear to weigh more than a mosquito, and was shaking her small fist at the ox's snout.

"Ye're the stupidest varmint God ever set breath to! I reckon a good wallop aside yer head wouldn't rattle much loose, or I'd blamed well try it, but that's what ye'll get if ye don't start payin' some heed here! And stay off me foot this time!"

Spying the harness on the ground in front of the wagon, and the two oxen already standing within their yoke, Matt guessed that she'd been leading the animal to join his

41

mates. As she reached for the rope about the beast's neck, he stepped forward. "Need some help, child?"

Matt realized his error when the sprite turned toward him, revealing a figure too well rounded to belong to a child. And the delicately crafted features framed by that wealth of flyaway hair were far too alluring. Her mouth was full and voluptuous, her sharp green eyes slightly tip-tilted and graced with luxuriant mink-hued lashes, and her pert little nose sported not a single freckle to mar its saucy charm.

Jade turned from her battle with the beast, startled by this unexpected intrusion and more than a little irritated at being mistaken for a child. But the scathing retort forming in her mind suddenly took flight as she beheld the man standing before her. The first thing that struck her was his height, for her nose came even with his breastbone, and she had to crane her neck backward to view the upper portion of him. Her gaze skimmed a wide chest and broad shoulders, up past the vee of crisp dark hair revealed by the open neck of his red plaid shirt, and clashed suddenly with the brightest, clearest pair of blue eyes she'd ever seen.

They were set in a rugged, tanned face and bracketed by fine lines that fanned outward toward prominent cheekbones. His nose was straight, his chin square, and his lips were curved in a quizzical half smile that made her heart skip a beat. Above all this, and tumbling across his forehead, was a shock of hair as black and shiny as a raven's wing. The only thing that saved him from absolute perfection, at least to Jade's thinking, was the cowlick sprouting up at the back of his hatless head.

"I . . . uh . . . I . . . Damn me, but ye're pretty!" she stammered mindlessly.

At this he threw back that glorious head and laughed, a deep husky sound that rasped deliciously along Jade's spine. "Handsome," he corrected smoothly. "Women and babies are pretty. Men are handsome, but I thank you for the compliment, though it's far from true."

"Now, don't ye be makin' me doubt what me own eyes

are seein'," Jade replied, flashing a dimpled smile at him. In the six months Jade had spent with Vera and the girls, she had learned the fine art of flirtation, and now she was putting that knowledge to work for her. Her lashes fluttered, drawing his attention to her sparkling eyes. She cocked her head slightly to one side in a come-hither gesture, laid her hand lightly on his arm, and purred, "Didn't yer mama ever teach ye 'tis not nice to lie, 'specially if ye want to impress the ladies?"

Matt couldn't help but smile at her antics. The little green-eyed minx was flirting with him for all she was worth, and doing a credible job of it into the bargain. Her fingers were softly stroking his arm now, and she was leaning slightly toward him, affording him a generous glimpse of creamy breasts confined within the lace-trimmed bodice of her dress.

For Matt, this was a rare occurrence, and he'd bet his bottom dollar she had no inkling he was a preacher, or she wouldn't be behaving so boldly toward him. Not that his appearance had given her any clue to his profession, for he was dressed like any other man working among the wagons—denim pants, boots, and a flannel shirt. For ready protection against snakes and wild animals along the trail, he also sported a gun belt and pistol now, the unfamiliar weight of which felt odd against his hip, though he was proficient with the weapon, as well as with the rifle and shotgun he generally used only for hunting game. Altogether, he certainly did not look the part of a minister today.

Still, he had to wonder at her attitude, which seemed a bit forward for the average woman. And wasn't her bodice cut a bit too low for modesty? As far as that went, most ladies of his acquaintance wore their hair bound back in some tidy manner, but hers curled wild and free, like that of some half-tamed Gypsy.

Before he could ponder more on the matter, she ran her tongue over her lips, presumably to moisten them and to make him notice their fullness, and said, "Me name's Jade. What's yers, sugar?"

His eyes widened. Jade? Had she said Jade? Oh, boy, what kind of situation had he gotten himself into here? He stared at her, noted her pouty frown, and realized he hadn't answered her question. "Matt. Matthew Richards."

He glanced toward the waiting animal, which was placid now that she'd left off trying to lead him where he didn't want to go. Matt understood exactly how the beast felt. "Uh, do you need help harnessing your team?" he offered once again.

Jade declined with a pretty show of reluctance. "I'll have to be learnin' how to do it meself," she told him, "and I'd best be at it quickly, since we start on the trail tomorrow." She cocked her head and smiled up at him. "Are ye headin' for Oregon, same as me and Billy and the girls?"

He couldn't help casting a swift look at her left hand, though the absence of a wedding band told him little, since many people were too poor these days to afford rings. "You have a husband and children, then?" he questioned, somewhat relieved at the idea that this small temptress was attached, while at the same time strangely disappointed.

She blinked at him in some confusion, then said, "Oh! You mean Billy?" She laughed softly. "He's not me husband. He's our piano man, for when me and the girls start up our new hurdy-gurdy."

Though appalled at her blunt announcement, Matt's curiosity got the better of him, and he heard himself asking, "And the girls? Who are they?"

"They're me friends," Jade informed him readily. "Five o' the nicest, bonniest ladies ye'd likely find anywhere. They're in town now, gettin' supplies, but ye'll meet 'em soon, I reckon, if we're all gonna be travelin' the same route. Ye are goin' to Oregon with the wagon train, then?"

"Uh, yes. Yes, I am," Matt replied distractedly, his mind still trying to absorb this latest bit of news. By luck of the draw, it seemed that Matt's wagon was to be located directly behind that of Jade and her companions when they headed out in the morning. Which meant that he and the five impressionable young orphans still in his care would be thrust into close association with a half dozen harlots! Some two thousand miles, and five long months, of practically rubbing elbows with each other! It promised to be an impossible situation!

Without another word, Matt spun on his heel, intent on finding the wagon master and rectifying this error immediately. No sooner had he taken a step, however, than he saw the very man he sought approaching him.

"Howdy there, Pastor Richards!" Sam Greene greeted him with a jovial bellow. "I see you've gotten acquainted with your new neighbors. Or one of them, at least."

"I have, indeed," Matt concurred, "and I was just coming to speak to you about making other arrangements, sir."

"Ain't no other arrangements to be made, Reverend."

"Mr. Greene, I have small children in my care, and it will not suit to have them in constant contact with a troop of trollops," Matt told him.

A quick gasp drew his attention once more to the petite woman behind him. He'd momentarily forgotten her presence and therefore had spoken rashly, without accounting for her reaction to his words. He was instantly contrite, and not a little embarrassed at his own inconsiderate behavior. "Begging your pardon, ma'am. I don't mean to be unkind, but—"

"Ye're a preacher man?" Jade interrupted, all but shrieking at him. She glared accusingly. "Ye stood there an' said not one word and let me . . . let me . . ."

"Throw yourself at me?" Matt offered with an arrogant male smirk. "Flirt outrageously? Play the tease?"

"Ye're despicable!"

"And what are you, Miss Jade?"

"I'm not what ye're thinkin', that's for sure! I'm a singer! An entertainer!"

He eyed her askance. "I've no doubt you are quite adept at your chosen trade, and I'm sorry if I hurt your feelings, but there are five orphans traveling with me to Oregon and I simply cannot have them exposed to the sort of 'entertaining' in which you and your friends are engaged."

Greene spoke up before Jade could respond to Matt's comment. "No worry over that, Reverend. That's why I placed their wagon ahead of yours in the column. To keep them in line, so to speak, don't you see? With you lookin' over their shoulder, they'll have to behave themselves."

To Jade, the wagon master said, "I've already explained the rules to your man, but I'll tell you now. Once we reach Oregon, you all can do as you please, but I won't stand for any shenanigans along the way. We've got many a God-fearing family in our group, and a long, difficult road ahead. So keep your skirts down and your feet on the ground, and we won't have any more problems than we can already expect to encounter."

Jade was fuming, so angry now that she could barely force words past her clenched teeth. "Ye'll both have a mouth full o' loose teeth as soon as I can get me hands on somethin' hard enough an' heavy enough to bash yer heads! I ain't never seen two more disgustin', overbearin' dunderheads, or a pair more in need o' a good swift kick in the pants!"

With a swish of skirts, she turned her back to them, stomping back to her oxen. "If y'all will excuse me, I've got me some apologizin' to do to these poor beasties, 'cause they sure as hell are a lot smarter than some critters I've met today!"

As Matt and Sam Greene stared after her, still stunned by her waspish rebuttal, they heard Jade croon to her team, "Come on, Tom. Let's go, Dick. You, too, Harry. We've got to get this wagon hitched b'fore the girls get back from town."

"Tom?" Matt echoed dumbfoundedly.

"Dick?" Greene repeated.

They shared a look of disbelief and rising humor. "Harry?" they crowed in unison. The two men burst out laughing.

"Well, if that don't beat all!" Greene claimed.

"Not by a long shot," Matt predicted, sobering a bit with the thought of what was yet to come. "As you said, there's a long road ahead of us. And I still don't relish the idea of monitoring a band of 'entertainers.' I'll have my hands full just watching after the children."

"Oh, I didn't mean to imply that I want you to be some sort of warden over that band of hussies, or that I expect you to be responsible for their behavior," Sam assured him. "I just thought with a preacher breathin' down their necks the gals'll curtail their business a mite and not cause so much of a ruckus." '

Sam's eyes began to twinkle with unholy glee. "Still and all, I reckon you won't have to worry 'bout getting bored on the trail, will you, Reverend?"

"Oooh, la la!" Lizette sighed dreamily on first catching sight of Matt. "Who eez zat marvelous man?"

Jade looked up and cast a glare toward the nearby corral, where Pastor Richards was currently trying his hand at breaking a half-wild horse for a fellow emigrant. A crowd of onlookers had gathered to watch and offer their encouragement, as half a dozen men had tried to ride the bronc and gotten thrown for their efforts. Now, it looked as if the Reverend was about to succeed where those before him had failed.

Only to herself would Jade reluctantly admit that Matt did, indeed, look magnificent atop that bucking stallion— sublimely, superbly male. A study in masculine grace and strength, with his thighs cleaving tightly to the horse's heaving sides, one arm thrown wide, and his shirt stretched taut across his broad chest. A reckless smile curved his mouth, the light of challenge flashing in his eyes, as he rode the animal to a quivering halt amid the cheers of his enthusiastic audience.

Jade gave an inelegant snort. "Calm down, Lizette," she told her friend. "It won't do ye any good to get yer mouth all watered up for that one. He's a preacher with a wagon full o' orphans. B'sides that, he don't cotton to trollops, and he doesn't want his wee charges exposed to us."

Mavis's brow rose. "Sounds as if you've met him already."

"Aye, and he might be wondrous to look at, but he's a stiff-necked buzzard."

"Now, honey, don't condemn the fellow right off," Bliss advised, her avid gaze following Matt as he dismounted, accepted his due congratulations, and strode toward his wagon. "He might be right nice once you get to know him better."

"The likes o' him don't want the likes o' us gettin' close enough to know him a'tall. And Mr. Greene made no bones in statin' that he deliberately put Reverend Richards's wagon right b'hind ours so the good man could supervise our conduct. Richards is a bloomin' spy, set on us to make sure we behave properly," Jade responded grumpily.

Bliss shrugged. "I wouldn't fret much over it. It's a long way to Oregon, and a lot can happen between here and there."

"What's gonna happen is we're all gonna starve in the first week," Fancy predicted dourly from her place at their campfire. The others cast dubious glances her way, and any hope of refuting Fancy's claim died instantly. Smoke was billowing up from the damp wood, with nary a flame to be seen. The meat in the pan was as raw as it had been when Fancy had set it over the fire ten minutes before. At this rate, it looked as if they might have their meal sometime around midnight, if at all.

"I knew we should've asked Vera's cook to come along with us," Peaches lamented. Then she brightened. "Maybe we could still hire one."

"And put her where? Strapped to the top of the wagon?" Mavis scoffed. "Those two wagons are groaning fit to fall apart now. Mr. Greene told Billy flat out that most of our furnishings would be decorating the sides of the trail by the time we reach Oregon."

"Yeah, well, that old blowhard also claims we won't be doin' any business along the way, but I'm willin' to bet otherwise," Peaches said with a sly wink. "Even if our fellow travelers don't feel so inclined, we'll be passin' through towns and stoppin' at several forts chock-full of lonely, randy soldiers."

"That guidebook recommended not packin' anything worth less than a dollar a pound," Fancy put in, "and I reckon we've stuck to that advice fairly well, considerin' the cost of the piano and those chandeliers."

"Not to mention the divans and the liquor," Bliss added with a nod. "We may be carryin' many a pound, but it's all worth a hefty price, too."

"We shall do fine," Lizette said. "Just as soon as one of us discovers ze trick of how to build a decent fire and anozer of us learns ze art of cooking."

"Billy should take charge of the fire, don't you think?" Bliss asked. "After all, that's a man's chore, isn't it? And he is a man, isn't he?"

"Golly, Bliss, I don't know. I guess I'd never thought of him that way," Peaches answered with a giggle. "Why don't you check on that for us and let us know what you find out?"

"He ought to be tendin' to the oxen, too," Jade complained. "I know he can't drive two teams at once, but he could surely harness 'em for us in the mornin' and unhitch 'em at night."

Mavis shook her head. "Billy isn't going to do anything more than he absolutely has to, Jade. You should know that. We can consider ourselves fortunate if he's more help than hindrance."

"Well, it'd be blamed nice if he knew how to cook, I tell ye. He couldn't be any worse at it than Fancy or me."

"Maybe he can sew a fine seam, Jade. Would that suit you? Then we could have him sew those pockets along the sides of the wagon cover, like that lady in the dry goods store suggested."

"Where is that lazy good-for-nothin', anyhow?" Fancy asked, eyeing the uncooked meat with disgust.

"Oh, he went back into town for a last taste of civilization," Mavis told her.

"How lucky for him!" Lizette sniffed, waving a hand

toward the darkening sky. "Zere he will eat a good meal, while we go hungry. And he will be sheltered, while we get soaked in ze rain. Are we supposed to put up zose tents by ourselves?"

"Only if we want to stay dry," Jade quipped with a resigned sigh. "Or we could huddle together in the wagons, like birds in a nest."

"Men!" Bliss declared in a fair imitation of Vera. "Dancin' peckers, the lot of them!"

Riding that bronc had gone a long way toward relieving some of Matt's pent-up frustrations, much of which had been caused by that redheaded spitfire he'd tangled with earlier. Now, back at his campsite, and despite his best efforts to the contrary, his attention kept wandering toward the wagon ahead of him and the six women gathered around it.

Though none of them was dressed outrageously, their attire was not that of the proper female. Their bodices were too tightly fitted and cut too low for decency's sake, their hair styled too elaborately. A dyed feather waved from the side of one floozy's head, and several of them sported dangling earbobs. Even at this distance, Matt could discern rouged lips and painted eyes, and he highly suspected that if the smoke from their fire was not so thick he would also detect the odor of cheap perfume in the air.

Their voices carried to him, though they were speaking too softly for him to catch their words distinctly. Still, one of the women appeared to be of French descent. Much to his discomfort, another bore a remarkable resemblance to Cynthia. From what little he could gather, the woman with the dark brown hair and eyes seemed to have assumed a position of leadership among them.

Though Jade, the little Irish wench, was not the most beautiful among them, his gaze was drawn back to her time and again. Matt told himself it was simply because she was the only one he'd met thus far, but this lame excuse rang a false note. If he were honest with himself, he'd admit he had enjoyed their earlier encounter—until he'd discovered that her charm was merely a practiced art, part and parcel of her trade.

The bare fact was, he'd enjoyed her attention too much—too much for comfort, both physically and mentally. To his surprise, and ultimate dismay, his body had responded to her siren's call quite spontaneously, like that of a sailor too long at sea, without conscious thought or forewarning.

Well, I don't know why you should be so astonished, he thought to himself with a shake of his head. *Following two years of enforced abstinence, it was bound to happen sooner or later, and toward anyone in skirts. You are only human, after all, fashioned of flesh and bone, like any other man. Consider it a welcome indication that you are still a normal, functioning male, despite the beating your pride received at Cynthia's hand.*

However, he wasn't altogether convinced that he would have had the same reaction to any other woman. There was something about that green-eyed hussy, something very beguiling, that struck an instinctive chord deep within him that no one else had ever before touched. It was like being abruptly awakened after a long, dreamless sleep—shaken suddenly alert, with heart thumping and every nerve alive and vibrating. Exhilarating. Exciting. Disturbing.

Again he shook his head, as if to dispel these troublesome thoughts and emotions. "You're becoming as balmy as a bedbug, Richards," he muttered silently. "Too long with only children for companionship."

He risked another look toward Jade, as if daring himself not to respond to her allure, and the sight that met his eyes brought a chuckle to his lips. The women were now attempting to erect tents for shelter against the coming storm, and were having no better luck at this task than they'd had with building a fire. Poles were standing askew, canvas flapping in every direction, ropes tangled amidst stray pegs, and the ladies were dashing about like chickens with their heads chopped off. Matt found himself with a front-row seat at the best comedy performance in town.

Jade was straining to hold a supporting pole upright, and a section of canvas with it, while a girl with a mop of mouse-brown hair tried to pound it into the hard-packed ground with a sledge hammer. As Matt watched in horrified fascination, the heavy hammer crashed down onto the pole, slipped sideways, and came within an inch of bashing Jade's skull. With a frightened screech, Jade backed away from the blow, pulling the shaft with her. In the next second she was buried under a billowing wave of canvas, wriggling and squealing like a stuck pig and cursing to beat the band.

Eventually, with her friend's help, she fought free, her head popping from the canvas like a jack-in-the-box, her copper hair straggling and her tongue on a rampage.

"Ye clumsy chit!" she raged—at least Matt hoped she'd said "chit," for now she was screaming loudly enough for him to hear her fairly well. "Dadblast it! Ye could've killed me, Bliss!" She blew a strand of tawny hair from her snapping emerald eyes and slithered out from beneath the tarp. "This time I'll use the hammer while you hold the pole," she announced as she grabbed the long-handled tool from Bliss.

Bliss stared at her for a moment, then burst into a fit of giggles. "Do you want a stool, shortie, so you can swing high enough to hit the top of it? Or maybe a ladder?"

Jade glared at her. Then, even from where Matt stood, he could see the impish gleam enter her gaze. "Fancy!" she called out. "Hie yerself over here so I can sit on yer shoulders and beat the bloomin' suds out o' this sass-mouthed beanpole!"

"Mavis and I are busy!" came the laughing answer. "Get Peaches to do it. She's got broader shoulders than I do, anyway."

"Yeah," Bliss taunted. "The better to hold Jade's big butt."

Bliss? Fancy? Peaches? Jade? Didn't any of these girls have normal names? Matt wondered.

Suddenly it started to rain, a drenching downpour that sent sheets of water streaming down upon their heads as if tipped from some gigantic bucket. Even as he dashed for the cover of his own tent, where the children were spreading out their bedrolls, Matt saw Jade make a leap for Bliss. At the same time, Peaches closed in on Fancy, and within seconds the four of them were rolling around on the sodden ground, screeching and clawing at one another. It was a sight to behold!

Small hands grabbed at Matt's pantleg, and a little head peeked around one thigh. Three-year-old Emily popped her thumb out of her mouth and asked, "What're those ladies doin', Papa Matt?"

"They're fightin' like cats in a sack," Ike supplied with all the wisdom of his dozen years.

"No, they're not," Beth corrected. At nine, and second oldest of the group, she had quickly assumed the role of mother to the other youngsters. "They're playin'. Aren't they, Papa Matt?"

At this point, Matt wasn't quite sure. By now they were slinging mud at each other and had pulled the older woman and the French girl into the fray. Slipping and sliding and tumbling over one another, wet skirts clinging high on their thighs, they tumbled about like a litter of gamboling, muck-caked kittens.

That thought had no sooner crossed Matt's brain than Carl Jansen ambled up and commented drolly, "What is it they say about all cats lookin' gray in the dark? Or the mud?"

Matt slid his friend a warning look, nodding toward the curious children. "And little pitchers have big ears, Carl. And even bigger mouths."

"And the memories of elephants," Carl added with a grin.

The men returned their attention to the skirmish just in time to see Jade flop down on the ground, tilt her head toward the sky, and call out on a breathless laugh. "One o' ye slippery ninnies toss me a bar o' soap!"

"See?" Beth proclaimed triumphantly. "I told ya! They're laughin' and playin'."

"I've never seen grown-up ladies play like that b'fore,"

Ike declared, "but it sure looks like they're havin' lots o' fun."

"Sure does," Carl agreed, his grin growing wider. Aside to Matt, he added on a confidential note, "I'll bet it's because they're such a special class of 'ladies,' don't you, Matt?"

Matt was still caught up with watching Jade, where she sat sprawled in the mud, her sodden skirts hitched up around her knees and her face lifted toward the heavens like an offering to a rain god. With her hair dripping about her lovely features and her clothes plastered to her feminine curves, she looked positively pagan. Like an untamed, wanton creature from some fabled realm that mortals were forbidden to enter. As if to further encourage his fanciful illusion, her tongue dipped out to lap a drop of moisture from her upper lip, and flames ignited in Matt's belly. He bit back a groan as desire slammed through him.

"Hey, Matt, are you okay?" Carl asked. "Did you hear anything I said?"

"Yeah. Special lady," Matt intoned dazedly. "Mistress of merriment and mayhem."

ᔷᔰᔦᔥ *Chapter 6* ᔥᔦᔰᔷ

As they were preparing to leave the next morning, Matt did a quick head count—and soon realized he was missing one small child. Zach, the baby, was too young to crawl off by himself. Five-year-old Skeeter, the little deaf-and-dumb boy Matt despaired of ever finding adoptive parents for, was clinging to Beth's skirts, and Ike was helping Matt hitch the team of oxen to the wagon. It was Emily, bright-eyed inquisitive Emily, who had disappeared.

With a frown, and an admonition to the others to stay put until he returned, Matt started to search. He did not have to look far for her, only the distance to the next wagon. There she stood, surrounded by Jade and her friends, watching them burn their breakfast. Atop Emily's dark curls rested a huge broad-brimmed straw hat, which dipped precariously over one eye, and a long strand of pearls trailed from her neck to her shoes. The thumb stuck in her mouth could not hide the delighted smile that lit her face. She appeared to be having the time of her young life.

"Ye think ye might grow into those big brown eyes o' yers one day, Em?" Jade was asking.

Emily nodded enthusiastically, and the hat tipped farther over her face.

"Emily!" Matt barked loudly. "What are you doing over here, young lady?"

Though he rarely raised his voice, much less a hand, to any of the orphans, Matt was so perturbed at finding

55

Emily with these wayward women that his tone was much sharper than he'd intended. So sharp that Emily nearly leaped from her shoes in surprise. As she spun about to face him, her foot caught in her long necklace, tripping her up. She toppled backward toward the fire, and if not for Jade, who reached out and pulled the child away from the flames, Emily might have been badly burned.

Naturally, Emily's immediate reaction was to begin bawling. Jerking her thumb from her mouth, she scrunched up her tiny face and let out a shrill cry that should have cracked windows for a square mile. Without seeming to pause for air, the child let out one ear-piercing howl after another.

Before Matt could step in and take matters in hand, Jade scooped the girl into her embrace. "Now, now, lass. 'Tis all right. No need to set up such a fuss over nothin'. He didn't mean to scare ye that way." Jade aimed an emerald-eyed glare at Matt. "Did ye?" she demanded fiercely.

"No, Emily. I didn't mean to frighten you so," Matt admitted more calmly. He approached the two and held out his arms to Emily. "I'm sorry."

Emily was having none of this lukewarm apology, however. She tightened her grip about Jade's neck and clung like a monkey to a banana tree. "Go 'way!" she sniffled, pushing her lower lip out in a pout. "You made me lose my hat!"

Indeed, the hat had fallen into the fire and was now reduced to a small mass of flickering flames. "Now, Emily, the hat was not yours to keep, dear," Matt pointed out reasonably. "Besides, you have a new hat of your own back at the wagon. One that fits you properly. Remember?"

Not yet mollified, Emily wailed, "But it doesn't have pretty flowers like Miss Jade's did."

"No, but it has a lovely blue ribbon to tie beneath your chin," Matt cajoled.

"Oh, me!" Jade exclaimed softly, nuzzling Emily's downy curls. "That sounds like a bonny hat, Em. Me own didn't even have ribbons!"

At last Emily showed signs of brightening. A tiny smile crept past a hiccup. "I s'pose so."

Matt held out his arms again, and Emily crawled into them. "I'm sorry I yelled at you, Emily, but I was worried when I couldn't find you. You're not supposed to wander away from the wagon."

To Jade, he offered a more grudging apology. "Since it's my fault that your hat has been ruined, I will make restitution. Just tell me how much it will cost to replace it."

"I wouldn't dream of takin' yer money, Reverend Richards," she purred cattily, her eyes narrowing at him. "Why, to some that might look as if ye were consortin' with the enemy, and ye wouldn't want yer sterlin' reputation tarnished now, would ye?"

Her barb struck its mark. Matt's rear teeth ground together in agitation. "I said I'd pay for the blasted hat," he repeated with a scowl.

She offered him a sugar-and-vinegar smile. "And I said ye could keep yer coin and stick it in yer own blarsted hat!"

"Fine! Just don't say I didn't offer. Have a good day, Miss Jade." He turned and started to walk away, then wheeled about again. "I see you managed to light your fire correctly this morning. Congratulations. If this continues, perhaps the children and I needn't worry about choking on clouds of smoke at every meal," he sniped, surprising even himself with his petty comment.

"All I had to do was conjure yer image in me head and breathe on the kindlin'," Jade retorted silkily. "It lit up like lightnin' hittin' a rotten stump."

Matt made a low sound in his throat and stalked off. As she bounced along in his arms, Emily giggled. "You sound just like a tiger, Papa Matt. Do it again!"

Jade's companions, who had sat transfixed throughout the confrontation between the gorgeous pastor and their friend, now found their tongues.

"Whew! You sure took a bite out o' his britches!" Fancy declared.

"Mercy, Jade! That Irish temper of yours has a mighty short fuse when it comes to that preacher!" Peaches added.

"I'll say!" Bliss concurred. "Land's sake, girl, you even treated Butch better than that! What is it about the good Reverend that gets you so riled?"

"He's an arrogant ass!" Jade hissed, still staring after him as if to glare holes through his clothes. "Acts as if he's afraid he'll get himself dirty if he comes within spittin' distance of us. Why, I'll wager he scrubs that poor baby raw, tryin' to get her clean after I held her!"

"Now, Jade honey, be fair. The man didn't start snappin' at you until you nailed into him," Mavis pointed out.

"Eef you ask me, I sink zeze two strikes ze sparks off one anozer," Lizette announced with a sly smile. "Zat is why Jade suddenly becomes ze she-cat and ze preacher ze tiger."

"Nobody asked you," Jade snarled.

Still, she had to wonder if there wasn't a wee grain of truth to Lizette's assessment. What was it about Matt Richards that got under her skin so terribly? So fast and so fiercely, like some irritating rash she couldn't help but scratch! There was just something about the man that put her tail in a twist!

Of course, there was the small matter of her dented dignity, after she'd all but ravished him only to discover he was a preacher! Begorrah! She'd wanted to crawl in a hole and pull it in after her, she was so mortified! And to think that this was the first man she'd felt any real attraction to since Sean!

Oh, she'd done her share of flirting with the gentlemen who'd frequented the hurdy-gurdy. But never with any actual emotion or intent behind it.

Then, out of the blue, she'd taken one look at Matt Richards and made an absolute fool of herself over a man who wouldn't touch her with a ten-foot pole! It was utterly humiliating!

"I'll eat dirt b'fore I throw meself at him like that again!" she swore to herself. "Great gritty gobs o' grime!"

* * *

Jade was eating dirt—and what she wasn't eating, she was wearing. They'd been traveling for three days now, and from the outset of the journey, the trail had alternated between oozing mud and clouds of choking dust kicked up by the plodding animals and slowly rolling wagons. Wagon wheels bogged down when it rained, and when the sun came out again it quickly baked the earth into jaw-jarring ruts. Either way, it was damned miserable for everyone. Dirt coated their clothing, layered their skin, and ground between their teeth.

Of their two wagons, Billy was driving the lead team, and the girls were taking turns learning to drive the other. None of them were adept at it, though Mr. Greene had laughingly told them they would be experts by the time the trip was done. Lizette dourly predicted they'd also have permanent calluses and bruises, and muscles bulging where no woman should display them.

"We look like charwomen," Peaches bemoaned as she trudged wearily alongside Jade.

Walking was another thing none of them had anticipated, but they'd quickly learned that the oxen were taxed enough just trying to pull the loaded wagons, without their weight added to the load. Literally everyone, with the exception of the drivers, the most feeble old folks, and tiny babies, walked most of the day.

"Every bone and muscle in me body is achin'," Jade complained loudly. "I've got blisters atop o' blisters so bad 'tis a bloody wonder I haven't bled to death through me feet!"

"You're the one who said she'd rather walk all the way to Oregon than set foot on a ship," Bliss was quick to remind her.

"When we reach Lawrence t'morrow, I'm buyin' me some boots at the first store I find. And I'm burnin' these torturous shoes!" Jade claimed. "And I'll be gettin' me a new hat, too. Lawsy! Me face must look like a raw steak!"

"Not unless it's been dipped in dirt, it doesn't," Fancy assured her. "Except for your nose, and it's gonna peel down to the bone and leave nothin' but your freckles behind."

"I don't have freckles."

"Ha!" Fancy snorted. "You do now, sweetie. That or you're comin' down with some rare disease."

"Well, I'd talk," Jade shot back. "Ye look like a spotted pup yerself!"

Behind them, on the high seat of his wagon, Matt smothered a chuckle. The "ladies" certainly were a bedraggled bunch today. They gave a whole new meaning to the term "soiled doves." Not that they didn't have just cause to complain, as did everyone on the train. But the journey had just begun, and if they thought the going was rough now, he could only shudder at how they would whine later, when the trail passed through the plains and mountains ahead. Then again, if they tired of the ceaseless travail, perhaps they would revise their plans and turn back—and he would be relieved of their constant, worrisome presence.

When he noticed how badly Jade was limping, Matt immediately berated himself for such an uncharitable thought. The girl was obviously in pain, and he shouldn't wish more on her. Still, he didn't need the kind of trouble she brought. Nor did he need the fire of longing that had rooted itself in his loins since their first meeting and refused to be extinguished.

Even as disheveled as she was now, dripping with dirt-streaked perspiration, her clothes wrinkled, her face sunburned, and her hair in a tangled mass that resembled a ratted horse's tail streaming down her back, Jade was fetching. A charming little scamp in the body of an angel. A fallen angel.

And why shouldn't she be lovely? Matt thought. Satan, yet another ousted angel, was supposed to have been extremely beautiful to behold. He heaved a disgruntled sigh. "Sin does, indeed, come attractively packaged."

Some of the other men on the train obviously thought so, too, for the "ladies" had a number of visitors as they moved slowly westward. Though a few married men happened along now and again, the majority of their callers appeared to be widowers or bachelors. As word spread, more men stopped by for a quick chat with these daughters of sin, until their wagon site began to resemble a beehive swarming with hopeful drones. It was becoming customary for one or more gentlemen to appear in the morning to make sure the girls got their fire started properly, or in the evening to deliver a freshly killed rabbit for their supper, or during the day to offer a brief horseback ride as respite from the drudgery of walking.

Though a couple of the girls had accepted rides from a few lucky fellows, and returned a while later looking more flushed and rumpled than before, Matt noticed that Jade had yet to accept such an offer. Also, as far as Matt could determine, none of the women had thus far entertained any of the men in their tents at night. Of course, that could be a result of the long, tiresome days they'd spent on the trail. These fallen frails were not accustomed to rising before the sun, or walking ten to fifteen miles per day, or driving a team of stubborn, mismatched oxen. Perhaps, like most of the other emigrants, they were too weary by the end of day to do more than crawl into their bedrolls and fall into an exhausted slumber until the next morning. That, or they conducted their clandestine business in the dead of night, waiting until their neighbors were sound asleep and oblivious to the immoral activity going on beneath their very noses.

After the third, seemingly endless day of travel, Matt was beat. With Ike's help, he'd unhitched the team, pitched the tent, and started the fire. Then he'd cooked their supper. Now, when his acquired brood should be clamoring for their evening meal, they were nowhere in sight. Each and every one of the children had mysteriously disappeared, and he was willing to wager exactly where he'd find them.

With determined strides, Matt headed for the next wagon, the one the rest of the travelers had dubbed the "cat cage," for the six "painted felines" traveling therein. Sure enough, there they were, all five wandering orphans clustered about Jade's skirts, staring up at her with varying degrees of adoration etched on their young faces. Even Ike appeared to be enraptured by whatever Jade was saying, and baby Zach was snuggled happily in her lap. The other "ladies" were not in sight.

Reminding himself what had happened the last time, when he'd gone in search of Emily, Matt took a moment to calm himself before he approached the group. Composure was hard to grasp, however. He could only imagine what Jade might be telling those guileless children. What corruption she was, at this very minute, implanting in those fertile, agile minds! The filth assaulting those tender ears!

They hadn't seen him yet, and Matt decided it might behoove him to remain silent for the moment. Keeping to the shadows, he crept closer. When he was finally within earshot, he stopped to listen—and nearly swallowed his own teeth in astonishment!

Jade's lilting voice wafted on the evening breeze, carrying her words clearly to him. "Then the queen of the fairies said, 'Please, Sir Leprechaun, ye must teach me how to dance. I can flit and fly ever so high, and twist and twirl with the wind, but I canna dance a step. I'm to be married soon, and I yearn to dance at me weddin'.'

" 'And what'll ye give me if I do?' the leprechaun asked with a wily look in his eye.

" 'A big pot o' gold,' the fairy queen offered generously.

" 'Nay,' the little man answered. 'Those can be had b'neath any old rainbow. I've more than I'll ever spend now.'

" 'A bushel o' diamond dust, then?' she said.

"Again the leprechaun shook his head. 'Not nearly rare enough.'

" 'What would ye have then?'

" 'Yer wings, fairy queen. I would have yer wings.' "

The children gasped in wide-eyed dismay, and Jade nodded knowingly and went on with the tale. " 'I canna give ye me wings, sir, for without them I could not fly. Me crown would go to another fairy, and me true love with it.'

"The leprechaun became nasty. ' 'Tis that or nothin', Queen. The price o' learnin' to dance is high, and I, too, yearn to fly.'

"Now, to speak in this demandin' way to the queen o' the fairies was courtin' disaster, and the hateful little leprechaun needed to be set down a bit. The queen was just the one to give this selfish elf his comeuppance. Ever so sweetly she said, 'Then fly ye shall, but not upon my wings. First, teach me to dance, and I will grant ye wings o' yer very own.'

"The leprechaun was delighted with the bargain, and he promptly taught the fairy queen how to dance. Then he demanded haughtily, 'I want me wings now.'

"Quick as a blink, the fairy waved her magic wand, and the leprechaun turned into a tiny little gnat, no bigger'n a wart on a frog's toe. 'Ye have yer wings now,' the fairy queen laughed. 'For all eternity. Now scat, b'fore I step on ye! And the next time we meet, show proper respect!'

"And the moral o' the story is twofold," Jade instructed her avid listeners. "First, greed can bring ye grief, so be wary what ye ask for. And second, mind yer manners, 'specially if ye're talkin' to a fairy queen."

As she delivered this final statement, Jade raised her head and stared directly at the spot where Matt stood watching from the shadows. He got the notion she'd known for some time that he was there, that she was silently daring him to confront her.

Stepping forward, he met her challenging gaze straight on. Then a familiar heat flooded through him as her emerald eyes seemed to take on a more sensual glow. Without a word spoken between them, he felt as if she was casting some kind of magical spell over him, as if she were not simply a scarlet woman but an Irish enchantress much like the fairy queen in the tale she'd woven for the children.

With effort, he tore his eyes from hers, focusing on the children. "Supper's waiting," he informed them quietly. "Go and wash up, please."

Beth collected the baby from Jade and the youngsters filed past him, sending him sidelong guilty glances as they went. Matt turned to follow. Jade's voice stopped him.

"Ye'll not punish 'em, will ye?"

He turned back to her. "They deliberately disobeyed me," he said sternly. "For that they will be reprimanded."

"How?"

"I'm not certain yet, but I believe a good scolding is in order, don't you?"

"For visitin' me?"

"For wandering away from the wagon and not asking or informing me where they were going."

"Ye'll not strike 'em?" she persisted with a fretful frown. "Or send 'em to bed without supper? Or preach and make 'em repent o' sins they didn't mean to commit?"

Matt was aghast at her suggestions. "Good grief, woman!" he protested. "What sort of man do you take me for?"

"I don't think ye want to know that," she answered bluntly. "I just need to know ye won't harm those wee ones."

Matt could not believe what he was hearing, no more than he'd expected to walk up and hear Jade telling fairy tales to his young charges. "I have never laid a hand in anger on any of those children, and I do not intend to start doing so now."

She was still not convinced. "Ye promise? On yer honor?"

"I swear it on the Bible I hold dear. Now are you reassured? May I go feed my hungry fledglings before their meal is little more than a burnt offering?"

She nodded, then added, "Thank ye. Maybe I misjudged ye after all."

"And perhaps I misjudged you as well," he conceded. "At least in part."

Again he turned to go, only to have her words bring him up short once more. "If there's any repentin' to be done tonight, preacher man, maybe those prayers ought to be yers, 'cause for a minute there ye were starin' at me like I was the only piece o' candy in the whole store."

She paused to let that thought soak in, then, on a sultry laugh that sent a shiver of desire skating up his spine, she added, "And I was wishin' I was that piece of candy—yer favorite flavor."

If she'd taken him by surprise, she had a bit of a shock coming back. Rather than stiffen up and stalk off in a huff, he offered her a lazy, heart-stopping grin and replied smoothly, "I'm partial to butterscotch and cinnamon, and I suppose, with your coloring, if those two flavors could be combined, they'd add up to you."

"Sugar and spice, and all things nice?" she bantered back coquettishly.

His smile widened. "More like nice and naughty, I'd venture."

Early the next morning, as the girls were attempting to prepare their breakfast, an older woman with a stern look about her walked up to their camp. "I'm Tilda Brunner," she announced brusquely. "The Reverend said you gals need someone to teach you to cook, and that you might be willing to pay for the lessons. Now, I'll tell you right up front that I don't cotton to women who sell their favors, but I need the money. So, are you interested or not?"

The six young women shared looks of surprise. After a moment of stunned silence, Mavis said, "That's right neighborly of you, Mrs. Brunner. And of Reverend Richards. How much would you charge to teach the lot of us?"

"I had in mind a dollar a lesson."

Mavis consulted her friends and met with agreement all around. "You're hired. When can we start?"

"No time like the present," Tilda suggested, shaking her head at the nearly raw bacon and burned eggs the girls had prepared for themselves. "I hope you laid in enough eggs. And I hope you had sense enough to pack them in cornmeal to preserve them."

Mavis nodded. "The guidebook we consulted did suggest it."

Tilda glanced around, her frown deepening. "Where's your milch cow?"

"Uh, we don't have one," Jade offered. "We didn't plan on needin' one."

"If you're going to learn to cook, you do. Besides providing you with milk to drink when the water is unfit, you can make custards and puddings and butter from it."

"We don't have a churn, either," Bliss informed her sheepishly. "None of us are what you'd call domestically talented."

Tilda sniffed and looked down her nose at Bliss. "Which means ye're all as green as spring grass when it comes to anything having to do with housekeeping. For your information, miss, you don't need a churn to have butter, at least not along the trail. All you need do is put your excess milk into a bucket and hang it beneath the wagon, and by the end of the day all that bumping and rocking will have churned the milk for you."

"Maybe we can buy a cow when we get to Lawrence," Fancy said. "Jade was gonna buy boots there, if they have a decent store."

"Well, you can't buy a cow in a store, but I'd suggest you get one somewhere. You can't cook worth beans without milk."

Tilda sent Lizette to wash the frying pan and Peaches to fetch more eggs. "Now, which of you gals is Jade?" she asked.

"I'm Jade. Why do ye ask?"

"The Reverend suggested you might want to learn how to make butterscotch cinnamon rolls. 'Course, we should teach you the basics of cooking first, so you don't ruin everything you try. We'll get around to the fancy baking later."

Jade's cheeks had flushed beet red. She turned away from the group, hoping no one would notice her reaction to Tilda's comment or ask her questions she didn't want to answer just now. She made the mistake of facing Matt's wagon, only to find him watching her with a delighted grin on his all-too-handsome face. Then he sent her a devilish wink, his eyes brimming with mischief, and went on about his business.

All that day, Jade had the hardest time trying to keep her eyes from straying in Matt's direction. When their wagons had begun to bog down in the mud, he'd come forward to help Billy push them free. As Matt had strained against the wheel, his shirtsleeves rolled up out of his way, Jade had gaped in rapt fascination at the way his arm muscles had bulged with the effort. Afterward, he'd changed into a fresh shirt, and she'd watched from the corner of her eye, her mouth going dry at the sight of his wide shoulders and bare chest, lightly furred with dark hair and slick with perspiration.

To make things worse, every time she looked his way, he seemed to feel her gaze on him, and would return it full-force. It wasn't long before the other girls caught this exchange of glances and began to tease her about it.

"I declare! Jade's makin' calf eyes at the preacher!"

"Yeah, and he's lookin' a mite dazed himself."

"What do you make of zat? Has Cupid's arrow struck its mark, do you zink?"

"Hey, Jade! What did Tilda mean this morning with that remark about the Reverend and butterscotch cinnamon rolls? You been keeping secrets from us?"

"I don't want to talk about it," Jade told them stubbornly when it proved impossible to ignore them any longer.

"But I thought you weren't all that impressed with the fellow, Jade. Or does the maid protest too much, perhaps?"

"I'm not a maiden."

Mavis laughed. "Well, you're not much of a courtesan, either."

"Or even a decent hussy," Bliss added, rolling her eyes. "Of course, there are tarts, and then there are tarts, and maybe the preacher has a real sweet tooth, huh? Right now he's eyein' you like you're the tastiest little pastry he's ever seen."

"I'm a singer, and someday I aim to be as great and as well-known as Jenny Lind. I'm sure not gonna fall for some man now, 'specially not one as ill-fittin' as that preacher, and ruin all me grand plans for a rich and glorious future."

"How do you know he's so ill-fittin', Jade?" Peaches asked with a shrewd wink. "Ya haven't even tried him on for size yet, honey. Why, he just might wear like a good kid glove."

"Mercy, Peaches!" Fancy declared, fanning herself with her hand. "Do hush, girl! You're gettin' me so hot and lathered, I'm about to die for want of a lover!"

"Well, hang in there, sugar. Lawrence, Kansas, is comin' up."

∞✧⊱ *Chapter 7* ⊰✧∞

*T*he wagon master had called a brief halt to consult with his scouts about the best place to make camp once they reached Lawrence, just an hour ahead on the trail. It was during this short rest break that Matt chanced to observe a disturbing encounter between Jade and one of the other emigrants from the wagon train. A young woman, obviously pregnant, was walking past Jade's wagon when she tripped over a lump in the tall prairie grass. She might have fallen if Jade, who was standing nearby, hadn't dashed up and grabbed her by the arm to steady her.

"Are ye all right?" he heard Jade inquire courteously. But when the mother-to-be saw who had aided her, she began to shriek hysterically. "Let loose of me! Get away! Get away!"

Jade immediately released her, a look of profound confusion on her face. "Careful now," she admonished as the woman backed hastily away from her "Watch yer step, or ye'll trip again."

"Don't come near me! Don't touch me! You'll give my baby the pox! Or some other dreadful disease all you harlots have! Oh, dear Lord!" she continued to wail. "If this child is born blind or malformed because of you, I'll come after you with an ax! I swear it!"

Shock registered clearly on Jade's stricken face. "What are ye talkin' about, lass? Ye're makin' no sense a'tall!"

"Yes, I am," the lady insisted. "I know all about your kind and the awful diseases you spread. My husband told

me things. Awful things. How the pox can make your hair
and nails fall out."

"I've never heard anything so ridiculous!" Jade retorted.
"Besides, ye needn't worry about catchin' any such plague
from me. I'm as healthy as can be."

The woman glared at her. "Maybe so, but you're dirty
to your soul for the vile sins you've committed, in bed and
against nature. Frank informed me how you trollops take
special potions to keep from conceiving children. He said
if you do find yourself with child, you kill the babes while
they're still in your bodies! You're a murderess, and you
deserve to fry in Hell!"

Jade's jaw dropped in mute astonishment. Her face
turned pale, and her eyes grew huge as she stared at
the raving woman. When she finally found her tongue,
she blurted, "No! I'd never do such a terrible thing! I
don't know why yer husband has told ye such foul tales,
but he's wrong! 'Tis all a rotten pack o' lies!"

"Tell that to Saint Peter on Judgment Day," the woman
shot back as she hurried away. "For all the good it will do
a daughter of the Devil!"

Matt was almost as stunned as Jade appeared to be.
Before he could determine what to do—whether to ignore
the situation as if he'd never witnessed the exchange, or
to go to Jade and try to comfort her in some way—the
decision was taken from him. With much relief, he saw
Mavis approach Jade and slip an arm around the girl's
quaking shoulders.

"Try to put it from your mind, honey," Mavis advised
soothingly. "You can't let their venom poison you."

Jade turned toward her friend, her cheeks wet with
tears. "Ye heard?" she sobbed.

Mavis nodded. "Couldn't help it, the way she was
screeching."

"Oh, Mavis! 'Twas so horrible! The things she said!
Where do people get such awful notions? Such lies?"

Mavis sighed and admitted reluctantly, "I'm afraid a
lot of what she told you holds more than a grain of
truth. You just haven't been with us long enough to learn

about it, especially since Vera ran such a clean house and looked after her girls so well. She helped prevent a lot of misery we'd all have faced if we'd have worked for someone else."

Jade shook her head and said miserably, "I don't understand."

"I know you don't." Mavis gave her a hug and nudged Jade toward the wagon. "C'mon, sweet pea. I think it's time we had a talk about the problems and perils of prostitution."

All the way to Lawrence, Matt's thoughts dwelled on what he'd seen and overheard. It stuck in his craw that for her attempt at kindness, Jade had reaped nothing but hatred and revulsion in return. That she had been so genuinely confused and astounded by the lady's accusations was equally disturbing, not to mention amazing. Why, it seemed the mother-to-be was better informed than the Irish harlot! It baffled him that Jade had appeared less enlightened, and thus more naive, than the young wife.

Of course, Mavis had served to explain that oddity, at least in part. Apparently, Jade was fairly new to the trade. Matt could not help but wonder how recently she'd joined that sisterhood of sin. And why. Who, and what, had driven her to such a life? More important, was it too late to save her from it if someone—himself, for instance—cared enough to try? Or would it be wiser to ignore his conscience and let someone else attempt her redemption, the better to resist the enticing green-eyed baggage who inspired such irrational feelings of lust in him?

Yes, perhaps that would be much more prudent, since the more he saw of her, and the better he got to know her, the more he found to admire about her. But could he avoid future contact, further involvement? Did he truly want to? Worse yet, was this absurd craving for her really lust, or was it actually something deeper? Something beyond his comprehension or control?

*   *   *

Two days later, during the noon stop, Jade entered Matt's campsite carrying Skeeter perched atop her hip. The boy's face was streaked with dirt and tears, there was a large rip in the knee of his britches, and he had his arms twined so tightly about Jade's neck that it was a wonder she could breathe. It was not need of air, however, but outrage that flushed Jade's face. Her expression rivaled that of an avenging angel.

Matt immediately went forward to take the crying child from her arms. "What happened?" he asked.

"I'll tell ye what happened!" Jade exploded. "Three big brutes, who need their rumps blistered royally, were beatin' up on wee Skeeter! No matter that they were all twice his age and size! For two cents, I'd go back and tan their hides meself, but they all went runnin' when I yelled at 'em."

Matt was on his knees, examining the lump swelling beneath Skeeter's eye, and paid only partial attention to Jade's next comments. "I couldn't tell how badly he's hurt, and he was cryin' too hard for me to bother askin'. 'Tis amazin' how little noise the lad makes when he cries, though."

Stripping Skeeter of his shirt, Matt winced at the red welts he discovered on the boy's torso. As he ran his fingers lightly along Skeeter's ribs, he said, "Nothing appears broken, thank God, but he took some hard hits."

"And kicks as well," Jade informed him angrily. "I'd like to thrash those young bullies! Give 'em a dose o' their own medicine!"

As Matt edged back a bit to inspect Skeeter's pantleg, and the knee exposed by the shredded cloth, the lad suddenly blanched and doubled over in obvious pain.

"What is it, Skeeter? Your stomach?" Matt asked, hoping the mute child could somehow understand and give him an indication of where the pain was located.

"Uh . . . I think ye'd best check his . . . uh . . . well, his private parts," Jade stammered. "He was holdin' . . . that area when I first reached him."

Matt's brow rose, at both the information she had just imparted and her obvious embarrassment in doing so. "Oh. I see. That would account for a good deal of his discomfort and his peaked complexion." He took his kerchief and wiped gently at Skeeter's face. "Between all the dirt and the bruises, I didn't realize he was quite so pale."

"Do ye think he'll be okay?" she questioned anxiously. "Gettin' hit in . . . there . . . won't be anything truly serious, will it?"

Despite his concern over Skeeter's injuries, Matt had to bite back a grin. "I imagine the family jewels will prove intact," he replied, slanting a look at her flaming face and catching the baffled expression his words had elicited.

"Family jewels?" she echoed confusedly.

Again he wondered that this soiled dove could, time and again, display such a seeming innocence. "His . . . private parts, I believe you called them," he explained. "I'll wager he'll recover nicely from any damage to the region, but I'll be sure to keep a close check on him, if it will ease your mind on the matter."

She nodded, now as mute as Skeeter.

He couldn't help but tease her a bit more, though he knew he shouldn't after she'd exhibited such kindness and concern for Skeeter. "Shall I report my findings back to you later?"

"Uh . . . no. Thank ye anyway."

"Thank *you*," he told her. "Most sincerely. If not for you, there's no telling how much more seriously Skeeter might have been hurt. Usually Beth or Ike look out for him when I'm busy." His face clouded. "You can bet I'll be asking them why Skeeter was left to fend for himself this afternoon."

"Well, I leave ye to tend to Skeeter now," she said as she started to leave. She hesitated before offering, "If ye ever need someone to watch over him or any o' the other children, just give a holler. I'd be glad to lend a hand."

Before he could answer, either for or against her suggestion, she was gone.

* * *

It was their first Sunday on the trail, but that didn't mean a day of rest for the emigrants. Rather, it meant delaying their departure by a mere half an hour, allotting that scant time for a quick prayer meeting between eating the morning meal and hitching their wagons.

"I ain't never heard a preacher give a sermon in less than half a day," Peaches said skeptically. "Back in Georgia there's a heap o' proclaimin' and prayin' between the openin' hymn and the last amen."

Tilda deftly demonstrated how to flip a flapjack before commenting on Peaches's remark. "I understand Reverend Richards is a Methodist minister. Could be they're a mite quicker than Baptist preachers."

"Couldn't be any more long-winded, that's for sure," Fancy put in with a short laugh. "Why, when I was a kid, I swore my backside was gonna grow fast to the pew and my stomach be touchin' my backbone b'fore church adjourned." She cast a curious glance in Jade's direction. "Are priests as blustery as all that, Jade?"

"I wouldn't know," she answered with a careless shrug. "My family wasn't Catholic."

"Do tell," Tilda said in mild surprise. "I thought all the Irish were Catholic. Guess it just goes to show how ignorant we can be about the rest of the world sometimes. I suppose we ought to take more notice than we do, instead of always getting so caught up in our own lives and petty problems."

"Broaden our horizons, Tilda?" Mavis suggested in wry amusement. "I'll wager we'll all have our fill of that between here and Oregon. Horizon after endless, dusty horizon."

As luck would have it, the girls found themselves with a ringside seat at the Sunday services, as all who wished to participate began to congregate around the Richards wagon, well within earshot of their own campsite. In lieu of a pulpit, Matt took his stand on the high wagon seat, where everyone could see and hear him, including the "girls," whether they wanted to or not.

After a prayer, in which he asked the Lord to open their hearts and minds to His word, Matt reminded his audience of the biblical flight of the Israelites from Egypt, comparing it to their own trek across America. He didn't rant or rave or thump his Bible for emphasis. Rather, he spoke calmly, eloquently, commanding the attention of his listeners in an astonishingly effortless fashion.

To Jade it almost seemed as if he were telling a story rather than delivering a sermon. As if he were teaching his flock, not preaching at them. His words were simple, easily understood, his message concise and to the point, with no flowery phrasing or scholarly terms beyond the comprehension of less educated persons. But what most amazed Jade, and several others as well, was the humor Matt injected into his biblical lesson, the easy smile that curved his lips and the twinkle that crept into his blue eyes.

"Let us all hope that the dear Lord will see fit to guide us to our destination in far less time than it took the Israelites to cross the desert into the Promised Land," he jested at one point.

Matt was decidedly no staid and stern minister of the Gospel, no standard-issue fire-and-brimstone preacher. This was a down-to-earth disciple of God who stood among his fellows, not apart from them. Who emanated a sense of empathy rather than of judgment, offering comfort and common sense in place of condemnation. At least that was the impression many of them gained that morning, along with their Sunday dose of Scripture, and they came away from the meeting feeling revived and assured of God's guiding hand in their lives.

"Gosh!" Peaches declared afterward. "I'm impressed! If we'd had a preacher like him when I was younger, my life might have turned out differently." She gave a short laugh and shrugged. "Then again, maybe not. I was a wild one back then. Still am, for that matter."

"We wouldn't know ye any other way," Jade assured her with a teasing grin.

*   *   *

Following his fight with the bullies, Skeeter appeared at Jade's wagon several times a day, often accompanied by his fellow orphans. Whether or not the youngsters had Matt's permission to visit her, Jade did not know. Baby Zach was too young to talk, Skeeter had yet to utter his first word in Jade's presence, and the other three had become adept at evading her questions on the matter.

Assuming that Skeeter must be painfully shy by nature, Jade did not press him to speak. Given time and patience, she imagined he'd overcome this problem and would probably chatter like a magpie ever afterward. Heaven knew Emily certainly did!

One day she took several old stockings, which the "girls" had managed to collect for her, and helped the children make hand puppets out of them. With crookedly placed pieces of yarn and lace, and odd buttons for eyes, the end products were a bit ragged, but the youngsters were pleased, and that was what counted most. Their smiles and antics made Jade glow with joy and love for them.

It was as Jade was prompting Skeeter to make his dragon puppet roar that she finally learned the horrible truth. It was Beth who enlightened her. "He can't do it, Miss Jade," the girl told her. "Skeeter can't talk or hear. Didn't you know? That's why we all have such a hard time explaining things to him, or understanding what he wants. That's why he fidgets so much while the rest of us are listenin' to your stories."

Upon hearing this, Jade was fairly well struck speechless herself. Tears pooled in her eyes and spilled down her cheeks. Slowly she gathered Skeeter onto her lap to hold him close to her heart as she gently stroked his hair. "I didn't know," she murmured. "Poor wee mite! But he can still feel. I'm sure o' that. When I hold him and touch him he can tell that I care. And he sees. He knows when we smile at him that we're happy about somethin', that when we frown we're displeased. That if we cry, we're sad or hurtin'. Don't ye suppose that's so?"

Beth, ever the little mother, patted Jade awkwardly on the arm. "Yes, Miss Jade. Skeeter might be deaf and dumb, but there's a lot he's smart about. That's what Papa Matt tells us. He says Skeeter just needs extra attention, and plenty of love."

Unbeknownst to anyone else, love was something Matt was contemplating at that very moment. Not love of God, or love for the children in his care, but his mixed emotions for one minuscule trollop with penny-bright hair and emerald eyes. Despite himself, his mind and body were running amok, and no amount of logic seemed to counter this irrational reaction. To his immense shock, it felt as if he were actually falling in love with Jade!

"It can't be!" he argued silently "Not with a harlot. Not after the harsh lesson Cynthia taught me about faithless females."

Though he harbored no bitterness toward women as a whole, his unfortunate marital experience had left him cautious about choosing another life's mate. He'd promised himself he'd be much more careful the next time around. Yet here he was, yearning after a freckle-faced strumpet!

"It's just lust, old boy. Plain and simple," he assured himself. But it certainly didn't feel that simple, when all he had to do was look at Jade and his throat constricted, his heart began pounding like a drum, and his brain suddenly took flights of fancy—and quite erotic excursions at that!

To top it all, the "lady" in question had several other qualities he admired. Not only was she beautiful, but she was kind, and funny, and patient and gentle with the children. Then there was that infernal, baffling aura of childlike innocence, which, when combined with her sensual looks, was fast driving him crazy.

"Hang it all! I need another wanton woman like I need the measles!"

An inner voice seemed to laugh at him.

He sighed heavily, instinctively knowing to Whom that voice belonged. *Please Lord, don't let this happen. Don't do this to me. Jade and I would be totally mismatched! The only possible advantage is that there'd be no rude awakenings such as I encountered with Cynthia. This alliance would be an uphill battle from the very start!*

Again that chuckle resounded in his mind, mocking his futile denial, willing him to bend to a will stronger than his own.

Matt entreated his Maker once more. *At least think about it, won't You? And if You're still certain this is what You want for me, I sure could use a little more time to get used to the idea. After all, I've only known the woman for a week and a half!*

Matt had a another dilemma on his hands, one that also involved Jade. He'd tried prayer and threats and bribery, and nothing was having any effect. No matter what he did or said, the children still insisted on visiting Jade and her lady friends. If Matt did not give them his reluctant permission, they would sneak off to see the women, despite any and all consequences.

To make matters worse, Ike was thoroughly smitten with Jade. He wandered around in a perpetual fog with a silly smile on his face and his chest puffed out like a bantam rooster's, chanting her praises. "She's so purty, ain't she?" he'd say with a sigh. "Her hair is the color of the sunrise, and her eyes are like . . . like . . ."

"Twin frogs?" Matt suggested wryly when Ike failed to find an apt comparison.

Ike spared him a disgruntled look. "For a man of words, you're sure no poet, Reverend. B'fore you go sparkin', you'd best practice up a bit, sir."

"I'll do that, Ike," Matt replied, hiding a grin.

Ike put on a thoughtful frown and asked, "What sort of man do you reckon Miss Jade admires most?"

Anything in pants, most likely, Matt thought to himself with a grimace. To Ike, he suggested gently, "Aren't you a little young to be thinking along those lines, son?"

Ike shrugged. "Nothin' wrong in lookin' over the herd and spottin' the best fillies."

"I don't imagine Miss Jade would appreciate being likened to a horse any more than she'd care to have her eyes compared to frogs. Looks as if we both need to improve our skills at courtship, Ike."

"I reckon so," the boy conceded. "But I ain't talkin' about marryin' Miss Jade and takin' her to Salt Lake with me, you know."

Matt leveled a reproving look at the boy. "Then what were you suggesting?"

The lad colored to the tips of his ears. "Uh, just gettin' her to take more notice of me, I reckon. To see that I'm not just a kid anymore."

"Don't be in such a hurry to grow up, Isaac," Matt counseled. "Manhood carries a lot of responsibility with it, and believe me, it's not all it's cracked up to be."

The more Matt considered this problem with Ike, the more he thought it might be wise to have a chat with the object of the boy's affections, just to make sure Jade was not encouraging the infatuation. He sought her out one evening after bedding the children down for the night.

Once again, he found Jade sitting alone at her campsite. She was leaning against a wagon wheel, staring at the fire a few feet away, and it wasn't until he was nearly upon her that Matt noticed the tears coursing down her face. Immediately concerned, he hunched down next to her. "What's wrong?" he questioned softly, not sure how to go about comforting her. "Are you ill? Do you want me to find one of your friends? Where are they, Jade?"

She sniffed and swiped at her tears. "They're around somewhere, out walkin' and such. They'll be back later."

Which, to Matt, meant they were most likely plying their trade in some bachelor's wagon or in some secluded spot along the riverbank. He wanted to ask why Jade wasn't doing likewise, but held his tongue. Instead he inquired, "Why are you crying? Are you sick, or hurt?"

Without warning, she turned her emerald gaze on him and said accusingly, "Why didn't ye tell me about little Skeeter? Until Beth said somethin', I thought he was just too shy to speak to me, too full of energy to be still and listen to the stories I told the children. How was I to know he can't hear or talk?"

"So that's what has you so upset," Matt said. "I'm sorry. I guess I'm so used to dealing with his impairment that I forget how it affects other people who are not prepared for it."

He waited for her to display disgust at the child's handicap. Cynthia, for one, had been openly repulsed by Skeeter, refusing to have anything to do with the poor tyke, as if she might somehow contract the ailment from him. Others often exhibited embarrassment for the child. But once more, Jade surprised him.

"How can ye be so calm about it?" she railed at him. "That wee child sits there lookin' up at ye with those big sad eyes, his world as silent as a tomb, while the rest o' us hear birds chirpin' and music playin' and fires cracklin'. 'Tisn't fair, Matt! 'Tisn't right for that poor little fella to go around not hearin' any of it, not bein' able to speak his thoughts or express his needs!" She was crying earnestly again, salty tears wetting her cheeks. "Me heart wants to break for him!"

Matt wasn't sure which of them moved, but suddenly Jade was in his arms, her head nestled against his shoulder as she sobbed in sympathy for the young orphan. "It's all right, Jade," he crooned, stroking her hair awkwardly.

She drew back far enough to look him square in the eye, her own sparkling with ire behind tear-spiked lashes. "It isn't all right! It will never be right! How can yer God do this to a helpless child?"

How could he explain, when he sometimes asked the same question himself? "God gives us all crosses to bear in our lives," he told her. "It's not always clear why. We simply have to trust that He has his own reasons, and that His plans are best. It's called having faith, Jade."

"Well, ye can have it!" she retorted. "Me, I want no part of a faith that cripples wee babes and makes orphans of 'em. If God is that cruel, then give me the Devil any old day o' the week!"

Matt cringed at her angry words. "Don't say that, Jade. I know it's hard for you to see right now, but God is kind and loving. He cares about each and every one of us."

"What about Skeeter?" she challenged. "How can God care about him, and still make him deaf and dumb?"

"He placed Skeeter in my custody, didn't He?" Matt argued. "And the Bible says God will never give any of us more burden than we can bear."

"Don't count on that, Reverend. I wouldn't be believin' everything I read in that book o' yers. O'course, I can't read, so I haven't got that particular problem, meself."

Her hair was so soft, so silky to the touch, that Matt was finding it harder and harder to concentrate on their conversation. Tendrils of it were catching on his work-roughened fingertips, clinging and stroking across his palms. "I . . . I could teach you," he offered finally.

She stared up at him, their eyes sending messages back and forth that had nothing whatever to do with the words being spoken. Her breath caught in her throat. "Teach me . . . what?" she asked faintly.

His fingers found her nape, caressing it lightly, making her shiver. "To read," he answered, his lips moving closer to hers.

"Why?" At that point neither of them was sure what she was questioning—the reason behind his offer to teach her, or the emotion threatening to engulf them both.

Matt had completely lost the thread of their discussion, his senses swamped with the feel of her, the sight and smell of her. All he could think of was tasting her, too. His mouth came down to cover hers, and all remaining conscious thought went up in smoke.

Their lips meshed, hers so soft, pliant, and so very warm beneath his. A small mew of pleasure, or perhaps surprise, issued from her throat, and flames ignited within him. His arms tightened about her, pulling her more fully into the embrace even as his tongue traced the crevice of her lips, urging them apart, searching for entry into the sweet, dark recesses beyond.

Jade gasped, her blood pounding a drumbeat in her veins, and Matt's tongue slipped into her mouth, gliding smoothly alongside hers, stroking the roof of her mouth in a gesture so erotic that she went weak with the thrill of it. Her head fell back beneath the questing pressure of the kiss, her mouth responding instinctively to the firm, gentle command of his. Her heart was racing, her breath coming in short spurts that left her light-headed. Never had she felt such wild, wanton delight as was now spiraling through her, making her skin tingle and her toes curl within her boots.

Matt's lips left hers, and she murmured in disappointment, then gasped anew when they found the tender flesh of her throat, trailing a path of fire from her chin to her ear. There, his tongue probed moistly, and she cried out softly, quivering in his arms. Vaguely, she recognized the hard length of him pressing against her hip, through their clothing, and wondered how she had come to be sprawled across his lap.

"Matt. Matt," she sighed, clutching at him with shaking hands. Her fingers wound into his raven hair, tugging his lips back to hers.

"One more," he whispered. "Just one more taste of you."

This second kiss was more urgent, more demanding, and she met his entreaty with matching ardor. Her tongue danced lithely with his, her lips clung and sipped greedily at his flesh. Yearning, sharp and sweet, built steadily, intensifying with every frantic beat of her heart, until she feared it would suffocate her.

When at last his mouth released hers, she sucked in a deep breath of air, collapsed against his heaving chest, and groaned, "Saints and salvation, Matt! Are ye sure ye're a preacher? 'Cause if ye are, ye're the sinnin'est one I ever did see, and blamed good at it into the bargain!"

He answered with an unsteady laugh. "Jade, my little Irish enchantress, I hate to disillusion you, but kissing and cuddling do not qualify as sins. At least not in my religion. I'm a Methodist minister, not a priest."

"And I'm not Catholic."

"That's good."

"Why?"

"Because I think I'm falling in love with you, and one of us would have to convert!"

❧❦❧ *Chapter 8* ❧❦❧

A stunned silence followed his announcement, until Jade hurriedly disentangled herself from his arms and scooted off his lap, putting a safe distance between them. Her face took on a wounded look, her eyes growing wary. "Don't," she advised quietly. "Don't fall in love with me, Reverend Richards."

"Why not?"

"Because I can never be what ye want, or what ye need."

"How do you know that unless you give it a try?"

"For cryin' out loud, man! I work in a hurdy-gurdy, and ye're a preacher! Can ye even imagine a more unlikely combination? B'sides, ye've made it as plain as the nose on me face what ye think o' me. In yer eyes, I'm a whore, and always will be."

"No, Jade. You could change, if you wanted to badly enough."

"Maybe I'm not wantin' to change. Has that crossed yer wee mind a'tall?"

His expression was one of disbelief. "Do you mean to tell me you'd rather be a prostitute than be married?"

"I'm an entertainer. A darned good one, too," she corrected stubbornly. "And someday I'll prove that to everyone, when I get to be famous and tour the world singin' for royalty."

"What about love? Honest, enduring, bone-deep love?" he persisted. "Will you also reserve a place for that in all your glorious plans?"

She shook her head. "Me heart is me own, and I never

intend to give it over to anyone else's keepin' again."

Realization dawned. "You've been hurt," he surmised. "Well, lady mine, you're not the only one to have drawn a losing hand in the game of love."

She stiffened and leveled a look at him that should have frozen him where he sat. "I'm not a lady, at least by yer definition, and I'm certainly not yers to claim. And I'll be double-damned if I ever play that game again."

He returned her glacial glare with a serene smile. "Don't bet too much on that, angel face," he warned. "I'm going to do my level best to see that you lose."

"Are ye now?" she returned indignantly. "And how might ye be fixin' to accomplish that feat?"

"I intend to court you until you can't resist me any longer."

"Do ye think ye'll live that long?" she taunted saucily.

He leaned forward to plant a kiss on the tip of her nose. "If the good Lord is willing and the creeks don't rise," he promised—and promptly left her to contemplate her fate.

Rain, rain, and more rain. Mud up to the hubs of the wagon wheels—or "up to the butt of a ten-foot Indian," as Mr. Greene so glibly put it. The Big Blue River was rising daily, threatening to overspill its banks, and Jade could only assume the various creeks were also getting their fair share of water.

Even as sodden and miserable as she was, Jade could not resist gloating to Matt about this development. "The creeks are risin', Reverend. Guess I win the wager."

"What goes up must come down, so don't count your blessings yet, Miss Jade," he counseled. "I have months in which to convince you."

Two weeks out of Independence, they reached a point in the trail called Alcove Spring. Here, they were forced to wait for a day and a half for the waters of the Big Blue to recede before they could risk ferrying the wagons across at Independence Ford, just a mile or so to the west.

The delay was well worth it, however, for the place was idyllic. Just a short walk from their camp, in a grassy, tree-shaded glade, a natural spring gushed forth, spilling over a rocky ledge in a small cascade. Below the stream, a crystal pool was so cold and pure it was as if it had just been melted from ice. Quite a welcome change from the storm-riled waters of the river.

Water kegs were gratefully refilled with little fear of contamination, since the oxen, the moderate herd of beef cattle they had brought along for meat, and the horses were all watered at the nearby river, leaving the spring and pond for human use. Then it was time for the dirty, bruised band of travelers to treat themselves and their clothing to the first good washing they'd had in a fortnight. It was as if they'd all been awarded a fortune in gold. In fact, there was a great deal of squabbling over which gender would get to use the pool first, for both men and women could not avail themselves of it at the same time. Only when the women threatened not to cook until they could do so with clean bodies did the men relent.

More complications then ensued. Matt found himself turning Emily and Beth and little Zachary over to the care of Jade and her friends, only to meet with immediate criticism from several of the Christian women in their traveling group.

"How can you even consider letting those innocent young children near such sordid riffraff?" one old dame accused.

"Why, they're liable to come down with some dread disease!" another declared.

"You're practically consigning those helpless girls to lives as Mary Magdalenes."

"Come now, ladies," Matt countered, shaking his head at their absurd claims. "In the first place, it has never been conclusively proven that Mary Magdalene was a harlot, though Christ did drive evil spirits from her body, after which she became one of his most devoted followers. Secondly, you must agree that it is far better for the baby and the girls to bathe with the other women than with me and the boys."

"You might have asked one of us to look after them

for you," Charlotte Cleaver commented, adding coyly, "I would have offered, had I realized you needed assistance."

Matthew dredged up a lukewarm smile for the young brunette who, for the past two weeks, had made it increasingly clear that she would lick the mud from his boots if he wished. Her adoration of him bordered on being worshipful, and was fast becoming bothersome. Not that the lady wasn't attractive, nor was she unsuitable in any overt fashion. She was neat, devout, virtuous, and obviously intent on ending her days as a maiden as soon as humanly possible, with Matt as her targeted spouse.

It was just that she didn't set his pulse hammering the way Jade did. When he envisioned making love to Jade, his imagination triggered all sorts of erotic reactions, whereas the thought of bedding Miss Cleaver left him completely devoid of desire, as droopy as an overcooked noodle.

"I appreciate the gesture, but the children will go with Jade, as planned," Matt announced. "After being trail neighbors for this long, they are acquainted and comfortable with her."

Throughout this discussion, Jade had silently endured the censure of the other women. Now she could not hold back a sneering smile. "Thank ye for yer vote o' confidence, Reverend. And I'm sure all these snooty biddies will keep a sharp eye peeled, just to be sure I don't try to drown the wee ones."

Jade had assessed the situation well. She felt as if she were walking a gauntlet as she and her companions took the three children to the pool. Once there, Jade was unaccountably shy about disrobing before the large gathering of women, which numbered about fifty or more. She hadn't been so self-conscious since the girls had helped bathe her that first morning at Vera's. It took all her courage to appear nonchalant as she tossed her clothing onto the bank and waded naked into the water with Emily and Beth on either side of her and three-month-old Zach in her arms. Only then, much to her chagrin, did she notice that the more proper women had entered the pool still modestly clad in their chemises, or at least their drawers and camisoles.

To make matters worse, Jade had never before had charge of any child, let alone one as young as Zach. The moment his toes touched the water, he turned from a placid, cooing infant into a slippery, wriggling worm! If not for Beth, who was used to looking after him, Jade feared she truly might have drowned the squirming, soapy bundle of energy.

While Jade helped bathe Emily, and washed both her and Beth's hair, Zach was passed from their hands to Mavis's—then on to Lizette, Bliss, Fancy, and Peaches in turn, until everyone was duly cleaned. All the while, they tried to ignore the flurry of whispers and sniping remarks being passed back and forth among the other women, snide comments spoken just loudly enough to be overheard by all.

"Look at those shameless hussies!"

"Jezebels!"

"Imagine taking off every stitch of their clothes! Why, I don't even do that in front of Harold, and we've been married going on twenty years!"

"And I'll bet old Harold has to seek his thrills in some pleasure palace, with more accommodatin' gals like us," Fancy surmised with a smothered giggle.

"Wouldn't you?" Mavis added. "Did you get a good look at that prune-faced woman?"

Charlotte Cleaver's voice floated over the clearing. "I think all loose women should be tarred and feathered, or marked with a scarlet letter, like the one in Mr. Hawthorne's book. They shouldn't be allowed to mingle freely with decent folk."

"They should be stoned to death, as in biblical times," another woman contributed. "Or at least put to the pillory or the dunking stool."

"Would ye listen t' that?" Jade exclaimed softly. "Leapin' lizards! Ye'd think we were still back in the days b'fore the wheel was invented!"

"Well, I for one am going to keep a keen watch on those women!" Charlotte declared. "Especially that red-haired tart Reverend Richards put in charge of the children. What can the man be thinking of?"

"Yeah, Jade," Bliss whispered. "Answer that one, sugar pie."

Jade tossed a long, dripping hank of hair over her shoulder, trying to assume a nonchalant attitude. "I'd hazard he ain't thinkin' o' Miss Priss there, at any rate, or he'd have asked her to watch the younguns."

As if in response to Jade's comment, yet another lady stated, "I wouldn't take it personally, Charlotte. From what I hear, the poor man is still recovering from his dear wife's death, and most likely isn't thinking straight when it comes to such matters. As I understand it, Mrs. Richards was one of the sweetest, most lovely ladies you would ever want to meet, and her sudden demise nearly devastated him."

Nell Jansen agreed. "Carl and I were neighbors of theirs back in Kentucky, and members of their church, and I'm here to tell you that Cynthia was a veritable angel. Matt hasn't been the same since she died, and he'll search a long way before he finds a woman to compare to her."

"Lawsy, Jade!" Peaches murmured. "You're competin' with an ever-bloomin' saint!"

"I'll not be competin' with anyone, thank ye very much," Jade asserted sourly, shrugging off the unwarranted twinge of jealousy that nipped at her. "I don't give a fig if his wife could stand on her head and whistle 'Dixie' at the same time. Makes no matter to me. I've plans of me own what don't include a man in my life, most especially a Bible-totin' preacher."

"Zen you won't mind if he turns his attention to Mademoiselle Charlotte?" Lizette queried skeptically. "Now, why do I not believe zis?"

"Think what ye will. I don't want that man."

Bliss laughed. "Sure, and a cat don't lick his whiskers either."

*   *   *

It was some time before Matt realized that Ike and Skeeter had disappeared, most likely together. Thinking the boys had decided to lay a fire for Jade, or perform some other chore that would gain Ike favor, Matt wandered toward the neighboring wagon. But he found no sign of either lad, there or anywhere within the circle of the wagon train.

The thought dawned on Matt that perhaps the boys had gone to fetch more water for the ladies. On the heels of that thought came another, one that stopped him in his tracks, then sent him racing toward the spring. "I'll whip him 'til he can't sit for a week!" he vowed, even as he prayed he was wrong in his assumption. "So help me Hannah, if that boy is doing what I think he is, I'll take a whole bundle of willow switches to his behind!"

As he neared the pool, another dilemma presented itself. How was he to look for the boys without intruding upon the privacy of the women bathing here? Certainly, he didn't want to disturb them, or, God forbid, to be caught creeping around in the bushes like some blasted Peeping Tom! But there was no help for it. If the boys were here, he had to find them before they got themselves into more trouble than they probably had already.

He'd edged his way cautiously around one end of the clearing, taking care not to be seen, or to inadvertently catch a stray glimpse of more than he should, when he sighted the red kerchief Skeeter always tucked into the rear pocket of his dungarees. The kerchief was still attached to its usual place—on the hunched-up rump of the younger boy, as he and Ike lay half hidden in the underbrush, spying on the unsuspecting ladies!

Muttering a quick prayer for forbearance, Matt caught hold of the backs of two sets of britches and yanked the boys from their hiding place. Mute as ever, Skeeter opened his mouth in a soundless yelp. Ike was only slightly more vocal, surprise making his startled cry catch in his throat.

"Don't you dare make any noise, young man," Matt hissed. "You're in Dutch enough as it is."

He latched onto the lad's ear before Ike could attempt an escape. "Whatever possessed you to go spying on the women, Ike? I've no doubt you knew it was wrong."

"I wasn't lookin' at all o' them," Ike whined, leaning to one side to ease the tug on his ear. "Just Miss Jade." His eyes were the size of ostrich eggs and still glazed with astonishment. "And I sure didn't know she was gonna go in the water as naked as a jaybird 'stead o' leavin' her underclothes on like most o' the other ladies done!"

Matt didn't mean to look.

He honestly tried not to look.

He looked.

He just couldn't help himself, couldn't find the strength to resist such powerful temptation. It was as if the Devil were sitting on his shoulder, twisting his head around and aiming his gaze through the thin veil of bushes separating him from the women in the pool.

And there she was, in all her glory. Jade. Standing hip-deep in the clear water, her wet, penny-bright hair streaming over her shoulders in sunlit splendor, she looked like some Roman goddess sprung to life. As he watched, his mouth suddenly as dry as a desert, his feet seemingly rooted to the earth, and his eyes helplessly riveted to her loveliness, she tossed her hair from across her chest, revealing one firm, pink-tipped breast. Matt could not avoid noticing that for all her lack of stature, the woman was marvelously well endowed. Her breasts were high and full, her waist small and flaring gently into smoothly rounded hips. Where the sun had kissed her skin, it was the color of honey, and where it hadn't, her flesh appeared to take on the translucent glow of fine pearls.

Though he stood in the shade, Matt felt his temperature rise dramatically—in tandem with a more invigorated nether part of his willful body. Perspiration dotted his forehead and upper lip, and his heart was drumming at double time in a chest so tight he could scarcely breathe.

This was the sweetest, hottest, most carnal torment he'd ever experienced in all his twenty-six years.

If Ike hadn't started squirming, trying to elude the constant pinch on his ear, Matt might have stood transfixed forever. Fortunately, the lad's movements served to break the spell, releasing Matt's attention from the sinfully enchanting tableau before him. Thoroughly disconcerted, and more than a little angry with himself and the boys, Matt promptly directed his steps, and those of his delinquent charges, toward the campsite and away from further temptation.

"March!" he ordered gruffly, guiding each of them by the scruff of the neck. "And if the two of you are extremely lucky, my temper will have cooled considerably by the time we reach our wagon."

❧❦ *Chapter 9* ❧❦

*F*or the first time in two weeks, the emigrants were able to take a well-deserved break from the constant trials of the trail. In celebration of their brief respite, music and revelry were the order of the evening. Ed Mueller brought out his fiddle, Margie Endicott her guitar, and Billy produced a harmonica in lieu of the piano half buried in the wagon. Thus inspired, Jade unpacked her flute and joined the impromptu band.

It wasn't long before many of the ladies and gentlemen, inspired by the lively music, began to dance. To Jade's surprise, even a good number of the more devout Christians joined in, including Reverend Richards. The mood was light and gay, and everyone was having a great time.

No one was more amazed or delighted than Matt when the music turned soft and dreamy, and Jade began to sing. As small as she was, he would never have dreamed that her voice would be strong enough to rise above the instrumental accompaniment as it did. Like a bird trilling at dawn, celebrating the day, her clear, vibrant tones issued forth to entrance her audience. Tears shone in many an eye as she sang poignantly of "Jeanie with the Light Brown Hair" and "Barbara Allen." Then she treated them to the more whimsical verses of "O, Susanna" and "The Man on the Flying Trapeze." By the time she began a rousing rendition of "She'll Be Comin' Round the Mountain," folks were joining the performance, clapping in time to the music, broad smiles wreathing their faces and weariness gladly forgotten as they danced with merry abandonment.

Jade had to smile as she watched Matt squire Beth and Emily over the grassy makeshift dance floor. It wasn't until Jade spied him dancing with Charlotte Cleaver that she again felt that strange stab of jealousy. A short while later, when he approached her and asked her to dance, Jade declined. "I'm busy playing," she informed him stiffly. "Go sport with yer dark-haired lass and let me be."

"To which dark-haired lass do you refer, milady?" he asked with a sly smile and an arch of one dark brow.

"Ye know. The one who thinks I'm leadin' yer poor little lambs astray. The one givin' ye looks as if ye hung the moon."

He didn't even have the courtesy to pretend to misunderstand. Rather, his smile grew into a grin. "Oh, you mean Charlotte Cleaver. Do I detect an air of pique here, Jade?" He clasped a hand to his chest in a theatrical gesture. "Dare I hope this means that you care?"

"I don't give a hoot what ye do, Reverend. Just go away and let me get back to me music."

"You play very well, Jade. And you have a voice angels must envy."

"And that surprises ye, does it?"

He nodded. "A bit. I didn't really take you seriously, but it seems you are, indeed, a woman of diverse talents."

"Thank ye—I think. Now, be gone with ye."

"I really do need to talk with you, Jade, and I thought we might converse while dancing. It would give me an excellent excuse to hold you in my arms again."

"Folks'll talk, ye know," she told him. "The gossips are already waggin' their tongues about ye."

"Are they?" He shrugged. "Well, let them say what they will. I really don't mind much. I suppose as long as they're gossiping about me, they're leaving some other person's life in peace."

"They're sayin' ye're not altogether in yer right mind

these days, still grievin' over the death o' yer dearly departed wife."

This brought Matt up short. "They couldn't be more wrong," he told her quietly, sincerely. "But that's a tale for another day. Just now I need to discuss a more immediate problem, and I truly do need your advice and help with it." He held out his hand to her, his bright blue gaze trapping hers. "Come dance with me, Jade. Please."

If her life had depended upon it, she could not have denied him. Not when his eyes were gleaming into hers with such compelling warmth, such wondrous promise.

Not until they began to dance did Jade realize that the band was playing "Buffalo Gals," much too spirited a tune to allow for conversation. However, at the end of that selection, they swung into a waltz, and she found herself swaying gently in Matt's arms, her nose mere inches from his chest. " 'Tis times like this when I wish I were taller," she complained softly.

Matt chuckled. "I think you are just right."

"Ye mistook me for a child at our first meetin'," she reminded him.

"Only for a moment."

"I thought preachers frowned on dancin' and such," she said, changing the subject.

"And I thought Irish girls could cook," he teased. "Just goes to show you how wrong we can be, doesn't it?"

She nodded, adding thoughtfully, "B'fore I met Vera and the girls, I thought women like them must all be horrible, but they're not. Vera took me in off the streets and gave me a home when no one else would. She fed me and clothed me and gave me a room o' me own, and treated me better than me own aunt did. A more kind and generous lady never lived. And the girls are the best friends I could ever want. They taught me to waltz."

"You're as light and graceful as a fairy queen," Matt said laughingly. His mind, however, was following more serious veins, considering what little she'd hinted of her background. He would have liked to have asked more about her childhood, and the events that had brought her to the life she now led, but he didn't want her to take offense or feel that he was being critical of her.

"Do ye think she could o' gone to Heaven, Matt?" she asked suddenly, plaintively.

"Who?"

"Vera. I know she ran a hurdy-gurdy and had her share of faults, but she wasn't evil, like ye'd suspect. She was more like a mother to us than a madam, and we all bawled like babies when she died. Underneath it all, she had a heart o' gold, and I'd hate to think o' God holdin' her mistakes against her. She don't deserve to go to Hell."

"Only God has the right to decide that, Jade. To weigh the good in a person against the bad. It is only by His grace, and according to His purposes that anyone enters His kingdom." He offered her a comforting smile. "Perhaps God, in His infinite wisdom, looked into Vera's heart and saw the love there. Maybe in the final minutes of her life, she sought and received redemption. Until we step through those pearly gates ourselves, and chance finding her there, we cannot know for sure."

"Guess that's about the same for anybody," Jade reasoned. "Some folks act real good on the outside and are nasty as all get out on the inside, while others might appear bad and measure up better in the end."

"Exactly. Only God knows what is in a person's heart, Jade. And there's no fooling Him."

"Well, I hope He's fair-minded, then, though sometimes it don't seem like it, when wee ones like Skeeter get a heap o' problems."

Speaking of Skeeter brought the boy to mind, and Jade suddenly realized she hadn't seen the lad that evening. "Where is he tonight, anyway? Skeeter, I mean," she questioned.

"He and Ike are restricted to the tent," Matt responded, a frown creasing his brow. "That's what I wanted to talk with you about, Jade, only I don't know quite how to explain it."

"Plain English will do fine. Right up front, with no fancy frills to confuse matters."

He laughed. "That's just one of the things I like about you, lady. You're refreshingly honest, if not downright blunt."

"So, what's the problem?"

He thought a second, then sighed. "I suppose you know that Ike is totally enthralled with you, to the point where it is getting out of hand."

Jade rolled her eyes and shook her head. "Well, I'm not goin' out o' me way to encourage him, if that's what ye're thinkin'. All boys go through that at some time or other. I'll wager ye did so yerself. It ain't fatal. Just give him a week or so, and it'll most likely pass."

"That's what I told myself," Matt admitted. "Until today, when I caught him peering through the bushes at you while you were bathing."

Jade's eyes went wide. "Faith an' begorrah!"

"Precisely, and that's not the worst of it."

"It's not?"

"No. He dragged Skeeter along with him."

"Saints alive! Anything else?" Jade asked hesitantly.

"That's quite bad enough, don't you think?"

"I reckon so. What did ye do when ye caught 'em?"

"Before or after I sneaked a peek at you, too?" he admitted, giving her a look that was a curious combination of fascination, admiration, and contrition.

"Ye didn't!" She stopped dancing and stared up at him.

"I did. My only excuse is that after Ike blurted out that you were bathing totally nude, I couldn't seem to help looking."

"But ye're a preacher!" She was still aghast at his admission.

"That doesn't mean I'm perfect. I come fully blessed with all the faults, feelings, and foibles of any other man." His tone turned sweetly cajoling. "It has been said that to err is human, to forgive divine. Will you forgive me, if I tell you that with just that one look I was spellbound by your sun-drenched beauty, so thoroughly enchanted that all I could see, all I could want, was you?"

"Blarney!" she retorted, her eyes snapping with indignation, though a blush crept up her throat and the night air suddenly seemed entirely too warm. "I ain't believin' a word of it."

His face drooped comically as he feigned exaggerated hurt. "You wound me, woman. I bare my heart to you, pour out my innermost feelings, and you tear them to shreds with your shrewish tongue! Is that any way to treat a suitor?"

"Yer not me beau, and all this nonsense aside, the lads aren't the only ones who should be repentin' inside that tent, Reverend Richards," she informed him tartly.

"I know. That's why I thought I'd better make a clean breast of it, apart from asking your opinion of what to do about Ike's infatuation. I wanted to tan his hide, but after bowing to temptation myself, the best punishment I could derive was to confine him to the tent and have him write, five hundred times, 'I will not lead others into transgression.' "

"And are ye writin' somethin' yerself, mayhap? Somethin' befittin' lecherous preachers?"

"I could. How about 'I will lust openly after my beautiful lady love. Not from the shadows, but in sunlight, and without shame before the world.' Would that suffice? Or would you rather I acknowledge my weakness and my affection for you in a public announcement to the entire wagon train prior to conducting next Sunday's sermon? Better yet, I could kiss you here and now, before God and everyone, and make my feelings clearly known to all."

She gaped up at him. "Ye wouldn't dare!"

His answering smile was decidedly wicked. "Wouldn't I?"

Before she could challenge him further, Jade found herself pulled more tightly into his embrace, her head securely bracketed by his hands, and his long, strong fingers laced through her hair. As she opened her mouth to object, his firm, warm lips swooped down on hers. His tongue initiated a swift, slippery duel with hers—and Jade's bones began to melt. Her thoughts immediately became muddled, even as her ears ceased to hear anything but the rapid beat of her own heart—or was it his she heard thudding so heavily?

A thousand stars danced in her head by the time he dragged his lips from hers and gazed lovingly down into her rapt face. "What do you have to say to that, sweet lady? Have I sufficiently proved how much I will dare for you?"

She nodded dizzily. "Ye've gone and done it now, Matt Richards," she warned him softly, dimly aware of the buzz of conversation in the background. "Ye've set the hounds to bayin', and there'll be no hushin' 'em. There will be the very Devil to pay."

"I've dealt with him before," he assured her, stroking her hair from her face.

"So have I, and he always seems to win."

"Not this time, sweetheart. Trust me."

"The last time I put me faith in a man, he stole me virtue and me purse, and I almost lost me heart in the bargain."

"Entrust your heart to me, and I swear I will cherish it for all eternity. Give me your love, and I will repay it a hundred times over."

"Why?" The single word emerged as a helpless wail.

"Because I love you, and I need you to make me whole."

"Why me? Of all people, why me, Matt?"

He smiled and shook his head, almost as much in wonder at this strange turn of events as she. "Only the good Lord knows—and so far He hasn't seen fit to let me in on the mystery. But I am certain that He brought us together, Jade, and that He means for us to stay together. I've never been so convinced of anything in my life."

She stared at him as if he were crazy. "I don't mean to offend ye, but ye've got bats in yer belfry, Reverend. Ye're definitely out there a-rowin' with one oar in the water."

"You don't believe me, do you?" he countered mildly. "Or is it that you don't believe that God places a guiding

hand on our lives? Some people call it luck, others desti-
ny. Kismet, fate, fortune, providence. It all boils down to
the same thing in the end, Jade. You and I are meant to
be a pair, two halves of a whole."

"Great!" she huffed, pushing herself free of his arms.
"A bloomin' idiot and a blasted fool, paired up into one
big nut! Yessir! If that ain't a match made in Heaven, I
don't know what is!"

"I want to be just like Miss Jade when I grow up," Beth
said, sighing dreamily.

Emily nodded agreement, her curls bobbing.

Ike looked doubtful, as if he thought it highly improbable that anyone could be as perfect as Jade.

Matt winced. There it was again. Evidence of the fine
web Jade had spun about them all—himself most of all,
perhaps.

What was it about this elfin trollop that had them all
trailing after her like mice after cheese? It certainly wasn't
her morals, though Matt had to admit that Jade always
watched her manners and her mouth when the children
were around. And she appeared to be just as enchanted
with the youngsters as they were with her. He only wished
she could be equally as receptive toward him.

Since he'd kissed her at the dance two nights before,
Jade seemed to be going out of her way to avoid him—
and to annoy him. All of a sudden she was taking far more
interest in her other male acquaintances than she had to
date. Naturally, the men were responding in kind, drawn
by her coy smiles and mischievous banter, not to mention her enticing loveliness. Matt was convinced she was
employing these tactics on purpose, trying to discourage
his regard. He was also determined that it would not work,
though the more men that flocked around her, the more
perturbed he became. This was too similar to some of the
games Cynthia had enjoyed playing, and he couldn't help
but dislike it.

For her part, Jade was not savoring the male admiration
as much as she might appear to be—or as much as she had

expected to. Usually, she adored flirting with the fellows within the limits she set for herself. It lent her a sense of power to have them hanging on her every word, vying for her attention, pleading for her favors; and in so doing, soothing that raw spot Sean had so callously inflicted upon her soul. But now, it wasn't nearly as much of a lark as it used to be. Not when it was designed to hurt someone as honest and kind as Matt.

She could tell it was grieving him to witness her open flirtation with other men. He wasn't doing much to try to disguise the haunted look that came over his face, or the dark pain that lurked in his expressive blue eyes, whenever he saw her cozying up to another man. It was causing her nearly as much anguish as he seemed to be experiencing.

"Hang it all!" she muttered to herself. "He makes me feel like I'm whippin' a puppy! Or drownin' helpless kittens!"

"Yep," Bliss agreed with a nod. "I don't know which of you looks more miserable. Why don't you give the poor fella a chance, Jade?"

"B'cause he's bent on ruinin' both our lives. He ain't lookin' for a quick roll in the hay, Bliss. The man wants a wife, and he's got it into his fool head that I'm the woman to fit the bill."

"Well, honey, you could do a darn sight worse, you know."

"No doubt. But can ye honestly see me as a preacher's wife? What I know about religion wouldn't fill a thimble."

"Maybe he's lookin' forward to teachin' you, and learnin' a few things from you in return. Did you ever think o' that?" Bliss offered her friend a smile and a broad wink. "I've heard it said that deep down, most men really want a lady in their parlor and a harlot in their bedroom."

"And I don't fit either pair o' shoes," Jade pointed out stubbornly, "though he seems set on squeezin' 'em onto me feet, regardless."

Bliss considered this, then cocked an amused brow in Jade's direction. "Maybe it's not as impossible as you think. Could be those shoes are like those boots you bought. They pinch and wear blisters at first, but the longer you wear 'em the better they fit."

Jade sniffed in disgust. "I'll not be changin' me ways to suit anyone, most especially a man."

"You missed my point, Jade. Your feet didn't change shape to fit your boots. The boots did the changin' to fit you." At Jade's quizzical look, she shrugged and added. "You think on it a while, sugar pie. Meanwhile, don't go snippin' your nose off to spite your face."

"Meanin'?"

"Don't cut the line b'fore you're real sure you don't want the fish that's already swallowed your hook."

✿❧ *Chapter 10* ☙✿

*T*hey'd crossed the Big Blue River and were following the route of the Little Blue along its northwesterly course. Almost three weeks into their journey, they were well on their way to becoming seasoned wagoneers, much better acquainted with each other and the hardships of prairie travel. Blisters were hardening to calluses on hands now proficient at the reins. Muscles that used to complain were now capable of carrying them miles with scarcely an ache at the end of the day. Mules and oxen pulled as unified teams, the animals no longer intent on balking or wanting to head off in separate directions. Wagon repairs were routine and, with neighbor helping neighbor, usually accomplished with fair speed and skill.

Travel in this spring of 1867 had its advantages over that of the first westward-bound pioneers, and some drawbacks as well. The trail was well marked by the ruts of the thousands of wagons that had gone before, and often by the graves of those who had died of cholera or snakebite or some other fatal accident along the way. Nowadays, travelers were advised to take care to avoid consuming or bathing in water that had been polluted in any manner, and those who adhered to the warning appeared to fare much better. Another advantage these days was that, with the land becoming somewhat settled, at least in parts of Kansas and Nebraska, there were plenty of opportunities to replenish provisions, trade lame animals for fresh, attend to major repairs, and gather the latest information via the telegraph.

However, on the opposite side of the coin, these latter-day emigrants found themselves having to stock up on firewood, a scarce commodity here on the treeless prairie, and the price was always high. The trees along the riverbanks had long since been chopped down, and the abundant supply of buffalo chips that had served the earlier pioneers as an excellent alternate fuel had been depleted. This far east, with much of their grazing lands now fenced and plowed, the buffalo no longer roamed in the vast herds of a decade before. Dried cattle chips were a passable substitute, but not in adequate supply, and were only available if there were other wagon trains traveling in advance on the trail, thus leaving these welcome "offerings" to those coming along behind.

While many of the river crossings could now be made by means of ferries that had been established by enterprising fellows, or in rare cases by way of a bridge, there remained treacherous currents and rough water to traverse, compliments of Mother Nature and her changeable spring temperament. Rain still fell, rivers rose, and wagon wheels continued to become mired in mud.

Additionally, a new crisis was arising—or more precisely, an old one was raising its ugly head anew. Earlier wagon trains had encountered relatively few problems with the Indians of the region, since they were merely passing through the territory and posed no real threat to the tribes or their way of life. But as more and more whites claimed western holdings—settling, bringing disease, building roads and forts and railways through prime hunting grounds, and running off the game, tensions had escalated accordingly. Treaties were signed, and promptly broken, even as more roads and rails were laid, more forts erected, more soldiers sent to the frontier to protect government interests. Each year, the discord multiplied, and conflict with the plains tribes was a growing problem.

Now the Indians were on the rampage again, renewing their war against the white soldiers and settlers intruding upon their lands. Just this past December, they had led eighty-one soldiers into a bloody ambush near Fort Phil Kearny in the Powder River region, in a slaughter now known as the Fetterman Massacre. There had been a brief break from fighting during the worst months of the winter, but the skirmishes had begun again with the coming of spring. While most of the fighting was taking place north of the Oregon Trail, along the Bozeman Road, a few war parties had been spotted elsewhere, and the U.S. Army had forbidden travel by single wagons into western Kansas until further notice. They also strongly advised any group of travelers to maintain constant vigilance against Indian attack and to be ready and able to defend themselves.

Thus far, however, Sam Greene's company hadn't seen so much as an eagle feather, let alone a red man, and the danger seemed remote. Besides, with such a large number of wagons traveling together, and meeting other trains along the route, they were supremely confident of their greater strength and firepower. In fact, many were the boasts, especially among the younger fellows, of how badly they would defeat any savages so foolish as to launch an attack. Indeed, many of the men seemed eager to engage the enemy and prove their superiority, until it seemed that only the women and children had the good sense to remain apprehensive and thankful for the blessed absence of the Indians.

Fort Kearny at long last appeared on the horizon, heralding the next phase of their westward trek. From this point, they would be following the Platte River through western Nebraska into Wyoming Territory. Shortly after departing from here, for all intents and purposes, they would be leaving civilization behind. No longer would there be numerous farms and ranches dotting the landscape with barns and windmills at every turn of the road, or towns spaced like clusters of stepping-stones along the trail unless one counted those ragtag shantytowns being spawned, and abandoned almost as rapidly, by the workers of the Union Pacific Railroad as the iron rails advanced slowly across the Nebraskan prairie.

The fort was a welcome sight, a place for the emigrants to recoup their energies and supplies and trade accounts of their adventures with other wayfarers pausing there. The trip's appeal differed according to the varying needs of the travelers. Though the trail had proven fairly easy until now, with surprisingly few serious accidents and no deaths, there were some who had decided that pioneering was not for them after all. A number of the disillusioned would take this opportunity to sell their wagons and arrange transport back east by rail. The wagon master, on the other hand, would be conferring with the commander of the fort, gathering additional information about the trail ahead and the Indian situation. Other emigrants were seeking fresh oxen and mules, or use of the fort's blacksmith shop to make repairs to their equipment.

While most of the women were eager to exchange tidings with the soldiers' wives and ladies from other wagon trains, Jade and the "girls" were looking forward to entertaining the troops stationed here. Almost the minute their wagons were secured and the oxen unyoked, the six women were delving excitedly into their trunks, searching out their most alluring attire. Dresses and petticoats flew like colorful wind-driven snowflakes through the crowded interior of the hastily erected tent.

"Where are my net stockings?"

"Who took my red fringe boa?"

"Has anyone seen my good ostrich feathers?"

"I can't find the crinoline for my can-can costume!"

"Screw your crinoline, Fancy. My black lace corset is missing!"

Fancy retaliated by poking her tongue out at Mavis. "You could always use the ox harness, sugar. God knows you could use the extra support for those overblown jugs of yours."

"Now, Fancy, no need to be so nasty," Bliss counseled with a giggle. "Just b'cause you have to pad your chest with cotton is no reason to snipe at Mavis."

"O' course, there is a grain o' truth to Fancy's claim, ye know," Jade put in with a grin. "I, for one, don't want to be anywhere near Mavis if her corset seams split wide open one day. It'll be like standin' next to an explodin' cannon. By the time her udders stop bouncin' a dozen innocent bystanders will be blinded and Mavis'll be lucky if both her kneecaps aren't busted."

Laughter filled the tent.

"You're a fine one to talk," Mavis grumbled, though she, too, had chuckled at the ridiculous picture Jade had painted. "It's not as if you have to stuff oranges down your front to fill out your gowns. I declare, a man with a four-foot nose could suffocate in your cleavage!"

"Oooh, poor Reverend Richards!" Lizette crooned. "He's sure to die!"

Peaches agreed. "Yeah, but he'll go with a smile on his face!"

At last the girls were dressed. As they scrambled out of the tent, they came face-to-face with Matt.

"Hullo, Reverend," they caroled as they strutted past him.

"You comin' over to the parade grounds?" Bliss asked by way of invitation. "Billy arranged with the major for us to put on a show. We're gonna do the can-can, and Jade's gonna sing."

In the weeks since the girls had been traveling with the wagon train, Matt had not seen them in their usual "working" attire. The lot of them now sported more face paint than any self-respecting Indian would apply. He was also certain he'd seen less fringe on a caravan of Gypsies and fewer feathers on the average flock of birds. Their bosoms were all but bare, and their skirts several inches too short, exposing long, elegant limbs clad in black net stockings. More flounced crinoline was showing than frilled overskirt, and he caught a glimpse of at least three sequined garters as they tottered past on heels much too precarious for the uneven ground. He thought it would be a miracle if one of them didn't break a leg before the night was done.

In answer to Bliss's invitation to the performance, he replied with a stiff frown. "I'm sure you will all be thronged by a multitude of adoring admirers, and my time might be better spent praying for your safety. I wonder if any of you truly realize the risks you take by exposing yourselves in such a flamboyant fashion."

Jade patted his arm with red-enameled nails, as if to comfort him. "Don't ye be losin' any sleep over it, Matt. We know how to take care of ourselves, and we all look out after one another."

"Be that as it may, men are readily incited to passion, and not always easily controlled. Even normally docile men can become violent when ruled by lust."

"We know what you're saying, Reverend. When a man's blood is up, his brain shuts down. We appreciate your concern, but it's a hazard of the trade and we've learned to contend with it," Mavis assured him.

"You shouldn't have to contend with it. Any of you. I'm sure, with a little help and instruction, you could all find more suitable employment. I'd be willing to assist you in such efforts."

"That's mighty kind of you, Pastor Richards, but you'll need a heap o' luck to attain any sort o' success," Peaches responded, her voice edged with bitterness. "I watched my own mama wither away for lack of enough food to hold body and soul together, and I swore I'd never see myself in that situation again."

Fancy nodded. "We may be riskin' life and limb, but we ain't hungry, and we don't have a passel o' ragged, starvin' kids lookin' to us to fill their achin' bellies, or shiftless husbands with nothin' better to do than keep us barefoot and breedin', like some poor women do."

Lizette added her own opinion. "Life eez full of peril, Monsieur Richards, and you cannot save ze whole world from it. Reserve your pity for zoze more in need of it zan we are."

"There is a difference between pity and honest concern," Matt told them. "I don't want to see any of you come to harm."

Jade smiled and patted his arm again. "Neither do we, and we'll be doin' our best to avoid it, so don't fret yerself into a tizzy. Ye'll turn gray b'fore yer time if ye do."

The girls turned to leave, their moods lightening with every step as they began to chat and laugh amongst themselves. They barely spared a glance as Matt took hold of Jade's shoulder to detain her.

"What now?" she complained with an exasperated sigh. "Haven't ye lectured us enough for one night?"

"Evidently not."

His bright azure gaze raked critically from her head to her toes. Though she was attired slightly more conservatively than her sisters in sin, she still looked entirely too wanton—and much too alluring. Her emerald silk gown, while longer than the can-can costumes the others wore, was drawn up on one side in yards of ruffled petticoats, revealing a single shapely leg to mid-thigh, where a beribboned garter attracted the eye. Her bosom threatened to spill over the top of her bodice, which was cunningly cut to expose the black lace edging of the corset she wore beneath it, not to mention a stunning amount of cleavage.

Rouge had been applied to her cheeks and her delectable mouth to enhance their natural appeal. Her lashes were darkened, and some sort of glittery green paint lined her lids, exaggerating the slight tilt of her cat-green eyes. A portion of her glorious mane had been brushed back and caught with a comb, the remainder left to stream freely over her opposite, and otherwise bare, shoulder in a shower of coppery curls.

"You look like a strumpet, Jade!" he concluded irritably, thoroughly irked that he could view her like this and still covet her, still think her the most desirable woman he'd ever known—or, more accurately, yearned to know in the true biblical sense of the word.

"Ye don't say!" she mocked back with deliberately widened eyes. "With such grand powers o' observation, ye should be workin' with the bloomin' detectives at Scotland Yard!"

"I'd probably have better success there than here, trying to convince you to listen to reason," he conceded.

"Then ye'd be doin' both o' us a favor if ye stopped knockin' yer head against a stone wall and let me get on about me business."

He sighed heavily. "I can't do that, Jade. I have to keep trying to make you see the right of things."

"What's right for you could well be wrong for me. I'm no bloody saint, Matt, and not likely to become one any time soon."

"I don't want a saint, Jade. I want you."

Without warning, she changed tactics. Leaning into him, she pressed her breasts tauntingly against the front of his shirt. Her eyes gleamed up into his, her mobile mouth curving into a beguiling, brazen smile that would have done the most celebrated courtesan proud.

"Then take me, darlin'," she dared boldly. "Here. Now. I'm all yers."

He stared down at her, his body rioting against his better judgment. "At what price, Jade? Your soul? Mine?"

She did not back down. Rather, she arched a delicate brow, licked her lips, and purred, "I thought ye said passion wasn't a sin in yer book, Reverend. Or was that a wee white lie?"

He shook his head. "No, Jade. Passion is a God-given emotion, but He expects us to employ it wisely, and within the proper bounds."

"Which are?"

"Matrimony. The sacred union between man and wife."

She wilted like a flower on a weak stem, then promptly stiffened and pushed free of his touch. "Ye're whistlin' in the wind again," she informed him scathingly. "I already told ye I've got me future planned. I'm gonna be rich and famous, like Jenny Lind, and do it all on me own. So go bark up someone else's tree, will ye please, 'cause ye're really startin' to annoy me."

"Good." He yanked her roughly back into his arms, flames of indignation snapping in his vivid blue eyes. "At least I'm getting through to you on some level, and I suppose that constitutes a degree of progress."

Holding her securely with one hand, he reached into

his pocket with the other, produced a handkerchief, and proceeded to scrub her lips clean of the rouge that stained them. "I'll have nothing artificial between us, Jade," he told her gruffly. "Not now, or ever. I've had enough of that to last me a lifetime, and I won't go through it again."

She didn't have time to ponder this last, curious statement, for his mouth swooped down to claim hers with an insistence that rendered her powerless to deny him. Sweet, hot tongues of fire lashed through her, melting her, molding her body and soul to his will. In his masterful embrace, with his lips plying hers, she was his to command, his willing, eager captive.

For timeless moments, they were both lost in the consuming desire that erupted between them. Lips suckled and savored, while tongues explored deeper, darker delights. Her hands rose, clutching wildly at his shoulders. His moved madly over her back, her sides—finally, inevitably, slipping between their straining bodies to cradle her silk-bound breast.

Jade's breath caught in her throat, and her breast swelled more fully into his palm. A tormented groan welled from his mouth into hers. Matt's long, agile fingers stroked the exposed slopes of her breasts, dipping into the sleek, warm valley between the satin-smooth globes.

Her violent shiver shook them both, at last awakening Matt to reason, wrenching him to an awareness of time and place, and how far and how fast their passion had taken them. Slowly, reluctantly, he tore his lips from hers, holding her to his chest as he drew in several ragged, reviving drafts of cool night air.

"I wish ye wouldn't do that," she murmured weakly, leaning against his strong, lean body for support.

"Do what?"

"Kiss me and touch me the way ye do."

"Why not?" he urged.

"Ye muddle me mind and make me want things I can't have. Ye make me want ye too badly."

He clasped her chin in his palm and tilted her face upward to meet his tender, compelling gaze. "Then take me," he said simply, turning her own words back upon her. "I'm all yours—anytime you decide to become my wife."

Chapter 11

With a dazzling smile, and a bow that threatened to pop her breasts free of their scant restraints, Jade acknowledged the applause following her final number and stepped down from the raised platform that served as a stage. As the other girls dashed past her, Billy launched into the music that was to accompany their can-can dance. The show was going over nicely, well received by the audience of soldiers and emigrants, though the men appreciated the performance more than the ladies, of course.

Pushing her way through the crowd of onlookers, and politely rejecting several fellows who wished to escort her, Jade made her way to the refreshment table set up to one side of the parade field. Before she could voice her request for a drink, a glass of punch was promptly pressed into her hand, compliments of Matt Richards. "It's plain fruit juice," he informed her dryly. "Probably not your beverage of choice, but better for you."

She favored him with a glare, "Ah, me self-appointed keeper decided to attend after all, I see."

"Bliss did invite me, if you recall."

"Who's lookin' after the children while ye're out lollygaggin' around?"

"Charlotte Cleaver kindly volunteered to sit with them for the evening. In fact, she all but insisted," he informed her with a smug smile.

Jade gave a derisive sniff. "Beth can look after the younger ones every bit as well as Miss Cleaver. Probably better. 'Course 'tis yer decision," she added with a nonchalant shrug, "but I'd beware o' lettin' that prune-faced spinster get both feet in the door, or ye'll likely never get rid o' her."

Matt's eyes twinkled with male delight at hearing the sharp note of jealousy Jade failed to disguise. "I'll take that under consideration," he responded wryly.

Jade raised the cup to her lips and was about to sip from it when a voice said softly from behind her, "I'd no idea ye could sing so sweetly, lass, or I might've thought twice about leavin' ye behind."

The cup froze at her lips. As Matt watched in curious surprise, Jade's eyes widened in shock. The color drained from her face, then rushed back again to stain her cheeks a bright pink. A soundless gasp hissed from her throat, and for a moment Matt feared she might faint. Then, quite visibly, he saw her draw a deep breath and gather her composure. Before he could ask her if she was all right, she turned to greet the man at her back with frosty hauteur.

"Well, as I live and breathe, if 'tisn't the long-lost Sean O'Neall. And what, may I ask, brings ye to Fort Kearny?"

"Why, I'm travelin' west to Oregon, same as ye are. It be a small world, after all, eh, luv?"

Jade feigned a negligent shrug. " 'Tis a free country. Ye can go where ye want. Doesn't make me no never mind, as long as ye steer clear o' me."

"Now, is that any way to be talkin' to an old friend?" he chided, clicking his tongue to his teeth.

"I always reckoned ye were a bit dense, boyo. It seems to have escaped yer notice, but we're not friends. Far from it."

Sean's eyes narrowed. He reached out to clasp her arm in his hard hand. "Why don't we go discuss it?" he suggested darkly. "Somewhere a bit more private?"

Jade stood her ground. "I think not, Sean. I choose me company more carefully these days, ye see, and I prefer a higher class of gentlemen."

Matt saw his opportunity and took it. "Excuse me, Mr.

O'Neall," he interrupted as he knocked Sean's hand free of Jade's arm with a deceptively casual gesture. "Jade is with me this evening."

Sean cocked his head, surveying his competition, and Jade almost laughed as the shorter man was forced to crane his neck a bit to meet Matt's gaze. However, his cockiness survived the effort, and he challenged boldly, "And what are ye to her, mister? If ye're not her husband, ye have no say in this."

"Speakin' o' spouses," Jade inserted quickly, before Matt could say something rash, "did ye ever find that rich wife ye were lookin' for?"

Sean's chest puffed out in a show of pride. "Aye. That I did. She's restin' in the wagon now, poor lamb. Gwen is breedin', ye see, and she's a mite more delicate than the Irish wenches back home, which is why we had to abandon our own wagon train and rest up a bit here. We'll be headin' out again with yer own group." He paused a moment to allow Jade to absorb this bit of unwelcome news, then added with a sly smile, "So ye see, lass, we'll have plenty o' time to renew old acquaintances."

To her credit, Jade did not show her dismay. Rather, she answered with cool disdain. "That'll happen as soon as the sun starts risin' in the West. I want nothin' more to do with ye, Sean. And ye can relay me sympathies to yer bride."

"Ye'll change yer tune when ye learn how well I wed," he predicted with a sneer.

"Can I assume ye've enough to pay back the coin ye stole from me, then?" she countered quickly.

Sean gave an ugly laugh and perused her costly gown with hot eyes. "From what I can tell, ye landed on yer feet nicely enough. Alley cats usually do."

She gave a curt nod. "Which is why yer money, or lack of it, does not impress me."

He reached for her again. "Perhaps we should continue this discussion in more secluded quarters, luv," he suggested once more, casting a warning glance from her to Matt, who stood ready to defend her. "Unless ye want yer fine gentleman to learn in embarrassin' detail exactly how well we know each other."

Jade's smile was canny, her emerald eyes glittering with animosity and blatant challenge. "Go right ahead, boyo. Do yer worst. Ye see, Reverend Richards already knows what sort o' woman I am, and what he doesn't know, he's good at assumin'. Ye won't be tellin' him anything new."

Sean was noticeably taken aback, and for a moment at a complete loss for words. At last he squeaked out, "Reverend?"

Matt offered a chilly assent. "I must say, Mr. O'Neall, I find your own absence of morals contemptible. It appears you have not taken your marriage vows much to heart, since you seem to be so willing to disregard your pledge of fidelity to your wife."

"If I were you, I'd look to me own affairs, Preacher," Sean advised hatefully.

"Oh, but I am, my misbegotten fellow," Matt told him with a superior smile. "You see, I am courting Jade, and I heartily resent your trying to lead my lady astray. I would also suggest that you remove your hand from her arm this instant, unless you'd care to have it broken."

Jade blinked twice and stared at Matt in dumbfounded amazement, wondering if her ears were suddenly playing tricks on her. Had she truly heard Matt threaten to do another person bodily harm?

Sean glared up at him, hesitated but a moment, and let loose of Jade's arm. His mouth twisted into a smirk. "What kind o' preacher are ye, to want a whore for a wife?" he jeered.

Matt met him look for look. "I'm a very fortunate one, to have met a woman as fascinating as Jade."

He then reversed the question and asked, "What sort of man are you, O'Neall? Can you view your own face in your shaving mirror and see a man worthy of respect? Or are you more often tempted to slit your own throat with your blade—before some irate father or husband offers to do it for you? It's never too soon to mend your ways."

"Save yer sermons for those who like bein' led around by the nose," Sean retorted scornfully. "Me, I'm doin' just fine on me own." He started to leave, then turned to Jade and added, "Let me know when ye change yer mind and want some more o' what ye craved so much b'fore, lass. I'll be waitin'."

She dared to laugh in his face. "Listen to ye, braggin' on yer own prowess! Well, boyo, I'm here to tell ye, ye're not near as good as ye think ye are, and that manhood ye're so blessed proud of will rot and fall off b'fore I come crawlin' to the likes o' you."

"Ye'll live to regret that, me girl," he warned, his eyes narrowed with malice.

She tossed him a caustic smile. "Does this mean we're not friends anymore, Sean?"

He stomped off in a huff, muttering obscenities.

"That, I take it, is the jackal who stole your virginity and your purse," Matt surmised dryly.

"Jackal. Snake. Louse. Weasel. Take yer pick." She met his questioning look. "Well, spit it out b'fore ye choke on it, Matt. I can tell ye're just dyin' to say somethin'."

His eyes searched hers. "Do you still care for him?"

"Are ye daft?" she squealed indignantly.

"I know he hurt you, and I know you're angry, with good reason—but love often survives such betrayal."

"I wouldn't spit on him if his hair was ablaze!" she declared adamantly. "B'sides, I was more smitten with him than in love. Sort of the same way Ike feels about me. I realize now that he wounded me pride more than me heart."

"I can't tell you how glad I am to hear that," he told her with a sigh of relief. "I was so worried that you might still love him, despite the despicable way he's treated you."

She wrinkled her nose in disgust. "I might be a fool, but I ain't stupid. And I try to make it a rule never to repeat the same mistake twice."

"So do I, Jade. So do I."

"Would ye care to explain that?"

He merely smiled and shook his head. "Maybe someday. It's not something I like to talk about."

"Tell me this, then," she persisted. "Would ye really have broken Sean's arm?"

Matt tossed back his head and laughed. "Only if he hadn't released you when he did."

She tried to look serious but failed, her smile refusing to dissipate. "Doesn't the Lord frown on bustin' other folks' bones?"

"Well, I'm sure He wouldn't applaud the measure, but I like to hope He'd forgive it if it were done to prevent harm to a potential convert—and the woman I love."

She sighed and rolled her eyes heavenward. "I'm never gonna understand ye or yer way o' thinkin'. Not if I live to be a hundred."

He grinned down at her. "You'll get to know me twice as fast—quite intimately, in fact—if you agree to marry me."

She sent him an exasperated glower. "Lands, but I wish ye'd learn to sing another tune!"

Jade was sitting on the ground with Beth kneeling in front of her, the girl's long blond locks tangled between her fingers. Beside them, Lizette held Emily on her lap, nimbly demonstrating how to plait the child's hair in an intricate fashion known as French braiding. "It eez quite simple, once you get ze hang of it," she said.

"Easy for you, perhaps," Jade groused. "I seem to need an extra set of fingers, or at least another hand."

A long shadow fell over her, dimming her view, and she glanced up to find Matt standing behind her.

"What's this?" he asked quizzically. "Hairstyling classes?"

Jade grimaced. "More likely how to pull a child's hair out in one easy lesson."

He chuckled.

Beth's head swiveled about and she peered up at him with a frown. "She ain't kiddin', Papa Matt. But Lizette says a woman has to suffer sometimes to be beautiful."

He bit back another laugh and pulled a sober face. "I see. I suppose we fellows are very lucky not to have to go through all that you do. Fortunately, when the good Lord created human beings and animals, He endowed the males with all the attractive plumage they needed. Of course, He did create man in His own image, so I suppose that accounts for His partiality."

"Well, ain't that just dandy! And what favors did He do for us women?" Jade inquired all too sweetly.

"Rumor has it He fashioned Eve from Adam's rib, but personally I think He must have used the funny bone instead. God has a wondrous sense of humor, don't you think?"

"Ye're a very peculiar person, Matt Richards."

He wagged a finger at her, his eyes twinkling. "Before you judge me so harshly, consider this. When the Tower of Babel was being constructed for the purpose of reaching into Heaven, God decided that this just wouldn't do. Since the people in those days all spoke one tongue, making communication among them easy, God decided that He would confound their language, and scatter them over the face of the earth, that they might not attempt anything so foolish in the future. This was the origin of the many diverse languages we have today.

"Now, many people believe that this was God's way of punishing them for this arrogant endeavor, which it probably was. However, I do not like to think it was simply an act of supreme wrath, but a lesson in humility. I also prefer to suppose that God was vastly amused with the result. Can you imagine how He must have laughed as everyone began to dash about in such grand confusion, bumping into one another, yelling and babbling in a thousand different dialects, hardly one person able to understand the next? Certainly, it must have seemed like a great comedy to Him, particularly since He had perpetrated it. And you must agree that some of the languages He invented sound downright hilarious to someone hearing them for the first time."

Lizette laughed in delight, while Jade gave them both

wondering looks that questioned their sanity.

"I have never regarded God in zis way before," the French woman said. "It eez a novel idea, and quite fascinating. Eez it not, Jade?"

"Ye've demonstrated yer point, Reverend, but it still seems a bit odd to think of God as havin' a sense of humor."

"Maybe to some, but I envision Him sitting on His heavenly throne, rocking in laughter as we humans run amok down here like bumbling idiots, creating more problems for ourselves than He ever intended us to bear; and then making even more of a mess of things as we try to maneuver ourselves clear of the tangle we've made of our own lives. I suppose, to Him, we often seem to be very silly creatures, indeed, and we must afford Him untold amusement."

"More so than exasperation or anger that we can be so ignorant and stubborn?" Jade asked.

Matt was secretly overjoyed that he had at last managed to spark a genuine interest in these two ladies, though he certainly would never admit that this had been his purpose all along. It was just one of the ways he often employed to open people's minds, and eventually their hearts, to God's word. He'd had much greater success applying this tactic than in trying to force the Gospel down their throats by ranting and raving and spouting threats of fire and brimstone.

"I suppose God feels all of those sentiments and more toward us, His most intelligent and willful creations, in varying measure. But again I remind you that He fashioned us after His own image. And, in doing so, if He endowed us with something as precious and pleasurable as a sense of humor, doesn't it stand to reason that His must be even more magnificent?"

Jade threw up her hands, defeated by his glib logic. "I suppose so."

His smile reeked of victory.

"Did ye have a reason behind this visit, or did ye merely feel compelled to plague us this fine mornin'?" she gibed.

"As a matter of fact, I came to invite you to accompany me to take a look at your new mare, to see if the two of you will be well suited to each other."

Completely confused now, Jade stared up at him in bafflement. "What are ye talkin' about? I don't own a horse."

"You do now. I just bought one for you. Or I will have once you look her over and approve of her."

Jade was flabbergasted, while Lizette laughed and the children cheered in gleeful support. When her jaw finally hinged itself properly once more, she railed at him. "Ye've got to be joshin' me, Matt. Ye can't be standin' there tellin' me ye bought me a horse and actin' for all the world as if 'tis no more than a bloomin' trinket. Hell's bells and little fishes! And where would ye be gettin' the coin to pay for such a bloody extravagant gift, might I ask? I may not be the smartest lass drawin' breath, but I know a preacher doesn't earn that kind of wages, and ye have all these wee mouths to feed."

"I can afford it, or I wouldn't be doing it," he assured her, grinning at her stunned reaction. "The children won't starve. And speaking of mouths, I really do wish you would watch yours in front of the girls. Next thing I know, they'll be swearing worse than Irish sailors."

She hissed at him, and he wondered if she meant to launch herself at him and sink her pearly, clenched teeth into him. She certainly looked angry enough to do so. "Just hie yerself back there and tell the man ye bought it from that ye've changed yer mind. I can't —I won't be takin' such a costly gift from ye, and ye were mad to think I might."

"Don't you even want to see her first? You might change your mind," he argued calmly. "She's a fine mare, and quite a bargain. Her owner is in a pinch for ready cash, or he wouldn't let her go so cheaply."

Jade contemplated a moment. It was tempting just to go look at the animal, and if the price was truly reasonable, perhaps she could purchase the mare herself. To be able to ride, rather than trudge alongside the wagon mile after endless mile, would be marvelous! "All right. I'll go. But if I like her, and if I want to spend that much, I'll pay for her meself."

"Oh, no," he told her, shaking his head. "If you decide you want her, the cost will come from my pocket, not yours."

"And how will that look to yer congregation, Reverend? Ye bestowin' such an expensive gift on a common hussy? Why, they'll think for sure that ye're samplin' me favors."

"Let them surmise what they will. Once we're married, the talk will die down. And you can just consider the mare an early wedding present, if it makes you feel any better about accepting her."

"Married!" Lizette exclaimed excitedly, leaping to her feet to embrace her friend in an exuberant hug. "You're getting married? Oooh, Jade! Zis eez just too, too marvelous!"

The two children began jumping up and down for joy, though little Emily was too young to fully understand what all the commotion was about.

Jade glared at Matt with flashing green eyes. "Now see what ye've done?" she accused.

He shrugged carelessly, a broad grin spreading over his face. "Seems to me it would be simpler all around if you'd just agree to marry me and be done with it, rather than try to explain to everyone why you don't want me, a fine specimen of a man, for your life's mate."

"Really?" she spat out. "To my way o' thinkin' it'd be a darn sight easier, and more to my likin', to shoot ye where ye stand."

He had the temerity to laugh at her. "Do you shoot any better than you cook?" he taunted.

This brought an enraged snarl. "I'll learn! Just ye wait and see if I don't!"

"Oh, calm down before you start foaming at the mouth and scare the girls witless. Accepting the mare doesn't mean you have to marry me."

"Then what does it mean? To you and me and everyone

else who'll be wonderin' and gossipin', 'specially after Lizette starts flappin' her lips?" she wanted to know.

"Only that you're considering the notion of becoming my wife. Is that so much to ask? Too painful to contemplate?"

Her lower lip poked out in a beguiling pout as one and all awaited her reply. "I suppose not," she conceded. "But remember, I'll only be thinkin' about it. It ain't fact yet, so don't go plannin' no celebration."

"It will be," he promised, planting a swift kiss on her protruding lip. "Oh, yes, green eyes, it will be both fact and celebration very, very soon."

Chapter 12

Riding her new mare was akin to announcing to the world that Jade was Matt Richards's personal, private property. "I might just as well be wearin' a bloomin' sign about me neck," Jade complained.

Matt merely grinned and told her, "I'd make one for you, but you wouldn't be able to read a word of it, and you are the one I most need to convince." He gave a sage nod of his head. "Yes, I can see we are going to have to begin those reading lessons soon."

Word spread like wildfire, and the reaction was immediate—and not altogether congenial. The audience that gathered around Matt's wagon early Sunday morning resembled more of an angry mob than a congregation of Christians assembling for worship services.

Blithely ignoring the dark, disgruntled mood of the worshipers, Matt bowed his head and led his reluctant flock in prayer. "Dear Lord, please bless us with love and understanding this fine morning. Open our hearts and minds to Your word and Your will, that we might find solace for our troubled spirits. Grant us tolerance toward those who would plague us, and caring for those who stand yet in the darkness of sin and uncertainty, in desperate need of your guidance. Let us not harden our hearts or become so complacent in our own salvation that we fail to bring others gently into Thy loving hands. In the name of our Lord and Savior we pray. Amen."

As he raised his head to look over the crowd, Matt noticed several sheepish looks on faces that had only moments before seemed set on rebellion. A handful of others, however, retained their mulish demeanor. He gave a mental shrug, reminding himself that there would always be those who would oppose him and his somewhat unorthodox methods.

He opened his Bible, directing others to do so as well, and read to them from the book of Matthew the portion of Scripture where the Pharisees were censuring Christ for eating with publicans and sinners, and Christ's answer to them. "Notice, people, that our Lord replies that He has come, not to call the righteous, but sinners, to repentance. Are we, as His faithful followers, less bound to do so? Secure in our own redemption, have we forgotten His example to reach out to others? In our efforts to shield ourselves from evil and temptation, are we not too often guilty of neglecting those most in need of God's grace, of judging our fallen fellows rather than rendering them aid and guidance? Would we not better benefit ourselves and others by showing more compassion and less disdain, or are we here only to selfishly serve ourselves from the divine plate of salvation?"

By now, only a few listeners appeared able to maintain their original obstinacy. One of these shouted out, "Is that your excuse for your behavior, Reverend? Embracing the enemy?"

Matt leveled intense blue eyes at his accuser. "If you are referring to my alliance with Miss Donovan, let me assure you that she is not my enemy, sir." This brought a smattering of lukewarm laughter.

Matt went on, his gaze roving to include all gathered about him, his tone admonishing. "Nor do I feel it necessary to tender excuses to any of you. My feelings for Jade, or hers for me, are a private matter between the two of us. They should be of no concern to anyone else."

"But it is our concern," another man insisted, boldly stepping forward to confront him. "You stand before us as a man of God, a leader of Christians, and you must set a proper example to those who look to you for guidance and wisdom."

"And that doesn't include fornicating with harlots!" an older woman asserted adamantly. She glared up at him, righteous indignation flaming from her rheumy eyes, her stance as rigid as if someone had strapped a broom handle to her backbone. "Charlotte Cleaver and Ethel Trumble both saw you as clear as day."

Several exclamations went up as Matt, temporarily dumbfounded, stared down at the elderly matron. Then he threw back his dark head and laughed. "My dear Mrs. Moorhead, what affection has passed between Miss Donovan and myself does not constitute fornication by any stretch of the imagination, so please set your mind at ease. Nor, if I were prone to such behavior, would I do so where others might witness it so readily. I might also suggest that before you or your cohorts charge others with wrongdoing, you should all get your facts straight. It might be a good idea for some of our better informed ladies to enlighten you, in as genteel a manner as possible, to the proper definition of fornication, that you do not unjustly accuse anyone again."

"I should hope so!" Nell Jansen declared scornfully. "Why, Carl and I have known Reverend Richards for years, and such an allegation is ridiculous!"

"Be that as it may," Charlotte Cleaver put in loudly, "it would seem that Reverend Richards's behavior is worrisome. We must consider the welfare of those young orphans in his care. Only the good Lord knows what those poor children have been exposed to, in such constant contact with those trollops."

"Oh, pipe down, Charlotte, b'fore you make a bigger fool of yourself than you already have," Tilda Brunner advised. "I've seen those gals with the children, and I'm here to tell you that any one of them would make a better mother than you. You're not so all-fired perfect yourself, or you wouldn't have been screechin' like a shrew at that little deaf boy the other night, while you were lookin' after them for the Reverend. The whole world was bound to hear you b'fore the lad would, yet there you were hollerin' like an idiot. And when the older girl, Beth, tried to come to his defense, I saw you grab hold of her

and shake her fit to rattle her teeth loose. I was mightily
tempted to intervene and do the same to you, but I figured
it was none of my business.

"Fact is," Tilda continued, "I would never have mentioned it if you hadn't brought the matter to light today,
professing such pretty concern for the same orphans you
were abusing so recently. Seems to me the pot shouldn't
go around callin' the kettle black, 'specially if it's just
plain jealousy talkin'."

"Well! I never!" Charlotte exclaimed.

"And you never will, if you don't stop being so petty,"
Tilda countered. "Any man in his right mind will sooner
choose a tenderhearted woman over a spiteful one."

"Now, ladies, let's have a little charity here. This is
supposed to be a church service, not a backbiting session,"
Matt reminded them and everyone listening.

From the rear of the congregation, a feminine, Irish-
lilted voice proclaimed softly, "Ye could've fooled me!
If this is what bein' a Christian is all about, hackin' every
livin' soul to bits with yer waggin' tongues, then I don't
reckon I want any part of it."

As Jade turned away, flanked by the children and her
friends, Matt's reproachful gaze swept the crowd. "Thank
you very much, brothers and sisters," he said mockingly,
"for your generous hand in leading another lost lamb
away from the Lord's fold. I sincerely hope we've all
learned a valuable lesson today—a lesson in humility, if
nothing else."

Later that afternoon, Jade was still fuming. "How can
ye be so calm about it?" she railed at Matt. "Ye act as
if it doesn't bother ye one whit, those folks accusin' ye
of doin' things that are bad for the children. Aren't ye
the least bit afraid they'll all turn against ye, take the
youngsters from yer care, and ex . . . ex . . . cast ye out
as their pastor?"

Matt smiled at her, though his eyes betrayed a more
serious mood. "I left my church in Kentucky, Jade, in
favor of starting up an orphanage in Oregon City, where

there are several churches already established by very competent ministers. While that does not mean that I intend to give up preaching altogether, the care of these homeless children is taking precedence at this time in my life. After I have established the orphanage, I may decide to head another church. Or I may not, depending on how the Lord leads me. Meanwhile, since I am the only pastor included in our traveling group, I will continue to attend those who seek my services."

"That's right nice o' ye, but yer followers are mightily put out with ye just now. They're all but claimin' ye're unfit to look after those young'uns. What will ye do if they try to take the children away from ye?"

Matt shook his head, his smile unwavering. "They won't," he said with conviction. "They might think about it, or even attempt it, but they won't succeed."

"Oh?" She cocked a mink-brown brow at him. "Ye're mighty convinced o' that. Mind tellin' me why?"

"God won't let them," he announced simply. "He set me on this mission, and He will see me through it, come Hell or high water."

"So all that bickerin' and opposition doesn't bother ye at all?" she questioned, eyeing him strangely, as if she couldn't quite fathom his calm faith in his Creator.

"What bothers me most is their maligning you."

"Why should it, when their opinion of me is the same as yers?" she asked haughtily. "Ye consider me a floozy, same as they do."

"Perhaps, but I see the good in you as well. I see your warm and tender heart, the patience you have with the children, your humor and intelligence and passion. Given the chance and the choice, I know that you can elevate yourself from your present station to claim a more satisfying, fulfilling role in life."

"As yer wife?" she scoffed.

He nodded. "Yes, and as the mother of my children. Our children."

The loving, intimate glow of those dazzling blue eyes, combined with the thought of bearing his child, sent a tingling warmth singing through her. Her belly clenched in intense reaction. Unconsciously, her hand drifted to her stomach. His own fingers covered hers, holding them there.

"That's right, Jade," he told her softly. "Think of it. Feel the ache deep within you, where your womb would harbor our babe."

His face lowered toward hers. As if they'd developed a mind of their own, Jade's fingers laced with his, anchoring their joined hands snugly against her belly. Her lashes fluttered closed a heartbeat before his lips claimed hers in a kiss so tender that it brought tears to her eyes. Her stomach muscles tightened even more, and she leaned into his caress, reveling in the feel of him, the gentle command of his flesh over her own. With just a touch, he seemed capable of rendering her mindless, of dissolving her wavering will before the steadfast strength of his. The kiss ended as sweetly as it had begun, leaving her staring with wonder into his brilliant blue eyes, eyes so filled with love and promise that her breath caught in her throat.

"Faith and begorrah!" she whispered. "What ye do to me! If I didn't know better, I'd swear ye're a wizard castin' spells o'er me soul."

"No," he murmured in return. "Just a mortal craving your heart. A man who loves you more than he can say, and yearns to share his life with you."

"Ye're daft to want me. We're complete opposites."

He gave a slight shrug. "Maybe so, but you're everything I desire, all I dream of. Sometimes I think I'm going to die for want of you. No matter how many times I attempt to convince myself that you're right, that we're not suited to each other, my heart tells me otherwise, refusing to listen to reason. Which is why I'll persist in my efforts to persuade you, despite the torment of waiting, though daily I pray that you'll soon take pity on me and accept my proposal."

"I can't," she said softly, regretfully, tears shimmering in her eyes. "I've ambitions o' me own that don't include takin' up a broom and an apron and a passel o' kids. Blast it all, Matt, can't ye see that? Can't ye understand? 'Tisn't that I don't care for ye, or for them, but y'all just don't fit into me scheme a'tall."

"Then I'll have to find a way to make marriage to me more alluring, more important to you, than these grand plans you've charted for yourself, won't I?" he countered, his hopes only slightly dampened. After all, she'd just admitted, in a roundabout way, that she did care for him, and that was a definite step in the right direction.

Thoroughly exasperated with his seemingly endless supply of patience, Jade stamped her foot. "Hellfire, but ye're stubborn!"

He grinned roguishly. "I prefer the term 'tenacious.' "

"I don't give a bloomin' drat what ye prefer! And as me dear ma used to tell me when I wanted somethin' I shouldn't, 'Wishin' ain't gettin'.'"

He just laughed, a determined glint making his eyes sparkle like sunlit seas. "There's nothing I like better than a challenge, sweetheart, especially one with such promising rewards."

They were on their way again, leaving Fort Kearny behind them as they trekked ever westward. The Oregon Trail ran along the southern bank of the Platte River, while the Mormon Trail followed its northern shore, only the wide, shallow expanse of muddy water separating the two. *Platte* was a French word meaning flat and shallow, and the river was just that, having been described as being "a mile wide and an inch deep." Yet another pioneer had said it was "bad to ford, destitute of fish, too dirty to bathe in, and too thick to drink." On either side of the river, the treeless plains were covered with short grass for about three miles. The land rose in sandstone cliffs that became higher and more broken the farther west they traveled.

Though they had again received warnings at Fort Kearny to be on the lookout for Indians making trouble along the newly laid rail lines, they saw nothing more dangerous than snakes, coyotes, and prairie dogs. With the latter, Jade was completely enthralled. She even contemplated trying to catch one and keep it for a pet, though she hadn't the vaguest notion how she would manage to do so. They were canny little creatures, and quite swift, popping in and out of their holes almost faster than the eye could behold. It was said that Indian youths perfected their skills with bow and arrow by using the nimble animals for target practice, a custom Jade found deplorable.

"They're so cute!" she crooned. "Why would anyone want to kill one?"

"They're stinking rodents with nasty teeth," Matt countered. "A burrowing nuisance to ranchers and farmers; and anything, human or animal, unfortunate enough to stumble into one of their numerous holes can almost be assured of a broken leg."

"I want one."

"A broken leg?" he queried, his mouth quirking with humor.

"No, ye twit. A prairie dog."

"People in Hell want ice water, but they're not likely to get it."

"Catch one for me, and I'll be eternally grateful."

"I already bought you a horse, you greedy minx."

"And I love her, but she's not a pet ye can cuddle, now is she?"

"Try nestling one of those prairie dogs you're so all-fired taken with, and you won't have any fingers left." His blue eyes took on a mischievous twinkle. "However, if you really need something to snuggle close to, I'm available."

True to his word, Matt set about the chore of teaching Jade to read and write. Early one evening, he called her over to his campsite and settled her near the fire with a slate on her lap. Emily sat nearby, laboriously outlining the letters of her name on a second lapboard.

"You and Emily will be learning together," Matt told her, "while Ike and Beth work on their sums."

"Ye've got a regular school goin' here, from the look of it. Ye sure ye don't mind takin' on another student?"

"Not at all, especially when I'll be teaching my future bride."

Jade frowned up at him. "Don't go puttin' the cart b'fore the horse, Matt. I don't recall agreein' to do more than think about it."

"You will marry me. Just as you'll soon learn to write your name." Retrieving the slate from her, he chalked out four large letters—*J-A-D-E*. "There," he said, handing the board back and fitting her fingers properly around the chalk. "Now you trace over it, following the letters as closely as you can. Don't worry if you're a bit awkward at first. Everyone is."

Jade frowned down at the letters before her and shook her head. "This don't look right somehow. Ye sure this is how me name's spelt? I'm sure 'tis done different in me Bible."

"Your Bible?" Matt echoed, a look of astonishment crossing his features.

"Aye. And ye can wipe that look o' disbelief off yer face b'fore I do it for ye," she warned him in disgust. " 'Tis me ma's book, and her ma's afore her. Now 'tis mine, me only keepsake of me family."

"I'm sorry, Jade," he apologized. "I didn't mean to imply you shouldn't own one. I'm merely a bit surprised somehow. You never mentioned it before."

"Ye didn't ask."

"Would you get it for me? I'd like to see it."

Jade puffed up like a banty hen ready for a fight. "Are ye doubtin' me word, Reverend? Callin' me a liar in yer polite way?"

"No, Jade. I simply want to see it and confirm the correct spelling of your name. Please?"

She eyed him askance, as if weighing the honesty of his answer. After a long moment she agreed, and trooped off to find the Bible she'd carefully packed in the bottom of her trunk.

When she returned, Matt took it from her and turned to the center of the volume, where the births, deaths, and marriages of Jade's antecedents were duly recorded.

The final entry listed the deaths of her parents five years previously. The entry prior to this recorded Jade's birth.

Matt stared hard at it for several seconds. Then he began to chuckle softly. "Well, I'll be blistered! Your name really is Jade, isn't it? Jadeen Agnes Donovan."

"And what's so blamed funny about it, I'd like to know?" she asked, glaring at him with her fists atop her hips.

"Well, for one thing, I thought you'd chosen the name yourself, as sort of a working title. I never dreamed you'd actually been born with it."

Jade nodded, admitting tersely, "Yer not the only one that's thought so, though it doesn't seem so odd a name to me."

"And Agnes?" he went on, laughing even harder. "Heavens! I love it! Aggie!" He was practically crowing now, tears of mirth glistening in his brilliant eyes.

Hers were glowing equally bright, but with belligerence rather than merriment. "Don't ye be calling me that!"

"Why not?"

"B'cause I'm not overly fond o' it, if ye must know, even if 'twas me dear granna's name."

"But it's perfect!" he claimed with devilish glee. "Much more suited to the wife of a preacher than Jade." He tried the new name out for the sound of it. "Agnes Donovan Richards. Aggie Richards. That has rather a nice, normal, solid ring to it, doesn't it?"

"Only in yer dreams, Reverend," Jade said, wrinkling her nose at him. "And they'll be nightmares if ye call me that again."

"Now, Aggie," he teased, reaching out to ruffle her hair as he aped her brogue, "don't be showin' yer Irish temper in front of the children."

She kicked him, the hard toe of her boot connecting solidly with his ankle bone through the supple leather of his own footgear.

"Yeowch!" he hollered. Grabbing his wounded limb, he began hopping about like a drunken crane while the children whooped with laughter.

His yelp of pain was yet echoing on the night air as she taunted, "Ye ain't seen me temper yet, Preacher, so that gives ye somethin' to look forward to, doesn't it? Maybe now ye'll think twice about wantin' to marry me." With that, she spun on her heel and marched back to her own wagon, the reading lesson postponed for at least one evening.

✣❧❧ *Chapter 13* ❧❧✣

Sean O'Neall was fast becoming the bane of Jade's life. Though his wagon was stationed a dozen or more behind Jade's in line, he managed to find the opportunity to make his way forward in the column several times each day. He'd succeeded in dimming much of the joy Jade took in riding her new mare and in treating each of Matt's orphan brood to a daily ride. Sometimes Sean spoke to her, employing that glib Irish tongue of his like a magical wand meant to enchant his victim, and Heaven knew she'd fallen easily enough for his brand of insincerity before. But never again. Now the honeyed brogue sounded in her ears like the warning hiss of a riled rattlesnake.

At other times, he said nothing at all, but the hot look in his eyes as they raked over her spoke louder than words. Sean O'Neall wanted what he'd so carelessly cast aside nine months before, and, in his usual arrogant way, he obviously thought that if he persisted long enough, Jade would succumb to his charms with scarcely a whimper.

In the course of this daily pursuit, he soon garnered the attention of Jade's friends.

"So that's the witless pile o' horse droppin's that left you to starve on the streets," Bliss sniffed, turning her nose into the air. "And now he thinks you'll have him back? Lawsy, but that man has more balls than brains, doesn't he?"

"Oh, but he eez rich now," Lizette pointed out, her mouth pursing in the fetching French moue she'd perfected. "Married in ze money. Zat eez supposed to make ze difference, *cherie*."

"Well, it's plain that he still wants Jade for something other than his wife," Mavis sneered. "No matter how much money he married into, the lousy bastard still has all the breeding of a cur. Jade has more polish on the tips of her fingers, literally and otherwise, than he'll ever hope to possess."

"Still, you have to admit he is a handsome rascal," Fancy said, in the interest of fair play. "And he's got a mighty smooth tongue to him."

"Sure, and 'tis a result o' lickin' the Blarney stone too long and hard," Jade commented caustically. "The man wouldn't know the truth if it stood up and bit him on the nose, so don't ye be believin' a word that comes tripping from his lyin' lips," she warned.

"Don't you go falling for his deceit, either," Peaches admonished. "Just remember, Jade, pretty is as pretty does."

"Don't fret, luvies. I've had me dose o' that pot o' poison, and I'm not fixin' to swallow a bit more o' it."

"Don't go riding off alone on that horse of yours, either," Tilda cautioned, not taking her gaze from the stewpot she was seasoning. "I don't like the looks he's been giving you. He's the type to take what he wants without botherin' to ask permission first. So stick close to the wagon, for safety's sake, or Reverend Richards will take strips off all our hides for not watching over you like we should."

"Reverend Richards is not me keeper," Jade announced sourly. "And y'all are no more accountable to him than I am. Ye hear?"

Lizette waved lacquered nails off to Jade's left. "Better for you to tell him zis zan for us, *cherie*."

Jade turned to find Matt standing a few feet away, casually propped against the wheel of the wagon and looking like the cat that ate the cream.

"How long have ye been standin' there spyin' on me?" Jade accused, narrowing green eyes at him.

"Long enough to know that your friends give excellent counsel. Advice you would do well to heed, Jade. O'Neall strikes me as a man who's dangerously obsessed with possessing you."

"Ye should know, Matt," she answered with a sardonic smile. "It takes one mule to recognize another, I reckon."

"There is a marked difference between us, my dear. I may want you, but my intentions are honorable."

She certainly couldn't argue with that.

"Steer clear of him, Jade."

"I intend to."

"Good. Because lately I've been spending a lot of time wondering what his nose would look like flattened to his face—and my thoughts would be more profitably applied in other, more charitable directions."

Three days out of Fort Kearny, they came to Plum Creek, Nebraska, or what little remained of it, since the entire settlement was in the final process of relocating from the south side of the Platte to the north, where the Union Pacific Railroad now ran. Numerous sod buildings stood deserted, as did the remnants of Fort Plum Creek. The sod fort had been built in 1864, following the Plum Creek massacre, an Indian attack on a passing wagon train that had left eleven men dead and one woman captured by the savages. With the arrival of the railroad the previous fall, the garrison had been abandoned. As had the Express station, which had seen the height of its activity during the brief, prerail era of the Pony Express. Even the small trading post was barely operating, most of its goods transferred to the opposite side of the river, where a more thriving place of business had been erected.

The trail-weary travelers rounded their wagons about the deserted buildings and prepared to make camp. Many emigrants from the train decided against pitching their cumbersome tents this night, choosing instead to make use of the convenient sod structures.

When Jade first entered the dank, dark shanty that was to serve as her bedroom that evening, she immediately changed her plans. "I'm thinkin' I'd rather sleep in the wagon, or under it." She gave a shudder of disgust. "This is worse than me Uncle Tobias's attic."

Beside her, Bliss grimaced. "It more resembles a root cellar than a place a person would live. One good rain and that dirt roof looks like it'll cave in. Why, I can even see the sky through some of those cracks!"

Fancy poked her head through the small door, took one look around, and headed back out again. "I reckon there are tombs with more light and less dirt. Ya'll can sleep in there if ya want, but I'm for either puttin' up the tents or bunkin' in with some handsome bachelor for the night."

Peaches was quick to agree. "Hell, I'd share space with the Devil before sleepin' in here."

"Well, girls," Mavis said with a sigh. "What do you say we give these quarters over to someone else and get those tents up?"

Obviously, Matt was of a similar mind, having already pitched his tent and started his campfire. "I thought you might have a change of heart about staying inside one of those soddies," he told Jade when she arrived for her nightly reading lesson. "Pretty dismal, aren't they? Of course, it's not as if the folks settling here have much choice, with the lack of lumber hereabouts," Matt pointed out. "And they can be fairly sturdy, with proper support and a new roof every year or so."

"They're too damp and dark for me likin'," Jade said with a shake of her head. "If I have to sleep on the ground, I'll do it out here, where nothin's gonna fall on me head but a bit o' canvas and a pole or two."

"Once we get to Oregon, we'll find a stout log house, or build one come spring," Matt commented as he handed over her slate. "With lots of windows to let in the sun, and wooden floors, and a big kitchen with a proper oven built next to the fireplace. You can sew curtains and maybe braid a few rugs to add some color to the rooms. Doesn't that sound cozy?"

Jade wrinkled her nose up at him. "I can't sew any better than I cook," she informed him curtly.

"You can learn, the same as you're learning to read and to cook. Tilda tells me you'll be ready to try your hand at butterscotch cinnamon rolls soon, and I can't wait to sink my teeth into them."

Those very teeth gleamed strong and white as he sent her a wolfish smile, his eyes shimmering like blue flames, and Jade got the distinct impression he was envisioning tasting buns of a more erotic nature than those baked in a Dutch oven. She stifled an odd impulse to check her clothing, just to make certain her dress hadn't mysteriously been transformed into a red cloak like that of Little Red Riding Hood.

"Ye're a rogue, Matt Richards. A scoundrel of the first order disguised as a harmless preacher."

He gave a deep, husky laugh that sent gooseflesh tripping over her skin. "And you love me all the more for it, don't you, sweetheart?"

"I most certainly do n— . . . uh . . . I . . ." Jade floundered, the denial mysteriously refusing to pass her lips, while Matt's smile grew wider and more confident with every moment. "Oh, just forget it!" She glared at him and swiftly changed the subject, asking in an annoyed tone, "Are ye gonna teach me to read, or not?"

"I intend to teach you much more than that," he countered with a wink.

"Not tonight ye're not, so hie yer mind back to these dratted letters. At the rate we're goin', me eyes'll fail b'fore I get past printin' me name."

Early the next morning, Matt invited Jade to accompany him on a short jaunt across the river. Several members of their wagon train were also crossing over, wanting a brief visit in the new town. Fancy and Peaches had gone "calling" the previous evening, intent on making a number of lonely railroad employees less forlorn. Like Mavis, some of the other women were simply curious about the group of Mormons camped along the trail on the north side of Plum Creek.

This site was where Matt led Jade and Ike, while Beth

and the other children stayed behind under Tilda's supervision. Here, he hoped to find a Mormon family willing to act as foster parents for Ike and to take the boy with them to Salt Lake City.

"What're we comin' here for?" Jade asked in a hushed voice as they entered the Mormon encampment.

Matt slanted her an amused look and answered in a normal voice. "You don't have to whisper, Jade. You're not Daniel walking into the lions' den."

"Well, it feels like it," she told him uncomfortably. "I've heard talk about these folks."

"They've probably heard talk about your kind, too, don't you suppose?" he countered with a superior grin.

"For cryin' out loud, Matt! Ye know what I mean. They say Mormon men have more'n one wife. Now, there's somethin' odd in that."

"Not to me," Ike put in quickly. "I kinda like it."

Jade had forgotten that Ike's parents had been Mormon, and she certainly didn't want to malign their memory. "Beggin' yer pardon, Ike, but it just doesn't seem right to my way o' thinkin'."

Ike shrugged. "I reckon it's all in what ye're used to."

"Look at it this way," Matt proposed. "Is it better for a man to have one wife and abuse her, or to have three and treat them all well? Is it any more right for a man to pledge himself to one spouse, and then find pleasure outside the marriage bed with other women, than to share his affections with several wives and not stray from home for his gratification?"

Jade stared at him in wide-eyed surprise. "Are ye sayin' ye agree with such a practice?"

"Not for myself. But I dislike seeing others constantly judged and found wanting simply because their beliefs differ from the usually acceptable strictures. I might also add that the idea of having multiple wives is nothing new. In early biblical times, before the birth of Christ, it was common among God's chosen people."

Matt made a sweeping arc with his hand, indicating the busy camp surrounding them. "Look around you, Jade.

Do these people appear evil to you? Do the women look downtrodden, the children unhappy? Or do they seem as any other families might?"

Thus bidden, Jade peered about with a critical eye. Everywhere she looked, people were busy getting ready to travel onward. Meals were being cooked, bedding shaken and folded, gear stowed into wagonbeds, animals tended, harnesses straightened. Children dashed here and there, many cheerfully helping their elders round up livestock or yoke oxen. Women chatted and laughed together as they attended last-minute chores. Men called out to one another, offering advice, aid, or simply a congenial greeting or word of encouragement. For the most part, the Mormon emigrants appeared no different from their Oregon-bound counterparts.

Even their manner of dress was more similar, less somber, than Jade had been led to believe. Many of the ladies wore long-sleeved dresses of colored and printed fabric, their hair drawn back into tidy braids and buns no more severe than those of most of the females in Jade's own wagon train. They sported the customary aprons at their waists and the requisite sunbonnets against the glare of the hot prairie sun. The men wore tan or dark trousers and plain shirts of varied hues. Some had beards, while others were clean-shaven. The majority wore hats of some sort, but of no unified shape or shade.

The difference that struck Jade most was the noticeable order and cleanliness of the camp and the people. Everything and everyone in sight was extraordinarily neat and organized. Faces shone from recent washing, their clothing had the look of being freshly laundered—even tidily pressed and starched! Jade marveled at how white some of those shirts and aprons appeared in the morning sunlight, and while she had no doubt that these emigrants would end the long day every bit as dusty and sweaty as anyone else following the Nebraska trail, she felt downright rumpled compared with them at this moment. Why, even their animals seemed to have received a recent brushing!

"They certainly seem an industrious lot," she offered generously. "I know our camp has never been this well ordered, and I can't recall the last time any of us found time to do more than shake the wrinkles out of our clothes as best we could. Do ye reckon they eat or drink somethin' that gives 'em more energy than the average person?"

Matt shook his head and chuckled. "I doubt it, Jade. They just keep going and stay busy."

"Well ask anyway, will ye? Lord knows, I'm so tired by the end o' the day I could just drop in me tracks sometimes."

"Aren't you afraid they'll give you some evil tonic concocted by the Devil?" he teased.

She rolled her eyes and sighed. "All right, Matthew. I admit it. They don't appear at all evil or threatening."

Matt approached an elderly gentleman and received directions to their captain's wagon. There, he conferred quietly with three more men while Ike and Jade waited a short distance away. Within a few minutes, Matt returned to announce, "Come along, Ike. There is a family here willing to take you on to Salt Lake City with them. Mr. Almann says he's heard of your uncle and that he'll make certain you are united with him and your other relatives."

Jade was astounded. "Matt! Is that what this visit is all about? Ye're gonna leave Ike with these people?"

"They're his people, Jade."

"They're strangers! How can ye be sure they'll treat him well? Ye can't just shove the lad off in the middle o' nowhere and leave him to go on to an unfamiliar city with folks he doesn't even know!"

"He didn't know me to start with, either. Or you," Matt pointed out. "At least these emigrants are of the same faith as Ike, with like beliefs and habits. It's right that he should be reunited with his own kind if he wants to be, Jade."

Jade turned to Ike. "Do ye want to go with these folks, Ike?"

"O' course I do, Miss Jade. They're just like me!"

For the first time, Jade had to wonder how hard it had

been for Ike to conform to ways and customs different from his own, to try to fit in with people who lived and thought unlike all he'd known and been taught.

"Well, I say we ought to meet this family b'fore we decide somethin' this important," she said, still not convinced it was right.

"Which is precisely what we are about to do," Matt concurred.

Josiah Almann was a ruddy-faced farmer with kindly eyes and a soft-spoken manner. By his wife Anna, a stout, friendly woman, he had two children, one of them a lad near Ike's age. Sarah, his second wife, was eagerly anticipating the birth of her first child in a few weeks. Ike and the Almann boy eyed one another speculatively for a few minutes, each lad silently assessing the other. Then, as if reaching some unspoken agreement, they shook hands and went off together to finish hitching the Almanns' team.

Jade might have felt excluded as Matt attended to the matter of filling Josiah in on what he knew of Ike's background. But just as she was beginning to feel uncomfortable about her presence there, Anna smiled and offered quietly, "Would you care for a cup of tea, ma'am?"

Surprised by the unexpected gesture, when others of her own party would never have been so considerate, Jade hesitated. "I know ye're fixin' to break camp, and I sure don't want to put ye to any bother."

"It's a shame to waste what's left in the pot," Anna told her. "Come. Sit."

Before Jade could quite fathom how it came about, she and Anna and Sarah were sharing tea and tales of the trail while Matt and Josiah discussed the joys and trials of farming.

"Have you and your husband eaten this morning?" Sarah asked. "If not, I'm sure we have some biscuits and gravy left from our meal."

"Reverend Richards and I aren't married," Jade admitted uneasily.

From his place behind her, where he and the farmer

stood talking, Matt put in, "Not for the lack of asking, Aggie."

She glared at him, for the interruption and for calling her Aggie. "I'll thank ye to mind yer own conversation and stay out o' mine, if ye please."

While the two Mormon women gasped at Jade's temerity, Matt merely chuckled. "She's pure red-haired, green-eyed Irish," he announced mildly, as if that explained everything, and promptly turned back to his own discussion.

Just as Jade and Matt were preparing to leave, saying their final good-bye to Ike, another gentleman approached the Almann wagon. They were promptly introduced to Thomas Bailey, Josiah's cousin. Though slightly younger than Josiah, Thomas towered over the other man. In fact, Jade was certain she'd never encountered a man as big as Mr. Bailey. Next to her minuscule height, he resembled a huge, burly bear, with a chest as wide around as a large water barrel, and limbs as thick as those on a fully grown tree! When he removed his hat, a shock of wheat-colored hair tumbled over his forehead, shadowing one of his chocolate brown eyes, and when he smiled down at her, his entire face seemed to light up from within.

"Glad to meet you, Miss Donovan," he intoned in a voice so deep it emerged as a gravelly growl. "I'm only sorry I didn't make your acquaintance sooner." His gaze swept slowly from her to Matt and back again before he added thoughtfully, "Since you'll be following the river for some miles, same as we'll be, would you mind awfully if I crossed over from time to time to call on you?"

Matt's congenial attitude melted into a frown. "You can save yourself the effort, Mr. Bailey, as Jade and I will be maintaining contact with Ike at various points along the route so that the boy does not feel we have deserted him too abruptly."

Thomas's bushy blond brow rose, humor glinting in his eyes. "It'll be no trouble, Reverend Richards. No trouble at all." He nodded his head to Jade, addressing her alone. "I'll look forward to seeing you again soon."

Matt hurried her out of the Mormon camp so fast that Jade couldn't even recall answering the man or thanking the ladies for the tea. Matt grumbled and glowered all the way. She'd never seen him so out of sorts.

"Sure, and what's put yer tail in such a twist?" she asked him finally, wearing an peevish scowl of her own.

"As if you didn't know!" he scoffed, his blue eyes glittering a warning that his mood had yet to improve and she would be wise not to press the issue.

"Mr. Bailey has every bit as much right to come calling on me as you do," she told him, disregarding the unspoken admonition.

He pulled his horse to a halt, and hers with it. Leaning toward her until his face was mere inches from hers, he stared into her startled eyes. "You are going to marry me, Jade," he insisted firmly. "Me. No one else. Is that perfectly understood?"

"Yer words are comin' through loud and clear, Reverend," she replied sharply, anger flushing her cheeks. "But as the sayin' goes, the show ain't over 'til the fat lady sings—and I'm not yer wife 'til I'm wearin' yer ring. So stick that in yer blasted pipe and smoke it!"

🌿❦ Chapter 14 ❦🌿

*T*heir first real disaster struck on the second afternoon out of Plum Creek. For some days now, they'd considered themselves fortunate in having fair weather, which had made traveling much more pleasant and faster paced than slogging through mud. However, in the predawn hours of this particular morning, they'd experienced one of those fierce thunderstorms that had become legendary to prairie wayfarers. Giant, jagged bolts of lightning had repeatedly seared both heavens and earth, striking with such force that the ground shook, the sky lit up for miles around with a blinding glow, and there was left behind a sulfuric smell reminiscent of brimstone. To the fanciful, and to others of normally sound mind, it seemed as if the end of the world had come. Oddly, while thunder and lightning abounded, the storm brought very little rain, and the small amount that did fall soaked quickly into the ground.

As if the storm was not bad enough, the animals had become as frightened as the humans. They milled about the corral of wagons, stamping and lowing and whinnying. Many managed to break loose from their tethers and hobbles, and crashed into tents and wagons, creating even more chaos. A good number escaped entirely, stampeding over the flat prairie at an incredible speed for animals customarily known to plod at a snail's pace.

A detail of searchers was quickly dispatched to round up the beasts and return them to camp, while another was formed to repair the damage to wagons and property.

Fortunately, the emigrants sustained few physical injuries. One woman received a broken arm when a skillet was knocked from its peg inside her wagon. A boy had gotten tossed about and now displayed a gash on his forehead. Others sported a variety of bumps and bruises, but nothing truly serious.

After their much-delayed departure, everyone breathed a sigh of relief. They were on the trial again, back to their usual, not-so-dramatic problems. Or so they assumed.

As the day wore on, a dull haze seemed to hang over the prairie, casting an eerie pall over the sun and the surrounding land. The very air seemed to grow thicker, heavier, harder to breathe. The teams and the horses grew fractious once more, nervously snorting and tossing their heads. The day grew steadily darker, and many wondered if there was yet another terrible storm ahead, perhaps this one capable of spawning a tornado.

Within a few hours, just after they had taken their noon stop and again resumed their journey forward, clouds formed on the horizon. Thick, boiling dark clouds chased briskly toward them on the westerly winds. Then they smelled it—an acrid, stinging odor. Smoke! These weren't storm clouds! This was a solid wall of choking, ash-filled smoke, headed straight for them! And where there was smoke, there was . . . Fire!

Alarm swept swiftly through the wagon train. Fire! That most dreaded of all disasters! A prairie fire! Roaring out of control! A blazing inferno, sweeping unchecked across the land, destroying and devouring everything in its path! And there was absolutely no way to stop it! Perhaps not even any way around it! They would all perish in the hungry flames!

Panic was nearly full-blown by the time the wagon master and his fellow captains turned the wagons toward the river, a quarter mile to the north. Word was passed back along the line. "Head for the river! Drive the wagons straight into it, as far as you can!"

"Make for one of the tiny islands, if possible, or the south side of the Platte if the current and depth allow!"

"Douse your canvas—your teams—yourselves!"

"Hurry! Whip 'em 'til they drop, but get those beasts and wagons to the river!"

"Pray! But don't slow down to do it!"

Suddenly everything was mass confusion. In their haste, anxious drivers veered directly into the paths of others, causing wagons to collide and oxen to stumble and fall. Conveyances bounced and careened precariously over the rough ground, tossing children and belongings about like loose marbles in a tilting drawer. The air was rife with the sounds of wagons rumbling, people shouting, animals bellowing, whips cracking, and wheels creaking in protest of this desperate dash for safety.

In the midst of this mad confusion, Jade threw the reins of their team into Mavis's hands. "Slow down enough for me to jump off!" she yelled.

"Are you crazy? Where are you going?" Mavis screeched back.

"To help Matt with the children. He can't watch over them and drive the wagon at the same time, and he doesn't have Ike to help him anymore."

With that, Jade took a quick breath and leaped from the rolling wagon. She hit hard, her knees buckling beneath her, but she rolled to one side and managed to keep from falling beneath the frantically turning wheels. She ignored the sting of her scraped elbow, levered herself to her feet, and launched herself at Matt's wagon as it barreled alongside.

Now that he'd finally gotten the crazed beasts up to some speed, try as he might, Matt could not slow them. Through the haze of smoke and the flying dust kicked up by hundreds of pounding hooves, he'd glimpsed a flash of red-gold hair as Jade fell from the wagon ahead of his. For an awful moment, he was sure she'd killed herself. Then, to his relief, she bounded to her feet and ran toward him. Her fingers reached out, grasping for the seat, her face a dusty blur as she ran beside him, her skirts flapping dangerously close to the spinning spokes. It took a second to transfer the reins to one hand, freeing the other to grab for her. Stretching, reaching, he managed to clasp her wrist and haul her aboard.

Fear gave way to fury. "Damn it, woman! What are you trying to do? Commit suicide? You could have broken every bone in your body!"

Clinging to the seat for all she was worth, Jade struggled to catch her breath. When she did, she hollered back, "Is that any way for a preacher to talk? Or any way to thank someone who's come to help ye?"

"Help me? You scared ten years off my life!"

She flashed him a weak grin. "Are the children all safe back there?"

"God, I hope so!"

Without another word, Jade crawled into the bed of the wagon, dodging swinging utensils and crazily swaying furnishings that threatened to snap free of their restraints at any minute. In the center aisle, midway back, she found the children huddled under a stack of quilts. Baby Zach was wailing at the top of his tiny lungs. Little Emily was whimpering and hiccuping and trying to suck her thumb all at once. Poor voiceless Skeeter didn't need to hear to be frightened nearly witless. Tears streamed down his freckled cheeks. Beth was almost smothered by the three younger orphans, her face as white as parchment.

Jade scrunched down among them and hauled all of them close to her, holding Skeeter especially tight. Of them all, he was the most confused and terrified, his fear multiplied by not knowing what was happening, or why. "It'll be all right," she crooned, smoothing four small heads, kissing four puckered brows. "Matt will get us there. He won't let anything happen to us."

Outside, on the jolting wagon seat, Matt wasn't quite so certain. He scarcely had control of the team, and could only hope they wouldn't topple the heavy wagon as they pulled it headlong down the slight incline at the riverbank, that he could slow them somewhat at that point and keep the wagon upright. To add to their peril, the front left wheel was wobbling hazardously, as if it hung there only by a prayer.

As he hastily added yet another frantic plea to his Creator, a new sound rose above the surrounding pandemonium. From inside the wagon, Jade's angelic voice warbled a familiar, if shakily rendered, melody. Even in his distraught state, Matt had to smile. Of all the numbers she might have chosen, Jade was singing "Shall We Gather at the River"! He hadn't even realized she knew that particular song, but evidently she'd heard his congregation sing it and quickly picked up the tune and the words. Matt shook his head in wonder. Jade must be mightily upset to have chosen a hymn to soothe the children, but she was comforting him with it as well, and he hoped it was giving her some measure of peace.

Several hundred tooth-jarring bumps later, the wagon plunged over the small rise and somehow landed upright in the river with all four wheels still attached. By now, the smoke from the approaching fire was so thick that Matt could hardly see the lead pair of oxen, let alone the wagon ahead of him. If one of the minuscule islands that dotted the Platte lay between here and the far shore, no doubt they would stumble upon it before sighting it. To compound the visibility problem, ash was floating on the breeze, settling on anything it touched and fast turning everything to shades of gray.

Thankfully, the river was shallow here, its murky surface a good foot and a half below the bed of the wagon. If it continued at this depth for the entire width of the river, the oxen would be able to maintain their footing, supposing there were no hidden holes for them to fall into. Nevertheless, Matt climbed down from the seat, knowing that he would have to lead the wild-eyed animals across lest they try to bolt and drag the wagon downstream, or worse yet, onto its side.

When the wagon plummeted into the river, Jade's stomach had nearly done likewise. Muddy water had sprayed up in a plume, drenching the canvas covering and showering a portion of its contents. She could not prevent the startled shriek that emerged from her lips. However, since the children also screamed, she doubted they even heard her. Again, she tried to calm them as best she could, heartily wishing she had someone to reassure her as well.

The wagon tilted slightly as Matt left his perch, alerting Jade to his departure. She knew she should assist him, despite her fears. "Beth, honey, I've got to go see if Matt needs help with the oxen," she told the frightened girl. "I'm countin' on ye to be brave now, and watch over the other children until I get back. Can ye do that, sugar?"

The girl nodded mutely, her blue eyes huge and teary, and Jade was tempted to stay right where she was. Instead, she gathered the little courage remaining to her, clamped her teeth tightly, and climbed awkwardly over the rear guard of the wagon—only to have her boots promptly overflow with mucky water.

That, however, was the least of her problems. The fire had advanced much closer than she'd expected it could in so short a time. Through the thick, choking smoke, a red-orange glow could now be seen as flames licked their way relentlessly across the prairie, ever nearer. Live, crackling sparks were flying amidst the ash, like thousands of fireflies turned treacherous, threatening to set new territory aflame. Even here, in the midst of the river, the heat was rising alarmingly, turning the very air she breathed into a scorching enemy.

Ignoring her sodden boots, Jade waded forward until she found Matt at the head of the team. "What can I do?" she shouted over the increasing roar of the fire.

Yanking down the sopping kerchief that shielded his mouth and nose, Matt yelled instructions. "I need cloth . . . rags . . . something to cover the oxen's snouts and eyes. Wet them. Soak one for your own face, and one for each of the children, or their lungs will sear." He reached out to brush a glowing ember from her sleeve. "First, douse yourself head to toe, or you'll be the next thing ablaze!"

Even as they trudged slowly through the muddy river, Jade scurried to do as he had bid her. As an added protection to the youngsters, she immersed several blankets and wrapped them about the terrified children, leaving them huddled together like small mummies. Then she grabbed a pail and began throwing water onto every part of the wagon, harness, and animals she could reach, all the while hoping her friends were taking the same precautions and that they would remain unharmed.

Somewhere on the fringes of her consciousness, Jade became aware that the emigrants were not the only ones crossing the Platte to safer ground. All manner of prairie wildlife was also fleeing the raging fire. The river teemed with creatures, large and small, all intent on escape. A family of skunks swam alongside a coyote. A rabbit floated by, flailing awkwardly in an attempt to keep its head above water. Snakes slithered along, too intent on eluding the fire to bother striking at what would normally amount to prey. Antelope splashed past, almost as graceful in water as they were on land. But when she spotted the bear, Jade clambered back onto the wagon, fervently praying the carnivorous beast would give them all a wide berth.

It seemed an eternity before her feet settled on dry land again. She wanted to drop in her tracks, and still they plodded on, lest they clog the shoreline and place those following behind in greater peril. Fortunately, aid was not long in coming, and from a source none of them expected. A short distance from the river, the Mormon pioneers had set up their camp and were welcoming their fellow travelers with open arms.

Considering how quickly Ike located them, Matt and Jade were certain he had been anxiously watching for their arrival. The lad rushed to throw his arms around Matt's waist in a heartfelt greeting, something the twelve-year-old would not have done under normal conditions for fear it would seem too childish. "We was real worried for ya," he choked out, his voice cracking. "Josiah told me to tell ya that you're all to come to his wagon for supper. The ladies have dry clothes and blankets if ya need 'em, and the men'll help ya set up camp and pitch the tents and such."

"Thank you, Ike. And thank Josiah for us." Matt enclosed the boy in a warm hug. "Tell him we'll be there soon, though I think we'd better wait to erect the tents until we're sure the fire does not jump to this side of the river."

After several minutes of confusion, they finally located Jade's friends and found a spot alongside them to situate Matt's wagon. Jade was relieved to discover that Billy and the girls had arrived without mishap, with minimal damage to their wagons and belongings. Even her mare, Marvel, though still extremely skittish, had survived the chaotic crossing safely.

In this, they were more fortunate than many of their fellows. Before the afternoon was done, while the fire still raged on the opposite side of the river, sorrowful news filtered from group to group—not all members of their company had made it across unscathed. Many were injured; seven had died. Another poor soul was not expected to live through the night.

Of those who had lost their lives, four had drowned in the shallow depths. Two had been small children, too young to swim; one was a woman whose skirt had become caught in a wagon wheel, dragging her along under the wagon, with none the wiser until it had been too late to save her; the other was a man who'd become pinned under a toppled wagon. A woman riding inside her wagon had been crushed when a heavy traveling trunk had fallen atop her chest. Another fellow had strangled when he'd become tangled in the harnessing when his oxen stumbled. A young lad had tripped and been trampled by a runaway team. An ember had caught in a little girl's bonnet, igniting her hair and clothing; the poor, tormented child now lay dying in her mother's arms, her life slipping slowly away.

Others suffered numerous, less serious injuries: burns, cuts, broken bones, wrenched muscles, lungs laboring from too much smoke. Though the Greene train had no doctor, there was a physician among the Mormons who graciously offered his services. Others produced salves and herbs with which to tend the lesser injuries of both humans and beasts, or set about helping their fellow emigrants make essential repairs to wagons and goods.

Once again, Matt found himself relying on Jade's benevolence. "I must console those who grieve for the loss of friends and loved ones," he told her, his eyes dark with sympathy. "Will you watch the children for me? See that they get fed and into dry clothes and bedded down for the night?"

Jade nodded. "Go and get yerself into some clean clothes, and don't worry about the young'uns. Me and the girls'll look after 'em."

"Can you find the Almann wagon by yourself?" he asked.

"If I can't, I'm sure they'll send Ike to fetch us," she assured him with a wan smile. "Now no more frettin', Preacher. Hie yer tail about yer business. And say a little prayer for that wee burned child for me while ye're at it, will ye?"

He planted a grateful kiss on her brow. "I don't know how I ever managed without you, Jade."

She gave a weary chuckle. "Pure dumb luck, most likely."

Chapter 15

Matt wasn't gone five minutes before Ike arrived, accompanied by Josiah Almann and Thomas Bailey. After giving Jade directions to his campsite, Josiah said, "Take the children and go along, Miss Donovan. Ike and Mr. Bailey and I will see to putting up the tent and setting things in order here."

"That's right kind of ye, but I have to help me friends first," Jade told him, gesturing toward the next wagon, where Mavis and the other four girls were struggling to get a fire and their own supper started while Billy tended to the oxen and harnesses.

If Jade and her companions looked bedraggled at the end of an average day on the trail, they certainly seemed a motley crew now. None of them had yet found time to repair their appearances. Half-dried mud still clung to them from the tops of their heads to the tips of their toes. Soot and dirt streaked their faces. Hair that had once been neatly combed was now fashioned in rat's nests of varied hues, half of it sticking out in stiff spikes and the remainder hanging in limp tangles. Seams had split, hems had ripped, sparks had seared holes of every size in their clothing, until they looked as if they'd dressed in the leavings of a ragpicker's cart.

"Ye'll have to excuse us," Jade said, a fit of giggles catching her by surprise as she suddenly became aware of the slovenly picture they presented, especially compared to the cleanliness and order of the Mormons. "I know we must all look akin to a troop o' tattered loonies from an asylum, but we clean up right nice most generally."

Upon this remark, several heads swiveled to deliver an assortment of frowns and grumbles in Jade's direction.

"Speak for yourself, sugar," Bliss commented wryly.

"Yeah, and if you want my advice, don't go looking in a mirror until you have a good long session with a pail of water and a bar of soap, unless you want to scare yourself spitless," Fancy retorted. "You look like you've crawled through a swamp on your face, girl!"

"More like an old dapple nag that's been rode hard and put up wet," Mavis offered with a snide smile.

Ike and the men were chuckling heartily. "Are you certain these women are your *friends*?" Thomas asked with a laugh.

Jade shrugged. "I thought so, but 'tis sort of hard to recognize 'em just now, past all the grime."

"We're Jade's friends, all right," Peaches agreed. "And if you think that's bad, you should hear what her enemies have to say about her!"

Jade pulled a face. Then, recalling her misplaced manners, she cordially introduced everyone. To their credit, the Mormon gentlemen did not bat an eye upon meeting women with such improbable names as Peaches and Fancy. Nor did they make any of the usual comments.

As Billy stepped forward to shake hands with Josiah and Thomas, he commented drolly, "You know, there was a day when I envied you fellas for having more than one wife, before I hooked up with these six ladies. How in the world do you stand it, listening to all that feminine squabbling and complaining day in and day out? It must be like having a sack of sick cats tied to your coattails!"

Josiah laughed. "Patience is a virtue we learn early in life," he answered with a twinkle in his eye.

Again, Josiah turned to Jade. "Gather what apparel you will need and take your friends and the children to my wagon. Sarah and Anna have a big pot of wash water waiting, and enough bread and soup to feed a small army. They will gladly help you with the little ones. By the time you return, we will have your quarters ready for all of you."

"Yes, Miss Donovan," Thomas put in with a winning smile, "after all the wonderful things Ike has told me about you, I will consider it an honor to do anything that will add to your comfort and pleasure."

At this, Jade's eyes widened measurably. "Th-thank you, Mr. Bailey. Mr. Almann," she sputtered, blushing wildly. Somehow, she resisted planting a sharp elbow in Lizette's rib cage as the woman tittered in open delight at both Thomas's courtly behavior and Jade's discomfort. Nor did she bow to the urge to swat Bliss, who was trying so hard to hold back a laugh that she looked like a blowfish about to explode. Even Mavis appeared in jeopardy of choking on something too large to swallow.

With a speed that belied her weariness, Jade collected fresh clothing for herself and the orphans, all the while wondering exactly what Ike might have told Thomas Bailey. Lord, what if the boy had admitted spying on her that day at Alcove Spring? If that were the case, she'd find a switch to take to that lad's backside! Aye, she would!

As the bedraggled group was making its way through the maze of wagons in search of the Almanns', they happened upon Sean O'Neall and his wife. This was the first time Jade had seen Gwen O'Neall at close range. Even considering the day's events the woman looked worse than the rest of them. In an attempt to be charitable, Jade reminded herself that Gwen was pregnant, and it had been a trying few hours for the most stout of men, let alone a gently reared lady expecting a babe.

Still, she did look horrid! Her pale hair hung in frazzled wisps about a face so pasty that it looked as if it were formed of pie dough. Her sparse blond lashes and brows practically blended into her ashen complexion, and her eyes were so light a blue that they added little color to her appearance. At the moment, Sean's beloved bride was berating him loudly, but even her obvious pique did not put a bloom in her cheeks or a glow to her eyes.

"I'm cold, I tell you!" the woman complained, her voice reminiscent of fingernails scraping across a piece of slate. "Stop being such a pinch-penny and add some more fuel to the fire! It isn't as if my father didn't give you enough funds to keep me comfortable, though Heaven knows that's practically impossible in this godforsaken country! I don't know why I ever let you talk me into this loathsome trip in the first place."

Sean's expression was surly. "I seem to recall ye thought it would be a grand adventure," he reminded her cuttingly. "B'sides, a wife goes where her husband takes her. And she's supposed to make at least some wee effort to be cheerful and content. But all ye seem capable o' doin' lately is whinin' and makin' me life thoroughly miserable."

"Hurrah for her!" Bliss announced, leaning close to whisper in Jade's ear. "If anyone deserves it, he does!"

"Had I guessed that all your wondrous charm and profoundly professed devotion would vanish so quickly following our wedding, I would never have married you!" Gwen wailed. "Here I am, carrying your child, and you don't even have the common courtesy to show due consideration for my delicate circumstances. Any proper husband would appreciate what I'm going through, would do his utmost to see to my every need, to meet my every desire. You should be fetching and carrying for me while I'm feeling so wretched, not expecting me to do so for you. After all, if it weren't for you, I wouldn't be in this condition, would I?"

Jade and Mavis shared a quick look, both rolling their eyes toward the heavens. Obviously, this woman knew a different class of gentleman than any of them had heretofore encountered. Moreover, she undoubtedly had mistaken Sean O'Neall for one of those rare, improbable fellows.

"No," Sean was agreeing with a sneer. "And ye're fast makin' me regret what wee pleasure I took in accomplishin' the deed, too!" he declared nastily. "Sure, and ye're not the most lovin' lass I've known either, ye thankless twit. Ye're spoiled to within an inch o' yer life, that's what ye are! Damn near next to worthless! If ye suppose I'm gonna spend me life caterin' to yer wants and wishes, ye have another think comin', dearie. 'Tis the wife's duty to see to her husband's comforts now and again, in case ye didn't know, and it's high time ye stopped yer eternal bitchin' and started lookin' after me satisfaction for a change."

Before Jade quite knew what was happening, she was being propelled forward, right past the quarreling couple. From close behind her, Peaches drawled clearly, "Mercy me! Is there trouble in paradise already, do you suppose?"

"Sure sounds like it to me," Fancy concurred.

Lizette disagreed. "To me it sounds more like two dogs, each snapping at ze ozer's throat."

"Don't y'all just hate it when folks air their dirty laundry in public?" Bliss added cattily. "It's so . . . common!"

"Best cover Baby Zach's ears, Jade," Mavis suggested. "No telling what he might hear next that he shouldn't."

Jade just shook her head and kept walking, shepherding her wee flock with her. "Come along, children. It's not nice to listen in on other people's fights, even if they are yellin' fit to wake the dead."

The wake-up signal brought Jade to groggy consciousness, and to the awareness that she had spent the entire night in Matt's tent with the children. A quick glance told her that Matt did not now share their sleeping quarters. Nor was there any evidence that he had done so. She was occupying his usual bedroll, and no extra blankets were within sight.

Slowly, she eased herself partially upright, smiling as she carefully dislodged Skeeter's head from the crook of one arm. After a bit of persuasion, during which she'd given in as quickly as wet newspaper, Jade had allowed Skeeter and Emily to place their bedrolls close alongside hers, and she was now wedged between the two cuddly tykes as tightly as jam stuck to two slices of bread. In fact, as she tried to raise herself farther from her bedding, she found her hair caught beneath Emily's plump little backside, for the lass had wriggled about until her bottom was snuggled securely against Jade's rib cage.

As Jade twisted about, trying to free herself from the two sleeping cherubs, her cheek burrowed into the pillow beneath her. Matt's pillow. After sleeping upon it all night, she had no doubt that she could select it, blind-folded, from a hundred others. The pillow was imbedded with the distinctive manly scent of him, a mysterious, delicious combination of odors that was uniquely his. All night long, that scent had assaulted her senses, leading to sweet, haunting dreams of him.

Allowing herself one more lazy minute of pure indul-gence, Jade closed her eyes and tried to recapture a half-remembered image from one of those beguiling visions. His image floated before her. That midnight-dark hair waving down across his forehead as his face hovered over hers. Those riveting blue eyes, as clear and bright as a crystal lake on a perfect summer day. The flash of white teeth as his lips curved into one of those wondrously enticing smiles that made him appear half rogue and half prince—and utterly, splendidly, undeniably male.

Though she wasn't aware of it, Jade's own lips pursed in reaction to the image she'd conjured in her mind. She sighed and, though reluctant to relinquish her delightful fantasy for the drudgery of another long, dusty day of travel, slowly forced her eyelids open once more. The sight that met her startled gaze nearly robbed the breath from her lungs. Matt was bent over her, his face scant inches from hers, his fingertip poised so close to her mouth that Jade's lips began to prickle in anticipation of his touch. His smile was tender, if a bit strained. His eyes were filled with wistful admiration and lingering sorrow.

"Good morning, sunshine," he murmured low, at last bringing his warm flesh to hers to trace her pouting lips. "I've wondered what you looked like first thing in the morning, all warm and sleepy-eyed and rumpled. You can't imagine the number of times I've pictured your glorious hair spread out upon my pillow, your cheeks flushed and your eyes as soft and misty as emerald velvet. The reality exceeds the wishful illusion by far, love."

His smile grew as he added teasingly, "However, my most treasured conceptions did not have you in my bed fully clothed from neck to ankles with two tiny guardians defending your honor."

As her lips shifted in reply, his finger faithfully followed their every movement—tickling, tingling along the sensitive skin. "They wanted to sleep with me. I couldn't deny them."

"I simply must pry their secrets of persuasion from them soon, whether it takes bribes or threats of torture."

His lips lowered, and they had scarcely grazed hers when Skeeter began to stir. On Jade's other side, Emily squirmed and gave a sleepy yawn. Matt chuckled and sat back on his heels, his eyes brimming with wry humor. "I should have known they'd choose now to wake up. I see I'm going to have to practice my timing a little more if I'm to sneak anything past your young sentries."

Rising, he stood gazing down at the three of them, his eyes clouding once more with fatigue and sadness. "Breakfast is ready, but you and the children will have to hurry. The burial service is scheduled to begin in half an hour, with the wagons rolling immediately afterward."

For lack of anything to say, Jade simply nodded, and watched thoughtfully as he exited the tent, his broad shoulders slumping beneath the burden of his appointed duty.

The funeral service was necessarily brief, but Jade thought it eloquent nonetheless, as Matt entreated the Lord to accept the souls of their departed brothers and sisters into His benevolent care. And to lift the hearts of those loved ones left behind, that their grief might be bearable.

As the emigrants turned their backs on the freshly covered graves, preparing to face the perils of the road ahead, Jade approached Matt. "All right, Reverend Richards. Ye've done what ye had to do. Now, hie yer behind into the back o' yer wagon and get some sleep b'fore yer eyes drop from their bloody sockets," she instructed him brusquely. "I'm drivin' yer team today."

"I'll be fine," he told her. "The lack of one night's sleep isn't going to harm me."

"Maybe not, but it'll no doubt make ye as grumpy as a bear with a sore paw as the day wears on." She cocked a brow at him, gracing him with a haughty smile. "I'm only lookin' out after the welfare o' the children, understand. I don't want 'em takin' the sharp edge o' yer tongue if yer temper begins to fray."

"You don't say?" His brow rose as if to challenge hers.

"I do," she stated imperiously, one hand riding the curve of her hip, the other pointing toward the loaded wagon. "I'm done listenin' to yer lame arguments, Matt. Climb in there and hollow out a space big enough to rest that long, lanky frame b'fore ye fall flat on yer face and bust that pretty nose o' yers."

He feigned a glare. "I may be tall, but I'll thank you not to call me lanky. I possess my fair share of muscles, which I'll gladly display for you if you doubt my word."

Wrinkling her nose at him, her eyes sparkling impishly, she sniffed. "Quit boastin' of yer attributes, ye bloomin' braggart. Time's a-wastin'."

As he hoisted himself into the bed of the wagon, he turned to deliver a final comment, his weary smile softening his words. "Just be sure you don't misplace any of the children, you bossy baggage." He shook his head in wonder. "For someone who only stands knee-high to a grasshopper, you sure do have a sassy mouth!"

With the prairie still smoldering as far as the eye could see along the south side of the Platte, they had little choice but to take the Mormon Trail westward in order to afford forage for their animals. Fortunately, the path ran almost parallel to the Oregon Trail along this stretch and would not take them far off their original route. Additionally, they should not have to follow it too far— only until they found the point where the grasslands had not been burned along the southern banks of the river.

For the time being, however, they traveled hub to hub with the Mormon emigrants. There remained a few among the Oregon-bound group who stood fast to their preju- dices, grumbling over the situation, but for the most part folks were grateful for the aid the Mormons had rendered so unstintingly.

One person who seemed especially thrilled to be in such close alliance was Thomas Bailey. Without fail, the gentle giant appeared each day to help Jade and her friends pitch their tent or take it down, or to offer his services in any way he might. The girls thought it was rather sweet of Thomas, and teased Jade unmercifully about collecting more beaus than she knew what to do with. Mavis, herself singularly tall for a female, took an immediate shine to the towering Mormon.

"Now there's a man a woman can look up to," she crooned, fanning herself with her hand. "If you decide you don't want him, Jade, send him my way. I wouldn't object to having him hanging 'round my front porch."

Meanwhile, Matt was becoming more peevish with each passing mile. "That man is making more of a pest of him- self than O'Neall has," he grumbled irritably. He gestured toward Thomas, who was grooming Jade's horse. "If he brushes that poor mare any more, her coat will fall out."

"He's just bein' helpful, Matt," Jade countered, hiding a grin. "I think it's right friendly of him, meself."

Matt gave a disgruntled snort. "Puppies are friendly, Jade, but they have an annoying tendency to wet on one's leg."

Jade giggled. "Oh, I'm sure Thomas won't do anything that bothersome."

"The hulking galoot would do worse, given the chance."

"Ye're just jealous 'cause he's bigger than ye are."

"I don't care if he has muscles coming out of his ears," Matt corrected in a testy tone. "And if I'm jealous, it's for better reason than that." He leveled his piercing blue eyes at her in accusation. "Every time I turn around, you're hanging on the man's every word, batting those long lashes and practically swooning over him."

"Matt Richards! Ye know darned well I haven't done any such thing!"

"Well, you haven't done much to discourage his attentions, either."

"I don't want to hurt his feelings."

Matt tossed his hands in the air in exasperation. "Why the devil not? You certainly don't seem to mind trampling all over mine!"

"Oh, for pity sake!" Jade exclaimed. "It's not as if I'm gonna marry him!"

"Tell him that!" Matt shot back.

"I will, if and when he asks me."

Chapter 16

*T*hat day came sooner than Jade antic-
ipated. Two evenings later, Thomas invited her to stroll
with him a short distance from the camp, assuring her
that they would not go beyond sight of the wagons, lest
she think his intentions less than respectful. With some
hesitancy, Jade agreed, though with every step she took,
she could feel Matt's gaze boring into her back.

Once away from the general commotion of the camp,
Thomas turned to her and with touching sincerity asked
Jade to be his wife.

"Ye honor me, Thomas," she told him quietly. "Truly
ye do. But I can't marry ye."

"Is it because I already have a wife?" he questioned.

Jade's mouth flew open, and she stared at him in mute
shock. As much time as the fellow had spent in their
camp lately, and as well as she'd thought she was coming
to know him, she'd had no idea he was already married. "That's reason enough, I reckon, if I'd have known
b'fore now. But the fact of the matter is, I don't love
ye. I like ye fine, but not enough to spend me life with
ye."

"Isn't there a chance you could come to love me?" he
persisted. "I'm a patient man, and I'm not hard to get
on with."

"Ye're an amiable sort, to be sure, but I've plans of
me own."

"With the preacher?" At her surprised look, he explained,
"I heard the other ladies talking."

"They shouldn't have said anything. Not yet, anyway."

165

Thomas shrugged. "He's a good man. If I can't have you . . ." His voice trailed off.

"I think I'd best go back now," Jade told him, not wanting to prolong the conversation. When he started to accompany her, she lay a staying hand to his arm. "I'd rather walk alone a ways, if ye don't mind. I need to gather me thoughts."

Jade arrived to find Charlotte Cleaver cozied up to Matt at his campfire. As she passed by, the woman sent Jade a smug look and shifted an inch closer to Matt, inclining her head toward his in a gesture of intimacy. Matt was not as quick to note Jade's presence, and she was almost beyond his wagon before he spotted her. When he did, he raised a questioning brow, as if to say, "Well, you don't want me, do you?"

By the time she stomped into her own tent, Jade was fit to be tied. Mavis was the only one of the girls there to witness her vexation. "I take it Charlotte is still passing the time with Matt," she commented lightly.

"Huh! She's hangin' all over him like wet laundry!" Jade railed, throwing herself down on her bedroll in a huff.

"Is that what's got you so miffed?" Mavis chuckled. "Sugar, in case you haven't noticed, the woman revived her campaign to snag that preacher the instant she heard that Thomas was calling on you. Guess she figured you'd left the door wide open and the poor man might need a friendly shoulder to cry on. She's gone out of her way to sway his attention toward her. In fact, it's a wonder she hasn't stripped naked and thrown herself in front of his wagon!"

"I noticed, and she can have him, for all I care! And ye're more'n welcome to Thomas Bailey, too!" Jade waved a hand toward the river. "I left him out there a ways, in need of a bit o' consolin' himself. If ye hurry, ye might yet catch him standin' around lookin' confused as to why I refused to marry him, though I ought to warn ye that he's got one wife, even while he's shoppin' for another. Men! Why God ever made such aggravatin' creatures is beyond me!"

Jade was still ranting and cursing, more to herself than to Mavis, as her friend slipped quietly from the tent and headed with determined strides in the direction Jade had indicated.

Sometime in the wee hours of the morning, as the sky was just lightening to shades of gray, and the tent was just as murky, Jade was awakened by a series of snorting, snuffling sounds. At first she assumed it was one of the girls just coming in and trying to undress without light; or perhaps Fancy snoring again, as she was prone to do on occasion. The noise stopped, and Jade had almost drifted back to sleep when she heard scratching begin.

Evidently, she was not the only one disturbed, for seconds later Bliss grumbled, "Dang it all! Whichever one of ya has the fleas, would ya kindly take 'em outside so the rest of us can get some sleep?"

"Must be Fancy," Lizette murmured drowsily. "She's been snoring again, too."

"Have not," Fancy yawned grumpily. "And I'm not the one itchin', either."

"Well, it sure ain't me," Peaches mumbled. "And I wish you'd all hush your yaps."

For a few minutes all was peaceful, though an odd, pungent odor began to pervade the tent. Then a loud shriek rent the air. "Ohmigod!" Mavis screamed, as the others jerked to full wakefulness. "There's a skunk in here!"

Pandemonium broke loose. Howling louder than a pack of crazed coyotes, the women scrambled from their bedding in a tangle of limbs and blankets, stumbling over one another in a mad dash to get outdoors. They spilled from the canvas shelter like three pair of carelessly tossed dice.

Matt lurched awake at the first frantic scream, his heart pounding in his chest. Without first giving heed to his actions, he leaped from his bedroll and yanked his britches over his drawers. Forgoing his shirt and boots in favor of haste, he bolted outside with but one thought in his befuddled brain—that of rescuing Jade from whatever peril threatened her.

Upon reaching the neighboring tent, Matt stopped short, hardly able to credit the sight that met his disbelieving eyes. By the pearly predawn light, he counted a half dozen of the most delectable, scantily clad hussies he could ever have imagined—all of them shrilling and hopping about in a flurry of bare arms and heaving breasts and flashing legs, like a troop of moonstruck nymphs.

Apparently, none of them believed in donning conventional, modest nightwear. Rather, they were attired in a rainbow array of revealing silk and satin concoctions, abounding with bows and frills. His stunned mind noted corsetlike garments teamed with brief French drawers, sleek camisoles and short ruffled petticoats, a dressing gown haphazardly held closed by a sagging sash.

And Jade . . . Jade was flitting around in what appeared to be a chemise designed to be worn beneath an evening gown, for it was cut very low in the front, where it laced together; and the straps that substituted for sleeves were dangling past her shoulders, caught on her upper arms. It was knee-length, fashioned of shimmering emerald silk that fitted faithfully to her torso, then flared from her tiny waist in a flounced skirt decorated with rows of gathered ebony trim. Above the snug bodice, the high slopes of her breasts gleamed as white as snow in contrast to the black ribbon edging them.

Matt's mouth went as dry as old bones at the bountiful display of tempting flesh paraded before his covetous gaze. The women's agitated cries finally broke through the shock still fogging his brain.

"That thing brushed my leg!" Bliss wailed. "I damned near wet myself!"

"Well, it tried to bite me!" Lizette exclaimed, her French accent mysteriously absent.

"What are we gonna do? We've got to get the critter out of there!" Fancy declared loudly.

"I'd rather burn the blasted tent down than go back in there. God knows, our clothes and bedding will never smell the same again."

"Oh, spit!" This from Jade, as she set her hands on her hips and glared toward the tent. "Ain't this just a fittin' end to a perfectly wretched week!"

Matt figured he'd better take charge quickly, before their ruckus roused the entire camp, treating one and all to the mindboggling sight of the girls in their skimpy nightwear. Surely, if that didn't incite a riot, nothing would!

"Ladies! What's all the commotion here?" he inquired, gaining their attention at last. Immediately, his ears were assaulted by a jumble of excited pleas as six voices tried at once to explain and request his aid.

He held up his hands for silence. "Calm down now, or you'll have everyone running over here to see what's wrong—and a whole lot more that they shouldn't see."

Six sets of eyes widened with the sudden realization that they were standing in the open in their most intimate attire. Bliss was the first to recover her wits. With a laugh, she said, "You're right, Reverend. If they want this much of a show, they should have to pay good money for it. Trouble is, there's a skunk in our tent, and the danged polecat's sprayed everything in it, blankets, clothes, and all."

"Yeah," Fancy added, wrinkling her nose. "It's just a miracle he didn't shower us any more than he did. Guess we were all runnin' so fast he couldn't get a good aim at us."

Now that she'd mentioned it, there was a noxious smell wafting on the breeze. Despite his best efforts, a grin crept across Matt's face. "A skunk?" he echoed with a sharp chuckle. "Good grief! The way you were carrying on, I thought sure it was a snake at least, if not something more threatening."

"Well, since ye seem to think it's so harmless, go in and get the varmint out," Jade challenged saucily, making the mistake of bringing his attention to her once more.

His gaze raked slowly over her, lust blazing in his eyes. In response, Jade's blood heated, followed quickly by a wave of gooseflesh.

Her own focus strayed to his broad, bare chest and the dark mat of hair covering it. Suddenly her palms began to itch, her fingers curling with the desire to weave through that fleecy pelt. Unconsciously, her tongue crept out to wet lips gone suddenly parched.

"Woman, you're going to drive me over the brink one of these days," he whispered huskily. "You know that, don't you?" He shook his head abruptly, as if to clear it. "If you have an ounce of mercy in you, you'll retrieve a blanket from my tent and cover yourself with it. Up to your neck and down to your toes."

"What about the other girls?" she murmured, her gaze still caught on his.

"They don't tempt me the way you do."

"Be that as it may," Mavis put in with a wry laugh, recalling them from their private fascination, "our trunks and fresh clothes are still in the wagon. If you'll let us use your quarters to wash and dress, we can all get fairly decent."

Matt nodded. "And I'll go roust the little rascal that created all this havoc to start with."

While the women changed, Matt located a broom, wound a kerchief about his face to filter the fumes, and reluctantly entered their tent. A short time later, after a thorough search, he was out again, minus the malodorous culprit. "He's not in there," he announced on a raspy cough.

"Well, he was," Jade told him resolutely.

Matt rubbed his stinging eyes. "Oh, I don't doubt that for a minute. Everything in there reeks to high heaven. However, the little stinker is gone now, probably scared into the next county by all your caterwauling."

"And left his stench behind. Lord love a duck! I sure hope the day gets better as it goes along, 'cause it sure has started out rotten!"

There was nothing for it but to bundle everything up in the canvas and tie it to the side of the wagon until they had time to launder and air it properly. At the noon stop, several of the Mormon women generously donated extra bedding for the coming evening, in addition to numerous jars of canned tomatoes, which they claimed to be the only cure for the pungent aroma. Thus, with their tent and belongings drenched in tomato juice, Jade and her friends bunked in with the orphans for the night—while Matt bedded down beneath his wagon, tormented by repeated dreams of Jade as he'd seen her that morning in that beguiling green gown.

The watery eyes, the runny noses, the coughs that had resulted from breathing in the skunk fumes seemed to linger longer than they should. While Jade and the other girls recovered almost immediately from the effects, Mavis grew progressively worse. As did Matt, though he hadn't been exposed to the stench for very long, certainly not the way the women had been while cleaning the canvas and everything inside the tent. It was also very peculiar that the children soon began to display similar symptoms, as did several other folks who hadn't been anywhere near the "cat wagon" following the skunk episode.

Baby Zach was especially fussy, to the point that Matt asked Jade to look after him. "Beth's not feeling all that well herself," Matt said, pulling his hat lower to shade his red, aching eyes. "He's running her ragged. Nothing she tries seems to quiet him."

Jade had never tended a sick baby. Truth be known, she didn't consider herself very skilled with a healthy one, scarcely knowing which end to diaper and which end to feed! Now Matt wanted her to take over Zach's care?

Jade decided her best bet was to consult someone more knowledgeable than herself. She promptly cornered Tilda.

"Well, he's either got the sniffles or he's cuttin' teeth, though he's a mite young to be teething just yet. He's what now, about four months old?" the older woman asked.

Jade nodded. "How do I know which is ailin' him?"

"You won't," Tilda cackled. "Not until a tooth pops through or his nose quits drippin'."

Jade put her cheek to the baby's brow. "I think he's got a fever, too."

Tilda felt the infant's forehead. "You might be right, but it's probably nothing to fret about. Babies do that when they're teething, and most other times when they're feelin' poorly. Does he have a rash on his bottom?"

"No more than I'd have if me drawers were always wet," Jade declared wryly, drawing a gruff laugh from the other woman.

"With so many folks goin' around hackin' and blowin', I'll put my money on the sniffles," Tilda pronounced. "I'll brew up a batch of sassafras tea and a nice pot of beef broth, and that should bring 'em around in no time."

Tilda had bet her funds on the wrong horse. By the next morning, Zach had, indeed, broken out in a rash. Not only on his bottom, however. Angry red blotches had spread from his face to his toes. Then Beth began to splotch, followed almost immediately by Emily and Skeeter.

Alarmed, Jade sent Bliss to fetch the Mormon doctor. The man arrived with the announcement that Mavis was in the Mormon camp, down with the measles, and that Hannah and Tom Bailey had taken her into their own wagon until she recovered.

Within minutes, the physician had diagnosed that the children were suffering the same affliction. "Don't worry," he told Jade. "Measles are rarely fatal, except to the Indians, and only last a few days." He went on to issue further instructions. "Steeped willow bark will help bring the fever down, and a pinch of salt dissolved in tepid water makes a soothing eyewash. Other than that, just make them rest and keep the sun out of their eyes."

"The salt I have, but where in this barren place am I supposed to put me hands on willow bark?" Jade asked fretfully.

The gentleman gave her a kindly pat on the shoulder. "I'll send some back. Martha always has some handy."

He'd no sooner ducked out of the tent than he popped his head back in again. "If I were you, I'd clear more space in the wagon than you'd planned on, Miss Donovan, and brew up a good amount of that tea. From the look of things, you've got another measles patient on your hands. Reverend Richards is peppered with them."

Of them all, Matt was her worst patient. Even Zach could not match him for demands, until Jade swore she would gladly give him over to Charlotte Cleaver's care. Except that Charlotte was in no position to do so, for she had contracted the disease as well. Fortunately, of Jade's friends, only Mavis came down with it, and the other girls eagerly offered to help Jade with Matt and the children.

For the first day and a half, the wagons rolled along as usual. They couldn't afford to be delayed along the trail very often, for fear of suffering the same disaster that had befallen the Donner party in 1846. They must stay on schedule as much as possible to ensure getting through the mountains before the passes were blocked by snow. However, when nearly a third of their party became ill, with every able-bodied adult and child struggling to attend the sick and drive the wagons at the same time, the train was forced to call a halt.

A good number of disgruntled Oregon emigrants were quick to place the blame for the current epidemic on the Mormons, conveniently disregarding the fact that the Mormon travelers were only now coming down with measles themselves.

"If anyone passed this disease to anyone, we gave it to them," Matt grumbled, scratching irritably at the prickly stubble of the two-day beard he hadn't wished to grow in the first place. Jade had forbidden him to shave it off, afraid he would scrape the rash on his face raw and leave scars. In fact, she'd hidden his razor from him and refused to tell him where. The little copper-haired pixie was turning into a termagant!

Jade slapped his hand from his face. "Keep yer fingers away from those spots and lie still or I'm gonna give yer knuckles a good rap with a wooden spoon! I swear, ye're ten times worse than any o' the young'uns."

She retrieved the washcloth from the pan of soda water and started swathing his chest. This was one part of her nursing that she'd truly come to appreciate! It was pleasure and torment wrapped into one, being able to touch him this way; to let her fingers sift through the soft, springy hair on his chest, to feel the warmth of his flesh beneath hers, to rub her hands along the muscled breadth of his shoulders and arms. She hadn't worked up the courage to bathe him below his beltline, though, even if she might somehow have managed it without the children noticing. Matt wouldn't have allowed it anyway, she was sure. Still, having him at her mercy was proving to be uplifting when her spirits began to sag at the end of a trying day.

If these periodic spongings were torment to Jade, they were pure torture for Matt. The soda was supposed to soothe his fevered, speckled flesh, but Jade's wandering hands were playing havoc with his dwindling powers of endurance. So far, he had resisted the urge to toss her to her back and give her a plentiful dose of her own medicine, primarily because the children were bedded down mere yards from him. Also, he felt altogether too miserable for such energetic antics just now, and he had no doubt he looked just as bad as he felt—not at all desirable. Oh, but when he was well again, he intended to pay her back in full for this fiendish teasing!

When she finished with him, Jade made her rounds among her smaller patients. Matt's eyes followed her movements as she went from bed to bed. Zach gave a fretful whine in his sleep; Jade patted his diapered bottom, brushing a damp curl from his tiny brow. Gently she tugged Emily's thumb from her mouth and kissed the napping girl on her flushed cheek. With a smile of encouragement, she urged Beth to take another drink of tea.

Skeeter held his arms out to her in a mute plea, and she scooped the lad into her lap and started to croon to him, rocking him gently to and fro. Matt had noticed Jade often did that with Skeeter, holding him near and singing to him. It was most endearing, especially considering the boy could not hear her.

"You're spoiling that scamp abominably, you know," he called out, careful to keep his voice low, lest he wake the others.

"I know, but this is the only way he can hear me sing," she replied, her eyes shining with tender tears as they met his.

His heart ached for both of them, woman and child. "Sweetheart, no matter how closely you hold him, or how much you wish it, he still can't hear you," he refuted softly, sadly.

She shook her head, a small smile curving her mouth. "Yes, he can. In his own way. Notice how he places his fingers on my throat, how his head rests against my chest? He's feeling the vibrations, Matt. He's feeling the music, absorbing it into himself, listening with his body and his heart."

Matt swallowed hard on the lump that had risen suddenly to his throat. "That is the most beautiful thing I've ever heard."

As he continued to watch her, Matt thought how wonderful she was with the little ones, despite her adamant objections to the contrary. She might not have had much previous experience with children, but her love more than made up for any ineptitude. And love them she did. It was so incredibly obvious—in the comforting touch of her hand, the caring tone of her voice, the spark that lit her emerald eyes. The same affections she also displayed time and again toward him, whether she was aware of doing so or not.

Matt sighed contentedly. She might not want to, certainly didn't intend to, but he would bet his last dollar that Jade loved him. Now all he had to do was get her to admit it—to herself, and to him.

Chapter 17

Sean O'Neall was a born opportunist, if ever there was one. Therefore, it came as no great surprise to Jade when he cornered her outside Matt's tent on a day when half the camp was sick and the other half busy ministering to them. With her arms full of freshly laundered linens, she could do little to avoid the hand that clamped roughly about her arm, pulling her to a halt.

"What do ye want, Sean?" she demanded, glaring at him over the stack of sheets.

"A stupid question, if ever I've heard one," he replied with a smirk. "Ye know what I want, lass. I want the same thing ye're givin' the preacher."

Jade gave a brisk nod accompanied by a curt laugh. "Sure, and I'll bring ye a gallon o' willow bark tea straightaway, then," she told him smartly.

"Keep a civil tongue in yer head when ye speak to me, Jade," Sean warned with a frown. "Ye might need me help soon, seein' as ye're about two steps from gettin' yer sweet behind tossed out o' this wagon train. Talk is, ye been takin' advantage o' the reverend while the poor man's too sick to resist ye. Seducin' him with yer wicked wiles when his resistance is at its lowest."

The look she sent him should have shriveled him to a smoldering cinder. "Now, I wonder how that rumor was born? Could it be that some Irish snake Saint Patrick missed has been slitherin' about lyin' through his fangs? Spreadin' tales seems to be a talent o' yers, Sean, and it seems wherever there's mischief brewin', ye're right there stirrin' the pot. One o' these days, boyo, someone's gonna take a mind to tossin' ye headfirst into yer own stew!"

"Yer sass is gonna turn to beggin' real quick, when ye need me to vouch for ye, luv."

"Don't I hear yer wife callin' ye? Go pester her a while. I've better things to do than listen to yer nonsense all day."

"That's right, O'Neall. Take the lady's advice." Matt's voice sounded from the tent entrance, gruff with warning "Run along home now, like a good boy."

Sean turned to meet Matt's dark glower. "Ha!" he laughed scornfully. "And who's gonna make me? Jade's not big enough, and ye're lookin' 'bout as strong as a spotted pup still wet from its whelpin'."

"We'll see who's weak and who's not," Matt responded, the light of battle gleaming in his eyes. He stepped forward. "Let loose of her arm, O'Neall, or are you the type who hides behind women when it comes right down to a good fight?"

Sean let loose of Jade, only to shove her into Matt. She felt him stagger slightly with the impact. "Ye can't do this, Matt," she cautioned, turning pleading eyes up to his. "Ye shouldn't even be out o' bed yet."

His gaze never wavered from Sean's. He simply reached out and swung her around behind him. "Go inside, Jade. Tend to the children."

Jade did no such thing. Though she knew there was no way to prevent the two men from brawling, she'd be darned if she would just slink inside like a turtle pulling its head into its shell. If these two stubborn jackasses were set on beating the living daylights out of each other, she was going to stay right here and watch—if for nothing more than to be sure that Sean didn't try something even more disreputable than to do battle with a sick man in possession of a mere portion of his usual strength.

With her heart in her throat, she watched as the two opponents squared off, each visually measuring the other, weighing the right moment to make his move. Matt, had he been up to his usual health, would have held the advantage. He was taller, his arms longer and more muscled.

But for all his lack of height, Sean was a compact, feisty little rooster, and Jade had the distinct impression this wasn't the first round of fisticuffs he'd been involved in, or likely the last. Unless Matt happened to kill him in the next few minutes—and if the fire in the good reverend's eyes was any indication, Sean would be wise to flee.

Except that Matt was obviously weakened from his bout with the measles. Even now, those blazing eyes were squinting against the bright sun. The fight hadn't even begun and already perspiration dotted his forehead and glistened on his bare chest. In a fair contest, he might be formidable, indeed, but here . . . now . . . barefoot and ill . . .

Sean was the first to strike, his fist flying forward to clip Matt's jaw. Matt's head snapped to the side; he staggered slightly but quickly found his balance. He adroitly sidestepped Sean's second swing and landed a blow of his own to Sean's unguarded midsection that nearly doubled the smaller man over. With his head still bent, Sean charged forward, ramming his hard skull into Matt's ribs. Under the impact, Matt's knees buckled, and the two men tumbled to the ground, Sean on top. But not for long. With an agile twist, Matt rolled Sean to his back, pinning him there.

"Call it quits, O'Neall. Walk away while you still can, before you have to crawl," Matt panted. Just this brief exchange had winded him, but not enough to completely sap his strength, for Sean was still securely caught beneath him.

After a long, silent moment, during which the two men continued to glare at each other, Sean finally nodded. "Aye. I'll go."

Immediately, Matt loosened his hold and slowly started to lever himself to his feet. In that instant, Sean reneged on his word. At the same time his hands reached for Matt's throat, he kicked out—one boot colliding with Matt's bare shin and the other knee catching him high on the opposite thigh. With a grunt of pain, Matt collapsed half atop his shifty rival. But this time he could not hold him there. Sean wriggled free, scrambling to his feet. Before Matt could recover, the devious Irishman leaped at Matt's unguarded back, winding his thick arms tightly around Matt's throat, pulling and squeezing with all his might.

Jade was certain Matt's neck was about to break at any moment, and if it didn't, Sean was surely choking him to death. She could hear Matt struggling for each breath as his face swiftly turned from its sickly ashen hue to dull red.

With a panicked cry, Jade threw down the linens and launched herself at Sean. "Stop it!" she screamed. "Ye're killin' him!"

Like a wild she-cat, Jade scratched and clawed at any shred of Sean she could reach. Catching a handful of his hair, she yanked his head back. Her teeth clamped down sharply on his ear, even while she shrieked into it fit to burst his eardrum.

With a yowl, Sean thrashed about, trying to rid himself of this bloodthirsty banshee stuck fast to his back. But Jade was not about to let loose that easily. She clung on like a limpet, until Sean was forced to release his stranglehold on Matt in order to fling Jade off him. No sooner was he free of her than she came bounding back, nails and teeth bared for business.

Matt stumbled to his feet, wheezing and weaving dizzily before finally steadying himself. His fogged vision cleared just in time to see Sean shove Jade roughly away from him for the second time. She landed on her backside, and Sean, enraged beyond reason, started after her.

"O'Neall!" Matt roared. The man pivoted in mid-stride. "C'mon, you little weasel," Matt challenged. "Let's finish this, once and for all."

The taunt worked. Sean stalked toward him, a feral gleam in his eyes and a jeering smile on his face. "Haven't had enough yet, Preacher?"

Once again they faced each other over the space of a few feet, slowly circling like wary wolves. Now it was

Matt who struck first, one fist cracking into Sean's cheek-bone while its twin smashed into his ribs. The maddened Irishman countered with a jab of his own that nearly drove the air from Matt's laboring lungs. There followed a flurry of exchanged blows, each of the fighters landing several sound punches.

Matt was gasping, his head spinning and his stamina at its ebb, when he gathered the strength for one final blow. His flying fist connecting squarely in the center of Sean's face, the crunch of splintering bone telling the tale. With an agonized howl, O'Neall went toppling backward, blood spurting from his nose as he fell. He made one futile attempt to rise, then collapsed like a rag doll stripped of its stuffing.

That was precisely how Matt felt at this point. Upon delivering the last hit, he went crashing to his knees. He could scarcely raise his head from his chest to view Sean's unmoving body. Sweat dripped from his hair into his face, stinging eyes already unbearably sensitive to the glaring midday sun. His stomach churned as the world began to reel in slow, wide circles. If not for Jade grabbing hold of one arm, and Carl Jansen supporting him on the other side, he would have fallen on his face.

He made a vain effort to smile at Jade through his split lip. Then, focusing woozily on the centermost of three swaying images of his friend, he mumbled, "When did you get here?"

Carl shook his head, which only served to make Matt all the more disoriented, and replied, "I arrived with the rest of the crowd."

"Crowd?" Matt echoed stupidly.

"Yes, old buddy, you've made a fine spectacle of yourself this time. You and your little Irish dove. Half the camp saw you displaying your grand, if sloppy, pugilistic skills."

Matt nearly passed out as, between them, Jade and Carl drew him to his feet and headed him toward the tent. On a hissing breath, he boasted, "Maybe so, but the best man won, and I'm the one left standing."

Carl gave a gruff laugh. "Sure, but only with help from your friends."

"Some friend," Matt pointed out wryly, his words starting to slur. "I nearly get killed trying to defend my lady, and you stand on the sidelines waiting to claim the body!"

By the next afternoon, the account of Matt's fight with Sean had made the rounds from one end of the camp to the other. Tongues were flapping faster than the wings on a hummingbird. Carl Jansen's wife, Nell, made it a point to stop by and tell Matt everything that was being said about him and Sean and, of course, about Jade.

Jade was just returning with a pail of fresh water when she heard Nell's voice coming from inside Matt's tent. She stopped just outside the entrance, not sure whether or not to go in, thinking perhaps this was a private session between preacher and parishioner. Her ears perked up as she heard Nell mention her name.

"For the love of God, Matt! You should be thoroughly ashamed of yourself! I can't believe you've done something so unconscionable! Fighting over that Jade person—that common trollop!"

Not for all the tea in China would Jade have left off eavesdropping now. She heard Matt chuckle. "It's not a sin to engage in a fistfight, Nell. For the record, I learned some of my best maneuvers from the boxing classes my fellow ministry students and I took in college. As for Jade, she is anything but common."

"Go ahead and laugh, but I'm warning you that your upstanding reputation is unraveling at an alarming rate. Gossip is flying thicker than goose feathers, and that awful brawl isn't the whole of it. Word has it that there is more afoot here than meets the eye, that you and that hussy are . . . uh . . . behaving indecently in the presence of the children."

"Not that it's anyone's business, but if you are trying to determine if either of us has yet seduced the other, the answer is no. However, I plan to correct that situation the minute I can get Jade to marry me. And rest assured that the children will be none the wiser when my bride and I consummate our wedding vows."

Jade would have loved to have seen the look that crossed Mrs. Jansen's face upon hearing this blunt announcement, but she was too keen to hear what else might be said to interrupt their conversation at this juncture.

Nell sputtered in embarrassment for a minute. When finally she replied, it was to rebuke him sharply. "If not for the fact that we have been friends for so long, I would slap your face for speaking so crudely. However, since you are sporting a score of wounds as it is, compliments of Mr. O'Neall, I imagine you are suffering enough pain at the moment. You look as if you tangled with a stampeding herd of buffalo."

Matt did look terrible, Jade knew, with his lip split and swollen to three times its normal size, his face bruised and abraded, and half the skin shredded from his knuckles. Jade suspected he might even have a cracked rib. And this on top of the measles, which were just now beginning to fade.

"I've heard O'Neall looks worse," Matt boasted. "He'll resemble a raccoon for a couple of weeks, at least."

"His physical condition, and yours, will no doubt improve," Nell allowed. "It's your mental state that concerns me more. I can't believe you are truly considering marriage to that tart! Why, poor Cynthia must be turning over in her grave!"

"Frankly, I don't much care what Cynthia is doing, or what she would think. My future with Jade has nothing to do with my past."

"But to go from a wonderful woman like Cynthia to one who sells her favors at the drop of a hat! Why, it's inconceivable."

"There is no comparison between the two of them, and I'm weary of people doing so. Regardless of what you think, Cynthia was not the absolute angel she appeared to be; nor is Jade the wicked witch you prefer to believe she is. In fact, Jade will be the better wife, all things considered."

"What a perfectly horrid thing to say! And Cynthia hardly cold!"

"It's been longer than you realize," Matt answered cryptically.

Determined to make him see reason, Nell went on. "Matthew, you simply cannot do this. If you need a wife so badly, and a mother for these children, there are plenty of decent ladies from which to choose."

"I've done my selecting, Nell, and that's all there is to it. I do not have to defend my actions to you or any other mortal being."

"What about God, then? Surely you don't think He approves of one of His disciples consorting with a harlot. A pastor and a prostitute? Merciful heavens!"

"Have you ever considered that He might have led me to her in the first place?" Matt suggested calmly. "That He made the choice and pointed me in the right direction?"

"You can't be serious!"

"Oh, but I am, Nell."

"You'll be tossed out of the pulpit on your ear," Nell warned. "Your parishioners won't stand for it, I tell you. Getting caught up in a skirmish is one thing, but wedding a harlot is quite another."

"If those narrow-minded people who object so loudly would bother to get to know Jade as I have, they would see the warm, generous, honest person she is," he countered.

"It's said that Mr. O'Neall and Miss Donovan knew each other previously," Nell commented slyly. "That they sailed from Ireland together and became intimate. If anyone should know her true character, he should."

"Sean O'Neall is a scurrilous scoundrel. Why anyone would listen to him is beyond me. People practically condemn me for courting Jade, and readily believe the worst of her. Yet they say little of O'Neall, a married man, chasing after a woman who doesn't even want him while he has a pregnant wife lacking for attention."

"Oh, folks are not painting him any whiter than you," Nell hastened to assure him. "It's just that they expect better of a man of God."

Matt sighed. "Well, I'm sorry to disappoint everyone, but I'm not striving for sainthood. I'm simply trying to follow where God leads me, and to do His bidding as best I can."

"Well, you certainly have a strange way of going about it."

Matt chuckled softly. "Perhaps I do, Nell. But does that make me wrong, just because my ideas differ from the accepted standard or my course veers a bit off the usual path? Remember, they thought Noah was fairly odd, too, when he claimed God told him to build that ark. But he had the last laugh."

❧ *Chapter 18* ❧

God did have a sense of humor after all, or so it seemed to Jade. Two days after his fight with Matt, Sean contracted the measles. By then the wagon train was pressing westward again, the majority of the emigrants sufficiently recovered for travel to resume, and Jade could only hope that Sean was thoroughly miserable at having to suffer his malady while on the move.

Travel they must, and quickly, for they were nearly a week behind schedule due to the unforeseen delays caused by the prairie fire and the measles epidemic. To add to their problems, the Mormon Trail had taken them several miles north of Fort McPherson, where they had planned to make another stop. Now their supplies would have to stretch until they could reach Fort Laramie to restock.

It was early afternoon when they came to where the Platte split to form the North Platte and the South Platte rivers. Here the Oregon-bound travelers would take leave of their Mormon counterparts, veering south a ways on the trail they'd originally mapped, while the Mormons would travel the northern fork. It would be several miles, and many days, before the two trails would nearly converge again, to run parallel once more on opposite sides of the North Platte River.

By now Jade, as well as others of her party, was fairly well acquainted with a number of the Mormon travelers, and were saddened to have to leave the company of these new friends. However, by this time she was also reassured that Ike would fare well with Josiah Almann and his family, which was one worry off her mind, at least. As she was bidding the boy and his temporary guardians farewell, Jade received another bit of unexpected news.

"There you are, Jade," Bliss announced breathlessly, running up to her. "Lands, girl, I've been lookin' all over for you! You've got to come help us talk some sense into Mavis, before it's too late!"

"Too late for what?" Jade asked in confusion even as Bliss grabbed hold of her arm and began to tug her along.

"To stop the blasted twit from marryin' Tom Bailey, that's what!"

"Oh, my saints!" Jade was agape. "Ye've got to be joshin'! Bliss. Tell me ye're not serious!"

"I am, and so is Mavis, unfortunately."

Bliss wasn't the only one upset by Mavis's announcement. The other girls were equally distressed. Upon arriving at their wagon, where Mavis was busily packing her belongings, they found the other women arguing loudly.

"It's one thing to show the fella a good time, Mavis, and quite another to tie yourself to him for life!" Fancy pointed out frantically, yanking at one end of the petticoat Mavis was attempting to stuff into her trunk.

"Honey, you'd stand a better chance of sproutin' horns than becoming a Mormon. Think about what you're doing, will you, please?" Peaches advised.

"I have thought about it, and this is what I want. We're all agreed, Tom and Hannah and I."

"Speaking of Hannah, are you not just *le petit* bit uncomfortable with ze idea of marrying anozer woman's husband while he eez yet wed with her? To be ze second wife? To be ze final member of zis *ménage à trois*?" Lizette put in.

Mavis turned to confront her friend with a serene smile that only served to further perplex the lot of them. "Not at all," she said. "Hannah's a dear girl, and I love them both more than I can say. I want to be a part of their family." She paused, then added with a twinkle in her dark eyes, "It's not as if I've never shared a man with another woman before, you know. Why, Bliss and I used to draw straws to see who would have the pleasure of entertaining Harv Henderson whenever he could get to town."

"I'd say this is a mite different," Bliss argued. "B'sides, you've already got a family." She waved a hand toward the other girls. "You've got us, Mavis."

Five heads nodded in concert as Jade added, "What of all our plans? Ye're our leader, Mavis. Our mainstay. The one with the level head, at least until now. What will we do without ye?"

"You'll all get along just fine. And so will I," Mavis predicted. "It's a fresh start for me, don't you see? A new way of life in a new place, with friends and family and a home of my own, and maybe a garden to tend and a baby or two, God willing." Tears brimmed in her eyes and her lips began to quiver. "Please don't hate me or make me feel like I'm abandoning you. I truly need this, believe it or not."

"Oh, Mavis!" Bliss wailed. "Are you sure?"

Beyond speech, Mavis could only nod.

"Zen be happy, *cherie*," Lizette said.

Peaches offered a watery smile. "We'll miss you. It won't be the same without you."

"Just don't forget us," Fancy blubbered past a sob.

"Never," Mavis promised, gathering each of her friends to her in turn for a last, loving embrace.

"And if ye ever need us, ye know where to find us," Jade managed to say.

Mavis grinned through her tears. "Why don't you marry that handsome preacher and put him out of his misery, Jade? The poor man is almost daft with wanting you, and you could do a darn sight worse."

"Go on with ye!" Jade sniffed. "Just b'cause ye're tying the knot doesn't mean we all want to get hanged with the same rope!"

It was a dismal group that bid farewell to their friend, wearing forlorn smiles as they waved good-bye. Upon hearing their sad tale, Matt tried to cheer them. "You'll see her along the trail from time to time, at least until we reach South Pass, and maybe farther."

"It won't be the same, though," Jade bemoaned. "Begorrah! 'Tis hard losin' those close to yer heart."

"I know."

Matt's eyes took on a pensive look as his own thoughts turned inward, and Jade could only imagine how devastating it must have been for him to lose his wife, the woman with whom he'd planned to spend the rest of his life. And now Matt wanted her to take Cynthia's place. But how could she? From what Jade had heard, the woman had been practically perfect in every way—while Jade had more flaws than she could care to count.

"I'm sorry, Matt," she murmured, though precisely for what she wasn't sure. Sorry for bringing sad memories to his mind? Miserable for not measuring up, for being totally inadequate compared to Cynthia? Sorry she could never be the kind of mate he needed and deserved to have at his side? Full of regret that she could not go back in time and erase the mistakes she'd made in her own life?

Matt blinked down at her. "Sorry?" he echoed, shaking off his dark thoughts. "I don't understand."

"For makin' ye recall yer painful loss. 'Twas thoughtless of me."

He shrugged and offered a half smile. "No harm done."

Since he seemed to be taking her apology well, Jade should have had the sense not to pursue the subject, but she couldn't seem to silence her tongue. "What was she like?" she ventured.

"Who?" he asked, his brows drawing together.

"Your wife. Cynthia. That is who we are discussing, after all."

In reality, Cynthia had been the furthest person from Matt's mind when Jade had mentioned losing those he loved. He'd been thinking of his parents and of his only brother. His father had died just prior to the start of the war. The senior Richards had taken a fatal fall while overseeing repairs to the barn roof. Six months later, Matt's mother had suffered a stroke and died in her sleep. Following the funeral, Jordan had joined the Union army, though he could have stayed at home when Kentucky decided to remain a neutral state in the war. For three years, Matt had received terse, sporadic letters from Jordan. Then the letters had ceased, and Matt had heard nothing from his brother since. Army records were a tangle, neither listing him dead nor missing in action, and Matt could only presume that Jordan was dead.

"Matt?"

Once more Jade brought Matt to the conversation at hand. With effort, he tried to collect his thoughts. "Cynthia?" he mused. His mouth twisted in a parody of a smile. "She was blond, beautiful, a porcelain princess," he said, confirming Jade's worst fears. To himself, he added cynically, *Cold, hard, heartless, shallow. A priceless, perfectly formed, artfully poised statue—to be admired, but rarely touched. At least not by me.*

"What a shame that ye lost her." Though Matt couldn't know it, Jade's sigh was more one of pity for herself than for him and his dead wife.

If Matt had realized what Jade had overheard about Cynthia, or that she was comparing herself in her own mind to his previous supposedly perfect wife, he might have revealed some of the bad points about Cynthia's nature. As it was, he saw no point in defaming Cynthia's character at this juncture or exposing his own humiliation and guilt about his former marriage. Thus, he simply shook his head, his laugh hollow as he said, "I doubt Cynthia was ever really mine to lose. Rather like a wish you make that never quite comes true."

"Do ye wish the two o' ye had had children of yer own?"

"I used to hope we would, but I gave up that dream long ago. In some ways, I suppose it's best that we didn't."

While Jade was yet pondering that comment, he continued, his smile tender and teasing as he leveled a warm gaze at her. "I think I'd much rather have children with you, my Irish minx. With your temper and my wit, they're bound to be little terrors, don't you agree?"

"I'm not agreein' to anything," she told him, slanting him a sidelong look. "Leastwise not when it comes to you and me."

"Sweetheart, I'm beginning to think you're hiding a wide streak of cowardice behind that sharp tongue of yours."

"I'm just cautious," she countered warily, thinking to herself that she was, indeed, a coward when it came to the notion of marrying him and trying to fit into Cynthia's shoes. "I prefer to tread carefully."

He graced her with a beguiling, slightly wicked grin. "And I intend to trip you up," he promised. "When you least expect it."

The route they were now taking skirted the south shore of the South Platte River. The water ran high here, the previous winter's abundant snows adding to the spring rains to swell the river to nearly overflowing. Sam Greene informed his party that it was far too dangerous to attempt to drive the wagons across. Rather, they would head on to the ferry station, some miles upriver, pay the necessary tariff, load the wagons onto barges, and cross safely to the other side.

As it happened, the Union Pacific Railroad was laying track along the opposite bank this same summer. For the three days it took to travel the distance to the ferry station, the clang of hammers slapping metal echoed across the water, even above the familiar rumble and creak of the wagon wheels. From sunup to sundown, the clamor continued, and when darkness fell sounds of drunken revelry drifted on the breeze long into the night.

To most of the emigrants, this was simply a temporary aggravation, soon to be left behind. Others were more than grateful for the high river between them, ranting repeatedly about the evils of strong drink and carousing. Meanwhile, Jade's companions were complaining along a different vein.

"Dang it all! Why'd we have to travel this side of the river?" Fancy groused, "We could be makin' a bloomin' fortune entertainin' those railroad boys!"

"Looks to me like they've got plenty of female friends already," Bliss noted, waving a hand toward the opposite shore, where several women were laundering clothing.

Lizette gave a ladylike snort, tossing her nose into the air. "Camp followers!" she sniffed.

Peaches laughed. "Oh, come down off your fancy French horse, Lizzie. Muck is muck, any way you care to rake it, and a whore is a whore any way she shakes it. Those gals are no better or worse than most of us."

"Speak for yerself, if ye please, and don't go paintin' all o' us with the same brush," Jade announced bluntly.

"Well, I don't care what y'all say," Fancy said. "I still claim we're missin' the boat by not gettin' in on the action over there in that rail camp. And no matter how many women they have, I'll bet they don't have anyone who can sing like Jade or dance the can-can the way we do or play the piano like Billy."

"Be that as it may, we're here and they're there, with no help for it," Bliss pointed out. "I, for one, am not about to risk life and limb tryin' to swim that ragin' river in the dark o' night just to give some railroad bum a thrill, no matter how much he'd be willin' to pay!"

It took much longer to transport all the wagons across the swirling, swollen river than anyone had anticipated. The water was turbulent, making the ferry lurch from side to side. Just watching those ahead of her made Jade's stomach clench, and by the time it was her turn she was ready to crawl back to Richmond rather than ride that bobbing flatboat.

"I'll not do it, I say!" she wailed, pulling back as Bliss and Peaches urged her aboard the tiny barge, where their wagon was already anchored.

"Well, short o' growin' wings, I don't reckon you have much choice, sugar," Peaches told her impatiently. "Come on now. We're holdin' up the rest of the train."

"What's the problem here, girls?"

Caught up in her anxiety, Jade hadn't heard Matt approach until he spoke. Now, with her friends still flanking her, she turned pleading eyes toward him. "I can't do it, Matt. Don't let them make me do it. Please!"

He'd never seen her face so pale, her eyes so huge and frightened. "What's wrong, Jade?"

"For some reason, she's bound and determined not to cross this river," Bliss informed him.

Matt frowned. "I don't understand. Jade, we've ferried over rivers before, and you never set up such a fuss."

"This one's wider, and the water is rougher, and I've seen shanties with more wood than is built into that barge! B'sides, me stomach's gettin' upset just watchin' it bob up and down! I had me fill o' bein' seasick on the way over from Ireland, and I'll be hanged if I'll go through that again!"

Now that she'd mentioned it, her face did appear more green than white. "Sweetheart, we're talking about a fifteen-minute ride, not fifteen days. Surely you can last that long. I'll tell you what. You can ride across with me and the children if it will make you feel more comfortable."

Jade touched a finger to her chin as she jutted it out at him. "I'd feel a darn sight more comfortable if ye'd just give me a wee tap on the jaw, like ye did to Sean a week ago. Just enough to knock me senseless long enough to get to the other side."

He stared down at her in amused amazement. "Jadeen Agnes Donovan! I'll do no such thing! I've never hit a woman in my life!"

"I'll do it for you if you want!" Bliss offered, stepping forward, her eyes gleaming with mischief.

Jade eyed her overly eager friend suspiciously. "Bliss, ye couldn't knock a tick off a dog's ear! I ain't aimin' for a split lip or a headache, ye twit. 'Tis pure, sweet oblivion I'm seekin', so I can sleep all the way across."

Bliss shrugged and grinned. "Oh, well, just remember I did offer to help." She turned to the others. "C'mon, girls.

We'll leave Jade and the good Reverend to work this out between them."

In the end, after several minutes of persuasion, Matt finally talked Jade into riding across with his wagon. "I'll be right there beside you, Jade," he promised. "Just try to be brave, will you, or you're likely to transmit your fears to the children."

"Be brave," she echoed on a grumble. "Sure, and next ye'll be offerin' me a blindfold and a cigarette."

Matt chuckled. "I don't agree with the idea of women smoking, but I suppose if you insist on being dramatic, I could offer you a last meal, be it a dry biscuit and a cup of milk."

Jade gagged.

For a little while, Matt was afraid he'd have to tie Jade to the wagon wheel to keep her aboard the raft. The orphans were behaving ten times better than she was. Thankfully, the ferry operator lost no time in setting them adrift, and then it was too late for Jade to do anything but hang on and pray for a swift end to her misery. "I'll get ye for this, Matt Richards!" she vowed between clenched teeth.

He grinned. "I'm shaking in my boots, Aggie."

Those boots were much the worse for wear, and Matt had long since lost his grin, by the time they finally made fast on dry land again. Jade had promptly made good her pledge, and Matt had found himself holding her head over the side of the barge the entire distance, while Beth, wise beyond her years, prudently kept the younger children occupied inside the swaying wagon.

Chapter 19

*I*t took the entire day to ferry all of the wagons across the river, and not without mishap. Midway through the repetitious process, the thick tow-rope tangled, frayed, and suddenly split under the terrific pressure. The barge tipped precariously with the rapid current, spilling the wagon atop it into the river. Fortunately, the oxen were not hitched to the wagon, and the accident occurred near enough to shore that the wagon did not sink entirely, though it was swept downstream some distance. Several men with sturdy ropes swam out and eventually managed to pull it to safety while the frightened family clung tightly to the perilously listing craft. All in all the damage was relatively minor, discounting that most of the contents of the wagon were drenched, some of the foodstuffs were too sodden to redeem, and the poor inhabitants were scared spitless.

Jade watched the event with her heart in her throat, her face as white as parchment, thanking her lucky stars that she and the children had gotten across safely several wagons before. "That might've happened to us," she exclaimed weakly, hardly able to speak.

"But it didn't," Matt said mildly. "God had His hand on us."

"Well, He must've looked the other way when that rope broke," Jade countered. "What a frightful time for that poor family!"

"Yes, but no one was hurt, and for that we must be

properly grateful. Flour and sugar can be replaced, blankets and clothing can be dried. A life is infinitely more precious."

It was nightfall before all the wagons had been brought across, the final two making the trip by lantern light. The emigrants made camp a scant mile from the rowdy, portable town of tents the railroad crews had hastily erected. As was usual, sentries were immediately positioned to safeguard the animals and wagons. However, this evening there were double the number of lookouts posted, to keep watch against any mischief the unruly rail workers might instigate. With enough beer under their belts, there was no telling what that band of hooligans might attempt, and there was no sense taking any chances.

Matt had drawn the last watch, from three till dawn, and was hoping to get to sleep at an earlier hour than usual. Therefore, he was getting somewhat irritated when Jade did not show up for her reading lesson soon after supper. He'd seen her flitting about her campfire a short while before, but now that he stopped to think about it, he could not recall seeing her, or any of the other girls, in the past half an hour or so. In fact, their fire was burning low and the area immediately around their wagon now appeared deserted.

A deep, thoughtful frown creased his forehead. "She wouldn't have," he told himself with a shake of his head. "Surely not. Especially after having been so upset today." He nodded as if to further convince himself. "She's probably just worn out. Most likely dropped off to sleep and completely forgot her lessons."

However, the longer he sat there, staring toward her darkened tent, the more uneasy he became. Finally, unable to stand the doubt a moment more, he heaved himself to his feet and went to investigate. "You're going to feel like a fool, Richards," he grumbled softly. "You're worrying for nothing."

Ever so quietly, he lifted the flap of the tent and peered inside. By the dim light of the fire he could make out bedrolls strewn about, brightly colored dresses and undergarments hanging out of trunks, and nary a living soul in sight.

Jade, and her four merry cohorts, were gone. And Matt knew precisely where to search for her, though why he felt compelled to do so was beyond his reasoning. "Drat it all!" he cursed. "I need this misery like I need three armpits! After Cynthia, you'd think I would have learned a thing or three about women and how conniving they can be! Why, oh why, has God seen fit to bless me with another wandering, wanton female? Of all the women I might have fallen for, why did it have to be this Irish hussy?"

The tent where the girls were performing was large, crudely furnished, and packed to the seams with raucous, half-soused rail workers. During the day, the canvas shelter served as the mess hall, and at night it doubled as a tavern. The floor was mud, overlaid with soggy straw. The bar was fashioned from a couple of planks of wood set end to end across the tops of barrels. Overturned kegs served as the only chairs, and the only three available tables, scarred and shabby, were presently in use as a makeshift stage.

Atop the foremost of these was Jade, in the midst of her third song of the evening. Behind her, dressed in their gaudy sequined can-can costumes, stood her four companions, smiling and teasing and swaying to the beat of the music as they awaited their turn at center stage. Billy stood to one side, accompanying Jade on his harmonica for lack of a piano. Not that anyone seemed to care what instrument Billy played—he might as well have been whistling or pounding a tom-tom, for all the crowd was concerned. And despite Jade's best efforts, she could barely make herself heard above the din of cheering, jeering voices. What with the haze of smoke from dozens of cigars, and the need to practically scream the lyrics, her voice was becoming more raspy by the minute.

She'd just launched into the final chorus of the number when one overexuberant fellow took it into his head to grab her leg. "C'mere, sweet thing!" he yelled drunkenly, his leering grin showing a broken row of tobacco-stained teeth. "I'll betcha sing even better with me on top o' ya!"

At this, several of his comrades took immediate offense, and as Jade hastily stepped back out of reach, the fists began to fly. Within seconds, every man in the place was punching someone else, until there didn't seem to be a single solitary male who wasn't joyously participating in the resulting donnybrook.

As a couple of combatants crashed into the table, nearly knocking it over, and her with it, Jade let loose a frightened scream. Behind her, the other girls were screeching and scrambling down from their own wobbly perches, too busy trying to save their own necks to worry over hers. Just as she'd almost regained her balance, someone grabbed hold of her arm and tugged, and Jade went toppling over the edge to land heavily across a wide, muscular shoulder. An equally strong arm clamped about her legs, and the next thing Jade knew she was being carted off like a sack of potatoes, hanging headfirst with a dizzying view of the floor and a man's backside.

With a shriek that would have done a banshee proud, Jade leveled her fists at that broad back, all the while wriggling like a prize fish on a stringer. "Put me down ye crazed galoot! Who do ye think ye are?"

"I've no doubt I'm the most gullible idiot on earth," answered a familiar, rumbling voice, now edged with unmistakable ire. "And just now I'm as mad as a hornet, so I'd advise you to use what little sense the good Lord gave you and try not to provoke me further."

The shock of hearing his voice froze her momentarily. Then, in complete disregard of her current vulnerable position and his dark warning, Jade resumed squirming and demanded loudly, "Matt Richards! Set me down this instant!"

His reply was less verbal, but instantly effective at gaining her attention, as the hand he'd been using to fend off the brawling throng rose to administer a resounding smack to her backside. Her outraged squawk was cut short as he gave a her a hearty bounce that stole the breath from her lungs. Several seconds passed, and they had gained the outside of the tent before she dared speak again. "You struck me!" she hissed, though less loudly now and a bit more warily.

"That I did," he agreed shortly, his strides not slowing as they passed swiftly down the muddy trail that posed as a street.

"Ye . . . ye said ye've never . . ."

"There's a first for everything, I guess, and under the circumstances it seemed an appropriate measure. Moreover, if you don't shut your mouth in the next few steps, I'll be sorely tempted to take further action. There's a horse trough just ahead that looks as if it might do the trick of muffling your tongue."

"Ye . . . ye wouldn't dare!"

"Sweetheart, you have no idea what I'd dare right this minute, so get smart and don't prod me—Aggie."

She did more than prod him. She bit him! Just a nip really, since that was all she could manage through his shirt and from such an awkward angle. But she did pinch enough flesh between her teeth to make him yelp in surprise.

"That does it!" he muttered. "You asked for this!"

In the next instant, Jade found herself catapulting through the air, only to land lengthwise, and with a tremendous splash, in the middle of the filthy horse trough. She sat up sputtering, vainly trying to swipe her sodden hair from her face.

"Ye lousy b—!" Her irate exclamation was cut short in a flurry of bubbles as Matt promptly dunked her head beneath the surface again. This time she bobbed up spitting water instead of words. Even if she could have stopped coughing long enough, she was far too furious to speak.

By now, the lampblack she'd used to darken her lashes was dripping down her face in muddy rivulets, mingling with the rouge from her cheeks. Her dress was soaked through and clinging to her like a second skin, and her hair was straggling from its pins, spiking out in every direction.

To add fuel to the flames, Matt was laughing heartily. "If you aren't a fright!" he declared, bending over her with his hands on his hips. "I've seen field nags after a long day pulling a plow that don't look as bad as you!"

She didn't bother trying to muster a fitting reply. She simply reached up, grabbed a fistful of his shirt, and gave a hearty yank.

As Matt's boots slid in the mud beneath him, he barely managed to spin himself around before falling bottom end first into the trough. As the resultant spray subsided, he found himself sitting beside Jade, waist-deep in the water, with his long legs dangling over the side of the trough. His hat was floating above his submerged lap, slowly sinking. Sloughing the water from his eyes, he turned toward Jade.

Her satisfied smirk shone clearly through the wreckage of her face paint. "Tit for tat!" she sneered.

He stared at her for a moment, then began to chuckle. "What a sight the two of us must make!" Reaching out, he wiped a smudge from her chin. "Shall we call a truce?"

She agreed grudgingly. "Just 'til we reach camp and can dry off. Now, kindly hie yerself out o' this dratted box. Ye're sittin' on me foot!"

After pulling Jade and his hat from the trough, Matt fished her high-heeled shoes from the water and handed them to her. "You might as well hold these," he advised. "They're not fit to wear as they are, and perilous enough when they're dry." Again he lifted her into his arms. "I'll carry you so you won't hurt your feet. But I must say, Aggie, you could have wrung some of the water from your skirts. You weigh a ton!"

"Ye're a real prince, Matt Richards," she snarled back. "A bloomin', blessed prince!"

Behind them, the saloon fight was still going strong and was now spilling into the street. Suddenly someone yelled over the fracas. "Hey! That fella's makin' off with our canary! We gotta get him!"

"To hell with him! Get her!" A united cheer went up as the mob charged toward them.

"Blast!" Matt muttered. "When I set you down, run as fast as you can. I'll try to hold them off as long as possible."

He swung around, and was about to lower her to the ground when a rider appeared from the shadows, walking his horse into the center of the street and stopping even with them. Dressed all in black, the horseman would scarcely have been visible but for the light of a lantern at the entrance to a nearby tent, which threw a golden glow over his rugged features. In one hand the stranger held a rifle, in the other a revolver. With a lightning-quick flick of his wrist, he cocked the lever-action rifle and fired it into the air, over the heads of the oncoming horde.

As one, the would-be assailants stopped, those in the rear bumping into those ahead of them.

"I'd rethink my plans, boys," the gunman drawled, his deep, even voice carrying easily in the ensuing silence. "It would be a darn sight healthier, if you take my meaning."

Jade heard and felt Matt's sudden, surprised gasp. "Jordan!" he breathed in hushed disbelief.

Though he never actually took his sights off the crowd, the horseman spared a quick glance in Matt's direction, his teeth flashing in a white grin. Quietly, he said, "Keep walking, Matt, while I maintain some distance between you and this mob. Where are you headed?"

"The wagon train. Down by the river."

The man nodded. "I passed it." His smile grew as he added, "If that bedraggled little spitfire is too much of a load for you to carry, you can put her up behind me."

Matt declined with a snort. "Thanks, but you take care of the dogs; I'll handle the vixen."

Jade was tempted to whack him, but thought she'd best wait for a more opportune moment. She settled for muttering beneath her breath.

The gunman kept his weapons trained on the throng, all the while backing his horse to keep in step with Matt. They were several paces along when a chorus of female voices called out frantically. "Wait! Wait for us!" Carefully skirting the disgruntled crowd, Bliss, Fancy, Peaches, and Lizette came running to join Matt and Jade.

Jordan chuckled, a low rumbling sound laced through with amusement. "Sweet Jesus, brother! That's quite a harem you've collected since last I heard from you! I can hardly wait to hear how all this came about."

"In due time, brother," Matt responded dryly. "After we get free of this mess. After I've had a few choice words with my beloved. And after you've told me why in blazes I haven't heard from you in three everlasting years!"

"Nice place you have here, Matt," Jordan teased, looking around the campsite. "A bit small, and not much to make it stand out from your neighbors', but it's portable and offers plenty of fresh air."

"Very funny, Jordan," Matt grumbled. "That reminds me. You have your choice of two spots to spread your bedroll—out in the open or under the wagon. The tent is barely able to contain me and the four children."

"Children? Four of them?" Jordan echoed, his eyes widening. "Glory, Matt! You've been busier than I thought. Which brings another question to mind. Why do I find it odd that you have yet to mention your wife? Cynthia, wasn't it?"

Matt's expression and tone remained bland as he stated baldly, "Cynthia died last fall. Her horse threw her. That's when I decided to sell our property and bring the children west. I intend to start an orphanage in Oregon."

Jordan eyed him curiously. "You seem to be taking her demise awfully well, brother dear. Come to think of it, you never wrote much about her."

"If you'll recall, we lost touch a few months after Cyn and I married." Matt's gaze became intense as he leveled an accusing glare at his brother. "What happened, Jordan? Why did you suddenly stop writing? Damn it all, I thought you were dead! For months, I waited and prayed to hear from you. I hounded the army for news of you. All to no avail. Do you have any idea what I went through, how deeply I mourned you when I eventually gave up hope of ever seeing you again? Right this minute, I can't decide whether to hug you or hit you!"

The two brothers faced each other over the space of a half dozen feet, silence growing between them, until Jordan made the first move toward Matt. "I'm sorry, Matt. You can't know how sorry I am, or how many times I longed to see you, to hear your voice just once more, only to find you gone when I finally did make it home. God, how I've missed you!"

The distance between them dissolved as they both lunged forward to enclose each other in a fierce embrace. Tears gleamed in two sets of blue eyes by the time they released each other and stepped apart. "Why?" Matt repeated more calmly. "What happened?"

Jordan offered a twisted smile that held little humor. "It's a long story, and not easy to tell."

Matt waved a hand toward the campfire. "Have a seat, and I'll stoke up the flames and heat up the coffee."

As Matt set the pot over the fire, Jordan asked, "Not to change the subject, which I know you won't let me do anyway, but would you mind telling me how you and Cynthia managed to have four kids in three years? You must have a set of twins in there," he added, jerking a thumb toward the tent where the youngsters were sleeping.

Matt shook his head. "No twins, and none of them are Cynthia's—or mine. They're orphans we took in. I managed to find good homes for all but these few before leaving Kentucky."

"And you're taking care of them all on your own?" Jordan marveled. Then he added on a sly grin, "Or is that where that bevy of beauties comes in, besides seeing to any needs you have of a more personal nature?"

"You seem to have forgotten my vocation, brother. I am a God-fearing minister, remember?" Matt reminded him, handing him a cup of steaming coffee and pouring one for himself.

With a twinkle in his eyes, Jordan retorted, "Oh, I didn't forget. I just thought you might have. After all, you're the one I found marching down that street with a drenched dance hall gal slung over your shoulder, both of you ranting at each other fit to be tied."

"Jade can be very irritating when she sets her mind to it, which is much of the time. I'm hoping she'll simmer down some once we get married."

Jordan choked on a mouthful of hot coffee, spewing it across the ground. "Married?" he repeated dumbfoundedly, gaping at his brother. "You? And her?" At Matt's calm nod, he gave a low whistle. "Well, will wonders never cease? When's the happy event to take place?"

"Soon, I hope. As soon as I can get my intended bride to accept my proposal."

"I see." Jordan's mouth pursed as he tried unsuccessfully to hold back a grin. "Having a little trouble convincing her, little brother? Would you like me to give you a few tips along those lines?"

"No. As a matter of fact, I'd much prefer you keep your advice to yourself, as well as any objections you might have," Matt told him succinctly. "What I would like, at this juncture, is to hear what you have been doing these past three years. You've sidestepped the issue long enough, Jordan, and I think we both need for you to talk about it."

Jordan sighed and settled back against the wagon wheel, his eyes darkening with his troubled thoughts. "I wrote you a thousand letters in my mind, Matt," he admitted quietly. "When I was lucid enough to compose them. There were long intervals when I was out of my head for long stretches of time. Pain. Fever. Exhaustion. Starvation." There was a lengthy pause before he added in a hushed, harsh voice, "Beatings so severe that oblivion was a blessed relief." Unconsciously, Jordan traced the faint scar that ran from the broken arch of his nose across his left cheek toward his temple.

"My God!" Matt gasped, appalled. "Where were you all these years?"

"You heard of Andersonville?" Jordan asked, turning his tormented gaze toward his shocked sibling.

"Dear Lord in Heaven!" Matt winced, hardly able to speak for the bile rising in his throat. Andersonville was the most notorious prisoner of war camp in all the South. For a Union soldier to be captured and sent there meant almost certain death. "How long?" Matt queried softly.

Jordan's eyes closed on a weary, heartfelt sigh. "A lifetime, Matt. And more. I wasn't released until some weeks after the war was officially over. Most of us were too weak to travel right away. It wasn't until the Union forces sent food and supplies that we surviving prisoners began to regain some of our strength."

"If I had only known—if you could have contacted me, I would have come for you, Jordan. I'd have sold my soul if I'd had to."

"I know that." Jordan sent his brother a sad, apologetic glance. "I know I should have gotten in touch then, but you can't comprehend the state I was in at that time, in mind and body and spirit. The brother you grew up with died in that prison camp, Matt. It was an entirely different man who emerged. I was a shadow of my former self, a brittle, empty, half-crazed shell. Scarcely human. And when I began to feel again, the emotions bombarding me were not gentle ones by any stretch of the imagination. I became so enraged, so filled with anger and hatred and bitterness, that I could barely stand myself."

Jordan's voice broke, and Matt waited, silently sharing his brother's pain, until Jordan could continue. "I couldn't come home that way, Matt. I just couldn't. I don't expect you to be able to understand it, but I had to have time to heal, to exorcise the demons inside me, before I could trust myself to be around the people I'd known before the war. You. Old friends. Neighbors. I didn't want you to see me that way. Nor did I want to take my anger out on any of you. I didn't want to hurt you. That's why I waited so long before attempting to contact you, delayed coming back for two more years. I wanted to make sure

I could still function as a halfway normal, sane person before I did."

"And did you finally find yourself again?" Matt asked, his eyes brimming with compassion for all his brother had suffered.

Jordan shrugged. "Mostly. I can hear a Georgian accent now without wanting to murder the speaker," he offered with a lame smile, "I can close my eyes and not smell the odor of rotting flesh. The nightmares have pretty much disappeared. And I've learned to control my more violent reactions, for the most part. These days, I take pride in the fact that I rarely explode in bursts of raw fury at the slightest cause. I suppose I pass for a reasonably rational member of the human race."

"How did you manage such an immense task on your own?" Matt wondered in obvious awe. "To overcome such terrible obstacles and anguish?"

"Oh, don't give me too much credit before you hear the rest of my story," Jordan suggested in a sardonic tone. "I conquered my problems the same way I earned them. By the gun. What the army didn't teach me, I learned on my own after the war. In fact, I'm surprised you haven't heard tales of me before now, because I'm rapidly earning a name for myself as one of the fastest gunslingers this side of the Mississippi." Jordan faced his brother squarely, his features hardened with self-derision. "Now tell me how proud you are of me, Matt. If you can. You never could lie worth a damn."

"I'm sorry, Jordan. I'm sorry for all you've been through and for all it's done to you. And while I can't honestly say I approve of your choice of careers, that doesn't alter the fact that you are my brother, my blood. I still love you, no matter what you've done, or what you go on to do. I always will."

"Thanks," Jordan said gruffly. "You can't know how much I needed to hear you say that."

"Yeah, well, I hope you know I've only started, that I'll be deluging you with advice and sermons from here on out. Trying to get you to hang up your precious guns and newfound reputation and settle down in Oregon with Jade and me. Or, failing that, to go on home and raise crops and horses in Kentucky."

Jordan chuckled. "It'd surprise me if you didn't, though I'm much better at raising Cain than crops." Then, with a perplexed frown, he commented, "Jade? Back in town, I could swear I heard you call her Aggie."

Matt's grin matched his brother's for pure orneriness. "I only call her that when I want to ruffle her feathers," he admitted, a mischievous spark lighting his blue eyes. "It works every time."

Chapter 20

The following morning, Jordan made a point of meeting the woman Matt intended to marry, though Jade was not quite as eager to make his acquaintance. Rather, she dreaded meeting this man, anxiously anticipating what Matt's brother would think of her. Most likely, he would consider her a trollop, unfit to lick his brother's boots, let alone become his wife. After all, that was what everyone else thought. Why should Jordan Richards be any different? In fact, she expected his reaction to be worse, given the fact that he was Matt's kin.

That Jordan was determined to confront her became immediately obvious when Jade stepped from her tent to find that the gunman had invited himself to breakfast with her, Tilda, and the other girls. His sharp blue gaze rose to meet hers, giving no hint of his thoughts as he continued to study her lazily, much the way a cat might eye a lame mouse. To Jade's dismay, a flush rose to her cheeks, and she suddenly felt as awkward as a newborn colt. This, in turn, made her angry, as did the knowing grin that crossed Jordan's face.

"Ye starin' at anything in particular, or is me nose on backwards this mornin'?" she asked tartly, her eyes flashing emerald fire at him.

Jordan chuckled. "Just curious to see what it is about you that has my brother enthralled. It might be those grass-green eyes, or maybe that riot of fire-splashed hair tumbling down your back. I rather suspect it's your sassy mouth, though, that has him tied up in knots."

"Well, why don't ye hie yerself back over there and untie him, then, if ye've nothin' better to do?" Jade retorted, pointing toward Matt's camp.

"To tell you the truth, I'm more comfortable right where I am. I'm not used to a passel of kids tugging at my pantleg first thing in the morning."

Despite herself, Jade smiled. "They take a mite o' gettin' used to," she allowed. " 'Specially Emily. I swear that lass's tongue is hinged at both ends, and she can think up the darndest questions."

"Then you don't mind if I stay to breakfast? Your friends were kind enough to invite me."

Jade shrugged. "Suit yerself, but I've got to warn ye, all o' us are still learnin' to cook. 'Tis a bloomin' wonder Tilda hasn't decided to charge us double for all the trouble it is teachin' us."

Tilda laughed. "She's right, you know. Never in all my born days have I seen gals so downright dumb about cookin'. But they're gettin' the hang of it, slowly but surely."

"Not without many a mistake," Fancy put in with a grimace. "And Tilda makes us eat each and every one, too!"

"I've eaten worse than you can dish up," Jordan assured them. Turning his attention back to Jade, he said, "We haven't been properly introduced. I'm Jordan Richards, Matt's older brother."

"Pleased to meet ye," Jade returned. "I'm Jade Donovan."

Jordan's brows rose in question, his eyes twinkling with merriment. "Oh? I thought your name was Aggie."

Jade's face turned stormy, her gaze again swinging toward Matt's campsite. "Drat that man, anyway! I've a notion to whack him atop his head so hard he'll have to unbutton his britches to talk!"

Jordan burst out laughing. Once started, he couldn't seem to stop, and it was several seconds before he could speak, tears of mirth dancing in his eyes. "You know, Jade, you and Matt might be good for each other after

all. He certainly needs someone like you to loosen him
up a bit, and you could probably use a man like him to
jerk you into line now and again. This thing just might
work between you, as long as you agree to give up your
present employment once you're married."

"Save yer breath, Mr. Richards. Ye're barkin' up the
wrong tree, 'cause I don't intend to marry anyone anytime
soon. And ye can relay that information back to yer
hardheaded brother for me, if ye'd be so kind. Maybe
he'll listen if ye're the one tellin' him. Every time I try,
he turns deaf."

"That's my baby brother," Jordan agreed, still wearing
a grin. "He's also stubborn to a fault."

"So am I."

"Maybe so, but I know Matt, and I'll put my money
on him any day. If I were you, Miss Donovan, I'd start
sewing my wedding dress."

"I can't sew, neither," Jade grumbled, pulling a peevish look.

Jordan chuckled. "Then you'd better learn quickly,
hadn't you?"

Now that the brothers were reunited at last, Jordan
decided to travel along with the wagon train for a spell.
He also volunteered to drive the wagon for the girls,
giving them a delightful break from the chore. Of course,
much of the time one or another of Jade's friends chose
to ride on the wagon seat next to him, whether it caused
the oxen more strain or not.

This didn't surprise Jade in the least, and Matt even
less so. Broken nose, scarred cheek and all, Jordan was
ruggedly handsome and seemed to attract women like
a magnet drew iron. As Lizette succinctly put it, with
a delicate shudder, "Ooh, la la! Zat Jordan, he eez so
deliciously dangerous, eez he not?"

Now that Jade did not have to take her turn at driving
the wagon, Matt naturally assumed she would spend her
free time with him and the children. Many a day, he urged
her to ride alongside him on the pretext of continuing her

reading lessons. "The more you practice, the faster you'll
learn."

"Sure," she retorted, "and if I don't go blind tryin' to
read on this bouncin' wagon, me eyes will go crossed."

"I promise I'll still love you if they do. Now, try that
last sentence again. Remember what I taught you, and
sound out the letters."

From the river crossing, the land rose sharply, only to
even out onto an extended prairie mesa. For the next day
and a half, the travelers and their animals had no fresh
water, for they had left the South Platte behind and would
find no streams again until they came to a favored resting
point in the trail known as Ash Hollow, more than twenty
miles to the northwest.

However, in order to get to Ash Hollow, they would
first have to descend this rippled plateau at a place called
Windlass Hill, so named because the downward grade was
so steep that the teams had to be unhitched and the wagons lowered by means of ropes. Since the early pioneers
had first negotiated this hill, it had become infamous for
its acute slope and the resultant hazardous descent. Many
a wagon had been lost here, and a number of lives as
well—and this was just a small taste of the route yet
before them and the mountains that still lay ahead.

Descending Windlass Hill was more difficult in many
ways than traversing the river had been. They had to
not only unhitch the teams but also considerably light-
en the wagons so the men could lower them down the
steep slope. Most folks made certain to remove anything
fragile they were transporting, or any item that couldn't
be securely lashed down or easily replaced.

"Well, if this isn't a fine how-do-you-do," Bliss complained. "I didn't think we'd run into this sort of problem
until we reached the mountains."

"How many times do you suppose we'll have to pack
and unpack these wagons?" Fancy wanted to know as she
and Peaches wrestled a flour cask to the ground. The
men were removing the heavier articles, but the women

still had plenty of smaller objects to maneuver themselves—lamps, the more perishable foodstuffs, mirrors,
and such.

Before the girls could venture an answer to Fancy's
question, Matt approached, looking somewhat stunned
and more than a little irritated. "What in blue blazes
possessed the lot of you? Did you all go daft when you
decided to bring along chandeliers and a piano? I couldn't
believe my eyes when I looked into that wagon Billy's
been driving!"

"Yeah? Well, just wait until you get an eyeful of what's
in this one!" Jordan announced drolly, peering into the
interior of their second wagon. "There's a red velvet
settee in here, a couple of huge wardrobes, and the rails
for at least three brass beds!" He climbed into the wagon
to further investigate the holdings. Minutes later, he let
loose with an exuberant holler. "I'll be double damned!
Now, this is the first thing I've spotted that looks like it's
worth haulin' two thousand miles! Matt, these ladies have
got half a dozen cases of liquor stowed in here! And not
the cheap brands, either."

Matt closed his eyes and groaned, wishing he could
open them to find he'd simply been dreaming, that this
was all a nightmare. When he dared look again, however,
nothing had changed. There were still tons of furnishings
to remove from two wagons which had appeared deceptively light until now.

Other emigrants, with less to rearrange, went ahead of
them in line, while Matt and Billy and Jordan labored
for hours. Eventually, the chore was sufficiently accomplished, and they took their turn at manning the ropes and
portable windlass.

Soon both of the wagons belonging to the girls, and
Matt's as well, were lowered without incident. The animals were led safely down and temporarily tethered to
one side. The women had escorted the children to the
bottom and left them in Tilda's care for the moment,
and were now busily carrying the smaller items by hand,
making trip after arduous trip on foot, their arms loaded

with goods. All that was left to transport was the weighty cargo piled atop the hill.

"We ought to leave half of this junk up here to rot," Matt grumbled, eyeing the heavy wardrobes and piano with disgust. "Lord knows I don't want the task of repeating this witless exercise a dozen times more farther along the trail."

"Why don't we just toss it down, and whatever lands in one piece goes back into the wagon?" Jordan suggested dryly.

"I don't care what you do with the rest of it," Billy put in, "but I'll carry the piano down on my back if I have to. Do you realize how scarce these things are out West? Why, they're practically worth their weight in gold!"

Matt nodded, his tired smile ripe with sarcasm. "Most likely because they cost a fortune to ship by sea, and because anyone with an ounce of sense would never attempt to cart one overland."

Jordan sighed. "Let's get at it, if we must. The piano is the heaviest piece. What say we give ourselves a bit of a break and drop the lighter things first?"

One settee made the descent without mishap. Its twin arrived at the bottom minus one leg. Likewise, one wardrobe sustained no damage at all, while the second received a large split in one side that would need mending later. Miraculously, the chandeliers carefully packed inside each wardrobe were totally unharmed. The four dressers all took the trip in stride, with but a few scratches and pieces of trim torn loose.

When it finally came time to lower the piano, Billy insisted on going down with it. "I'll try to help steady it along the way. Even easing it over on its back, and with the quilts cushioning it, there are so many rocks that I'm afraid it will be damaged beyond repair."

Matt shook his head. "I don't think that's a wise idea, myself. This monstrosity is so unwieldy, there's no telling which way it might bump and bounce."

"Matt's right," Jordan concurred. "This isn't the safest undertaking."

"I'll take my chances," Billy maintained. "It's much too valuable to risk having it needlessly abused."

"Then I'll go with you, and attempt to steady it from the opposite side," Matt offered. "Jordan can operate the winch."

All went well for the first part of the descent, Billy, Matt, and the piano reaching a spot about a third of the way down, where a small parcel of ground was level enough to allow the bulky burden to rest evenly while the three men gathered their strength. After a brief respite, they began again, as slowly and steadily as they could manage. They were now traversing the roughest portion of the course.

Suddenly everything began to go wrong. One end of the piano struck a large boulder, taking a tremendous bump. About that time, a section of rope slipped off one corner, and the instrument swung clumsily to one side. Immediately, Billy signaled Jordan to stop the winch. He dashed to the forward edge, intent on keeping the piano from breaking loose entirely, trying to brace it with his shoulder and at the same time attempting to stretch the rope back over the unsecured front corner.

"The rope won't reach!" he yelled to Matt. "It's slipped too far to go back again!"

"Maybe it's caught on something," Matt suggested. "Hold on. I'll have a look."

Carefully, Matt inched his way around the unstable instrument, cautiously examining the underside. "I found it," he said at last. "The cord is hooked on a rock, too far in for me to reach."

"Signal Jordan to pull back a ways," Billy said. "Maybe that will release it."

"Get out of the way, then. If this thing goes, you don't want to be in front of it."

"I can't let go now. Just tell Jordan to raise it."

Though still apprehensive about such a maneuver, Matt waved for Jordan to reel in the line. Slowly, the cumbersome mass moved backward. Then, just as the rope came loose from the snag, the piano shot forward. For a moment, it strained at its bonds, then it broke free of the weakened restraints with all the force of a stone launched from a sling. As it did, it shifted to one side, and before Matt could scramble out of the way, it crashed down, pinning his left leg to the ground.

Matt heard the snap of the bone before he felt the intense flash of pain that seemed to spear through his entire body. Bright lights flashed in his head, and, as if from some distance, he heard himself scream. Though he was sure he was about to pass out, his vision began to clear almost instantly, even as his leg began to throb.

It was then that he realized it was not merely his own scream he'd heard. Above him, Jordan was yelling frantically. Several feet beyond, Billy lay crushed and unmoving on the rock-strewn slope. The piano was still tumbling down the hill, shattering into a thousand splinters as it went, keys clinking crazily and strings twanging in a final, ghastly tune.

Jade was running before she heard the first scream. Heedless of the runaway piano, or any possible danger to herself, she scrambled up the hill—tripping over rocks, stumbling, never slowing. Until something heavy smacked into her back and sent her sailing to the ground. Seconds later, the earth rumbled ominously. Loose stones and debris rained down on her. A shadow passed overhead, gone a moment later.

Weight lifted from her legs, and hands tugged her swiftly to her feet. "Are you all right?" Carl Jansen asked anxiously. "Tarnation, girl! You'd have run straight into the path of that piano if I hadn't tripped you when I did!"

"Th-thanks!" Jade stammered breathlessly. Without another word, she turned and started up the slope again, her knees so weak they scarcely held her upright. Tears streamed unheeded down her cheeks as she struggled, half-crawling over rocks and ridges, literally clawing her way toward Matt, sobbing out his name time and again.

With less distance to traverse, and a downhill route, Jordan reached his brother first. To his immense relief,

Matt was alive, his face contorted with pain as he sucked in each breath through gritted teeth. "How bad is it?" Jordan asked, feeling helpless, but knowing not to attempt to move the wounded man before first determining the extent of his injuries. "Where do you hurt?"

"My leg," Matt gasped.

Jordan didn't have to ask which one. Matt's left leg was scraped and bloody and twisted at an impossible angle—in fact, several angles.

"Where else? Your neck? Your back?"

"I don't know. I haven't tried to move much yet, but I think the leg's the worst of it. At least I hope so." Matt halted, a wave of pain temporarily stealing his voice. "How's Billy?"

Jordan glanced toward the other man and shook his head. "He's not moving. I think he must be dead. That damned piano rolled right overtop of him."

"Go check, Jordan. See if you can do anything for him."

Jordan was bending over Billy's crushed body, trying to feel for a pulse, when Jade stumbled to a halt just beyond him. Horror drained all the color from her face as she stared down at the battered body of the piano man. Without a word, she pivoted, heading up the hill toward Matt as fast as she could scramble.

"Matt! Oh, God, Matt! Please, please be alive!" she prayed. Throwing herself to the ground at Matt's side, her tears nearly blinding her, she sobbed, "Lord, I beg ye to have mercy and let him be all right. I'll promise anything. Anything!"

In the throes of agony, his eyes scrunched shut, Matt could not reply for a moment. At last, pain lending an irritable tone to his words, he ground out testily, "Then marry me, you Irish baggage!"

Chapter 21

$\mathcal{J}$ade's head jerked up, and she blinked furiously to clear her vision, almost afraid of what she might see. Hope dawned in her eyes, her lips quivering as she whispered, "Oh, Matt! Saints be praised! Ye're alive!"

He grimaced. "And I intend to stay that way and hold you to your oath."

"What oath?" she asked hesitantly.

"To marry me. You said you would promise anything, Jade, and I'm calling in the marker, sweetheart. Right now. Before you take it into your head to conveniently forget your hasty plea to the Almighty."

Jade frowned. "Now, Matt, I was upset. I feared ye could be dead. I don't recall half of what I was just babblin'."

"A vow is a vow, Jade," he told her somberly. "And one made to God is especially binding. Besides, I have witnesses. They heard you, too, so don't think you can easily worm your way out of this." He nodded weakly toward Carl, who was standing close behind her, and to Jordan, who had returned to kneel at Matt's other side.

"He's right, Miss Donovan," Carl concurred. "I heard you, plain as day."

"So did I," Jordan admitted. "You might as well surrender graciously, Jade, and save your wits to fight another day—after the wedding."

"Oh, for cryin' out loud! This is ridiculous!" she spouted. "The man is addled. Raving. He's lyin' here in pain, his leg bent six ways from Sunday, with Lord knows how

216

many more injuries, and the lot o' ye are more interested in whether I'll marry him than in gettin' him off this hill and tendin' to his wounds! I swear, I've never seen the likes o' ye!"

"Say it, Aggie," Matt groaned. "For heaven's sake . . . for mine . . . for yours, just spit it out once and for all."

"All right, dadblameit! I'll marry ye! Now are ye happy? Now will all o' ye act like ye've got the sense God gave a goat and find a way o' gettin' this daft man to camp without breakin' any more bones?"

Jordan eased her mind by saying, "I've already sent someone for blankets. We'll make a stretcher of them and carry Matt down on it. A couple of other men are seeing to Billy."

"Is he still alive?" Matt asked hopefully.

With a shake of his head, Jordan told him, "No, Matt. I think he must have been killed instantly."

"I suppose we should be grateful he didn't suffer."

"I'll be grateful if we can locate someone adept at setting bones."

"The Mormon doctor!" Jade exclaimed. "If someone would be willing to ride to the Mormon camp, I'm sure Dr. Worley would come."

Carl nodded. "I'll go. Can't be but two miles to the river, if there's a way of getting across it."

"Sprout fins if you have to, Carl," Jordan advised. "Just hurry!"

Matt was definitely going to live. How well his left limb might heal was yet to be determined. It had taken the good doctor three hours to set the bones properly, press Matt's hip back into place, apply makeshift wooden braces, and attend to all the lesser injuries.

"That leg has been broken in three places, twisted, crushed, and generally lacerated," Dr. Worley announced afterward. "How your foot escaped with only two toes broken is beyond my reckoning," he marveled, aiming his remarks toward his woozy patient, who was now thoroughly sotted, compliments of half a bottle of the best whiskey Jade could furnish. "In addition to that, your hip was dislocated and your back was wrenched. Whether you will ever walk again without benefit of a crutch or a cane depends entirely on how favorably the bones and muscles mend. To be completely honest with you, you can count yourself blessed to do that well."

"I'll . . . I'll walk, Doc," Matt insisted drunkenly. "You'll shee."

"You might," the doctor agreed, "if you stay off of that leg for the next few weeks. If you follow my instructions to the letter. And if you're extremely fortunate."

"Oh, I'm 'bout the luck-luckiest fella there is," Matt slurred with a sloppy grin. "I'm gettin' married."

"He's also as stubborn as a lop-eared mule," Jade muttered.

"And lucky as hell to be alive," Jordan added on a heartfelt sigh.

"A-Amen." Matt intoned. On a final hiccup, he passed out cold.

"That young man is going to be hurting like all get out when he wakes up," Worley told Jordan and Jade. "I'll give you some ointment for the abrasions and some medication for the pain. It might even help that hangover he's bound to have. Keep his leg elevated and immobile tonight, and don't remove the splits when you apply the salve. His leg must remain stable. If possible, try to rig up some sort of hammock in the wagon so he can ride more comfortably on the trail. I'll try to get back across the river to check on him in a couple of days."

"Anything else?" Jade questioned anxiously.

The doctor regarded her curiously, then asked, "Are you the bride-to-be?"

Jade nodded. "Why?"

"Well, miss, I hate to dampen your spirits, but I'm afraid you're either going to have to postpone the ceremony or forgo your nuptial bliss for a time. Unless you can find a way to do it without putting undue strain on that leg of his."

She blushed to the roots of her hair, her face flaming.

Jordan laughed outright. "I have a notion Matt will have a thing or two to say about this," he predicted. "Most likely, the wedding will take place as soon as possible. As to the rest, they say you can't keep a good man down, and it wouldn't surprise me if Jade has a few tricks hidden up her . . . uh . . . sleeve, as well."

Jade's "sleeve" didn't hold nearly as many tricks as most people thought. Two short weeks of lovemaking with Sean hardly qualified her as the vastly experienced tart everyone supposed. In retrospect, after having lived with the "girls" for more than half a year, Jade recognized how naive she'd been—and still was, for that matter.

Just listening to their ribald comments concerning their customers had given Jade new insights into her lone experiment into fleshly pleasure, and it hadn't taken her long to conclude that Sean had been a selfish lover. Primarily concerned with his own needs, he'd attended to hers only insofar as those delights might enhance his. In fact, she now suspected that her former lover had been rather inept, though in what specific aspects she could only guess, her knowledge along these lines still somewhat scant and muddled, and essentially gained secondhand. There were simply some things one had to experience for oneself in order to fully understand them, she supposed, especially those dealing with feelings and reactions of an intimate nature.

However, if Matt had his way, Jade would be immersed in those murky realms up to her neck before long. She also imagined he would be expecting a good deal more expertise than she possessed. How ironic that those same talents with which others assumed she was so familiar were the very ones she lacked, and might soon require, if her upcoming marriage was to be consummated without causing further damage to Matt's leg. Under other circumstances, or perhaps with another bridegroom, the matter might never arise—the wedding, or at least the ensuing act of sealing their vows, postponed until a more convenient time. But Jade suspected that Matt was just mule-headed enough to risk injury to see both deeds accomplished to the fullest measure.

In a quandary, Jade sought Bliss's advice.

"Well, if this ain't a queer barrel of fish!" her friend exclaimed after Jade had explained her predicament. "On the one hand, it sure would be nice to make the man eat his own words, to let him find out for himself how wrong he's been to believe you're such an accomplished harlot. On the other hand, if he's got his mind set on making love after the wedding, you're gonna have to do most of the work—and be mighty careful about it, too—or you're likely to give him more pain than pleasure."

"Don't tempt me," Jade muttered.

Bliss laughed. "Now, Jade, who are you tryin' to fool? When Matt was hurt, I saw the way you charged up that hill like Grant takin' Richmond. You'd have challenged the Devil himself to get to that man, to assure yourself that he was alive. You're crazy in love with him."

"Or just plain crazy," Jade argued. She sighed. " 'Tis a pity they don't have a convent handy out here. I swear I'd run off and join it."

"You're not Catholic," Bliss reminded her wryly.

"I'd convert. Gladly."

"No, you wouldn't. You like men too well to do somethin' that drastic. And that says a lot about your gumption, after the way Sean loved and left you. Some women would be real gun-shy, not to mention bitter, after gettin' treated like that."

Jade rolled her eyes. "Make up yer mind, Bliss. First ye're paintin' me almost as pure as driven snow, and in the next breath ye're sayin' I'm hot after everything in pants!"

"I wouldn't go that far," her friend admonished with a grin. "But you have to admit you do love to flirt. You get a real thrill out of entertainin', standin' up there singin' and smilin' and teasin' dozens of men to distraction. Makin' 'em practically drool just imaginin' what it'd be like to have you. It gives you a peculiar sense of control over 'em, doesn't it?"

Jade frowned. "I never thought of it quite that way, but I reckon there's some truth to what ye're sayin'. Is it the same for you?"

"You bet your bloomers it is, sugar. And since it's about the only power a woman really has over a man, I put it to good use whenever I get the chance. A woman who knows what she's about can get a man to agree to just about anything. You simply have to use the right bait at the right time, set the hook, and reel him in."

Reminded of Bliss's previous advice, some weeks ago, about not cutting her line until she was sure she didn't want the fish, Jade commented, "Sure, and ye must have done a heap o' fishin' in yer past, Bliss. Ye seem to know a great deal about it."

Bliss shrugged. "The main difference between fishin' and manipulatin' a man is to remember that you've got to convince the man that he's the one steerin' the boat— in the direction you wanted to go all along."

"Maybe I'd have handled Sean better if I'd known that a year past," Jade said. "Then again, Sean is a rotten apple any way you care to cut him. Luckily, not all men fall into the same bushel. I think I picked me a better one in Matt."

"I reckon so," Bliss agreed. " 'Course, you were a mite more choosy this time. Searchin' out the sweetest fruit in the batch."

"Sweet, but tart, too," Jade corrected. "And plenty bruised just now."

Bliss nodded and winked saucily. "Hold that thought, sugar, and listen well while I tell you how to squeeze the most juice out of him with the least effort, come weddin' night."

As Dr. Worley had predicted, Matt was much the worse for wear the next morning. The beating his body had taken the previous day was making itself felt in every bone and muscle Matt possessed, and some he hadn't known he had, while huge purple bruises melted into each other across his entire body. His disposition wasn't particularly sunny, either.

Thankfully, Jordan was on hand to handle his brother's most immediate needs, and Jade was glad to let him do it. Measles was one thing, the patient being somewhat mobile. If not for Jordan, someone else—most probably Jade—would have had to help Matt relieve himself, and she wasn't quite up to tackling that chore as yet. Just thinking of that part of his anatomy, and all that Bliss had told her the night before, was enough to set Jade blushing to the tips of her ears.

Matt was his most arrogant self today. First, he wanted to officiate the burial services for Billy. Jordan put a stop to that nonsense in short order. "Perhaps you were too stewed to recall, but the doctor told you to stay off that leg if you want to keep it to walk on. Though you might like to think you're indispensable, dear brother, we have everything in hand. Carl has volunteered to take your place and say a few kind words over Billy's gravesite. While the others are attending the services, and Jade isn't here to see your bare assets, I am going to help bathe you."

"I'd rather have Jade do that. She managed well enough when I had the measles."

"Be that as it may, I am here to attend to it now. She's not your wife yet, Matt, and while you may want to forget that small fact, other folks aren't apt to. So just behave yourself, and try to remember that you were raised to be a gentleman."

"Oh, ho!" Matt exclaimed. "Listen to you, giving me advice on how to conduct myself! If that isn't the pot trying to call the kettle black! And speaking of my bride-to-be, I'd like to discuss wedding plans with her, if you would be so kind as to fetch her for me."

"Later. She and I took turns watching over you last night, and I sent her to get some rest."

"Where are the children?"

"The girls are watching them for the moment. With the amount of liquor you put away yesterday, I thought your head might shatter if you had to listen to Emily chattering and Zach squalling."

"Are they still bringing wagons down the hill?" Matt wanted to know. "Has anyone else been hurt?"

"So far, so good," Jordan reported. "A few broken wheels and bent axles, but nothing major amiss."

Only half of the wagons had been winched down Windlass Hill the day before. With luck, the remainder would be lowered today, convening with the others at Ash Hollow for a brief respite in the pleasant, wooded glen before continuing their westward trek. Ash Hollow, with its cool streams, clear pond, and flower-splashed meadow, provided the first fresh water the travelers had encountered since departing the South Platte River. Its trees offered the first real shade they'd found in weeks, practically since they'd left Independence. It was a haven, a perfect relief from the trials of the trail.

In this, Matt was fortunate, for the men had been able to erect his tent beneath the branches of a towering ash, where it was sheltered from the bright June sun. Otherwise, by mid-morning, the canvas quarters would have been sweltering and he would have been a good deal more miserable than he already was.

He was resting in relative peace later that morning, listening to the low drone of honeybees on the warm air and trying not to doze off as he waited for Jade to make an appearance. Jordan had just left to attend to a few camp chores, and Matt was alone for the first time that day. His lids were closed, and he was half asleep when he felt slender, cool fingertips caress his forehead. Smiling, he sighed. "What took you so long? Have you been avoiding me?"

"Not at all. I just had to wait until your watchdogs left their posts," answered an unfamiliar female voice. Well, not unfamiliar, precisely, but certainly a surprise, as Matt's eyes popped open to find Charlotte Cleaver leaning over him.

For one of the few times in his life, Matt could not think of anything to say. It took him several seconds to find his tongue. "Oh . . . uh, Miss Cleaver," he stammered. "I wasn't expecting you. That is, I was expecting someone else."

"That Jade person, no doubt," the lady surmised.

"As a matter of fact—"

"As a matter of fact, sir," Charlotte interrupted, settling herself primly at the edge of his pallet, her hands folded neatly in her lap, "I have come to converse with you on just that topic. It is the general understanding throughout the camp that you still intend to marry that vile woman. Correct me if I am mistaken."

Matt opened his mouth to speak but never got the chance, as Charlotte barged ahead. "I have stood by and watched you make a laughingstock of yourself over her for entirely too long now, and though I am not usually so forward, I feel I must speak my mind. She is not the sort of woman with whom you should align yourself. You are a preacher and she is a . . . well, for lack of another term . . . a harlot. My word, sir! How can you even contemplate such a thing? How can you bear to look at her, knowing how many men she must have . . . entertained?"

"Miss Cleaver . . ."

Again she cut him off. "Pastor Richards. Matthew. If you want a wife to tend to your home, a mother for those orphans, you need look no further. If you will forgive my saying so, I can offer you those things much better than that tart can. You and I would have ever so much more in common. Why, I hear she can't even read or write, while I am proud to state that I am quite literate. Imagine the cozy evenings we could spend together, reading before the fire. In addition, I am a fine cook and a God-fearing lady who would rear those youngsters to walk a pious path, while that Jezebel would lead them straight to the Devil. Dare you chance that? Have you even thought of all the consequences marrying her would bring? And all for absolutely no reason, for I am prepared to marry you, if you wish, and be the devout and devoted wife you so deserve."

At last Charlotte paused, and Matt quickly took his opportunity. "I suppose you mean to save me from myself?" he asked curtly. "You need not sacrifice yourself to such a cause, Miss Cleaver. I am in full control of my faculties, and I know quite well what I want and what is best for me and the children. My mind is not off its hinges, by any means, simply because I mean to marry the woman I love. Nor do I think Jade and I will be as incompatible as everyone seems to think."

Despite his pain, his aggravation with Charlotte, and the anger her words against Jade provoked, Matt's Christian conscience urged him to turn the other cheek and reject her with some gentleness. "I'm sorry if that offends your sensibilities or anyone else's. Also, while I appreciate your offer and what it must have cost you to come here today and tender it, I must decline. Please understand that it has nothing to do with you, but everything to do with the feelings Jade and I share."

"Lust!" Charlotte huffed in disgust. "Animal passions! Well sir, if that is part and parcel of your needs, I can accommodate those as well, if I must."

As if to prove so then and there, and before Matt could do anything to prevent it, Charlotte pitched forward. Grabbing either side of his head to hold him fast, with her lips as tightly pursed as prunes, she planted her mouth firmly over his.

Predictably, considering the way Matt's luck had been running lately, Jade chose that exact moment to arrive. "Faith and begorrah!" she announced loudly as Charlotte gave a startled shriek and jerked hastily back from her stunned captive. "And they dare to call me a slut!"

Jade stalked toward the two of them, her eyes spitting fire, "Miss Cleaver, if ye'd like to keep that stringy brown mop ye call hair, ye'll hie yerself out o' here b'fore I get me hands on it. And if ye're at all wise, ye'll keep a clear distance in the future—from me and me man!"

Thoroughly disconcerted, Charlotte uttered another strangled cry and fled the tent as fast as she could gather her quaking limbs beneath her, prudently giving Jade a wide berth as she went. Matt, unable to escape so conveniently, was left alone to contend with Jade and her riled Irish temper—which was fast rising to awesome heights.

Chapter 22

$\mathcal{J}$ade was hopping mad, so outraged that for a few seconds all she could do was glare daggers at Matt.

"Now, Aggie, don't go flying off the handle," Matt cautioned warily, holding his hands up as if in surrender.

That loosened her tongue fast enough. Pointing an accusing finger at him, she growled, "Don't ye 'Aggie' me, ye low-down, double-dealin', belly-crawlin' varmint! I ain't the one in the wrong here, mister! I ain't the one askin' one woman to marry me, and kissin' up to another in the same breath, ye schemin' wolf in sheep's wool! Why, I ought to break yer other leg for ye!"

"Jade, honey, if you'll just calm down a moment."

"Calm down?" she echoed on an angry shriek. "It ain't as if I just broke a fingernail, or snapped me garter!" she informed him sarcastically. "This is a mite more serious. Ye . . . Ye . . ." Her voice broke as tears filled her eyes. Hastily, she blinked them back. "I thought I could trust ye, Matt. After Sean, I should have been more careful with me feelin's, I suppose, but ye bein' a preacher and all, I figured ye'd be more honest with me."

"Jade, let me explain."

"Why bother? I saw ye kissin' her with me own eyes, Matt. That was damn well plain enough!" Again she pointed her finger, this time toward the tent opening through which Charlotte had fled. "Is that what ye want, Matt? If so, just tell me straight out, but don't be stringin' me along for the fun of it."

"Hang it all!" he yelled back. "If you'll just pipe down and let me get a word in edgewise, I'm trying to tell you that I don't want Charlotte Cleaver. I never did; never will. I want you. Only you. Always you!"

"Ye were kissin' her," Jade stated firmly. "Ye gonna try to deny that?"

"Yes, I am, Miss Know-it-all. I was not kissing that woman. She was kissing me. There is a vast difference."

"Didn't appear to me that ye were fightin' her off much," Jade countered stiffly.

Matt gave her that look—the one an adult gives an especially dull-witted child. "Just what was I supposed to do, darlin'? Slap her face? Wrestle with her? Jump up on my broken leg and throw her out? Besides, she caught me off guard. Of all things, I never expected her to throw herself down on top of me and kiss me like that. Especially after I refused her proposal."

"Her what?" Jade squealed, her emerald eyes glowing like a cat's, her nails curled into her palms like claws.

Matt winced. "Charlotte came today to try to talk me into marrying her instead of you," he admitted sourly. "I turned her down flat."

"Ye must o' done a mighty poor job o' convincin' her, then, is all I can say," Jade argued.

Matt sighed. "What you witnessed was simply her final attempt to change my mind. Which it didn't. Now, are you satisfied of my innocence? Am I acquitted of a crime I didn't commit?"

Jade's lower lip jutted out. "That sort'a depends on how much ye enjoyed it, I reckon."

Matt groaned, rolling his head on his pillow. "Tarnation, woman! You're bound and determined to hang me, aren't you?"

"Well?" she persisted.

"No, I did not particularly enjoy the kiss, Jade. It surprised me, but it didn't move me to passion. Fact is, it was like kissing a peach pit."

Jade blinked at him. "A peach pit?" she repeated stupidly. A smile tugged at her mouth.

Matt grinned back. "A hard, dry, wrinkled peach pit. Now, are you ready to believe me at last?"

"I suppose so," she relented. "As long as nothin' like this happens again. I ain't gonna marry ye, Matt, and have ye chasin' after other women. I've had me fill o' philanderin' lovers, and I won't be wed to one."

"My sentiments exactly, so keep that foremost in mind," he told her, his tone quiet but deadly serious, his gaze intent. "Once we're married, Jade, I'll be the only man in your bed."

"And I won't share mine with a ghost," she insisted stubbornly.

He frowned. "Would you care to explain that last remark?"

"I won't have ye constantly comparin' me to yer late wife, Matt, or wishin' she were there in me place."

He stared at her in astonishment. A moment later, a rough bark of laughter broke forth. "Sweetheart, that will be the furthest thing from my mind. Believe me. In fact, it will please me immensely if the two of you turn out to be as different as day and night."

Jade frowned. "And would ye care to explain that a wee bit more?"

He shook his head. "I'd rather forget about it entirely. Just rest assured, Jade, that I love you, dearly and with all my heart. And for better or worse, my affections will not stray."

She came to kneel at his side, her eyes aglow with emotion. "I love ye, too, Matt. I reckon I didn't realize how much until yer accident, when I thought I might have lost ye. And when I saw ye kissin' Charlotte Cleaver . . ."

"As I said, she was kissing me, but go on with what you were saying, love. It's music to my ears."

"I liked to died, Matt. Sure, and I saw red, I did. For a moment there, I wanted to murder both o' ye."

"I'm sorry you had to witness that," he told her solemnly. "I'd rather lose my leg than ever intentionally hurt you."

"Don't say such a thing!" she cautioned him anxiously,

giving a little shiver. "Don't even think it! Begorrah! 'Tis like temptin' Fate when ye do! Ye're gonna get well, Matt, and that's all there is to it."

"I'll get well faster once we're married," he teased with a boyish smile that melted her heart.

She eyed him skeptically. "Just how do ye figure that?"

His grin widened. "How could I not, with all the tender, loving care you'll lavish on me? Consequently, I see no good grounds to delay our marriage any longer. I think we should exchange vows immediately. Today, if possible. Tomorrow at the latest."

"And how will we manage it? Ye're the only preacher we have, Matt," she reminded him. "Surely, ye can't perform yer own weddin' ceremony, can ye?"

"No, but Judge Talbert can marry us. Unless you're concerned about wedding a man who may always walk with a limp, or a cane." His eyes assessed her carefully, awaiting her reaction, hoping he wouldn't see revulsion overtake her pretty features.

Rather, she puffed up like a brood hen and gave him a furious glare. "Matt Richards, I declare, if I ever hear anything so absolutely absurd pass yer lips again, I'll smack 'em!"

"I'd rather you kissed them," he invited, his blue eyes gleaming up into hers. "Then you can run and find Judge Talbert. Or, better yet, have Jordan do it, while you go do whatever it is a bride has to do to get ready for her wedding."

"Not just yet," Jade replied, a look on her face he couldn't quite discern. Rising, she fetched a wet cloth and bent to rub it briskly across his mouth. "There!" she stated, nodding her head in satisfaction. "I'll not stand for havin' the taste of another woman on yer lips when I kiss ye."

"You didn't have to scrub quite so hard, Aggie," he informed her with a grieved look. "Besides, your kisses are a darned sight sweeter than peach pits any day."

"Just ye remember that in the future, sir, when some lady decides to tempt ye."

"You're all the lady I could want, Aggie, and more."

She rewarded him with a long, hot kiss that left him with more parts swollen than his injured leg, and an entirely different sort of pain—one he hoped would soon be assuaged.

Of necessity, the marriage took place inside Matt's tent, with the groom lying flat on his back, his broken leg propped on a stack of blankets. With Jordan's aid, he'd donned a white dress shirt, a black-and silver brocade vest, a tie, and his black broadcloth coat. The seam of the left leg of his matching trousers had been slit to accommodate his heavily splinted limb, but given the limitations of his injuries he looked appropriately dressed for the occasion.

His bride knelt next to him, nervously holding his hand and clutching a small bouquet of wildflowers the children had picked for her. To everyone's surprise, and to the indignation of a number of the hastily invited guests crowded in and around the small tent, Jade was attired in an actual wedding gown, complete with satin slippers and lace veil that made her appear quite the innocent and demure bride. The gown was somewhat aged from its original pristine white, now more the color of rich cream or soft candlelight, which appeased the onlookers somewhat. About her throat she wore a blue ribbon, pinned to which was a delicate cameo.

Matt was just as stunned as the others to see his bride appear in the beautiful gown. When he asked where she had gotten it, Jade leaned close to whisper something in his ear that set him grinning broadly. It would remain their secret, and that of the "girls," that Lizette had graciously donated the gown. It seemed one of her former customers had had a fetish for brides, and had given her the gown to don whenever he visited her. To whom the dress had originally belonged was questionable, though Lizette suspected it might have been his mother's.

Jordan later commented that the assemblage of guests more resembled warring factions than witnesses to a wedding, with the tearfully smiling "cats" clustered to one side, and a half dozen of Matt's frowning friends and former neighbors grouped together in opposition. The four children stood on the middle ground—Emily balanced on Jordan's arm with her thumb in her mouth, Beth standing behind the bride and groom holding the sleeping baby, and Skeeter snuggled beside Jade clutching a handful of her skirt.

Much to his wife's displeasure, Carl Jansen had consented to be Matt's best man, thus freeing Jordan to give the bride away, since Jade had no one else to do so. Jordan, again dressed all in black, and sporting his holster and gun, wore a determined look that dared anyone to openly object to the proceedings.

Tense silence reined as Judge Talbert began the ceremony.

In short order, he reached the spot where he asked, "If anyone can show just cause why these two people should not be joined in holy matrimony, let him now speak, or forever hold his peace."

There was a shuffling of feet, and a few inarticulate grumbles, as Jade held her breath, waiting for someone to dispute their right to marry. However, with Jordan glowering a dark warning, his hand hovering near the butt of his revolver, no one spoke outright. She heaved an inward sigh of relief as the judge quickly continued.

They repeated their vows with touching sincerity, Matt replying in his deep resonant tone, Jade's voice more hushed and tinged with a noticeable quaver. There was another slight sputtering of surprise when Jade intoned softly, "I, Jadeen Agnes Donovan, take thee, Matthew Richards, to be me wedded husband." Clearly, a good many of those listening were shocked to learn her given name, and that she hadn't just called herself Jade for purposes of her profession. Of course, a few still wore doubtful looks, and most likely would for some time.

Near the end of the rite, much to Jade's wonder, Jordan handed Carl a plain gold wedding band, which Carl then passed to Matt. Gently, his eyes glowing with emotion,

Matt pressed the ring onto Jade's marriage finger. As prescribed, he recited solemnly, "In token and pledge of our deep and abiding love, with this ring I thee wed."

Jade scarcely heard the judge pronounce them man and wife. Next she knew, Matt was urging her downward, his lips softly meeting hers in a tender kiss that sealed their vows. Tears she hadn't even known she'd shed glistened on her cheeks, wetting his as well.

Then Judge Talbert's voice was booming, "Congratulations." With a grand wave toward those gathered about, he announced, "I present to you, with great pride, Reverend and Mrs. Matthew Richards."

After a pregnant pause there came a spattering of polite applause, which swiftly grew in volume as Jade's friends took up the cause. En masse, the "girls" rushed up to Jade, bussing her on the cheek, wiping at her joyful tears, taking their turns at kissing and teasing the groom. Not to be left out, though not fully understanding all the commotion, the children joined in, laughing and hugging everyone who would indulge them. Matt's friends, more reserved in their felicitations, nevertheless bent to tradition as well, and came forward to congratulate the newlyweds.

In the midst of this havoc, a new voice suddenly rose above the tumult. "Not to be meanin' any disrespect, Judge Talbert, but I'm wonderin' if ye have the authority to lawfully marry these two. Ye bein' from Ohio, aren't ye a bit out of yer jurisdiction out here?"

In the wake of Sean O'Neall's blaring query, an immediate hush fell over the crowd. All ears waited expectantly to hear the judge's response, even as the blood drained from Jade's face. In contrast, angry color rose to stain Matt's flesh, his eyes blazing blue ire. Jordan's wrathful gaze mirrored his brother's, his mouth set in a grim line as he stepped forward, his hand resting on his gun.

Placing a restraining hand on Jordan's arm, Judge Talbert faced the arrogant intruder. "Young man, I assume from your pronounced brogue that you are newly arrived to this country. Therefore it is understandable, if not entirely forgivable, that you should interrupt such a glad occasion with such an untimely and ignorant inquiry. However, I shall endeavor to enlighten you to the error of your thinking. I hold a federal judgeship, as opposed to a state office, and have been duly appointed by none other than the president of these United States himself. I have full authority within each and every state and territory under the American flag. Does that sufficiently clear your mind on this issue?" he concluded with pompous dignity.

Sean's stiff features registered his anger at being so thoroughly and publicly chastened. His reply was worded politely, yet sharply edged with spite and double meaning. "Beggin' yer pardon, sir, but Jade bein' a close acquaintance o' mine, I just wanted to make sure 'twas all legal and such, ye know. Wouldn't want to see her shamin' herself by carryin' on like a married 'lady' when she really wasn't one a'tall."

"It might behoove you to concern yourself with your own business and not go poking your nose where it isn't wanted, Mr. O'Neall," Matt advised tersely from his place on the floor. "Jade is my wife, and my concern, not yours. You have a wife of your own to look after, though you seem to be doing a poor job of it from all accounts."

Low murmurs of agreement rippled through the gathering. It was well-known that Sean O'Neall was not the most attentive husband, that he spent more time gambling and carousing and stirring up trouble than in seeing to his pregnant wife's comforts. Even now Gwen O'Neall was just recovering from her own terrible bout with the measles, still bedridden, while Sean blithely neglected her needs in order to trespass on a wedding he hadn't been invited to attend.

To reinforce Matt's statement, Jordan added his own decree. Standing head and shoulders above him, glaring down at Sean with fierce loathing, he growled, "I'd put my brother's suggestion to serious consideration if I were you, little man. Otherwise, you're liable to slit your own throat with that sharp Irish tongue of yours and bleed to death one of these fine days."

True to form, Sean drew himself up and faced the challenge before him, regardless of his disadvantage. "Are ye threatenin' me, by some chance, Mr. Richards, b'fore all o' these fine folks?"

Jordan's answering grin was diabolical to behold. "Nope. I rarely issue warnings, but I do make predictions—and promises, which I damned well keep."

While Sean was yet contemplating a suitably scathing reply, Matt spoke up. "I can fight my own battles, brother. I've sent that pup crawling off with his tail tucked between his legs before, and I can surely do it again if the occasion arises—with or without a bum leg."

Jordan's smile widened. "Be that as it may, Matt, I'd consider it a personal privilege if you'd allow me to escort Mr. O'Neall back to his own wagon now, so the rest of us can get on with celebrating your wedding."

Without waiting for Matt's assent, Jordan summarily grabbed Sean about the collar and the seat of his britches, hefted him a good foot off the ground, and carted him from the tent like so much rotten garbage. Sean went cursing and flailing, providing quite a show for those who watched his hasty, helpless departure.

It was Bliss who eventually broke the tension by exclaiming softly, "Well, I declare! This is certainly the most interestin' weddin' I've ever attended!"

Chapter 23

Not so much because they approved the pastor's marriage, which many of them did not, but because it gave them the perfect excuse for a well-deserved celebration, the emigrants decided to throw the newly united couple a wedding party. As soon as the sun had set and they could put aside their evening chores, they threw together a small feast and took a portion of it to Matt's tent. There, they handed the offering to Jordan, leaving him to best determine the proper time, if ever, to give the lovebirds their nuptial supper. Then they were off to enjoy their own share of revelry, music, and dancing, apart from the bride and groom.

Meanwhile, the "girls" had taken Jade in hand. Amid much good-natured arguing over which nightwear was most appropriate, most alluring, and most beautiful, they finally had her dressed—or rather, undressed—for her wedding night. Then, of course, they debated whether she should wear her hair up, braided, or unbound. Though it was most likely to tangle, loose and flowing won out, on the wager that Matt would probably enjoy running his fingers along its silken length.

By the time they'd brushed her hair to a coppery glow, buffed her nails, creamed her skin, and filled her head with more well-meant advice than she could ever possibly recall, Jade was a bundle of raw nerves. She could scarcely walk on rubbery legs as her giggling friends escorted her, suitably concealed in the folds of a voluminous cloak, to her eagerly awaiting groom. In the end, they practically had to push her into the tent, after which they quickly closed the entrance flaps and tied them securely from the outside, effectively "locking" the newlyweds inside with each other. From his bed beneath the wagon, Jordan would be standing guard throughout the night to further insure Matt and Jade's privacy, while the girls took charge of the children for the evening.

As she stumbled into the lamplit interior of the tent, Jade was so jittery that her stomach was threatening a revolt. She clutched the cloak about her, fighting the urge to shut her eyes and wish herself anywhere else but here.

Matt was waiting for her, lying on his bedroll, bared to the waist, his lower body covered with a thin blanket. The sight of his broad, furred chest made her mouth go even more dry.

"I . . . I thought sure a preacher would wear a nightshirt or somethin' to bed," she stuttered stupidly, her eyes resembling large, shining green pools.

Matt smiled tenderly. "And I never thought you'd be this nervous on your wedding night," he told her quietly. He held out a hand to her. "Come, Jade. The girls sent over a bottle of champagne from your cache. We'll share a glass, talk a bit, and take things as they progress."

She went to sit beside him, glad to be off her wobbly legs, not sure how much longer they would have supported her. "Would you care for something to eat?" he asked. Gesturing toward a small camp table on the far side of the tent, he added, "Our fellow travelers got together and provided our wedding supper."

Mutely, Jade shook her head, her arms still folded over her quivering tummy. Finally, she offered in a barely audible murmur, "If ye're hungry, though, I'll be glad to fetch a plate for ye."

His eyes gleamed up at hers. "It's not food I'm hungry for right now, Jade." On a low chuckle, he waved a hand toward her cloak. "Would you care to take off your wrap and stay a while, love?"

That was the last thing Jade wanted to do at the moment, but knowing she'd have to remove it eventually, she figured sooner was as good as later. Slowly, with shaking fingers, she loosened her hold on it and shrugged it off her shoulders.

Matt took one look, and the breath locked in his lungs. He'd never seen a gown such as Jade wore. Certainly, it wasn't the average sort of bed attire any lady of his previous acquaintance might don. Even Cynthia, with her love of rich fabric and expensive clothing, would never have contemplated purchasing a nightshift of this type, if you could even term this garment as such. It looked like something an Eastern queen, or perhaps a pasha's concubine, might wear. Assuredly, it did not inspire thoughts of restful sleep.

Sewn of sheer, shining gold silk, the gown draped to her form with daring faithfulness. Stark in its simplicity, with not a shred of lace in sight, it was sublimely sensual. The upper portion was sleeveless, fashioned with inch-wide straps across the shoulders, which graduated in width as the material widened to embrace her breasts— barely! From bosom to navel, the garment laced sparsely down the front, leaving a tantalizing, cross-patterned expanse of creamy flesh exposed. From the waist, the skirt fell in gossamer folds, slit the entire length of the sides to bare her long, shapely limbs.

To the fortunate observer, the fabric itself seemed to reveal more than it concealed, for through the shimmering weave Matt could just discern the dark crowns of each breast, and had she not been sitting so modestly, he was sure he could have seen the triangular shadow at the apex of her thighs. Even as his eyes lovingly caressed her body, her nipples hardened and peaked, prodding boldly at the scant bodice.

Slowly, Matt reached out to trace the crest of one breast, his knuckle brushing lightly over the scarcely hidden nipple. Jade sucked in a hasty breath, the action pushing her breast more firmly against his lingering hand, as if further inviting his touch.

"You look like a goddess come to life," Matt told her, his deep voice full of reverent awe. "Almost too perfect to touch. Your skin glows like honey, your eyes are emeralds displayed against a sunrise, your hair a glorious copper flame atop a golden candle."

Indeed, her skin and eyes had taken on an added radiance, both from the lustrous color of the gown and the tremendous tension building within her. But, to Matt's mind, a true goddess could never have felt this soft, this warm, this enticing.

A burnished lock of her hair curled about his fingers. He tugged at it gently, urging her to bend to him, until her warm, moist breath heated his lips. Their mouths meshed, first in tentative exploration, then more fervently as his questing tongue slipped between her parted lips to drink from the sweet dark well beyond. Tongue frolicked with tongue—gliding, tangling, teasing. Slowly stoking the embers of desire.

So gradually that Jade scarcely noticed, her nervousness vanished, only to be promptly replaced by growing tension of a more amorous nature. Matt's kisses were fast heating her blood, and when his fingertips skimmed the shell of her ear, a delicious shiver shook her. His lips were still sipping at hers, his teeth nipping lightly, when his hand again brushed her breast, the shifting silken fabric creating the most exquisite friction. She could not contain the low moan of desire that escaped into his mouth.

Of its own accord, her back arched. In response, his hand slid beneath the slippery material to fully cradle the milky globe in his warm, work-roughened palm. He captured her extended nipple, plucking at it gently, rolling the rosy crest smoothly between his long, strong fingers. A sweet, sharp stab of longing traveled from her breast to her belly, making her muscles clench tightly as her womanhood went hot and wet and aching.

Caught up in sensual bliss, Jade's hands swept the breadth of Matt's chest, her fingers sifting through the downy hair sprinkled across it. Her nails scratched lightly over his jutting male nipples, and he gave a gasp of pleasure. "Yes, love. Touch me," he implored, his voice gruff with yearning. "Warm me. Heal me."

Once begun, it seemed she could not get enough of the feel of him. The furry tickle against her palms. The firm, heated texture of his flesh-bound muscles quivering slightly beneath her curious caresses. As they exchanged kiss for passionate kiss, stroke for tantalizing stroke, her head spun with delirious delight. The very scent of his skin seemed to intoxicate her.

Soon, even this was not sufficient for either of them. Freeing her breasts from their silken confines, Matt caught Jade about the waist and hauled her upward, his mouth leaving hers to trail a stream of playful bites and teasing kisses from her cheek to her chest. His steamy mouth enveloped one breast, his lips suckling ardently at the turgid crest, and Jade felt the tug to the depths of her womb. On a mewling cry, she melted against him, his to command. When she thought she could not possibly stand one additional moment of this marvelous torment, he worked his way slowly back toward her mouth, his tongue laving every inch of her trembling skin along the route.

Their lips reunited in mutual, eager craving, tongues darting in a nimble dance of desire. His hands stroked her silk-clad body, then delved deftly into the side slits of her skirt to caress her stomach, her hips, her buttocks, skillfully and progressively working their way toward their ultimate goal. Jade complied mindlessly as he parted her legs, his agile fingers swiftly finding the nubbin of desire he sought. She gave a muted gasp, reflexively clenching her thighs and tightening her muscles, effectively trapping his hand where it lay.

"What?" he questioned softly. "Was I too sudden? Too rough?"

"No. It just came as somethin' of a shock. Like gettin' struck by lightnin'."

He chuckled. "Well, I hope it's a lot more enjoyable than that, sweetheart." He wiggled his fingers tauntingly, brushing them repeatedly over the tiny mound, and she writhed in response.

"Matt, oh, Matt!" she panted. "Stop! Don't stop! I've never felt anything so . . . so . . . wondrous!"

He wasn't done there. He teased and rubbed and tantalized until she was delirious with need. One long finger slid smoothly into her, finding her slick and hot and wanting. "I can't believe how tight and wet you are," he murmured thickly.

His words came faintly, for in that instant Jade felt her mind and body shatter. Her entire being spun crazily out of control, as if her very spirit had been hurtled free of its physical frame into a spinning star-spangled abyss.

Matt felt her inner muscles tighten spasmodically, and knew she'd found her release. As her velvet walls pulsated about his finger, his manhood throbbed violently, and it was only by dint of will that he maintained control of his own responses.

At length she recovered her wits somewhat and lay limply across his chest, her breath coming in short, fast spurts. "That was amazin'!" she exclaimed.

He grinned triumphantly. "Turnabout is fair play, don't you agree, honey?" he said, catching her hand and directing it beneath the blanket.

As he wrapped her slender fingers around his swollen member, Jade marveled at how smooth and fevered and hard he was. Satin over fired steel. Iron encased in steaming silk.

The initial impact of her touch on that most sensitive and vulnerable appendage brought an immediate groan of ecstasy from deep within Matt's chest. "Well, maybe that's not such a good idea after all," he suggested, removing her hand before she could do more than run her dainty fingers along the length of him. "I'm too near to bursting now, and I want to do it right—embedded so deeply within you that we become forever one."

As he attempted to shift her more fully atop him, Jade scrambled to recall what Bliss had told her. "Wait! Wait!" she cried excitedly. "Ye gotta stop this!"

Matt froze, a look of disbelief on his face and his blue eyes blazing. "Stop what, Mrs. Richards?" he asked tersely. "Making love to my wife?"

"No, ye gotta stop tryin' to do this all by yerself, ye dunce!" she spat back, her gaze locked to his. "Lawsy! 'Tis a bloomin' miracle ye haven't hurt yer leg already!"

Matt relaxed, relieved that she didn't mean to call a halt to the proceedings. "Little darlin', the only limb aching at the moment is the one you are about to put to good use."

He watched her blush, again thinking how remarkable it was that she'd retained such an impression of innocence in her profession. Her former profession.

"Well, ye'll just have to let me take charge from here," she told him firmly. With that, she eased herself over him, straddling his waist. "Now, Matt, I don't want ye to move a muscle, hear? Just lie back and enjoy it, if ye can, and tell me if I cause ye any pain."

Though he sincerely doubted he could strictly follow her orders and not move at all, he was willing to give it a try, for contrary to what he'd told her, his leg and foot were throbbing some, despite the medication he'd taken earlier. "It's your show, green eyes."

Carefully, Jade edged backward, bracing herself on her arms and trying not to put her weight on Matt's hip. She could only imagine what Dr. Worley would say should he dislocate it again!

Slowly, inch by inch, her lower lip clamped between her teeth, she settled herself hesitantly upon his stiff staff, ignoring the slight discomfort she was causing her own body, which was not at all accustomed to such intimate invasion, despite the fact that she was not a virgin. Halfway down, she heard him moan. Thinking she'd hurt him, she halted instantly, perched in midair.

"For mercy's sake, don't stop now!" he implored. "Glory, woman! Nothing's ever felt this good!"

She lowered herself farther, finally taking the entire length of him within herself. "Oh, Matt!" she exclaimed on a whisper. "I feel so full of you! I can feel ye touchin' me far up inside!"

He, too, could feel himself butted securely against her womb. The heat of her was incredible, her body gloving his so tightly that he could scarcely bear it! The pain in his leg was forgotten, eclipsed by intense pleasure.

Slowly, easily, Jade began to rock upon him. To and fro, side to side, alternating her movements. Then, assured that she was not causing him distress, she commenced drawing herself up and down the complete extent of him, riding him as gently and as lovingly as she could.

Her lazy, deliberate movements nearly drove Matt mad. It felt so heavenly, so blessedly glorious! With each silken stroke, she was driving him closer and closer to the brink of ecstasy. Every twist of her body on his, every time he slid into her so snugly, he could feel that final splendor reaching for him with outstretched arms—just out of grasp. It was frustrating! It was wonderful! It was the sweetest torture he'd ever imagined! All he could do was grit his teeth and hope to endure!

Try as she might to keep her mind clear, Jade was fast losing herself in the bliss. Joy was beckoning once more, cloaking her in a cloud of mounting emotions. Her actions became totally instinctive as she gave herself up to the wondrous delights awaiting her.

Just at that awesome moment, as she teetered on the edge of passion's pit, she felt Matt stiffen beneath her. Her glad cry blended with his, as together they took that final, headlong plunge into rapture.

A short while later, they lay quietly contemplating the wonder they had shared. Slowly, rhythmically, Matt sifted his fingers through the shining copper veil of Jade's hair spread across his chest, silently thanking God for this beautiful, sensuous woman who was so giving of herself, so different from his first, self-centered mate. Her head was nestled in the crook of his shoulder, her hand rested lightly above his heart, the ring upon her finger gleaming like a golden blessing. Catching her fingers in his, he brought them to his lips, gently kissing the place where his wedding band rested.

"Where did ye get it?" she murmured drowsily.

"Get what?"

"The ring."

"It belonged to my grandmother, originally. Jordan inherited our mother's wedding ring, and Grandmother's came to me. I had it packed away in one of my trunks. Why do you ask?"

"Well, it was kind'a obvious ye couldn't run down to a store and buy it, or send Jordan, since we're out here in the middle o' nowhere. I . . . I thought maybe it was yer first wife's."

"Cynthia's?" Matt scoffed softly. "No, Jade. You may set your mind at ease. This ring never graced her hand."

Jade sighed. "I'm glad."

"So am I," Matt admitted tenderly. "I'm also overjoyed, and still a little stunned, that you are really mine at last. It's like a dream come true." His lips brushed the top of her head. "I love you so very much. You know that, don't you?"

"I love ye, too, Matt," came her whispered reply. "I just hope 'tis enough."

"Enough for what, sweetheart?"

Jade's cheek shifted slightly on his shoulder, and he felt a single teardrop, warm and wet, fall to his chest. "Enough to see us through the rough times ahead."

His arm tightened about her, binding her more securely to him. "Love shared is love multiplied a thousandfold, Jade. The more you give it, the more it grows. Between us, we'll have an abundance—to last a lifetime and longer."

His promise echoed softly in their hearts as they drifted slowly off to sleep, still entwined in a lovers' embrace.

Chapter 24

*E*arly the next morning, before either Jade or Matt was yet ready to face the day, Jordan cheerfully and loudly announced breakfast. Jade scarcely had time to yank a blanket about her before the tent flap was raised and Jordan entered, bearing a tray heaped high with steaming flapjacks, syrup, fried sausage, and fluffy golden biscuits. "Compliments of Tilda and her ever-diligent students," he told them with a wide, toothy smile. He added with a mischievous wink, "I hope I didn't catch you at a bad time."

"You never did exhibit much finesse, Jordan," Matt grumbled in reply.

Jordan walked right up and placed the tray on Matt's lap, and for a moment Jade feared he meant to join them at their meal. Her wide-eyed look of disbelief must have given Jordan a hint to her thoughts, for he laughed outright. "Enjoy your breakfast, lovebirds," he teased, waving a hand at the small feast. On his way out of the tent, he called back over his shoulder, "Better hurry, though, 'cause your small brood of chicks is getting anxious to greet Papa Matt and Mama Jade."

Their all-too-brief honeymoon was fast waning. The tedious tasks of everyday life on the trail awaited them.

Half an hour later, Jade was dressed and tending to camp chores, much the same as she did any other day, her four little charges shadowing her wake. The wagon train was laying over until the following morning, giving the weary travelers time to mend tack, care for their animals, wash their laundry, and attend sundry other repairs and duties before continuing onward.

Despite his injuries, even Matt was not to be exempt from the work, for Jordan soon appeared with an armload of harness and extra strapping. "Since there's not much else you can do, I thought you might want to keep busy by looking these over for weak spots," he explained, dropping the pile at Matt's bedside.

"What's Jade doing?" Matt asked irritably. "I haven't caught a glimpse of her since she went trotting out of here with the breakfast dishes. I hate being cooped up in this tent where I can't see what's going on."

"I'll see what I can do about it later," Jordan promised. "I'll also keep an eye on your wee bride for you. As for her trotting, though, I'd say she's down to more of a waddle at the moment. Or maybe a slow shuffle." He grinned broadly. "I'd hazard a guess that you two found a way to maneuver around your injuries just fine. Fact is, Jade looks worse for wear this morning than you do, Matt. Which is very curious, don't you think?"

"No, I don't," Matt answered with a scowl. "Neither do I find this an appropriate topic of conversation. Family or not, there are some subjects which I consider strictly private."

Jordan shrugged. "Still and all, given her reputation, you'd think she'd be much more accustomed to such vigorous activity, not mincing about like she'd been strapped to the back of a galloping horse for a month, following one short evening with her somewhat disabled bridegroom."

"Not that it's any of your business, brother," Matt said tersely, his features registering his annoyance, "but Sam Greene instructed the 'doves' to curtail their usual endeavors during the course of the trip. Naturally, it would follow that they might be a bit out of practice, shall we say."

"Oh?" Jordan's brows rose above twinkling blue eyes. "Well, maybe Jade is, but her friends sure aren't. I can vouch for that personally—and thank them mightily!"

"I really don't want to hear about your romantic exploits, Jordan," Matt told him sourly. "Any more than I wish to discuss mine, or Jade's, with you. If you have a need to confess the intimate details of your sins, either offer up a private prayer for forgiveness yourself or go find a priest who's willing to intercede on your behalf."

Jordan chuckled and shook his head. "My, my! You certainly are an old grouch, aren't you? Why, after a night with your green-eyed sprite, I thought you'd be singing a brighter tune today, regardless of all those broken bones."

"It might help cheer me if my closest kin would cease badgering me about my wife and her former profession," Matt countered. "I get quite enough of that from my friends and congregation. It seems there is an abundance of people in this world who tend to strain at a gnat and swallow a camel. Meaning, of course, they make a huge fuss over small issues, while they accept greater faults without much comment."

Jordan nodded. "I agree. But before I condemn others for wearing missionary blinders, I'd check my own vision, if I were you. Because I have a hunch there is more to your little Irish nightingale than meets the eye—or less, perhaps."

It was strange, considering Matt's talk with his brother, that he should chance to eavesdrop on yet another interesting, related conversation a short time later.

While Matt was examining the harnesses, Jade and the children appeared from time to time to check on him and to keep him company. After sharing the noon meal with him, Jade encouraged him to rest a bit to save his strength. The heat of the day was fast warming the tent, and Matt was feeling drowsy. He was half asleep by the time he heard Jade collecting the laundry and ushering the children quietly from the tent.

Now, just as peace and sleep were a nod away, he heard Bliss call out from the nearby wagon, "Jade! Wait up!"

Jade answered with hushed impatience. "Shhh! Ye'll be wakin' Matt, and he's just dropped off to sleep, the poor lamb."

Matt had to grin at this. One broken leg, and he'd gone from good shepherd to poor lamb, had he?

Bliss had joined Jade just outside the tent. Matt could see their shadows outlined against the sun-dappled canvas. "Where are you off to?" Bliss asked more quietly, though still clearly enough for Matt to hear.

"The river. I thought the young'uns might like to splash a bit while I wash the laundry. Saints, but 'tis amazin' how many clothes this pack o' ragamuffins can dirty in no time a'tall!"

Bliss chuckled. "Your days of washin' out a dress or two and a handful of unmentionables are gone, sugar. This crew will have you hoppin' from sunup to sunset. It sure is a good thing you got used to watchin' over them like you did, a bit at a time, or you'd be in a fine fix now, wouldn't you? If I were wearin' your shoes, I'd probably be runnin' for the hills, lookin' for a handy Indian to put a quick end to my misery."

"If ye found one, ye'd have the unsuspectin' fella eatin' out o' yer hand within five minutes, Bliss, beggin' for yer favors," Jade predicted.

"Speaking of which, how did it go last night?" Bliss asked curiously. "Did my suggestions work all right for you?"

"Like a charm, with nary a peep o' pain out o' him. I have to thank ye for that, Bliss. If ye hadn't told me what to do and how to go about it, there's no tellin' what damage I might have done. Pain or not, he was bound to see it through."

Inside the tent, Matt's jaw was drooping in astonishment. Heat scorched his face. He simply could not believe what he was hearing! In anticipation of their lovemaking, and its possible problems, had Jade actually discussed her wedding night with her friends? Had they truly counseled her concerning the dilemma his injuries presented? Lord have mercy! Was nothing sacred to these women?

His eyes nearly popped from their sockets as Bliss unwittingly informed him further.

"If you hadn't been so dead set against acceptin' any and all offers to warm your bed, you wouldn't have had to come to me for advice. You'd have known the best way to go about it. And you'd be a darned sight richer into the bargain."

"Like I told Vera when I first hired on, I'd rather sing for me supper than earn it on me back. Though I don't fault ye for it, I can't be as casual and calm as the rest o' ye are about takin' lovers." Jade gave a short, wry laugh. "I reckon I thought, with my luck, they'd all end up as rotten as Sean."

Bliss gave a shrug. "Could be. Doesn't matter much anyway, now that you're married to Matt—though I can't help wishin' he thought better of you. You really ought to tell him that Irish no good was your only lover."

"Even if he believed me, it doesn't make much difference, really. One lover or a thousand, 'twas still wrong and can't be undone. Matt's willin' enough to forget me past, to build a future together with me, and that's what counts most. And now that we're married, I'm gonna bust me buttons to be the best wife I can be, and then some."

"That's great, honey, but just remember, bein' grateful is one thing, licking his boots is another. You can get a mouthful of mud doin' that—and wind up with a bellyful of grief."

Once the women had gone, Matt had plenty of time to himself to ponder what he'd overheard. A part of him was angry at Jade for not being totally honest with him about her past. It made him feel like such an idiot, such a fool, to discover the truth at this time and in this manner! Why hadn't she explained, right from the start, instead of letting him go on thinking she was selling herself so cheaply? Why hadn't she corrected his misconceptions?

Another part of him cringed to think what a self-righteous ass he'd made of himself these past weeks, insisting that she could change if she truly wanted to. How pompous he must have sounded! Yet, she'd hardly said a word to refute his mistaken impression of her, other than to proudly state that she was a talented singer and entertainer.

Pride. The word lunged out at him, and suddenly his anger began to subside as he tried to view things from Jade's perspective. If he'd stood in her shoes, might he not have reacted in much the same way? Wasn't that, in large measure, the very reason he preferred not to reveal his problems with Cynthia? Because his pride stood in the way? Perhaps Jade hadn't wanted him, or anyone else, delving into the private secrets of her past any more than he wanted his own mistakes exposed and dissected.

Still, she should have trusted him. And he should have known, should have guessed that she was not the harlot she seemed to be. Even his own brother had suspected Jade was less accustomed to lovemaking than one might assume, while Matt had remained steadfastly blind.

Oh, not that Jade was entirely blameless. She could have come right out and set him straight on the matter. And it wasn't as if she was totally virtuous. After all, she had given herself to O'Neall. And she did entertain in dance halls and the like, painting herself up like a floozy and flouncing about in those revealing gowns. Moreover, she'd picked up a good number of bad habits and language from the other "girls." Lord knew, she could curse like a mule skinner when her temper was riled! Given all that, what else was he to think, for heaven's sake, when she played the part so well?

But now he knew the truth. The next question was, what was he to do about it? Should he confront her with what he'd learned, and how? Should he demand an explanation—or apologize for being such a dunce all this while? Or should he simply say nothing, amend his faulty thinking, and start treating her like the new, fairly unskilled bride she was?

Another thought struck him, hitting hard. Good grief! No wonder she'd seemed so nervous last evening. If she hadn't thought to consult her friends beforehand, their wedding night might well have been a tangle of errors and confusion. One wrong move and he could have found himself howling in pain. And there he'd lain, none the wiser, confident in his own abilities—and hers! Relying on her to know precisely what she was doing, what he was expecting her to accomplish!

Matt shook his head in wonder. Lord save the world from blundering idiots such as he! God did, indeed, look out for fools and children! Most especially nearsighted self-righteous fools!

When Jade and the children returned from the river, Matt was just waking from a nap. As Jade moved about the tent, spreading clean blankets and linens on the bedrolls, Matt's gaze seemed to follow her every move. Each time she looked up, he was watching her with brooding blue eyes. Frankly, this first day of being a bride, having to take over chores she wasn't adept at, not knowing precisely what her wifely duties were and weren't or what Matt expected of her, was enough to make her nervous in itself. Those intense, unfathomable looks he was now giving her were making her all the more jittery.

Finally, she could stand it no longer. "Is somethin' wrong, Matt? Is yer leg painin' ye?"

"A bit, but that's to be expected."

"Do ye want a dose o' yer medicine, then?"

"Not yet."

"Are ye hungry? I was gonna wait and have Tilda help me with dinner, but I can probably muddle through on me own if ye'd like an early meal."

"No, thank you. Later will do."

"Would ye like a book to read? A cup of water? Anything?"

"No. I'm fine."

"Then would ye kindly stop starin' at me like ye're doin'?" she huffed in exasperation. " 'Tis givin' me the fidgets."

He smiled then. "Sorry, sweetheart. Just admiring my beautiful bride."

"Oh," she answered, taken aback. "I thought maybe I was makin' the beds up wrong or somethin'."

His smile widened. "I don't think there is a right or wrong way to do it, Jade, as long as the oilcloth is underneath the lot to keep it dry. I just sort of tuck everything in and let it go at that."

Beth spoke up with a giggle. "Yeah. Once he even stuffed Emily's doll in with her pillow, and she almost bawled her eyes out b'fore we found it for her."

Matt pointed a finger at the girl, giving her a fake frown. "You promised never to tell on me, Beth. Just for that, you have to let me win at checkers tonight."

Beth wrinkled her nose at him. "You always win anyway, 'cept when you cheat."

Jade laughed in delight. "Matthew Richards!" she tsked. "Imagine ye cheatin' at checkers! Wait 'til yer faithful flock hears that!"

"Aggie Richards!" he mimicked back. "Tattle on me and you'll rue the day!"

"Ye don't say," she teased smartly, her hands on her hips. "What ye gonna do, boyo? Beat me?"

"No more than a swat or two on your bottom with a broom," he boasted.

"Ha! Ye'll have to catch me first, and right now I can run a blamed sight faster than ye can."

Matt's eyes twinkled merrily. "There's more than one way to bag a green-eyed cat, darlin'."

Matt was exceptionally congenial the rest of that afternoon and evening, despite the boredom of having to lie on his back all day and the pain Jade witnessed in his eyes from time to time. When Tilda and the girls arrived for the cooking lesson, he offered to entertain the children for her while she was outdoors preparing supper. Afterward, he praised her efforts, though the dumplings were almost as chewy as the chicken, and the broth was salty enough to cure leather.

"Ye can thank Jordan for the meat," Jade told him, offering a nod toward her brother-in-law. "He went huntin' and came back with three fat prairie hens."

Feigning a cough, Matt furtively spat a pellet of buckshot into his palm. As Jade glanced away, he threw it at his brother. "Overload your shells, by any chance, Jordan?" he inquired wryly.

Jordan grinned back. "Actually, I borrowed your shotgun, Matt. I don't own one myself. I normally get by with my rifle and revolver. If anyone overloaded his . . . uh, shells, or is about to overload anything else, little brother, it's you."

Matt rolled his eyes. "I suppose I'll have to put up with such impudence for a while, until I'm back on my feet. After all, you are doing most of my work."

While Beth and Jade washed the dinner dishes, Matt and Jordan discussed the tasks Jordan had seen to that day. It was no small list, starting with greasing the wagon wheels and axles, repacking three wagons, cleaning and trimming the oxen's hooves and applying a special salve to them, and replenishing the water barrels.

Matt shook his head in amazement and dismay. "Tarnation, Jordan! I never meant to heap all of this onto your shoulders. I hope you know how much I appreciate your help."

"Don't worry about it, Matt. And don't look so blasted guilty. It's not like you asked to have your leg broken, you know."

Coming in on the tail end of the conversation, Jade said miserably, "If it's anyone's fault, 'tis mine, and the girls'—and poor Billy's. We're the ones who insisted on bringin' that dratted piano along. And look what it got us. Billy's dead, Matt's laid up in pain, and the piano's in splinters."

"No one's to blame, Jade," Matt assured her kindly. "Besides, if that pile of wires and keys hadn't rolled over on me and crushed my leg, you'd still be dithering around trying to decide whether or not to marry me. So I guess I got the best of the bargain."

"Sure," Jordan agreed. "Besides, instead of having to haul the blasted thing across country, the piano is now being put to better use," he added with a touch of irony. "We were running low on firewood."

🌸❧ *Chapter 25* ❧🌸

$\mathcal{J}$ordan stayed long enough to play a couple of rounds of checkers with Matt and the children, while Jade watched and tried to absorb the fundamentals of the game. Matt promised to teach her soon.

"Watch him," Jordan cautioned as he levered himself from the floor and prepared to leave. "He'll cheat every chance he gets."

Beth and Jade shared a look and burst out laughing. "I know," Jade answered, poking her tongue out at Matt. "Beth already warned me about that."

Soon thereafter, Jade tucked the youngsters into their bedrolls on their side of the tent, which was now partitioned off from the adult side by means of a blanket strung from ceiling to floor—a measure intended to provide a modicum of privacy to the newlyweds. While the little ones were drifting off to sleep, Matt suggested that Jade sit down next to him for a reading lesson. All too soon, much before Jade was ready, the youngsters were sleeping soundly, the reading lesson at an end. It was time for her and Matt to turn in for the night.

Feeling unusually shy, Jade offered quietly, "I . . . uh`. . . I can help ye out o' yer clothes if ye want, Matt."

A mischievous twinkle lit his eyes, a slight smile crooking his lips. "That would be more comfortable for sleeping, thank you."

Tentatively, she reached over him and unbuttoned his shirt, peeling it carefully from his broad shoulders. All the while, Matt lay there like a limp rag doll, grinning. Those devilish eyes danced with amusement. Finally, he whispered loudly, "I won't bite, Aggie. Honestly."

She puffed up like a peevish robin and yanked his arms free of the sleeves. "Where's yer nightshirt?" she demanded shortly, irritated at herself for feeling so anxious, and at him for being so blasted smug in the face of her agitation.

"Forget the nightshirt. It's warm in here. I'll make do with a sheet." She eyed him darkly, waiting. "Well?" he prompted at last, "aren't you going to assist me with my britches, like a good little wife? Charlotte Cleaver would, in your place," he taunted.

"I'm sure she would," Jade muttered, glaring at him. Her hands hovered over the buttons of his denim trousers. "For two cents, I'd yank yer pants up to yer neck and cinch yer belt to the tightest notch."

Matt chuckled. "Good thing I'm not wearing a belt, isn't it?" His hands covered hers, bringing them firmly over the thick cloth and the swollen flesh they hid. "Have I told you how adorable you are when you blush, Jade? Or how much I love you?"

Guided by his fingers, she worked the metal buttons through the stiff openings. Four hands pushed the heavy material from his hips, until Jade slid the trousers from his long legs.

Much to her surprise, Matt was wearing a pair of cotton drawers beneath his britches. Since Sean had never bothered with such modest measures, and she hadn't laundered any of Matt's earlier in the day, Jade was unprepared to find her husband wearing them. This was the first she'd seen a man sporting the undergarment, and she stared in frank fascination.

"Is it the drawers that amaze you so, sweetheart, the fact that I wear them, or that part of me which is straining for release and making a tent of them?" Matt questioned softly, his eyes sparkling with mirth at her dumbstruck reaction.

She merely nodded.

He laughed. "Your turn, love."

"What?" she asked distractedly.

"Unless you intend to sleep in your dress tonight, I'd suggest you disrobe, darling."

"Oh, yes," she concurred. She glanced about, as if slightly bewildered and wondering how to accomplish the simple deed. "I don't have a proper nightshift," she murmured.

Matt took pity on her. "Your chemise will suffice. Or, since I'm not using it, you can wear my nightshirt if you want. It would probably look much better on you than me, come to think of it."

Jade cast a sidelong look at the lamp, and another toward Matt, who was watching her intently. Without another word, she turned her back to him and quickly shed her dress, her one petticoat, her boots and stockings. Clad only in her drawers and chemise, she rummaged about in a small trunk until she located her hairbrush. Before she could decide where to settle herself, Matt patted the blanket beside him.

"Come. Sit here, sweetheart, and I'll help you with your hair."

Jade seated herself at his side, her back toward him. Within seconds, Matt had deftly unplaited the braid and was pulling the brush through her loose tresses with long, sure strokes. Her hair tumbled down her back in a thick ripple of burnished waves.

"Your hair is glorious," he marveled. "It's as soft as cornsilk, as thick as honey, like spun sunlight gathered into a shimmering, fiery cascade. Angels must envy it."

"I don't know much about angels, but this sure feels heavenly," Jade purred blissfully. "I've never had a man brush my hair b'fore."

"That doesn't surprise me, after what I overheard this afternoon. Your conversation with Bliss came as quite a revelation to me."

Jade gave a surprised jerk and froze where she sat. Her mouth went so dry that when she attempted to swallow, she thought she might choke. "Ye heard?" she finally managed to squeak.

"Every blessed word," he admitted evenly. "You might have told me, Jade."

"What difference would it have made?" she asked hesitantly, still not able to determine his mood.

"None, now. But at the start, I might not have thought so badly of you. And last night, I would not have presumed your experience to be so great, or relied so heavily upon your limited skills. I would have been more prepared to handle matters myself, to progress more slowly, to guide you more gently, perhaps."

Jade turned toward him, her eyes searching his. "I still wouldn't have come to ye pure and innocent, Matt, like I wanted to."

"No, but if you had said something before, maybe our intimate relations could have remained confidential."

"Ye mean without Bliss knowin'?"

He nodded. "Yes."

"Saints alive, Matt. What makes ye think I'd have talked to ye about our weddin' night? O' course, I asked Bliss. She's a woman. And who would know best how to go about such things without causin' more misery to yer leg?"

"And how much distress did your efforts to save me pain cause you?" he questioned softly. "Jordan mentioned that you were moving about a bit more gingerly than normal today."

"Lord love a bloomin' duck!" Jade exclaimed, completely mortified. "Ye talked to yer brother about the beddin'?" She gave a low groan. "Sure, and I'll ne'er be able to look the man in the eye again!"

"Now, Jade, he simply remarked that your steps weren't as spry as usual," Matt assured her, stretching the truth as much as he dared.

"I see," she replied curtly, her temper rising. " 'Tis fine and dandy for ye to be discussin' our private affairs with yer brother, but not for me to talk to Bliss about 'em. Is that about the size of it, Reverend Richards?"

"No. What goes on in our bed is no one else's business but yours and mine. However, I am grateful that Jordan brought your discomfort to my attention, since you failed to make mention of it, and most likely would not have." His gaze was both stern and concerned. "I wouldn't intentionally harm you for all the world, Jade, and I've been worried all day. Are you all right? You weren't hurt too terribly?"

Her face flamed to match her hair. "I'm right as rain. Fit as a fiddle. Grand as . . ."

"The truth, Aggie."

She sighed, her eyes skittering away from his as she admitted, "Just a wee bit tender, but nothin' to fuss over."

"You're sure."

"Yes."

"Then put out the lamp and come to bed."

When she returned to lie down next to him, he drew the light blanket over the two of them and pulled her close to his side, pillowing her head on his shoulder. "Go to sleep, love. It's back to the trail tomorrow, and we can both use all the rest we can get."

He was silent for some moments, until he said quietly, "Don't ever be too shy, or too embarrassed, or too frightened to discuss your concerns with me, Jade. No matter how intimate or trivial they may seem. I'm your husband, your helpmate, and I want to share your thoughts and problems. That's what marriage is supposed to be about— uniting and caring."

"I care," she whispered back. " 'Tis the unitin' part that needs practice."

"We'll work on it together," he promised softly, his lips lightly stroking her forehead.

She swore she felt the warm caress of his smile in that kiss. With a smile of her own, she turned more fully into his embrace, arching to fit her lips to his. Sleep could wait a bit longer. Making love with her husband suddenly seemed a much better use of their time.

*   *   *

On the fourth day out of Ash Hollow, as they gradually plodded up a slight but steady incline, they came upon a pair of distinctive landmarks that had inspired previous travelers to near-poetic narrative. Two strange formations of earth and rock stood side by side within sight of the trail. The first had been dubbed Jail Rock. The second and larger, multitiered and some four hundred feet high, had long since been labeled Courthouse Rock, since it bore a striking similarity to a municipal building in Saint Louis. Other pioneers had likened it to a crumbling cathedral, the Tower of Babel, and the Capitol in Washington, but the name Courthouse had stuck.

More striking yet was Chimney Rock, which they reached the following day. The lower section was broad, similar in shape to a haystack. From its top, thrusting ever higher and thinner, rose a towering spire, much like that of a church steeple—or a chimney. It loomed an estimated five hundred feet tall and was most awesome to behold.

"It looks like a giant tipi," Jordan remarked.

"Or a funnel resting cup-side down," Jade added.

Matt shook his head in wonder and admiration at this example of nature's handiwork. "It appears to me more like an ancient stone chapel set down in the wrong time and place. I can almost imagine some primitive tribe of Aztecs or Incas worshiping in just such a place."

Chimney Rock was also a significant milestone along the trail, as it unofficially marked the end of the prairies and the beginning of the journey onto the great plains. However, the emigrants had little time to celebrate this momentous event. With their day's route only half traveled and the noon stop soon at an end, they hurried on, following the path now marked by a crooked line of telegraph poles leading west toward Forts Mitchell and Laramie.

As usual, Matt groused at being returned to his make-shift hammock, constructed from a canvas cot and suspended beneath the arched ribs of the wagon. "I feel like a blasted pig in a poke!" he grumbled irritably. "Or perhaps a hog spitted for roasting is a more apt description. All I lack is an apple stuffed into my mouth!"

"Don't tempt us, brother," Jordan advised him, only half in jest. "Here you are, lying about in leisure the day long, treated for all the world like a pampered prince with the rest of us at your beck and call, and all we hear out of you are complaints."

"Ha! If anything, I'm a trapped animal for the lot of you to torment! If you assume it's a pleasure swaying along in this contraption, as helpless as a fish in a net, wondering when it might break loose and send me tumbling, you have another think coming, Jordan."

His brother sent him a taunting grin and whacked him lightly on his drooping backside. "Save your objections for your doctor, Matt. This was his ingenious suggestion. Until then, just lie back and enjoy the scenery and the breeze."

"Breeze?" Matt jeered. "Ever since you raised the cover along the sides of the wagon, I've been choking on dust."

"We could always lower it again and cut off your view altogether, as well as what little air you're getting. Leave you to stew in your own juices, so to speak," Jordan offered unsympathetically. "And if you don't stop being so damned cantankerous, I'll take you up on that notion about the apple. That is, if Jade doesn't gag you first."

From her seat at the front of the wagon, Matt heard Jade reply smartly, "It wouldn't help. He'd only mumble past it!"

If Matt had hoped to see an immediate reversal in attitude toward Jade from the other travelers now that she was his wife, he was sadly disappointed. The crowd that gathered around his wagon that next Sunday morning was smaller than usual, and those who did attend markedly ignored her, though they did shake hands with Matt following the sermon and wished him a speedy recovery. That was when Matt conceived the idea of having Jade lead the singing at future services.

"You could even perform a hymn by yourself, or perhaps play a selection on your flute," he told her, bubbling over with enthusiasm for his latest brainstorm.

"I don't know, Matt," she said doubtfully. "Like as not, they'll stone me for darin' to sing a religious number, Jezebel that I am."

He grinned conspiratorially and winked. "Think of it as entertaining the troops, sweetheart."

"Hmph! Enemy troops, no doubt."

"You'll win them over. Slowly, perhaps, but surely."

Jade simply shook her head and mumbled, "Sure, and 'tis right glad I am that one of us has such colossal faith. Or such farfetched fancies."

In the next couple of days, they passed more odd rock configurations. Among them was Castle Rock, which looked like some huge medieval stone fortress, and Table Rock, with its flat-stepped summit. Beyond these, they came to Scott's Bluff. Its name had derived from that of a fur trader, Hiram Scott, who had died there nearly forty years before. The wind-sculpted escarpment was immense, half again the height of Chimney Rock and wider at the base than any of the formations they'd previously encountered, with numerous crags and gulches and turretlike projections.

At this point, the trail left the North Platte, circling to the south side of the bluff. To the north, along the river, was an impassable expanse known as the badlands. Even the Indians had long ago labeled this area *Me-a-pa-te*, which meant "hill that is hard to go around."

Skirting the left flank of the cliff brought them through a wind-plagued, sloping gap in the surrounding ridge, known as Mitchell's Pass. Here, the westerly gusts were so strong they shook the wagons, clawed voraciously at the madly snapping canvas, and threatened to suck the breath from straining lungs. Dirt swirled up like miniature twisters. Within seconds, throats were parched and everything in the wind's path wore a thick coating of finely ground earth.

While Jade sat up front, struggling to keep the shuddering wagon and the stumbling oxen on course, Matt was inside, experiencing the wildest ride of his life. His suspended bed was swinging recklessly, like a tiny boat caught in a hurricane. Back and forth it went, and Matt with it, lurching about in every conceivable direction, a peculiar pendulum gone berserk.

The wagon stopped briefly, long enough for Jade to pitch the youngsters into the bed of the wagon and lash down the sides. "We're on the downhill track," she informed him breathlessly. "The wee ones can ride from here to Fort Mitchell."

"Wait!" Matt yelled when she would have scurried back to the driver's seat. "Fetch Jordan to get me down from here. I'm afraid this thing is going to break loose at any moment, and if it does I'm liable to crush the children."

"There's no time," she told him hurriedly. "We're holdin' up the train as it is. B'sides, the fort's only a couple of miles farther. When the wind shifts just right, I can see it through the dust. Just hold tight for a bit more, darlin'."

By the time they finally reached the fort, drawing the wagons into a tight circle on the lee side of its walls, Matt was dizzier than he'd ever been in his life. It took several minutes for the world to stop spinning about him, for blurred images to resolve themselves into distinct shapes and features.

"You look a mite green about the gills, brother," Jordan announced.

"So would you, if you'd been careening around in here like a monkey clinging to a storm-tossed vine!" Matt grumbled.

As Jade aided the dirt-caked, shaken orphans from the wagon, she started to giggle.

"It's not funny," Matt muttered, annoyed at her lack of pity. "Moreover, you could exhibit a little sympathy, if only for the sake of courtesy. After all, I didn't laugh at you when you got seasick fording the river."

"I'm sorry," she gasped out, "but I just got the silliest vision in me head."

"Of what?" he asked curtly, sending her a disgruntled frown. "Your husband sailing through the side of the wagon and landing facefirst into a cliff?"

"No, but I did imagine ye soarin', so to speak," she admitted, going off into another burst of jocularity. When she calmed enough to speak again, she brushed away merry tears. Softly, her Irish brogue enhanced by the impish glee in her voice, she began to sing the popular lyrics of "The Man on the Flying Trapeze"—most appropriately, those lines boasting of the fellow's daring "swinging" ability.

Jordan started laughing so hard, so abruptly, that he nearly dropped Matt on his head. An hour later, the tent erected and Matt installed safely within, Jordan was still chuckling. And whenever he started, Jade was powerless to stop her own chortles.

"You two are just a barrel of laughs," Matt complained. However, now that the episode was past and the ill effects were diminishing, he was beginning to see the humor of it. A grin teased the corners of his mouth. "I suppose next you'll want me to dress in my long flannel drawers so you can put me on display and sell tickets."

"Now there's an idea," Jordan concurred with a wide grin. "I always suspected you took up preaching just to get attention."

"We can't do it," Jade proclaimed on a muffled snicker. "We're fresh out o' popcorn and peanuts."

"My, what a shame!" Matt commiserated comically. "And I was even going to grow a flowing mustache to compliment my costume."

That evening, in the darkened tent with the children fast asleep behind a shielding blanket, Jade and Matt were involved in a bout of heated passion. In the midst of their lovemaking, at a crucial juncture, Jordan's voice drifted to them from his bed beneath the nearby wagon. He was humming a now-familiar tune.

Helplessly, Jade collapsed onto Matt's chest, shaking with hilarity. Matt gave a reluctant groan of laughter and frustration. "Drat his infernal hide! I'm going to throttle that cackling buffoon! First chance I get, I intend to strangle him with his own tongue!"

❧❧❧ *Chapter 26* ❧❧❧

*T*heir overnight sojourn at Fort Mitchell was all too brief, for early morning found them on the road again, bound for Fort Laramie, two days down the trail. Just prior to their departure, Dr. Worley paid Matt a short visit, having ridden over from the Mormon campsite on the opposite side of the river. After inspecting Matt's leg, and chuckling at his patient's complaints about "that perilous contraption" he was forced to ride in, the physician announced that the limb appeared to be knitting nicely in the week and a half since the accident.

"I'll check in on you again at Fort Laramie," he promised. "If all goes well, perhaps we can dispense with the hammock soon. For now, however, stay strictly off of that leg."

The wagon train was a full day's travel out of Fort Mitchell when one of the scouts took note of a toppled telegraph pole next to the trail. Several men went to investigate the matter, concerned but not unduly alarmed. Buffalo had long been known to use the poles as scratching posts, often knocking them askew or felling them altogether in their enthusiasm. Many a line had been severed in this manner, and the army was continually having to repair the breaks.

Now that the travelers were progressing into Wyoming Territory, where civilization had yet to encroach so heavily, they could expect to encounter some of the burly beasts, though not in the vast numbers of days gone by. If luck was with them, they would soon have an adequate stock of "buffalo chips" to supplement their dwindling reserve of firewood. Most guidebooks maintained that, once dried, the dung burned much more efficiently than wood, lasting longer, igniting more easily, and producing less smoke.

The fellows examining the fallen pole returned to the train more excited than when they'd left it. They hurried to confer with Sam Greene, and soon word was filtering back through the column of wagons. There were no signs of buffalo, no tracks or dung or tufts of pelt anywhere near the broken telegraph pole. However, one of the scouts had discovered what he thought might be a moccasin print, though the ground was so hard he could not be certain. Still, it was a chilling thought to contemplate that Indians might have severed the wire. That they might be lying in wait around the next bend in the trail, hiding behind the next outcropping of rock, ready to ambush the wagon train.

Suddenly everyone was on immediate alert. Scouts rode out ahead of the main body. Men checked their rifles and ammunition. Women gathered their children close, admonishing them not to wander from the wagons. Every eye scanned the surrounding countryside, straining to see against the bright glare of the sun. Talk died to worried whispers, and even the animals seemed to note the growing tension as the wagons creaked slowly along.

A mile farther west, they passed another break in the telegraph line. This time there was little doubt that buffalo were not responsible. The pole was standing upright. The wire had been cleanly cut, presumably by a sharp instrument—perhaps a knife or a tomahawk. Many a scalp tingled upon learning this. Many a heartbeat quickened.

By the time they corralled the wagons for the noon break, nerves were stretched taut. The scouts returned to camp, having seen nothing more threatening than a coyote and a couple of rattlesnakes. Mr. Greene and his assistants hastened to reassure the emigrants.

"Like as not," the captain told them, "those savages have done their mischief and are long gone from the area. Besides, now that we've rounded the wagons, we're safe enough. If they're gonna attack, they're more apt to do it while we're on the move, wagons strung out from here to Sunday, not while we're circled into a defensive position like this. So you can all calm down now and enjoy your meal and the short rest."

Most of the travelers took his advice, though they didn't let down their guard altogether. Jordan helped Matt from the wagon, bracing him against the front wheel and propping a loaded rifle within arm's reach. "Just in case," he told him, casting a wary eye out over the barren plain. All about them, others were also keeping a sharp lookout, with their weapons close at hand.

Soon, the meal was finished. Beth was feeding Zach his bottle, while Jade and Emily dried the dinner dishes and began storing them into their box on the side of the wagon. Matt was dragging a washcloth across Skeeter's chin. Jordan was preparing to hitch the teams to the wagons.

One minute the surrounding terrain was silent and empty. The next, the air was filled with the sounds of war whoops and the thunder of galloping hooves as a band of mounted Indians charged over the horizon in a cloud of dust. Pandemonium erupted. Men cursed, shouted, and grabbed for their guns. Women and children scurried for cover. Babies cried. The first shots resounded over the din of panic.

Leaving the oxen to their own devices, Jordan bounded into the wagon, quickly tossing down two small trunks, the ammunition box, and Matt's shotgun. "Shove the baggage under the wagon!" he hollered. "Make a barrier!"

Before they could react, he was dashing to the forward wagon to help Jade's friends do the same.

"Jade! Get the children beneath the wagon!" Matt cried, taking up the call. Even now, he was crawling forward, pushing one of the trunks before him.

All around them, others were doing likewise, grabbing anything that was handy to use as a barricade against the barrage of bullets and arrows. Fortunately, the Indians did not make an immediate straightforward assault, which allotted the emigrants precious time to establish a hasty defense. Rather, the warriors fell into a well-organized pattern of advance and retreat.

In cunning fashion, a number of the savages advanced far enough to launch a volley of shots as their fellow braves raced their ponies around the encircled wagons, just out of range of fire. Their weapons discharged, the first party fell back to reload and regroup, a second battery now taking the forward positions. The wily plains fighters seemed to know just how far they could safely advance, and were annoyingly adept at discerning when to retreat, thus causing the shaken pioneers to waste considerable ammunition at the start.

However, it did not take long for the emigrants to settle into the rhythm of the battle. Many of them were seasoned veterans of the recently ended war between the North and the South. Though few were skilled at fighting off Indians, most were capable marksmen, and once the fight was under way they began to time their shots well, making every bullet count.

As the men, the boys, and some of the women exchanged fire with the Indians, the remaining ladies and older girls were busy reloading the empty guns as fast as their trembling fingers could manage. Though she'd never done it before, Jade caught on quickly. With Skeeter and Emily and the baby huddled about their skirts, both she and Beth kept Matt's weapons supplied with bullets. Beneath the next wagon, the "girls" aided Jordan. Much to her surprise, Jade noted Bliss lying on her stomach next to Jordan, firing her own rifle with enviable competence.

"If we live through this, I want ye to teach me how to shoot," Jade yelled as she passed Matt a loaded pistol.

She watched as he took careful aim, his shot striking a brave high on the shoulder and knocking him off his horse. As near as she could tell, Matt hit his target with remarkable regularity, though he seemed inclined to disable his opponents rather than inflict mortal wounds. Which, considering his vocation, was understandable, she supposed—less of a shock, actually, than the fact that he was as proficient with a gun as he was with a Bible.

When a fair number of their warriors had fallen to gun-
fire, the Indians quickly changed tactics. Without warning,
completely encircling the pioneers, they abruptly charged
from all points at once, galloping their ponies at full speed
toward the wagons. The eerie war cry they sent up was
enough to curdle Jade's blood in her veins. Beside her,
Beth gave a wail of fright. Emily's sniffles escalated to
loud sobs. In her terror, Jade squeezed Zach so hard that
he, too, began to shriek. Only Skeeter remained strangely
quiet, locked in his world of silence.

Several of the mounted savages managed to break
through the barrier, launching their ponies through small
spaces between the adjoining wagons into the center of the
circle. Suddenly shots were being leveled in all directions,
and the underside of the wagons seemed paltry protection. A cacophony of screams and whoops and shouts
assaulted the air, combined with the frightened whinnies
of the horses and the deep lowing of cattle. The anxious
animals milled nervously about in the enclosure, trying to
avoid the cross fire.

Across the way, a wagon canvas erupted into flames,
further exciting matters, as the family dodged arrows while
attempting to extinguish the blaze. Elsewhere, a wounded
man aimed his pistol point-blank into his attacker's painted
face. Three wagons down, Tilda valiantly applied her trusty
iron skillet to a warrior's skull, giving her son time to come
to her aid.

In the midst of all this, Jade was frantically reloading
Matt's guns, at the same time trying to keep one eye on
their blind side and the other on the children. Somehow,
she missed the exact moment when Skeeter came up
missing. One second he was there beside her, and the
next he was out in the open, dashing toward a young
brave who was trying to steal Jade's horse.

"Skeeter!" With no weapon in hand, and no thought
for her own safety, Jade scurried out from her shelter
and ran after him. Like a mother lion defending her cub,
she launched herself forward, snatching Skeeter from the

path of the Indian pony's slashing hooves. Together, she and Skeeter fell.

Jade scrambled to her feet, the frightened boy held tightly in her arms. At her first step toward safety, she was brought to a halt by a sharp tug at her scalp. Then her feet left the ground, and she and Skeeter were dangling in midair at the war pony's side. As she swung about, suspended by her hair, her fearful gaze caught the glint of a knife blade—and the fierce face above it. The warrior's obsidian gaze was riveted with covetous fascination at the bright copper curls in his grasp.

Horror ripped through her. Frantically, she squirmed, trying in vain to free herself. Somehow, even in her absolute terror, she retained enough sense to drop Skeeter. "Run!" she screamed, forgetting that he could not hear her.

In that moment, time seemed to stop. All she could hear, all she could see, was the savage who held her. The wild, victorious gleam in his eye. That threatening blade edging ever closer to her skull.

She didn't hear Matt's mad roar as he realized her peril. All around her, the battle raged on, but the sights and sounds were now beyond her comprehension. There was only her—and her captor—and that sinister knife.

Just as she was sure that her next breath would end in excruciating agony, Jade closed her eyes. For the life of her, she could not recall a single word of prayer. Only one word kept resounding in her mind. Matt! Matt! Matt!

Little did she realize that she was sobbing his name aloud. Nor did she know how each terrified wail was ripping through Matt's soul, even as he sucked in a steadying breath, drew a careful bead, and prayed to God that his aim was true. He hardly dared to watch, dreading the outcome, as his finger plied the trigger and the deadly missile left the rifle chamber, not to be recalled.

The bullet whizzed past Jade's head so closely that it clipped strands of her hair before exploding into the warrior's chest. The impact hurtled her assailant from his pony. He toppled, pulling Jade with him.

She landed heavily, stunned, confused, not knowing what had happened—or why. Her eyes opened to meet the lifeless stare of the man lying beneath her. Slowly, she levered herself away, her trembling hands slick with sweat. No, not sweat. Blood! Fearfully, she glanced down, not yet sure if the blood was his or hers. Crimson blossomed across his bare bronze skin and the front of her dress, and the knife that lay between them. Shock held her brain frozen, and it was several seconds before she perceived that she felt no pain, before she identified the obscene hole in the warrior's breast.

Jade began to quake in reaction now, her sobs choking her as they grew into shrill shrieks. She was still screaming as Matt dragged her back to shelter beneath the wagon. There, he knelt beside her, drew her into the haven of his arms, and began to rock with her. "It's all right now, love. It's over. You're going to be just fine, sweetheart."

Even as he was comforting her, his hands were busy seeking the truth of his claim, searching for any wound she might have sustained. Her dress was half undone before he was assured, with profound relief, that she had not been pierced by the wicked blade that had become wedged between her and the Indian as they'd fallen.

"Sk-k-keeter," she stammered between clattering teeth.

"He's right here, honey. Not a scratch on him."

However, now that Matt was convinced that Jade, too, was unharmed, he had to see that they remained so. Gently, he pushed her aside, again taking up his gun. "Think you can still load for me?" he asked.

Jade forced herself to the task, trying not to think of the bloody corpse lying half a dozen steps from her, willing her stomach to stop lurching and her quivering fingers to obey her commands. Within a short time, the fighting eased. The war party retreated to a knoll some distance away, where they paused.

"What are they doing?" Jade wondered aloud.

Matt shook his head. "I'm not sure. I'd guess they're either regrouping for another attack or they intend to leave."

"If they're leavin', why don't they stop dallyin' and go?"

"Perhaps they want the bodies of their fallen comrades," Matt suggested. "I seem to recall hearing that they always try to retrieve their dead for proper burial, but I'm not sure how accurate that information might be."

Jade shivered. "Well, they're welcome to 'em, once we've left. I just hope they don't come chargin' at us again like all the devils let loose from Hell."

"The trouble with that idea is, once the wagons are strung out along the trail, we're much better targets."

"Then what are we to do? We can't stay here forever tryin' to outwait those savages. Lord knows how many more of 'em might come along."

"Or how long we can keep fighting them," Matt added grimly. "We have our own wounded to tend." His blue eyes scanned the enclosure. All about them, emigrants were using this lull in the battle to care for the injured. Matt could only hope there were few deaths among their number.

Unconsciously, Matt rubbed at his aching leg, unwittingly drawing Jade's attention to it. "Saints and salvation!" she cursed. "Ye came after me on that leg, didn't ye?"

He dredged up a grin. "I couldn't very well leave it behind, now could I?"

Jade shook her head at him. "I'll not forgive meself if ye've done permanent damage to it just to save me," she informed him. "It hasn't even been two weeks since ye broke it."

"Sweetheart, did you stop to weigh the risks before you raced out there to rescue Skeeter?"

"There wasn't time."

He nodded. "That's right. Decisions were being made in haste and the heat of the moment." His gaze strayed to the Indian he'd killed. "And may God be merciful on us for some of the deeds we were forced to commit today."

Jade stared at him openmouthed. "Ye regret killin' that beast?" she asked in astonishment. "Sorry ye were forced into it to save me worthless hide?"

"Yes," he admitted quietly, somberly. "I am. Not that I wouldn't do it again, if need be, to keep you from harm. For you are the most precious person in my life. I was so afraid that if I only wounded him, he might still have the time and strength to harm you, so I deliberately aimed to kill. But that was no beast I shot, Jade. Make no mistake. He was a living, breathing, human being, with a mortal soul, and only the color of his skin to set him apart from any of us. And now he is dead."

"Better him than us," Jade argued vehemently. "Don't be forgettin' he and his friends didn't arrive for no prayer meetin', Matt. They were set on murderin' us."

Matt sighed heavily. "I know. That's the pity of it, of any war. Men slaying other men for land or property or rights. Murder committed in the name of religion, or nations, or passion is still murder, no matter how you try to glorify it. That warrior probably had a family dependent upon him, perhaps a wife and children who might go hungry now. Certainly someone will mourn his death, will shed tears of grief over his grave. How can I not regret that?"

Jade reached out to stroke his cheek, wishing there was some way to ease the pain in his heart. "Put that way, I reckon ye can't. Ye can only be thankful that none o' us are wearin' his moccasins, and pray that God will see us safely to Oregon."

He smiled softly. "How did you get so wise so fast, love?"

Jade shrugged and offered a tender smile in return. "I've been hangin' 'round this preacher I know, and I guess some o' his sermonizin' must've rubbed off on me," she teased. "If this keeps up, I'll be measurin' me head for a halo soon."

"Not too soon." His eyes gleamed lovingly into hers. "I want you around for a long, long time, lady mine."

Chapter 27

*T*he situation was extremely tense for the next couple of hours, as the uneasy emigrants waited to see if the Indians intended further attacks and the savages continued to hover in the distance like a band of hungry vultures—all but those who lay dead and the lone warrior Tilda had bashed with her skillet. That fellow, now revived, sat tightly bound and gagged, a bullet still lodged in his thigh. For the moment, until they could decide what to do with him, he would remain their prisoner.

It was nerve-racking to wait like this, doing little, with the hot summer sun blazing down as if to bake the very life out of every living thing. All they could do of consequence was tend to the wounded and pray. Time seemed to creep by, every anxious minute like an hour.

At one point, someone suggested that they take their chances, simply pack up and head west rather than sit here on the open plains like ducks on a pond. Another fellow proposed that they wait until dark, then start out, claiming he'd heard that Indians did not attack at night for fear of evil spirits of some sort. No one seemed inclined to trust that notion, however, any more than they now believed that Indians were not prone to charging circled wagons.

A scout courageously volunteered to ride for Fort Mitchell to get help from the military, but the majority voted to delay that idea until it was absolutely necessary. Most felt that, even on the swiftest horse, the man stood little likelihood of outrunning the entire band of mounted warriors and their weapons.

Together, Jordan and Matt suggested that a group of men gather the bodies of the dead Indians and deposit them some distance from the wagons, at a point where their comrades might retrieve them. "If that's all they are wanting, perhaps they'll then leave us in peace."

"And maybe they won't," another argued. "I'm not riskin' an arrow in the back to cart those stinkin' red carcasses anywhere. Let 'em come and get 'em themselves, or wait until we're gone."

"I just hope we're *gone* by our own means, with our scalps still attached to our heads," Carl Jansen put in.

"Yeah, and what are we gonna do with that jackal?" someone else asked, pointing to their captive.

No one knew. So they waited, undecided and growing more anxious all the while. The warriors appeared to have settled in for the duration. Then, miraculously, for no apparent reason, the savages mounted their ponies and galloped away.

"What in blazes?" Jordan muttered, echoing the confusion in everyone's minds.

"Stay alert, folks," Sam Greene advised. "Those critters are wily rascals. Could be they just want us to think they're leavin' to throw us off our guard."

"Wait!" one of the scouts exclaimed. "Lookee there!" He pointed toward the east, to a cloud of dust barely visible on the horizon. Soon a hazy mass appeared, accompanied by the sound of pounding hoofbeats. One and all, the emigrants held their breath, praying that this was not another attack.

Suddenly a bugle sounded, and everyone nearly wilted with relief. When the army troop rode into view, a united cheer rose up for the gallant soldiers rushing to their rescue.

Sam Greene put out a welcoming hand. "Captain," he declared sincerely, "I've never been so glad to see anybody as I am to see you and your boys."

The captain nodded. "When the telegraph lines went dead, we suspected you might have run into trouble." He dismounted, and indicated for his men to do likewise.

"I'm Captain Bastian. What are your casualties?"

"We came out better than we might have," Greene admitted. "Only one dead. It looks like the other nine who were wounded are gonna make it. One wagon gone up in flames, and a couple of others with canvases burned."

"You got off lightly," the officer concurred. "You must have some crack shots in your midst."

"That we do, sir, includin' one eagle-eyed, bum-legged preacher and a lady who wields a mean skillet. She nabbed our only prisoner for us," Greene informed him proudly.

"I can take your captive off your hands if you'd like," Bastian offered.

Greene immediately agreed. "That'd suit me just fine, Captain. Truth is, we didn't have the foggiest notion what to do with him. You gonna take him back to Fort Mitchell with you?"

"No, we're going on to Fort Laramie." He motioned in the direction from which he'd come. "Half of my unit is following behind, riding shotgun for another wagon train that arrived the day you left Fort Mitchell. We'll combine forces, for added strength in numbers, and accompany the lot of you to Fort Laramie. From there, you'll be on your own, unless you can get another escort on to Fort Fetterman. I'd suggest you get your company ready to head out immediately."

"We have to bury Joe Small," Greene reminded him.

"Then you'd best be quick about it, though you might prefer to take the dead fellow along, at least until we make camp tonight. Bury him here and chances are good that the Cheyenne will dig up the body."

The family whose wagon had burned salvaged what little they could of their possessions and stored their meager belongings in their neighbor's wagon for the time being. At Fort Laramie they would most likely be able to buy new supplies, perhaps even a new wagon, if they could afford it. Any heirlooms they had treasured were sadly reduced to mere memories, however.

The combined caravan of wagons rolled out, the travelers much more wary and battle-wise than they'd been before. Even with their military escort, they could not shake the need to keep constant watch for Indians. They did spot some now and again along the trail that afternoon, usually just a brave or two keeping well back from the trail, silently watching the passing wagons. At each encounter, they were reminded anew of their lucky escape from total disaster.

It was just before dark, as they were preparing to stop for the night, when they came upon the smoldering remains of a single wagon. It was tipped onto its side a few yards off the edge of the trail. Immediately, Captain Bastian halted the column and ordered two of his men forward to investigate. Jordan and several men from their party joined them.

From this short distance, the waiting emigrants could see the charred skeleton of the wagon, its contents strewn haphazardly about on the surrounding ground. Barrels and trunks and odd pieces of furniture lay where they had been tossed, lids pried open and goods rifled. A length of scorched cloth blew in the evening breeze.

At first glance, there appeared to be no signs of life. Even the animals were gone, presumably stolen by the rampaging Indians. The death-stiffened bodies of two men lay unmoving on the fire-blackened earth. The entire scene seemed wrapped in an eerie silence.

Suddenly one of the soldiers gave a shout, leaped back, and reached for his pistol. Jordan was quicker. Faster than the eye could see, he drew his revolver, yelling a warning at the young recruit. For a moment both men stood facing each other, neither moving. Reluctantly, the private lowered his gun.

Only then did Jordan advance slowly toward the spot that had drawn the soldier's attention. Those watching saw him hunch down as he peered through the spokes of a wheel. Holstering his weapon, he held out his arms as if coaxing someone toward him.

It seemed an eternity before a small, soot-covered child crept forward. The youngster stopped short of Jordan's reach, turned, and held out his own grimy hand. A second child crawled from the shadows, obviously hesitant to emerge.

"Faith and begorrah!" Jade exclaimed, as stunned as everyone around her.

"What is it? What did they discover?" Matt called out, unable to see from inside the wagon, where he was once again ensconced in his hammock.

"Oh, Matt! Jordan has found two children who look to be about Skeeter's age. They're ragged and dirty and scared near to death, but they're alive!"

"What about their folks?" Matt asked, though he could almost predict the answer before she gave it.

"I don't see a woman, but there are two men lyin' dead out there."

Matt's voice came quietly, but with conviction. "Go help Jordan with the children, Jade. Bring them here."

"But, Matt . . ." Jade poked her head into the wagon. "Ye're thinkin' o' takin' 'em in, aren't ye?"

She could just discern Matt's sorrowful smile in the murky interior. "Of course, love. That's what orphanages are all about, you know."

"We can't keep tryin' to run an orphanage out of a wagon, Matt. There's only so much space to be had, and we're fast runnin' shy of it."

"There's always room for one more. Or two."

"But . . ."

"Go, Aggie. Those homeless waifs need the comfort of a woman's arms around them."

"And I need more chicks like a bear needs a bonnet!" she grumbled, climbing down from the wagon seat. He could still hear her mumbling as she marched off to do his bidding. "Hell's bells and little fishes! I can't keep track o' the ones we've got now! What am I gonna do with two more?"

Jade's pique lasted only as long as it took her to cross the space to the wreckage. Two tear-streaked, grief-stricken faces rose to meet her gaze—and Jade promptly lost her heart. "Come here, lambs," she urged, dropping to her knees and holding her arms out to them.

The two small lads rushed into her embrace, nearly toppling her to the ground as they buried their faces in her bosom and began to sob. "Their ma?" she asked softly, her eyes seeking Jordan's.

He shook his head, then gestured toward the wagon. "Dead. Their father and uncle, too. From what these two boys have said, they managed to run and hide along the riverbank during all the commotion. That's how they escaped. Their older sister wasn't so fortunate. We think the Indians must have ridden off with her."

Jade gave a horrified gasp. "Oh, merciful heavens!"

Jordan glanced around at the carnage. "Not today, I'm afraid," he muttered bitterly. "The angels must have had better things to do."

After camping there for the night, they held a brief burial ceremony early the following morning. Matt insisted on officiating the service for Mr. Small and the Everett family. At Captain Bastian's suggestion, they interred the dead directly beneath the trail, then drove all the wagons over the graves to pack the earth down well. According to the cavalry officer, earlier pioneers had long ago discovered that this was the best method of insuring that wild animals did not disturb the bodies.

The two newly orphaned boys traveled with Matt and Jade and their growing troop. Only a couple of women, those still most adamantly opposed to Jade, bothered to voice any objections to this arrangement. Typically, Charlotte Cleaver protested most loudly, but to no avail.

Much to everyone's surprise, once they were properly washed, the lads turned out to be seven-year-old towheaded twins. They were as alike as two peas in a pod, and Jade was certain she would never be sure which was Larry and which was Harry. Stunned and choked with grief over the loss of their family, the pair were unnaturally quiet, rejecting friendly overtures from Matt and the other children. Only Jade seemed capable of reaching through their sorrow with much success, and they clung as close to her as possible, like abandoned puppies seeking warmth and comfort. She was the one they allowed to dry their tears when nightmares plagued their sleep, to listen with heartfelt sympathy to their tormented tales, to soothe them with soft lullabies and assurances.

It was a balm to the spirits of one and all when Fort Laramie came into view just as the final rays of the setting sun were fading in the western sky. The emigrants were safe, for the moment—or as safe as they could be at this remote outpost with no walls surrounding it for protection against attack.

While the travelers were organizing their campsites, Captain Bastian reported to the commander of the fort, relaying all the details of this latest trouble with the Indians. At his request, a company of soldiers was ordered to leave at first light in search of the Everett girl, though no one held much hope that she would be found, at least not alive. If she'd survived, the braves had probably taken her back to their camp, and it would be a miracle if anyone heard from her again.

Fort Laramie was a major stop and supply point on the trail. Until recently it had been a convenient place for holding discussions with the Indians, and many treaties had been negotiated there in the past. However, with the building of the new forts along the Bozeman Road in Indian territory, the various chiefs were not inclined to talk peace, and had indicated that they would not do so until the white men left these tribal lands. At present, the only Indians residing at the fort were three enlisted Pawnee scouts and the Cheyenne prisoner Captain Bastian had turned over to the commander there. The warrior was immediately secured in a locked cell, under vigilant guard.

Tenderhearted Fancy soon discovered that they had chained the captive in a filthy, airless room with no intention of attending to his wounds. She came running to Matt with her tale of woe.

"You should have seen it!" she told him with wide, sympathetic eyes. "I was out gettin' the lay of the land, so to speak." This, Matt correctly interpreted as an exploring mission for likely customers. "I was talkin' to this darlin' corporal when four soldiers came right past us, draggin' the Indian between them like a sack of meal. Lawsy! I took one look at that big, gapin' hole in his leg and nearly lost my stomach right then and there! Not a soul has bothered to bandage it, and I'd wager my best lace corset the bullet is still in there, festerin'."

Fancy gave a delicate shiver and grimaced. "They opened a door not six feet from where I stood and shoved the fella inside. Matt, I saw that room, and it isn't fit for a pigsty! There's not one window, and the stench almost knocked me off my feet. But that isn't the worst of it. They've shackled that man, hand and foot, to the wall! Like some mad dog! Last I saw, he was unconscious and bleedin' like a stuck hog, and they just left him like that! Can't you do something? Please? A rabid wolf shouldn't be treated that way!"

Matt had to agree. "I'll talk to Captain Bastian. Perhaps they have a surgeon who could see to him, though I don't expect to encounter much compassion from anyone. They probably intend to hang the fellow, or shoot him, as an example to others of his kind. Most likely, they'll consider any endeavor toward tending his injuries a waste of time and effort."

Matt was correct in his assumption, and Fancy was beside herself when the camp physician flat-out refused to "administer aid to the enemy." Even Jordan was riled, recalling his own terrible experience at Andersonville.

"There's no call for such despicable treatment of any prisoner, no matter how vile his crime," he railed, his eyes shooting angry sparks. "I know there's no love lost between the Indians and the whites, and for good cause, but it wouldn't hurt to show the poor bastard a little common decency before fitting the rope around his neck."

When the Mormon wagon train pulled into Fort Laramie the next morning, Dr. Worley paid a call on Matt. After expressing satisfaction at the way Matt's leg was beginning to heal, he presented his grateful patient with a pair of crutches he'd thought to bring along with him. Then, upon hearing about the fort physician's hardened attitude, the Mormon doctor proposed a visit to the camp commander. There, he volunteered his services for their Cheyenne prisoner. It took some smooth persuasion, but the colonel finally agreed.

Late that night, the prisoner escaped. Just prior to dawn, the alarm sounded. Everyone was surprised, but none so much as Fancy's friends when they learned that she had been the one to help the Cheyenne flee. According to the shamefaced private who had been guarding the captive, Fancy had approached him sometime after midnight, seducing him with her wiles and a full bottle of whiskey. He did not recall passing out or having the keys removed from his belt. Nor had he witnessed the Indian and the dance hall girl stealing a horse and riding away together.

The private now sat in the same cell the warrior had so recently vacated.

The other girls were distraught.

"We've got to go after her!" Jade wailed. "I can't believe she went with that savage of her own free will."

"She set him loose, didn't she?" Peaches pointed out glumly.

"I can see her helpin' to free him," Bliss put in, shaking her head. "She's so damned softhearted it's a shame! Hell, back in Richmond she was always draggin' stray animals into the house."

"*Oui*, but perhaps she only meant to release him," Lizette contributed. "Not to go with him. He must have abducted her."

Mavis, who had come over from the Mormon camp to join them as soon as she'd heard the news, said solemnly, "I think you're wrong. While y'all have been running around like headless chicks, I've been going through Fancy's belongings. Some of her favorite things are missing. Maybe she did go willingly after all."

Matt proposed another dilemma, one they hadn't even considered. "You do realize that by aiding the Indian in his escape, Fancy has put herself into a heap of trouble with the law? The colonel agrees that she should be found. He'd like nothing better than to see both her and the warrior swinging from the same gallows."

"Under those circumstances, rather than wish for her return, maybe you'd better hope otherwise," Jordan advised somberly. "If she's lucky, the Cheyenne might show some pity."

Matt gave a grave nod. "At any rate, there's not much we can do to help her but pray."

"For what, Matt?" Jade inquired softly, tears glittering in her eyes. "For a quick, merciful end?" To her missing friend, she called out sorrowfully, "Oh, Fancy! What have ye done, lass?"

Chapter 28

Tilda was supremely miffed that Fancy had freed the Cheyenne warrior. "That Injun meant to have my hair on his belt, and now she's gone and set him loose to try again!" she railed. She slammed the skillet so hard against the rocks bordering the fire that it sounded like a brass gong. The "girls" all retreated a few paces, none caring to be Tilda's next victim, and wondering if it might be wise to curtail their cooking lessons for a while, until the older woman had calmed down.

Hesitantly, Jade spoke up. "I can understand how ye feel, Tilda. Truly. I nearly lost me own hair in that attack, and I still shiver every time I think on it. We ain't sayin' what Fancy did was right, but we can't despise her for it, either. Not while we're so worried sick about her."

"She was a good girl, despite what some might think of her," Bliss put in. "She's just too softhearted for her own good. Always has been."

"Softheaded, too, I reckon," Tilda grumbled, though her glower lessened to a concerned frown. "Lord knows I don't wish any harm to come to her. Fool though she is, she's a sweet little twit, and soon as I get over bein' so mad, I intend to pray heartily for her well-bein'."

Others were not as charitable in their views. The entire military contingent was up in arms, Colonel Filbus most of all. "That trollop has caused more trouble than she's worth," he announced angrily. "And more than she could possibly know. My informants tell me they suspect that Cheyenne was some sort of important tribal leader. His death would have been quite a feather in my cap. Now I've had to dispatch troops to try to recapture him, in addition to those I sent out to look for the Everett girl, which leaves me severely undermanned. I was supposed to send a unit on to Fort Fetterman, but that will have to wait until the search parties return."

Colonel Filbus had scarcely begun to vent his displeasure when Sean O'Neall climbed atop his bandwagon and began to fan the flames anew. "I told ye those bawds would be trouble," he proclaimed smugly to his fellow travelers. "Perhaps ye'll listen now. I say they should be tossed from the train now, while we have the chance to be rid of 'em. And that goes for the preacher and his harlot as well. Let's be free of the whole lot."

Many of the emigrants were inclined to agree. Because of Fancy's escapade, their own departure for Fort Fetterman was being delayed in order that they might have an army escort along the way. They, too, would have to cool their heels until the search parties returned—or go on by themselves, which they were loath to do. Thoroughly disgruntled, they did not hesitate to shift the blame onto Fancy's cohorts. Whether it was fair or not, they were all being judged for Fancy's folly.

Matt tried to convince the malcontents of the injustice of blaming the innocent with the guilty, but tempers were running high and he had little success. Jordan tried to reason with them, also to no avail. Surprisingly, it was Colonel Filbus who put a stop to the rising rebellion.

"I will not have those wantons set loose here," he declared adamantly. "Just one has managed to turn the fort into an upheaval. I certainly do not need more of the same on my hands. There is no predicting the amount of mischief they could cause until transport east could be arranged. Oh, no. I refuse. When you depart, that particular basket of vipers goes with you. And it can't be too soon, so make certain none of your traveling party causes any further problems or I'll send all of you packing, with or without your escort."

As the colonel marched off, Bliss stated huffily, "I'd rather be called a dove or a cat any old day than a dratted snake! I've a good notion to go after that man and sink my 'fangs' into his big fat a—" A sharp nudge from Jade's elbow brought Bliss to the realization that Matt stood nearby and that six wide-eyed children were hanging on her every word. " . . . ankle," she finished lamely, much to Jordan's amusement.

"If ze Indian had to take somebodies with him, why could it not have been zat awful Sean?" Lizette lamented. "Ze sought of zat skunk staked over an anthill eez *très charmant*. Eez it not?"

"What?" Jade asked with a puzzled look.

"Very delightful. Charming. Appealing. Sean on ze anthill."

A devilish smile tilted Jade's lips. "Oh, yes," she agreed. "I can't think of anything more fittin' for him."

She cast a quick glance at Matt to find him shaking his head at her, a long-suffering look on his face. "I can see it's going to take a while for you to learn to turn the other cheek," he chided lightly, meaning only to tease her.

Jade simply shrugged, hiding the sharp twinge that came with thinking she'd disappointed him. She was going to have to work more diligently at being a preacher's wife. But, darn! It was so hard!

Matt hated to see Jade so downhearted. When the cavalry troop returned to report that they'd lost the Cheyenne's trail some distance from the fort and had absolutely no idea where he and the girl might have gone from there, Jade was nearly inconsolable. It did no good to remind her that she should be thankful that the soldiers had not found Fancy's dead body—not when orders had been sent around that the wagon train was scheduled to depart the following morning.

"We can't leave her, Matt!" Jade wailed.

"Sweetheart, it would appear that she left us."

"We can't know that for sure."

"No, but we must cling to that thought, for it makes it easier to bear. If it was her choice, we can only hope she acted wisely."

Jade was distraught that evening and Matt, more mobile now on his crutches, was determined to help. When she burned the stew, he quietly urged the children not to complain and to eat what they could of it. When she tugged Emily's nightshift on backward, he unobtrusively corrected the mistake. He changed Zach himself, lest, in her mental fog, Jade should try to diaper the wrong end of the baby.

By the time the children were asleep, Matt was desperate to find a way to comfort her, to distract her thoughts from worries over Fancy. He would have liked to have made love to her, but his splinted leg still hindered his movements to such a degree that Jade was always the one who had to assume the most dominant position, and that wasn't quite what Matt had in mind this evening. He wanted to take charge, to make love to her, to lavish her with kisses and caresses until she was mindless with desire and could think of nothing else. He wanted to send her on a mad flight to the stars, where nothing but joy awaited her.

Jade had let her hair down and was unbuttoning her dress, preparing for bed, when an idea suddenly struck him. It was somewhat risky, bordering on outrageous, but it could work.

"Wait," he told her, grabbing her arm. "Fasten your dress again and come with me."

She frowned in bafflement. "Where? Why? What about the children?"

"Don't fret. We're not going far. We'll hear them if they waken. Now, no more questions. Just do as I say."

Jade shook her head, wondering what had gotten into him. He certainly was being mysterious—and commanding. Still, she didn't have the energy to argue. It was easier just to go along with him.

Matt was right. They didn't go far. Just to their wagon, which was stationed a few feet from the tent.

Once there, Matt drew up short, nearly changing his mind before recalling that Jordan was occupied in a rousing card game at the moment, and most likely would not return to his bedroll until much later. For this, Matt was exceedingly grateful. He definitely didn't need his brother hanging around just now. Not with what he had planned.

He lowered the tail section, sending up a word of thanks when it did not squeak, and boosted Jade aboard. "Crawl in," he whispered, climbing awkwardly after her and raising the rear gate again and lashing the canvas down tightly. "Try to be quiet. Find the lantern if you can."

He located it first, when his head banged into it. "Never mind. I found it." He proceeded to light it, turning the flame down to its lowest level, and hung it safely out of the way.

"What are we doing here?" Jade questioned softly.

"Having a clandestine affair," was his mischievous and unexpected reply.

"Beggin' yer pardon?" Jade was sure she couldn't have heard correctly.

"If I can manage this without breaking my other leg, you'll soon be begging for more delightful things than that," he told her with a perfectly wicked grin.

He set his crutches aside, found his balance, and reached for her. "Come here, my lovely green-eyed sprite. I want the pleasure of undressing you—completely—for the first time since our wedding."

"Ye've gone daft, ye have," she assured him, her breath catching in her throat as she beheld the wild gleam in his eyes. Of their own accord, her feet carried her forward, to stand directly before him. "Some . . . someone will see," she murmured.

"No," he assured her, even as his fingers deftly dealt with the row of buttons securing her bodice. "The wagon is stocked to the rafters with fresh supplies, with the two of us caught cozily in the center of them."

Reaching behind her, he untied her sash. The dress hung loosely about her, needing only a slight tug past her shoulders to send it fluttering to the wagon bed. Within seconds, her chemise followed, pooling at her feet. A small pull at the drawstring of her drawers sent them sliding to her ankles. She was left standing in her boots and stockings.

"Now, see that box?" he drawled, pointing. "I want you to stand on it."

Jade frowned. "What for?"

"So you'll stand taller, be more accessible to me since I can't kneel. Though I can still bend from the waist, I can't curve my leg with this splint holding it stiff. It makes things a bit awkward, to be sure, but if you'll just trust me, I intend to show you a few tricks I'll bet even your friends haven't tried."

She climbed atop the box, muttering, "If I didn't know ye better, I'd swear ye've been nippin' the bottle, Matt Richards. Oh!" Her yelp of surprise came when Matt's mouth, now level with her breasts, suddenly claimed a jiggling nipple. She swayed slightly and clasped her arms about his head to steady herself.

His laugh was muffled as he cautioned, "Easy, honey, don't smother me. Think how hard that would be to explain."

Then he was suckling, nipping, laving her breast with his tongue, and Jade went weak with the pleasure of it. She could only cling to him and glory in the waves of sensation rushing through her. His hands stroked her bare, quivering flesh, weaving a shimmering pattern of fiery goose bumps from her nape to the backs of her knees.

"Delicious," he crooned, switching from one moistened breast to the other. "And Adam chose an apple over this, the poor fool."

Jade couldn't begin to reply. When she tried, a soft moan of delight was all that came from her throat.

When Matt grasped one bare buttock in each of his warm hands, she gave an involuntary lurch that nearly sent them both tumbling. "Steady, love," he warned, shifting his hold to her trim waist. Before she could guess his intent, he lifted her, made a quarter turn, and suddenly

Jade was falling backward. With a startled shriek, she landed sideways in the hammock, still clutching Matt's hair.

"Ouch! Aggie, let go." With every sway of the suspended cot, she was tugging dark strands loose. "If I wanted to be scalped, I'd find an Indian to do it properly."

"I can't! I'll fall!"

"No, you won't. Trust me. Let loose now and grab hold of the edge of the cot. And try not to knock me off my feet. My balance isn't the best right now, you know."

Hesitantly, she opened one eye to glare at him. Slowly, one finger at a time, she released his raven locks, clawing for one handful of canvas at a time. Much to her wonder, not only did she not fall, but when she finally got her bearings it was to find Matt standing squarely between her outspread thighs. "Oh, my stars!" she exclaimed, a bright blush staining her face.

He chuckled. "You want stars, sweetheart? I'll certainly try to oblige." With that, he pushed her hanging bed to a more favorable, more perpendicular angle, and bent forward to brush his lips against the coppery curls at the juncture of her legs.

"Matt?" she whispered uncertainly. "What . . . no . . . this . . . ye can't . . . oooh!" If her short flight into the hammock had been dizzying, what Matt was doing with his tongue was positively stunning. Shattering. Beyond belief! Ripples of sweet, torrid desire assaulted her, so intense that she could scarcely breathe. She tried to squirm away, the pleasure nearly too much to bear, but in her vulnerable position she only managed to lodge herself more firmly against his hot, tormenting mouth. The sharp yearning built with every incredible lash of his tongue, and with every silken stroke she rose with it. Higher. Further. Her senses deluged to bursting. Suddenly she seemed to explode from within, her trembling spirit flung heavenward amid a radiant shower of swirling stars and rainbow clouds. She cried out in wonder at the awesome beauty enveloping her.

Matt's voice came softly, as if from some great distance, crooning words of love that wrapped about her heart and pulled her gently back to him. When, at last, her senses ceased spinning, he was holding her, welcoming her home with a tender smile that set his eyes aglow.

"I . . . I . . ." she stammered, unable to find the words to properly express what she'd just experienced, the incredible gift he'd given her.

"Stars?" he asked quietly.

She managed a weak nod, and was still trying to collect her scattered thoughts as he tugged her boots and stockings off. She watched past lazy lids as he began to remove his own clothing, struggling to keep his balance as he pushed his denim britches over his splints and bandages. Her eyes widened as his turgid member sprang into view.

He grinned. "Now here's where it might get a bit tricky, darlin', so hold tight and bear with me." Employing the long, flat box she'd stood upon, Matt used it as a step stool to raise himself to a more advantageous height, at a level with the cot upon which she remained sprawled. Still standing, he clasped hold of her hips and brought her forward, claiming a space for himself in the inviting vee of her thighs. "You can't know how much I've wanted to make love to you," he told her, his eyes shining into hers.

"Ye have," she whispered back, gasping as his smooth, swollen manhood stroked intimately across that sensual nubbin of feminine flesh, rubbing erotically, exciting her anew.

"Not like this. Not lying over you, slowly stoking your desire, making myself part of you as you writhe beneath me."

He bent, his mouth seeking hers, his tongue delving deeply past her parted lips. The soft furring of hair on his chest tickled lightly over her breasts, teasing the sensitized peaks into tight rosebuds. Her belly quivered in joyous anticipation. Within his grasp, her hips shifted slightly, seeking closer contact with his.

"Patience, sweetheart," he murmured, his breath warm against her throat, his lips gliding on a shivery course to her ear. "Let the longing grow. Let it build. Until it fans the embers of our need into flames too hot to endure."

Jade was already smoldering. As he continued to caress her, to kiss her, to tantalize her with whispered words, her temperature soared to fever pitch. Her blood seemed to simmer heavily in her veins, making her body quicken and her skin tingle. Small mews of pleasure and frustration issued from her lips. Her hands clutched at him, urging him to come inside her, to end this exquisite torment.

"Now. Please. Now," she implored shakily.

At last he surged into her in one long, silken stroke, and Jade thought she would die from the sheer delight of it. Matt's low groan of bliss echoed her own wondrous gasp.

"I can't believe how hot you are. How wet. How smooth," he marveled in a voice made husky with desire. "Like plunging into a heated pot of honey. I could drown in you and revel in every glorious moment."

She wriggled beneath him in ardent entreaty. "More," she moaned. "Love me . . . more."

For answer, he gave the cot a light push, and she swung slightly away from him, though not enough to disengage their throbbing bodies. Like a pendulum, the hammock rocked forward again, merging them more completely, driving him deeply into her sheltering sheath. Again they gasped aloud, stunned by the power of their union.

"Oh, Matt! Matt!"

"Yes." He hissed the reply through gritted teeth and gave the hammock another small nudge.

Time and again, as the cot continued to swing to and fro, they moved scant inches apart, only to come together again with devastating impact. Matt was panting, passion glazing his skin with a fine sheen and lighting his eyes with a fervent glow. Beneath him, Jade trembled, her body arching toward his like a bowstring drawn taut by the hand of an archer, her head tossed back as splendor rose within her.

Rapture erupted with volcanic force, quaking through them in a series of colossal convulsions that went on and on. Ecstasy spilled forth from within, bathing them in golden glory, shimmering all about them as they reeled helplessly, caught up in its captivating clutches. Their voices blended in sweet, glad harmony, as together they weathered the cataclysm to its final, quivering vibration.

Weak, sated, they clung to each other, Matt's damp brow resting on her heaving breast, Jade's fingers filtering through the dark, wet hair at his nape. Finally he raised his head and sought her gaze, awe and humor blending in his eyes. "I thought I'd be glad to see the last of this hammock, but now I'm not so sure. Perhaps we should keep it up for a while, now that we've found such a delightful use for it."

She laughed softly. "Ye like havin' me at yer mercy, do ye? Holdin' the reins, so to speak?"

He nodded, grinning down at her. "I most certainly do, and so far this is the only means I've found to accomplish that, at least until my leg is healed and I can move about normally."

"Ye've a devious mind, Matt Richards. Yer congregation would surely be amazed at how resourceful ye can be when the need arises."

"More than need was arising, sweetheart," he reminded her smugly. His hand stole between them, resting on her stomach. "And this particular circumstance might better be termed 'creative' than 'resourceful'. It would be my most heartfelt pleasure to get you with child. To watch him grow within you. To see him nurtured at your sweet bosom."

She bestowed a tender smile upon him, brushing an errant, boyish lock from his forehead. "Then we'd best hurry for Oregon, love, where we can make room for any babe that might be born of yer vigorous endeavors."

She paused, then added with an impish twinkle in her eye and a sultry tone to her voice, "And I'd really like to keep the hammock strung for a time, Matt. I'm developin' a queer fondness for it, I am."

❧❦❧ *Chapter 29* ❦❧❦

Matt, Jordan, and the "girls" were the only ones who were dismayed at having to leave Fort Laramie the next morning, and that only because they felt they were abandoning Fancy to whatever Fate had in store for her. Certainly, Colonel Filbus was more than happy to wave them on their way. Therefore, it was some consolation that the Mormon and Oregon trails followed the same route now, and would not diverge again for more than two weeks, after covering over two hundred and fifty miles together. This meant that they would have the pleasure of Mavis's company once more, and be able to spend some time with Ike and the Almann family and the many other friends they'd made among the Saints.

The trail out of Fort Laramie began to climb in earnest now. Laramie Peak loomed larger with every passing mile, an ever-present reminder that the emigrants were now heading into the foothills leading to the Rocky Mountains. The oxen teams labored to pull the heavy wagons and, once again, many a family was forced to lighten the load and forsake treasured possessions along the way.

Matt was first to encourage the girls to jettison more of their outrageous collection of furnishings. Jordan readily agreed. The women were not quite so eager to part with their precious goods, however.

"We'll be needin' most all of it when we reach Oregon," Bliss protested. "It's bad enough we don't have Billy and the piano anymore, but we've got to have beds and whiskey and such. Whoever heard of a pleasure palace without those?"

"At least get rid of those blasted chandeliers," Jordan argued. "They weigh a ton, and I'll bet my last bullet they'll never make it through the mountains without mishap. Better to discard them now and save wear and tear on the team."

"Do you have ze slightest idea how much zose cost?" Lizette countered, horrified at the thought of leaving such valuable items behind. "It would cost us a fortune to replace zem, to have ozers shipped to Oregon."

"Jordan is right," Matt put in. "They're too heavy. You'll risk killing your oxen if you insist on carting extra weight with you. And those animals might be the only things standing between you and certain death, you know."

With much reluctance, and even a tear or two, the ladies watched sadly as the pair of brilliant, tiered chandeliers was consigned to the dusty trailside.

"If we meet up with some Indian wearin' crystal ornaments on his warbonnet, I'll know where he got them," Peaches lamented.

"It does seem a shame to leave them here," Jade concurred, turning limpid green eyes toward Matt in a final appeal.

He wasn't falling for it, however. "Forget it, Aggie. Somehow I just can't envision them hanging in the entrance of an orphanage."

For that matter, Jade was having trouble picturing herself fitting into such a conservative setting, be it orphanage or church or simply any home she might share with Matt. It was almost inconceivable, akin to imagining an orchid thriving in a desert. Nevertheless, since Matt was not about to give up his dreams, and his parishioners were never going to accept her as she was, Jade set about trying to change herself, to make herself over into the plain, staid sort of woman she presumed would be the proper mate for a minister of God—or the administrator of an orphanage.

Jade hadn't thought it would be easy, but neither had she imagined that changing would be so very difficult.

After all, Mavis seemed to have done it successfully. Jade figured if she could learn to cook and sew and control her temper, that would be a fair start.

She began by singing at the Sunday services and by passing out extra hymnals among the folks in attendance. Though many sneered at her efforts, she tried not to mind their snubs, to be thankful for those few who relented and gave her credit for trying.

To Jade's surprise, Nell Jansen seemed to have decided to give her a chance to prove herself worthy of her new station in life. It was a reluctant acceptance, to be sure, but acceptance nonetheless, and for reasons Jade could not determine. Perhaps Carl had suggested it, or maybe it was in honor of their longstanding friendship with Matt. Regardless, Nell appeared to be unbending ever so slightly toward the new Mrs. Richards.

Matt noticed this as well, and was delighted. Consequently, when Jade mentioned that she was thinking of asking Tilda to teach her to sew, Matt suggested that she ask Nell instead. "She's a fine seamstress, and I know she would be pleased to help you. Besides, it will give the two of you an opportunity to get to know each other better."

If not altogether pleased, Nell was at least willing to give it a try. "I think the first thing we should do is to make you a nice simple dress, one with a more modest bodice. Or perhaps a skirt and blouse combination would be better."

Jade offered a wan smile. "I was sorta hopin' ye'd help me sew up a new nightdress, since I own nary a one that's proper enough to wear in front of the children."

Nell's jaw fell open at this unexpected request. "I . . . uh . . . of course, Mrs. Richards. That would make a fine first project. And while we're at it, perhaps an accompanying robe would be in order."

To Jade's dismay, she was all thumbs when it came to a needle and thread. No matter how hard she tried, her thread tangled and her seams went awry. She lost count of the number of times Nell made her rip out what she'd so laboriously sewn and begin again. And thimble or not, her needle always seemed to prick unprotected flesh, until Jade's aching fingers began to resemble pincushions and the white cotton cloth became blotched with stains.

"Dear girl, ladies do not put their fingers into their mouths," Nell remonstrated as Jade gave yet another yowl and began to suck on her injured digit.

Jade scowled. "Well, what in tarnation do they do when they poke themselves and start to bleed all over the danged place?"

"They wrap the small wound in a handkerchief until it stops," Nell told her with a dark look. "Most certainly, they do not curse."

"I wasn't cursin'."

"You most assuredly were. Words such as *tarnation* and *danged* should never pass a lady's lips."

"Maybe not, but I'll sure bet they pass her mind once in a while."

Nell's mouth twitched slightly. "Occasionally, perhaps," she allowed. "But they remain unspoken."

Another hazard of associating so closely with Nell Jansen was that the woman was constantly reminiscing about Matt's first wife, never missing an opportunity to sing Cynthia's praises. Even as she was pointing out Jade's numerous faults, under the guise of helping her better herself, Nell was lauding Cynthia as nearly perfect.

"I've never seen two people more suited than Matt and Cynthia were." She sighed sadly. "Her death came as such a shock to us all, but poor Matt was positively devastated. Especially since she was carrying their first child at the time, and he lost them both." Nell wiped a tear from her eye. "My, what a child that would have been, too, with their combined looks and talents."

"Matt told me she was very beautiful," Jade offered generously, swallowing the bitter taste of her own jealousy.

"An absolute angel in every way. So pretty it was almost a crime, and so kind and gentle that you couldn't help loving her. In all the time I knew her, I hardly heard her utter a word of complaint, just as I can't recall ever seeing her disheveled. Her hair was always done up so nicely, her taste in clothing impeccable. Though I've tried, I cannot imagine Cynthia on a trip such as this, where it is nearly impossible to stay clean and tidy for more than an hour. She would have managed it somehow, I assume, and put the rest of us to shame."

"I suppose she could sew, too," Jade muttered, attempting to work yet another knot from her thread.

"Beautifully, in fact. Her needlepoint was something to envy. She was also accomplished at the piano. She used to play at our church services, you know. I imagine that's why Matt has urged you to play your flute; he probably misses having Cynthia provide the musical accompaniment for the hymns."

As the days went by, Jade grew so sick of hearing Cynthia's praises that she wanted to scream. It was thoroughly demoralizing to be compared with such perfection and to know that you fell far short of the mark. However, it also served to make her all the more determined to improve her image and her meager skills.

Matt had taken over driving the wagon, leaving Jade free to tend the children and visit among her friends. One day, she dropped back in line to chat with Mavis.

As they walked along, herding the children ahead of them, Jade took note of how much more modestly Mavis was attired these days. Her dark hair was pulled back into a neat knot at her nape. She wore a plain, pretty blue dress with a clean white apron over it. With her face scrubbed to glowing, she appeared altogether wholesome, not at all the Mavis they used to know.

It suddenly struck Jade that this was just the image she'd been trying to achieve. Clean. Orderly. Demure. It never occurred to her that such a severe hairstyle might compliment Mavis's facial structure but look awful on her. Or that, given her own diminutive height, an apron might only make her appear more elfin. Or that a poke bonnet, in place of her own jaunty straw hat, would all but swallow her pert face, not to mention that seeing beyond the brim presented a hazard in itself. All she saw was a look more in keeping with that of a preacher's wife.

The next morning, as they were preparing to break camp, Jade emerged from the tent and promptly got more attention than she'd bargained for—and not at all the sort she was expecting. As he turned to greet her, Matt stood stunned. He could scarcely believe his eyes! There stood his darling wife—at least he assumed it was she—decked out in Mormon garb and looking like a dowdy old lady shriveled with age!

"What in bloody blue blazes have you done to your self, woman?" he bellowed, too shocked at her changed appearance to bother to monitor his tongue or volume.

Before she could answer, Jordan came loping around the corner of the wagon, intent on discovering what had his usually calm brother so ruffled. He took one look at Jade and exclaimed, "Holy shit! What's this, some sort of masquerade?" Then he convulsed in uproarious laughter.

On his heels came the "girls." All three skidded to a halt and gawked in open-mouthed astonishment.

"Glory!" Peaches declared at last. Sauntering up to Jade, she peered beneath the huge brim of the poke bon net. "Is that you in there, Jade?" she asked, and gig- gled.

"O' course, 'tis me!" Jade huffed, thoroughly miffed at all of them. Here she'd gone to all this trouble to look presentable, and all they could do was make fun of her! "Who'd ye think it was?"

Bliss chuckled. "Well, sugar, we weren't quite certain. Betsy Ross, maybe, but you sure as hell don't look like yourself in that getup."

Lizette was holding her sides and rocking with mirth. "Ooh! Zis eez too, too absurd! *Cherie*, you look like ze little girl playing dress-up in her mozer's clothes!"

Jade burst into tears. Ripping the bonnet from her head, she tossed it to the ground and stomped on it, grinding it into the dirt. In the process, she dislodged her tight, tidy bun, and red-gold curls immediately started to frizz out in every direction. "There! Are y'all satisfied now?" she shouted.

Fortunately, Matt had recovered sufficiently from his surprise to regain a portion of his own composure. He approached her cautiously, not sure how receptive she was to an apology just yet. "Now, Aggie, don't pitch a fit. If you could see yourself, you'd have to admit that you do look ridiculous dressed as you are. It just isn't you, sweetheart."

"What *is* me?" she wailed, throwing off the arm he attempted to place around her shaking shoulders. " 'Tis gettin' so I don't know meself anymore."

"You're everything you always were," he replied gently, turning her to face him, placing his palm beneath her chin and raising it until their eyes met and held. "All that your few short years have made you. The same lively, copper-haired, emerald-eyed sprite who stole my heart and ran away with it. Sugar and spice and a pinch of sass all rolled into one delectable package."

Despite the crutches that hindered his movements, he pulled her close, gathering her to his chest. "Don't try to change yourself for me, sweetheart. Or for anyone else but yourself, because I love you just as you are— or were."

He tugged at the knot of frazzled curls until it loosened, sending her hair tumbling down her back. His chuckle vibrated through her ear. "Land's sake, Jade! Your hair was pulled back so tightly that your eyes were slanted nearly to your ears. Even your freckles were stretched. You looked like a red-haired Chinaman! That or a pixilated pixie!"

She leveled a well-aimed kick at his shin. The good one. He let out a howl and stumbled backward, releasing her. For several seconds he tottered crazily on his crutches, fighting for balance. "Hang it all! What did you do that for?"

"That's for makin' jokes about me size, ye overgrown buffoon! I may be small, but I'm damned sure big enough to take on the likes o' you."

*   *   *

Jade was in a pout for the rest of the day, even after she'd changed back into her usual attire. "There's simply no pleasin' some folks," she complained loudly as she stomped alongside the wagon. She glared at Matt, who was perched on the seat, hoping he'd heard her.

Beside her, Bliss snickered. "It appears to me you're the one grumblin' the loudest, sweet pea. What's put you in such an all-fired snit anyway? You've been actin' as queer as a spinster with an intimate itch."

"I'm tired o' competin' with a ghost!" Jade muttered, lowering her tone to a confiding whisper. "All I've heard lately is how utterly perfect Matt's first wife was. 'Tis a bloomin' wonder she didn't walk on water."

Bliss's eyes grew wide. "Oh. And who's been fillin' your ears with all that nonsense? Matt?"

"No, but Nell Jansen thinks the sun rose and set on Cynthia's head. And it ain't nonsense. I've heard others talk about her like she was some blasted saint, too. So have you."

Bliss laughed. "Nobody's that perfect, honey, and you're a cockeyed fool if you believe it. The woman had to have some faults. She might have been silly as a goose. Maybe she had a tin ear and a voice like a squeaky wheel. Or could be she was lazy as sin, in which case the sun probably rose and set on her rosy red butt while she was snorin' the day away."

Jade grinned. "I'd sure like to think so, but so far I haven't heard nothin' bad about her from anyone."

"Why don't you ask Matt?" Bliss suggested with a sly look. "After all, if anyone would know, he would. He lived with her."

"I couldn't!" Jade protested on a soft gasp. "He never talks about her. It's like he can't bear to think about her and all he lost when she died. He loved her."

"He loves you now," Bliss reminded her easily. "Seems to me you keep losin' sight o' that, sugar pie, and every time you do it gets you into trouble."

* * *

Cupid was a very busy fellow these days, it seemed. Before long, it became obvious to everyone that Peaches was smitten with one of the soldiers traveling with them from Fort Laramie. He was a handsome middle-aged major who was being transferred to oversee the closing of Fort Casper now that Fort Fetterman was nearing completion. Major Sutton, originally from Vermont, was equally taken with Peaches and her enchanting Southern drawl.

Meanwhile, Lizette was focusing a great deal of time and attention on a smooth-talking, dandified gambler who was a member of the second wagon train, which had joined up with them west of Fort Mitchell. John Halin was bound for California, and was doing his level best to persuade Lizette to go with him to San Francisco, where he intended to start a new gambling house.

Not to be left out of this moonstruck madness, Bliss was acting like a mare in heat every time Jordan came within ten feet of her, which was more often than not. For his part, Jordan seemed to enjoy her company immensely, though Jade was concerned that Bliss was taking their amorous liaison much more seriously than he was. She mentioned this to Matt one evening.

"I'm not meanin' to be a busybody, but have ye noticed what's goin' on between yer brother and Bliss these days?"

"Yes, but I'm trying to keep out of his personal affairs now that Jordan has finally stopped prying into ours."

"Well, I'm startin' to worry about Bliss. I don't think she's takin' things as casually as Jordan is. Fact is, I think she's bustle over bosom in love with him, and I'm afraid she's bound for heartbreak. Has Jordan mentioned to ye how he feels about her?"

"His intentions?" Matt asked with an upraised brow.

Jade nodded.

Matt shook his head. "Not a word. But Jordan is one to keep his thoughts and emotions pretty much to himself most of the time."

"Do ye think ye might ask him? Just to set me mind at ease?"

"No, my little matchmaker, I will not. However, if he broaches the subject himself, I'll try to get some idea of his feelings."

"Do ye suppose I should say somethin' to Bliss about not gettin' her hopes set too high? She's liable to take an awful tumble."

"My advice would be to keep your pert little nose out of their business and attend to your own. Bliss is not exactly ignorant when it comes to men. She strikes me as the sort who knows her way around the bedpost. If I recall correctly, she's the one who imparted all that invaluable wisdom to you on our wedding night."

Jade colored prettily. "Ye're never gonna let me forget that, are ye?"

"Not until I do, and that's not likely. It was a very memorable evening, sweetheart." A wolfish grin curved his lips and lit his eyes. "Has she offered any further suggestions lately? Something even more erotic, perhaps? I'm in an adventurous mood tonight."

"Sorry, darlin'," Jade crooned, batting her long lashes at him. "Looks like we're gonna have to come up with our own naughty notions."

"No problem," he assured her with a bold wink. "I'm a very inventive fellow, remember? And I've got you to help fire my imagination."

❧❧✥ *Chapter 30* ✥❧❧

*A*t Fort Fetterman they checked for word of Fancy's whereabouts, but after a full week there was no news beyond the fact that neither she nor her Indian had been found. After leaving some of the soldiers at Fetterman and picking up a few new replacements, the wagon train rolled on toward Fort Casper.

They camped the following night near a small stagecoach outpost called Deer Creek Station. Here, Josiah Almann took Matt and Jordan along in search of a vein of coal with which the Mormon emigrants were long familiar, the information having been passed on by their religious brothers. The coal was a welcome supplement to the scanty wood supply, for though the bordering mountains appeared lush from a distance, in actuality they were dry and rocky, dotted with only short clumps of sagebrush and greasewood. The surrounding countryside was little better.

As if to correct their faulty impression of this thirsty, barren land, Mother Nature decided to display her power the next day. The wayfarers awoke to lead-gray skies, with brisk winds that swept the clouds into boiling masses. It was not a good portent, particularly since the emigrants had hoped to make Fort Casper by nightfall.

The rain held off for quite some time, however, and it was not until they had circled for the noon meal that the storm hit. As the first huge drops of rain pelted earthward, Jade abandoned her cookfire and scurried to gather the children inside the wagon. Beth, bless her heart, had already scampered for shelter, baby Zach on her hip and Emily trotting alongside.

"Where are the others?" Jade called out over a loud rumble of thunder.

"The three boys all left together, sayin' something about bringin' back buffalo chips," Beth related. "But I think they're really wantin' to find a real live buffalo so they can brag to the others about spottin' one first."

Jade glanced around at the wall of rain and grimaced. "They sure did pick a fine time to wander off," she mumbled half to herself. "I hope they didn't go far, or I'll tan their hides for disregardin' all the warnin's Matt and I have given them."

"They won't," Emily answered after plucking her thumb from her mouth. "They're too scared o' Injuns."

Jade took a moment to locate Matt's large black umbrella, then went back to the campfire to tend the pot of sodden stew she'd been warming for dinner. It was no easy chore, especially with the wind threatening to tear the huge umbrella from her hand. She just hoped she wasn't asking to be struck by lightning, with the clumsy contraption suspended above her.

By the time she was ladling the stew into bowls, the twins dashed into camp, their fair hair plastered to their skulls and their clothes soaked through. "Ye're just in time, lads," Jade said, shaking her head at them. "But just look at ye. I'll bet there are swamp rats drier than the pair o' ye. Ye'd best go find some fresh clothes first off, and yer slickers, too. And don't dawdle or yer dinner will be cold."

"Yes'm," they chimed as one, making her smile at how alike they were in most everything they thought and said.

They were clambering into the wagon when Jade stopped them by asking, "Where's Skeeter? Wasn't he with ye?"

"He was for a while," Harry answered.

"But then he sorta distappeared," Larry finished for him. "Ain't he back yet?"

"No, and I'm beginnin' to get worried," Jade admitted with a frown. "I thought ye knew better than to leave him alone, since he can't hear or talk. Didn't Matt caution ye about that?"

Two blond heads drooped in shame. "Yes'm, but we got to playin' and wasn't payin' him much heed, I reckon," Larry confessed.

Harry's head bobbed in agreement. "We're real sorry. We'll go right back and look for him if ya want."

"You just stay put," Jade ordered. "I'll go get Matt."

Within minutes she returned, Matt and Jordan with her. "Where were you boys playing?" Matt asked. "Where did you last see Skeeter?"

In the end, it was easier for the twins to show the men where to search than to try to explain where they'd been. "You stay here with the girls," Matt told Jade when she tried to go with them.

"If he comes in by himself, I'll get Peaches to have Major Sutton give a toot on the trumpet so ye'll know to quit lookin'," Jade volunteered.

"Good idea." He planted a swift kiss on her furrowed brow. "Don't fret. We'll find him." Then the two men and the boys were gone, Matt on horseback to ease his leg, the others on foot.

Locating one small boy in the surrounding hilly country-side in the middle of a thunderstorm was no easy feat. While Jade waited anxiously, her fear growing with every passing minute, the four searchers were having little luck. There was no sense in shouting for Skeeter, since he would not be able to hear them. Nor could he yell to let them know where he might be, which made finding him all the more difficult. And with the rain washing away any tracks he might have made, they would practically have to stumble across him by accident.

The longer they looked for him without success, the more worried Matt and the others became. How far could one five-year-old wander on his short legs? Where could he be in all this rolling, treeless terrain? Had he fallen and hurt himself? Had he met up with a rattler and been bitten? Was he lying unconscious out here somewhere? Why could they find no sign of him?

Finally, after almost an hour, Jordan shook his head. "It's useless, Matt. The twins are ready to drop. Let's go back and get more horses and men to help us look. We can cover more ground that way."

Jade held her breath as she watched them return, then let it out again on a trembling sob. Skeeter was not with them. She ran to Matt, seeking the haven of his arms as he dismounted. "Mr. Greene's itchin' to move on. I told him we ain't leavin' 'til we find Skeeter. What are we gonna do, Matt?"

He stroked her wet head. "We're going to keep searching, even if we have to stay behind and catch up with the others later."

While Jade took the twins in hand, Matt and Jordan went to speak with Sam Greene and Major Sutton. While Greene sympathized, he did not want to delay travel for one missing child. It was only when Major Sutton volunteered his troops to aid in the search, thus depriving the wagon train of its military escort should the other emigrants go on ahead, that Greene rethought his plans. "Damnation, man! We're still in Indian territory!" he declared.

"Precisely. And a scared little boy is out there—lost, hungry, and perhaps injured," Sutton replied firmly. "Worse, the poor lad can neither hear nor speak. Should we simply abandon him like some worthless animal?"

A flush ran up Greene's neck, equal parts embarrassment and anger. "All right! Let's call a meetin' and get the search under way, then. The sooner we find the boy, the sooner we can all be on our way."

In short order, nearly every able-bodied man was included in the search party. Sutton took charge, breaking them into groups and allotting each a different section of ground to cover. "My corporal will stay here, and once the boy is found and brought to camp, he'll sound the signal to the rest of us."

That signal never came. Throughout the long day and into the night, the men continued to search, ignoring the storm that raged about them all the while. Periodically, they would report back to camp, brace themselves with a hot cup of coffee or soup, grab a lantern, and head out again.

Each time a group returned, Jade would rush to meet them, her heart in her throat. Hoping. Praying. Only to meet with disappointment.

Tilda and the girls prepared supper and helped look after the other children. They also attempted to console Jade, urging her to lie down and rest, or to eat something, but Jade was too distraught. "He's so little," she lamented repeatedly. "So helpless."

As the hours dragged on, other emigrant women, wives and mothers themselves, began stopping by to offer their sympathy. Some brought tea, or muffins, or simply their heartfelt prayers for Skeeter's safety. Though she was grateful for their support in this time of duress, Jade was too steeped in misery to register surprise at this magnanimous gesture from ladies who wouldn't have spoken to her the day before.

It was Bliss who commented mockingly on this turn of events. "So this is what it takes to break down the barriers and make folks wake up to what's really important in the world. Ain't it a cryin' shame!"

"And at what cost?" Tilda added, wiping her own damp eyes. "A child's life?"

"No!" Jade exclaimed, clasping her clenched hands to her breast. "Don't say that! They're gonna find him! Skeeter is gonna be just fine!" But the longer they waited, the more she doubted her own words.

Just before dawn, the storm finally passed, but the eastern sky was still dark with receding clouds, dulling the coming sunrise. Morning arrived, bringing light and warmth but no word of Skeeter. Shortly thereafter, the men began drifting back into camp—wet, bone-tired, muddy, and disheartened.

"We must've combed every hill, every gully, every clump of sage within twenty miles," one fellow claimed. "I swear I rode almost to Fort Casper and back, and turned over most every rock between here and there."

"Where could that danged kid be?" another asked in weary wonder. "I know he ain't no bigger than a minute, but he's still taller than any bush out there. In that red shirt he was supposed to be wearin', you'd think he'd stand out like a wart on a witch's nose. 'Specially now that it's daylight."

A third man suggested somberly, "Not if the poor tyke fell in the river, he wouldn't. With all that rain, it's runnin' pretty fast and deep in places. He might have been swept under, or carried along in the current for miles."

Matt and Jordan rode in, just as drenched and red-eyed as the others, and with no better success. All they could do now was to wait for the remainder of the searchers to report back and hope for the best.

It was not to be. A quarter of an hour later, Will Sutton and his group returned, nearly the last to do so. From his saddlebag, the major withdrew a shredded patch of scarlet cloth and one small, battered boot. He solemnly handed them to Matt. "We found the boot several yards down the riverbank, almost buried in the mud," Sutton said gravely. "Several miles downstream, we finally spotted that piece of his shirt, but no sign of the boy. My guess is that he fell into the water and drowned. There's no telling where his body might be. I'm sorry."

A doleful silence followed the major's announcement as all eyes turned toward Matt and Jade. For several seconds, Matt stood stunned, feeling as if he'd just been poleaxed. Tears stung his eyes as he balanced himself on his crutches and reached out to Jade, his heart aching.

Beside him, Jade felt the blood drain from her head. She swayed dizzily. Then the most devastating pain lodged in her chest, making her gasp for air. It felt as if her heart were being ripped from her body, the force of it doubling her over, her arms wrapped tightly about her waist. A long, keening wail of grief rose from her throat, expressing her intense agony more eloquently than words ever could.

She barely felt Matt grab hold of her, had no realization that without his support she would have fallen to her knees in the mud. Blinded by tears, she didn't see the awful sympathy on the faces of others who witnessed her sorrow with burdened spirits. "No!" she screamed. "No! Not Skeeter!" She gasped for breath, only vaguely aware of Matt's presence. "Please!" she begged. "Please, Matt! Tell God He can't have him! Make Him give him back to me!"

By the time the train rolled out, leaving the sad scene of Skeeter's demise behind, Jade was huddled on a pile of blankets in the wagon, weeping inconsolably. For a few minutes, after learning that the company would be leaving immediately, Matt had thought he was going to have to tie Jade down to make her go. She'd been like a madwoman, ranting and screeching and thrashing in his arms. Then, thankfully, she'd collapsed, and he'd bundled her into the wagon as quickly and as gently as possible.

Sitting atop the wagon bench, listening to her broken sobs and feeling every bit as miserable, Matt hung his head and prayed that their grief would soon ease. How often, in the course of his ministry, had he seen others laid low by such loss? How many times had he counseled wisely, telling his bereaved parishioners that time and God would heal their heartache? Similar sorrow had touched his life before, with the deaths of his parents and Cynthia, each tearing a portion of his heart away. Jade had lost her parents as well, so he knew this was not the first time she had grieved for someone she loved. Still, every time it happened the wound was fresh, the pain no less devastating.

Yet, this was different. This time a child had died, and it was harder to understand when the little ones were taken, harder to bear. Skeeter had been so special to them, perhaps because of his impairments and the fact that few others had seemed to care for him. And now he was gone, and like Jade, Matt wanted to lash out at God for taking him. Instead, he bowed his head and prayed for strength, for himself and for Jade, and tried to imagine Skeeter in Heaven—laughing, talking, hearing, singing. Whole and healed and happy for the first time in his pitifully brief life.

A day later than anticipated, the emigrants crossed the Platte River for the final time by way of the bridge leading to Fort Casper. From there they would travel overland on a southwesterly course to the Sweetwater River and Independence Rock, some fifty miles ahead. They would also be leaving their military escort behind at Fort Casper. Once again they would be dealing on their own with whatever disasters awaited them.

Jade and her friends were leaving much more than that behind. Peaches approached them with the rather shamefaced announcement that she would be staying on at Fort Casper.

"I really hate to desert y'all now, especially when you're grieving so over losin' little Skeeter," she told them. "But Will has asked me to marry him, and I've said I would."

"Lord have mercy!" Bliss exclaimed. "First Mavis, then Jade, and now you! And with Fancy gone, that'll leave only Lizette and me to start up the hurdy-gurdy! It'll hardly be worth the effort of dragging all those beds across country if we've got no one to put 'em to good use!"

"I'm sorry," Peaches offered with a shrug. "Well, in a way I am, but I'd be lyin' through my teeth if I didn't admit that I'm happier than a kid at Christmas to have found Will and fallen in love with him." She grinned. "If it'll make you feel any better, you can leave my bed right here, and my new husband and I'll put it to better use than it's seen in a long time."

"Well, I should hope so!" Lizette declared, giving Peaches a big hug. "We're going to miss you."

"I'll write. Y'all have to promise to keep in touch, too." She turned to Jade, who was sitting forlornly on the rear gate of her wagon, gazing sorrowfully at the Platte River. "Sugar, I know how you hate to go on and leave him," Peaches murmured, her own heart aching for her friend.

"I just can't believe he's gone," Jade whispered, her voice cracking. "There wasn't even a body to bury. How do I know he's not still out there somewhere, wanderin' around, lost and frightened? How can I leave, not knowin' for sure?"

The girls were taken aback. They had all accepted Will Sutton's word and had resigned themselves to the sad fact that Skeeter had drowned. Now, hearing the doubt in Jade's voice, they, too, began to wonder if the major could have been wrong. What a tragedy that would be!

"Jade, honey, if that boy is out there, someone will find him," Peaches assured her. "We were only a few hours from the fort, so if anyone runs across him, they'll be stoppin' here, and Will and I will hear about it. I promise I'll keep an eye out for him, and if I learn anything at all, I'll send a letter. Better yet, a telegram, so you know almost as soon as we do."

"Ye swear it?" Jade asked. "Ye'll keep lookin'?"

"Every day 'til Will and I leave for Fort Fetterman. And then I'll post a notice where everyone headin' west can see it and be watchin' for the little fella."

Tears swam in Jade's eyes as she grabbed Peaches's hand and held it tight. "Thank ye, Peaches. If I've got to go on, at least I know that ye'll be here in me place. Ye can't know what that means to me."

Chapter 31

That evening, Matt conducted the brief ceremony uniting Major Sutton and Peaches as man and wife. A hastily organized gala followed. Almost everyone attended, bringing food and good wishes, for on the heels of Skeeter's disappearance they all needed something to lift their spirits.

Though Jade was more in the mood for a wake than a wedding, she did not decline to witness Peaches's marriage or to bid her happiness. She got through the evening by clinging tightly to the thought that Peaches would remain here at the fort, continuing the search for Skeeter, which Jade must abandon. She could not fathom how she could ever repay her friend for such an immense favor.

Those women who had offered their sympathy and support the night before now sought Jade out to extend their condolences for her loss. Some of them had lost children of their own. Others could only imagine how she was feeling and empathize from that standpoint. But all were gracious and understanding, proffering their friendship as well as their profound regrets. At long last, Jade was being accepted into their midst, at a tremendous cost.

Sunrise saw them bidding farewell to the newlyweds and Fort Casper. Jade took one last, long look at the North Platte River, thinking how ironic it was that it looked so calm and placid beneath the morning sun, not at all like a raging river bent on claiming lives. Then, slowly, she turned her face westward, toward the mountains and the life that awaited her in Oregon.

313

Matt had to resist the urge to look back. He was suddenly reminded of the story of Lot's wife, who had turned back for a final view of Sodom and had promptly been transformed into a pillar of salt. Though it was foolish, he breathed a sigh of relief when Jade cast her eyes forward and did not look back again.

The area through which they now passed was increasingly rough and mountainous, as evidenced by such landmarks as Emigrant's Gap and Devil's Backbone, also known as Rock Avenue. Moreover, it was dotted with alkali springs and poisonous water holes. For this stretch, the emigrants had to water their animals from their own supply barrels, and keep close watch lest the beasts try to drink from the noxious creeks and ponds. Fortunately, they reached Willow Spring, the only reliable source of water until they hit the Sweetwater River a full day later, early on the second day.

It was the third day of July when they rounded their wagons at the base of Independence Rock. Despite all their trials, they were right on schedule, for the rock had attained its name from the fact that many wayfarers bound for California and Oregon had reached this spot on or about Independence Day. This great, granite mound was adorned with the signatures of thousands of pioneers who had previously stopped here. Since the newly arrived emigrants had forgone a similar opportunity at Register Rock out of Fort Laramie, fear of further delays and of Indian attacks pushing them onward, they now looked forward to carving their names alongside their predecessors'. They would also celebrate their country's birthday with song and dance, a small feast, and a brief rest.

With great relish, and enormous pride, Jade carefully notched her name into the stone alongside Matt's. Their names, and this date, would forever be etched into history, and she had entered her own signature with her own hand, something she could not have done if Matt had not taken the time and patience to teach her. They celebrated the auspicious occasion with a kiss—and a promise of more to come.

It was also on this night that Jade first wore her new nightdress. The white cotton garment covered her from neck to wrists to ankles, leaving nothing but her head, hands, and feet in sight. Slim bands of pale green ribbon laced through the cloth at the hem, at the gathered ruffles of the sleeves, and across the neckline, where they served double duty as a drawstring closure.

Jade had already washed up, brushed out her hair, and donned her nightdress by the time Matt entered the tent. Upon first seeing her in it, he stumbled to a halt. His wondering eyes took in the cloaking folds and the petite woman whose body was hidden somewhere within, then rose dubiously to meet hers. Her gaze was just as uncertain as his, with a hint of hopefulness lurking in their clear green depths.

"Well, say somethin'," she prompted when he failed to speak. "Do ye like it or not?"

She held her breath as he again perused her person.

Though he was no tailor, this time Matt noticed the slightly crooked seams, the few odd blemishes here and there in the fabric, one sleeve hanging just a tad longer than the other. Intuitively, he knew that this was the secret sewing project Jade and Nell had been working on these past weeks. Though he much preferred Jade's chemise, which bared more of her sweet flesh to his view—or the sleek, sensual gowns from her hurdy-gurdy days—he vowed not to disappoint her now.

A smile crept over his face. "It's perfect," he announced at last.

She released her pent-up breath in a gush of relief. "Do ye really think so?" she persisted.

"Well, it certainly covers you well, and that is what you were aiming for, I take it?"

She nodded. " 'Tis much more respectable for wearin' in front of the young'uns, don't ye agree?"

"Absolutely. And the ribbon goes well with your eyes." A slight frown creased his brow. "It looks roomy enough, but aren't you too warm with all that cloth covering you?"

"A bit, but the nights do get chilly the higher we travel, and Nell says a lady never bares her body, no matter how uncomfortable she might be."

Matt chuckled. "Nell always has been a priggish puss. Nice, to be sure, but she regularly gives me the impression that her corset is laced too tightly for her own good."

Jade tried not to laugh at the mental image this conjured, but a smothered chortle escaped. Then another. Soon she was giggling openly. "Matt, ye're terrible!"

He shrugged, smiling. "Perhaps, but it's the truth. And as long as I'm being so honest, I have to tell you that as lovely as you look in that new nightdress, I still favor having you naked in my arms, regardless of any ridiculous rules Nell is pouring into your head." He sent her a roguish wink. "She'll be none the wiser, the poor thing. And she obviously has no idea of the pleasure she and Carl have been missing out on all these years."

"What about the children?" Jade questioned.

"Fast asleep on the other side of the partition," Matt pointed out. "And you can always wriggle quickly into your gown again when you hear them begin to stir."

He held his arms out to her. "Come here, sweetheart. The sight of your bare toes peeping out from beneath your hem is tempting me to distraction, whetting my appetite for more."

Minutes later, snuggled beneath the covers in the dark, he whispered, "I don't suppose Nell imparted any words of wisdom about the notion of suckling a person's toes, did she?"

Jade laughed softly. "I've never heard o' such nonsense."

With amazing dexterity, considering the clumsy splints still binding his leg, Matt maneuvered about until he caught hold of her ankle. His hot breath tickled, a mere inch from her foot, as he warned, "You have now, sweetheart."

An instant afterward, Jade gave a frantic lurch and a hastily stifled yelp.

At breakfast the next morning, Emily commented innocently, "I was dreamin' 'bout baby pigs last night, and they was squealin' and gruntin' so loud I thought I was waked up. Ain't that funny?"

Jade promptly choked on her biscuit. Matt thumped her on the back, grinning widely. "Yeah, *piggies* sure are cute, aren't they, Em? Especially the wee pink ones. I like them the best."

On the tenth of July, in the heart of nowhere and at the hottest part of the day, they arrived at a marvelous stop on the trail. It had long been labeled the Ice Slough, for the miraculous wonder that lay hidden just a few inches beneath the peatlike sod. Here, at this high altitude, an underground river that only partially thawed out even in midsummer provided the emigrants with— of all the unbelievable things—ice! Huge, glorious, solid chunks of it!

The weary wayfarers immediately declared a holiday and began digging into the earth to retrieve this curious and delightful gift. As the men labored, the women gathered casks and pots in which to carry the ice.

As they stood impatiently to one side of the work area, Tilda commented, "You know, it's a shame we haven't got one of those ice-cream-making contraptions, or we could have ourselves a real treat. My sister had one, and we'd all get together at her place in the summer and make up two or three batches, all in different flavors. It sure was delicious!"

Lizette's eyes lit up. "Zen you know how to make ze ice cream, Tilda? Would we have all ze necessary ingredients?"

"Sure do. All but the gadget to put 'em in."

"Oh, but we do have such a machine," Lizette assured her. "Somewhere in one of our wagons."

"We do?" Jade questioned in surprise.

"*Oui*. If we can locate ze blasted sing."

Tilda rallied them to action. "Well, don't just stand there like ninnies. Go find it!"

"I don't even know what we're supposed to be lookin'

for," Jade complained as Lizette grabbed her arm and pulled her along toward their wagons.

"It's a big, round tin container wiz a smaller one inside and a crank on ze top."

"And it's probably buried at the bottom of a ton o' other useless 'necessities' we carted along with us."

"You'll be glad we brought zis one," Lizette promised.

Though it took them a while, they finally located it. Meanwhile, Tilda had passed the word along, and it turned out that several other ladies had also packed ice cream makers, much to the surprise of their husbands. By the time they'd gathered together, there were eight ice cream cranks in all.

In a united effort, other women quickly rounded up the required ingredients, each donating a measure of milk, cream, sugar, eggs, and salt, until everyone had contributed something to the supply. One lady produced a jar of canned cherries, another a prized pot of orange marmalade, a third a jar of strawberry preserves.

Inspired by the thought of the delectable treat in store for them all, the men and boys now got into the act, and there was no lack of volunteers to do the cranking. Of course, it took quite some time. In fact, supper had been eaten and the sun had set before the ice cream was at last pronounced ready. But no one seemed to mind the work or the wait, or the evening chill that had promptly invaded the mountain heights, as they gleefully anticipated the creamy delight.

A festive air abounded as the entire population turned out to witness the lifting of the first lid. A glad cheer arose, and a line quickly formed, everyone standing with cup in hand, laughing and chattering and sharing the pleasure of the moment. Of course, once the ice cream was evenly divided among so many people, each person came away with only a small serving, but all appreciated what little they received, savoring it down to the final, refreshing taste.

"I wish we could stay here longer and make more

ice cream tomorrow," Beth said, licking her lips and shivering.

"Yeah," Larry agreed, running his tongue inside his cup for the last bit of flavor. "This is the bestest stuff I ever tasted."

Harry, sporting a drippy white mustache, mimicked his twin. "You bet."

Emily simply nodded vigorously, too busy sucking her sweet, sticky thumb to answer.

Even baby Zach had gotten a portion of the treat, and had gobbled it down with enthusiasm.

Jade's smile was tinged with sorrow as her gaze sought Matt's. "Skeeter would have loved this," she murmured, her lips trembling with both cold and the urge to cry.

Matt drew her closer to his side, sharing sympathy and body heat. "I know. Try not to dwell on it, sweetheart."

" 'Tis hard." She blinked hastily to clear away a veil of tears. "Just as it's gonna be difficult to part with so many of our friends tomorrow."

By noon of the following day they would reach the Lander Road cutoff. There, those emigrants bound for Oregon and California would split off, heading west, while the Mormon train would veer south, toward Fort Bridger and on to Salt Lake City. This was the last evening they would spend with Mavis, Ike, and the rest of that group, and the thought of parting lent a poignant touch to the festivities.

They were all gathered about, enjoying one another's company for the final time, when Sarah Almann gave a small, surprised squeal and clutched at her protruding stomach. She turned large brown eyes toward her sister-wife and said softly, "Anna, dear, would you walk me back to the wagon, please?"

Anna rose, smiling at her husband's second wife, who was now so round with child she appeared about to burst. "It's time?" she asked quietly.

Sarah nodded.

Jade watched with avid curiosity as Anna and Josiah aided Sarah to her feet, and the two women walked off slowly, arm in arm. Turning to Dr. Worley, who was still conversing with Matt and the other men, she asked, "Won't they be requirin' yer help?"

The good doctor chuckled and shook his head. "I very much doubt it. Anna is an accomplished midwife. She knows what to do. And if they run into difficulties, they know where to find me." He paused, a twinkle in his eyes. "Now, if you'd care to go along and learn how it's done, I don't think they would mind."

Jade hastily declined the offer. "Thank ye, but I think I'll visit with Mavis a bit longer while we have the chance."

Mavis was looking wistfully after the departing women. "I hope Thomas and I have a baby soon," she said with a sigh. "Hannah suspects she's in the family way now, and I'm torn between being happy for her and being eaten alive with envy."

"Matt wants us to have a child, too," Jade confided. "As if we didn't have 'em hangin' from the rafters now."

They were still talking when word arrived that two more ladies had gone into labor. One was birthing her fifth child and was expecting an easy delivery. The other was having her first, and her frantic husband implored Dr. Worley to attend her.

"I guess I'd better go have a look at her, if just to calm the poor man," the physician said, relenting. He rose with a chuckle. "With the first one, the father often experiences more anxiety than the mother."

Jordan shook his head in wonder. "What's goin' on all of a sudden? Three women all delivering at once! Isn't that a bit odd, Doc?"

Worley waved a hand toward the sky. "Not really. Take a look at that moon." It was fat and full, glowing like a beacon in the star-filled night. "I can't explain the why's or the wherefore's, but more babes seem to arrive during a full moon than at any other time of the month. Maybe it's the pull of the tides or some such thing. I really don't know."

He left them with a parting thought and a mischievous wink. "I do know that the gestation period for humans is generally two hundred and eighty days. It does tend to make one ponder what the parents were doing beneath another full moon, ten lunar months previous to the grand appearance of their offspring." He laughed again. "Or perhaps it was just the ice cream that brought this particular infant invasion to a peak."

Chapter 32

*G*radually, everyone drifted away from the campfires. While Jade got the children ready for bed, Matt arranged the various bedrolls and erected the blanket partition.

"There," he announced with satisfaction. "Our wall is in place once more."

"They can still hear us," Jade was quick to point out, reminding him of Emily's recent comment about piggies.

"Then we'll have to be very, very quiet, won't we?" he suggested with a knowing grin. "Especially you, my little squealer."

Jade poked her tongue out at him. Her husband appeared to be in a mischievous mood this evening, and she had to wonder if Doc Worley had been right about the full moon affecting people. Matt certainly was feeling his oats tonight. And unless Jade missed her guess, Jordan was presently sporting with Bliss in the next tent, while Lizette was sharing her gambler's sleeping quarters. There was definitely something amorous in the air.

A short while later, as Jade was about to pull her night-dress on, Matt told her softly but firmly, "You won't be needing that, at least not for the moment." He patted the space next to him in invitation.

When she started to put out the lantern, he said, "Turn it down low, but leave it lit. Tonight I want to see every beautiful inch of you."

She claimed her place on the bedroll, only to have him confiscate the blanket with which she would have covered herself. She offered a wry smile. "My, my, ye sure are the bossy sort this evenin'. Makes me wonder what ye have up yer sleeve, Reverend Richards."

He waved one bare arm at her. "Not a thing, my suspicious little wife. However, I do have something stashed away right here." He reached out to grab a small bowl, and brought it forward for her perusal. The bowl had been packed with ice, which was now partially melted, and resting within the mushy remains was a cup of ice cream.

At her questioning look, he grinned again, waggling his eyebrows in a wicked fashion. "I saved my portion for something special. Since I couldn't have it over apple dumplings, I decided to see what it might taste like on your warm, naked body."

Jade stared at him in wide-eyed astonishment. Finally, she managed a breathless exclamation. "Ye amaze me, truly ye do! I'd never have guessed ye'd turn out to be such a lecherous rascal. I'm thinkin' 'tis a good thing ye married me instead of that prim and proper Charlotte Cleaver."

Matt nodded, his white teeth flashing behind his smile. "She'd have been running for the hills long before now, I suppose."

Gently, he pushed Jade down upon her back, his fingers dipping into the cold cup as he added, "But you're a much more adventurous sort, aren't you, sweet? My perfect match, from the top of your head to the tips of your pretty pink toes, each tantalizing particle of you—every one of which I plan to savor very thoroughly before this night is over."

The first touch of his fingers, chilled and gooey with ice cream, made Jade catch her breath sharply. "Saints and salvation, that's cold!" She gave a quick shiver.

Matt laughed. "Do that again, honey. That cute little shimmy was incredibly provocative."

Jade obliged, not that she could help doing so with his frosty fingers coating her bare flesh with ice cream and goose bumps. It was all she could do not to screech aloud, and that only because she had her jaws clamped tightly closed. Still, whimpers of pleasure sounded in her throat, goading Matt on in his imaginative artwork.

He painted creamy rings around her alert nipples, each successive circle more narrow than the last, until he at last dripped a dollop of the melting dessert directly atop the peaks. "Your breasts resemble miniature snow-capped mountains," he crowed in delight. "Or sugar-dipped cakes. But I'll bet they taste better than any confection a master baker could devise."

As his lips closed over one dimpled crest, his mouth against her chilled skin felt as hot as an iron fresh from the fire. Jade would not have been surprised to see steam rising from her chest, so great was the contrast of temperatures. On a fevered moan, she arched upward, grasping handfuls of his dark hair and clutching his head firmly to her bosom.

"Sweet," he murmured. "So impossibly sweet!"

By the time he had suckled and licked every drop of ice cream from that breast and switched hungrily to its mate, Jade was aflame with desire. But Matt was not yet done tormenting her. He trailed a long, thin stream of the half-frozen treat down her torso, filling her navel to overflowing. Then he proceeded to lap the sticky sweetness from her quivering flesh, dipping his tongue into her navel time and again, much like a hummingbird gathering nectar from the heart of a flower.

When he was finished there, his attention veered toward uncharted territory. Like an artist gone mad, he smeared her lower limbs with the flavored concoction and lapped his way upward and inward, so slowly and seductively that Jade was certain she was going to lose what little remained of her mind before he was through. She lurched wildly as he parted her legs and dribbled more of the chilled, tasty delight on that most heated and aching place between her trembling thighs. His mouth hovered over her, his breath warm and teasing. Then he bent to taste the sweet delicacy awaiting him, and she could not hold back the low moan as ecstasy burst through her. It was as if she'd become a part of the sun, only to explode with it into a million blazing fragments. Again and again and again, each time more powerful than the last, until she was sure she would forever be lost in this shattered, glittering splendor.

She drifted earthward to find Matt gazing raptly at her, watching every blissful expression that etched her passion-dazed features. "You are so glorious!" he whispered. "So unbelievably responsive. I'd given up all hope of ever finding a woman like you. Then, when I least expected it, I turned around and there you were, like a gift . . . a treasure."

He kissed her then, his lips still tinged with the flavor of orange marmalade ice cream—and of her. Suddenly the most incredible urge came over Jade. A craving to taste Matt as he had her. To run her tongue and her lips over every part of his body. To revel in the feel, the smell, the very essence of this man she loved so desperately.

She pushed at his shoulders, willing him to look at her. Her eyes shone up into his as she murmured, "If ye wouldn't mind, I'd like me own turn at this game now."

For a moment he looked stunned. Then a smile arched his lips. "Oh, you would, would you?"

She nodded, her look a beguiling blend of shyness and boldness. Matt likened it to that of an impudent cherub. "But the ice cream is gone, down to the last delicious drop," he told her with feigned dismay and a touch of smug satisfaction.

Her smile was ripe with impish playfulness as she wriggled beneath him, rubbing her bare, sticky flesh along his. "I'll wager there's a lick or two on ye now. The fun will be findin' 'em."

With that, she pushed him off her, onto his back. He went willingly, with a wide grin. Throwing his arms wide, he declared, "Do your worst, temptress. I'm at your mercy."

She gave a low, sultry laugh that set his blood racing. "Ye bet yer boots ye are, love. Now just lie there and take yer just deserts like a man."

"I've already had my dessert," he gibed, deliberately misinterpreting her words. "And it was scrumptious."

"Then 'tis high time I had mine," she announced saucily.

She started with his ears, swirling her tongue inside the rims, nipping lightly at his lobes, laughing delightedly as Matt gave a violent quiver. Her moist mouth followed the sensitive cord running along his neck to the dip of his shoulder, then traced it back again, sprinkling tiny love bites and kisses along the way. He moaned, but made no move to escape her exploration or to direct her in any manner.

Her lips found his throat, resting over the pounding pulsebeat, her tongue laving it and speeding its beat. Then she moved lower, peppering his furred chest with kisses, burrowing her nose into the ticklish cloud of soft dark curls. As her lips grazed tauntingly over his male nipples, they rose to greet her inquisitive, lashing tongue.

Again he groaned, and shifted slightly beneath her touch. "Oh, honey, you are such a tease, such an enchanting little witch! It feels as if every nerve in my body is standing at attention, anticipating your next move."

"And ye'd throttle me if I dared to stop right now," she answered, laughing.

Her hands stroked along his sides as far as her arms would reach, her nails scarcely scoring his bare skin and raising gooseflesh in their wake. Her mouth traced a course of its own, her tongue searching out his navel and darting inside. The muscles of his stomach contracted tightly, and she chuckled anew.

"Now ye know how it feels," she quipped, and promptly did it again, just for good measure.

One wandering hand found him, her fingers folding around his turgid manhood, stroking, assessing, meting out their wordless praise of his bold masculinity. A gruff purr, like that of some great cat, rumbled through his chest.

She moved lazily downward, across his lower stomach, her lips whispering over his taut, fevered flesh. Her flowing tresses brushed his tense thighs as lightly as the wings of a butterfly. Each slight move she made brought her closer to her ultimate goal.

At last, when he thought he could stand the sensual torment no longer, her warm lips teased lightly along his throbbing shaft. He caught his breath in suspense. Then her hot, sweet mouth was enveloping him, and he knew he'd never felt anything so wondrous. His fingers caught in her hair, clenching spasmodically as her mouth caressed him with loving strokes that threatened to send him hurtling over the edge of reason. Though he withstood the exquisite torture as long as he dared, finally he tugged her head away.

"No more. No more," he chanted as he rolled over, pulling her beneath him and parting her thighs.

"Mind yer leg," she warned breathlessly, already arching up to meet his first strong thrust.

He gave a gratified groan and murmured, "Don't fret. Right now I wouldn't feel it if the darned thing fell off!"

Then he began to move—plunging deeply, retreating, in an ever-increasing rhythm set to the drumbeat of their hearts. Immersing himself time and again in the honeyed haven of her hot, silken body.

Rapture claimed them suddenly, without warning, hurtling them skyward, spinning them toward the heavens. They soared among the clouds, floating in a timeless, star-spangled world where only the two of them existed and pleasure knew no bounds.

It was aeons later when Matt at last shifted, pillowing her head on his shoulder and pulling the blankets over their cooling bodies. Sleep stole sweetly over them, while the moon reigned supreme in the night sky.

Jade was helping Matt break down the tent and fold it prior to strapping it to the side of the wagon. Every now and then, she would stop and tug the front of her dress away from her body, grumbling loudly, while Matt watched with a huge grin.

"Go ahead and laugh, ye big buzzard!" she said. "If I get attacked by bees today, it'll be yer fault. I've washed three times, and I still can't get rid o' that sticky mess ye ladled on me. What I wouldn't give for an honest-to-heaven hot bath!"

She was still complaining when Mavis dashed into their camp, her face aglow with excitement, pulling Thomas hurriedly along beside her. "Thank goodness I caught you before you had everything packed," she declared.

"Why?" Jade asked.

Simultaneously, Matt questioned, "What's going on?"

Mavis answered with a smile as wide as all outdoors. "We want to adopt one of your orphans. Thomas and Hannah and I have discussed it, and we truly want to do this."

Jade was speechless. Matt was not. "Which one of the youngsters did you have in mind?"

"Well, Thomas won't come right out and say so, but I'm sure he'd prefer a boy."

Thomas nodded. "A man can't have too many sons, so they say."

"It seems you have a choice between Zach or the twins, then," Matt said.

"As cute as the baby is, I'd just as soon have an older child," Mavis confessed. "Infants still scare me some."

"Then ye'll have to take both the twins," Jade told her friend. "Matt and I would hate to see Harry and Larry torn from each other, especially after losin' the rest o' their family the way they did."

Mavis turned beseeching brown eyes toward Thomas, and he melted like butter in the warm sun. "Woman, when you look at me like that, I'd fetch you a rainbow if I could."

Matt laughed in sympathy. "I know the feeling well."

Mavis clapped her hands in joy. "We can do it, then? We can take both of them?"

Thomas nodded again, almost knocking his nose into the top of Mavis's head as she leaped toward him and twined her arms about his neck. "Oh, just wait until you see them, Thomas. They're absolutely darling! Mirror images of each other! You're going to be such a proud papa!"

"I saw them last night," he reminded her. "Of course, their faces were smeared with ice cream at the time, so I didn't really get a proper look at them, but they appeared to be a handsome set nonetheless."

He peeled his exuberant wife from his neck and glanced around, trying to spot the boys. "Where are they now? We'd like to take them and their belongings with us right away, if you wouldn't mind."

"I'll fetch them," Matt volunteered. "They're helping Jordan hitch the teams to the other wagons." He turned to Jade. "Why don't you gather their things, sweetheart? It's almost time to break camp."

Jade was suddenly assailed with second thoughts. Her doubts registered clearly on her expressive face.

Mavis was having none of this. "Now, Jade. Don't you even think of changing your mind. I've got my heart set on having a family of my own, and you're not about to rob me of the chance. I'll look after those two like they were my own, and I'll be a good, loving mother to them."

"I know ye will, Mavis. And I know Tom will be a good father, too. It's just that I'm gonna miss 'em somethin' fierce!" Another realization struck her hard. "I'm gonna miss you even worse!" she exclaimed on a sob.

"Oh, I'm gonna miss you, too!" Mavis wailed.

In the next second, the two women were clinging to each other, their tears falling freely. Poor Tom stood by, looking distinctly uncomfortable and helpless. This was how Matt found them when he returned with the twins.

"What's all this?" he inquired, though he was fairly sure he knew.

The women parted, each swiping at her wet face. "Who was it said 'partings are such sweet sorrow'?" Mavis said, sniffing.

"I believe it was William Shakespeare," Matt offered.

"Well, he's a danged fool," Jade mumbled, searching her pocket for her handkerchief. "There's nothin' sweet about 'em."

Short minutes later, Jade watched forlornly as the twins trotted off with Mavis and Tom, chattering like magpies. She sighed heavily as Matt's arm closed over her slumped shoulders, cuddling her close. "How do ye like that? They've practically forgotten me already."

"They'll remember. At least for a while," he consoled.

She turned a wan smile on him. "I reckon it's better that they're leavin' with smiles instead o' tears. I want them to be happy."

"They will be. Mavis will see to that," he assured her.

"Hmph!" Jade gave an unladylike snort. "She'll have those two spoiled rotten inside of a week!"

"Just like you did," he concurred, nudging her toward the wagon.

"Mark me words, Matt. Those two are gonna lead her a merry chase." She was still bending his ear, making all sorts of predictions, as the wagon train rolled out, every turn of the wheels taking them that much closer to Oregon.

Chapter 33

In comparison to the rest of the Oregon Trail, the Lander Road was relatively new, having been in use for only the past eight years. Also, it was the only section of the route that had been surveyed and constructed by the government for the benefit of those emigrants heading westward. This cutoff was a vast improvement over the older route, which led down to Fort Bridger and then north again to Soda Springs. The Lander Road cut almost straight west, saving approximately one hundred dreary miles of travel and offering a much improved route, with good grass and water along the way, as well as some timber. It did, however, take the wayfarers through a larger portion of the Rocky Mountains, and it was therefore fortunate that the road had been carefully charted.

Late afternoon of the second day found them camped along the Little Sandy Creek in a place called Antelope Meadow. The surrounding scenery was nothing short of spectacular. The meadow itself was lush with thick grass for grazing and summer wildflowers of every imaginable color, while to the northeast the Wind River Mountains provided a magnificent backdrop to this verdant valley.

Here, the men decided to try their luck at hunting. Despite his healing leg, and over Jade's objections, Matt would not be left behind. He saddled his horse, hauled himself awkwardly atop his mount, and rode off with the other hunters. Two hours later, he returned, tired but triumphant, having successfully shot one of the four antelope the men brought back with them.

The fresh venison was evenly distributed among the wagons, and was much appreciated by everyone. So was the nearby stand of cedar for fuel. It was a pleasant change to cook with decent wood again—and to have abundant game.

Still, as mellow as Jade felt, with her stomach full and her spirits reviving, she could not help but berate Matt for his foolhardy behavior. "Ye know Doc Worley told ye to take it easy with that leg for the next couple of weeks yet. And what do ye do, first chance ye get, but ride off on that horse o' yers!"

Matt grinned and resisted the urge to rub his aching limb. "Do you know how cute you are, standing there frowning at me with your hands on your hips?" he countered smoothly.

"Hmph! Did ye come across another Blarney stone out there, Matt Richards? Or do ye simply think I'm daft enough to swallow all yer sweet talk and forget what a risk ye took today?"

"Oh, for pity's sake, Jade. Stop treating me like an invalid—or an infant. I'm a grown man, and perfectly capable of deciding what is and isn't good for me. My leg is almost healed, and a little healthy activity isn't going to harm me."

"A good whack aside the noggin' with me rollin' pin might," Jade warned, glowering at him. "It might also serve to knock a wee bit o' sense back into yer head."

Matt stared back at her, his eyes twinkling. "Are you threatening me, dear heart?" he asked with some amusement.

Jade's lower lip protruded in a pout. "What if I am?"

"Well, it's rather like a mosquito taking on an elephant, don't you think? Aside from that, try swinging your puny weapon at me, and your pretty little backside is sure to pay for such rash imprudence."

"B'fore or after ye finish seein' stars?" she quipped.

He shook his head at her. "That sassy mouth is bound and determined to get you into trouble, isn't it? A good dose of soap might cure it. Shall we find out?"

"Ye wouldn't dare!"

One dark brow rose. "Wouldn't I?" he inquired softly. "Seems to me my hand has smacked your bottom before," he reminded her. "A bit of soap between your teeth shouldn't present much of a problem. Except that you could be blowing bubbles for a few days to come."

Though his tone remained mild, Jade saw the challenge lurking in those blue eyes. Prudently, she decided to back down. "All right. I'll stop naggin' at ye about yer leg, but if ye injure it again through some foolishness, don't come to me for comfort."

"Oh, I'll be very careful," he assured her with a devilish smile. "I want to be able to chase you with that cake of soap one of these fine days."

The terrain, though breathtakingly beautiful, grew steadily rougher. They had crossed the continental divide, but still had a large section of mountains to traverse. Once again, they encountered grave markers of those unfortunate pioneers who had succumbed to the trials of the trail. So far the emigrants could consider themselves fortunate not to have met with more numerous disasters and to have lost relatively few lives from among their own party. Of course, they still had several hundred miles of trail ahead of them, including the lengthy trek along the Snake River and through the Blue Mountains and the Cascades in Oregon.

By the time they reached Pine Canyon, the estimated halfway point along the Lander Road, they had been on the cutoff for over a week, averaging about thirteen miles per day. Though this pace was somewhat slower than their passage through the plains, it was adequate to the rigors of the trail and a good deal faster than they would have gone had they traveled south to Fort Bridger. The emigrants were well pleased.

Fort Piney—or Piney Fort, as it was sometimes called—was not a fort at all. Rather, it was a small log structure that had operated as a supply depot for the crews that had originally constructed the Lander Road. It had long been abandoned, and now served only as a convenient camping spot. The old corral was still intact, however, which offered the wayfarers a handy place in which to safely pen their animals. Not to have the beasts tethered so near to the wagons and tents, or in the open where they might stampede or be stolen by Indians, was a welcome novelty.

Here, in this lush, peaceful region, tragedy struck again. The emigrants had taken this day to hunt, replenish their wood supplies, repair their wagons, and rest their teams. Taking advantage of the opportunity at hand, the women were washing their laundry in the clear, cool stream, laughing and gossiping and thoroughly enjoying the brief respite from the road.

Suddenly the sharp, piercing cry of a baby rent the air. No mere whimper, this was the steady, frightened shrieking of an infant in severe distress. One and all, the women abandoned their laundry and went running toward the sound. Similarly alerted, several men, Matt among them, came bounding from the campsite, rifles in hand. All arrived to witness the same horrible sight.

There, his cradle securely wedged in the mossy nook of a pile of boulders, where his mother had placed him not fifteen minutes before, lay little Andy Landford. Next to him, striking repeatedly and viciously, was a large diamondback rattlesnake. The poor infant's face was already turning blue, his wails reduced to pitiful moans, his tiny limbs twitching erratically.

One look, and Peg Landford let loose a frantic scream and lurched forward, intent on rescuing her child regardless of the danger to herself. Reflexively, Jade threw out her arms, blocking the woman's way, while two other ladies grabbed Peg's arms and held her back. The young mother fought them, thrashing with all the strength of a demented animal, but they held tight.

The men acted as quickly as possible, though there was some rapid debate among them.

"Where's Jordan Richards?" one fellow asked.

"Off hunting," Matt answered briskly.

"Damn! He's our best marksman!"

"Let Matt do it," another suggested. "He's nigh as good."

Matt wanted to refuse, afraid of shooting the baby while aiming for the snake. Yet how could he decline? Poor Peg was almost out of her mind, and that damned snake was still sinking its long, lethal fangs into her son! With no time to weigh alternatives, Matt raised his rifle and carefully sighted down the barrel. One swift breath to steady his aim. A simple one-word prayer. One abrupt pull on the trigger, and the resultant blast.

Relief flooded Matt's being as he saw the rattler's head, raised in midair for yet another savage strike, burst from its body. His shot had been true, hitting the snake and missing the child. Not that it would have made much difference in the end. Little Andy was sure to die—was even now scarcely breathing as his hysterical mother rushed to gather him to her bosom.

Stepping quietly to Matt's side, Jade crept her arms about his waist. Tears glistened on her pale cheeks. "Even with yer fine shootin', there's no hope for him, is there?" she said, echoing Matt's own sad thoughts.

"I'm afraid not."

Though other members of their party had previously been bitten by rattlers along the trail and had survived with nothing more than a few hours of fearful discomfort, Andy was much younger and smaller than the others. He had also been bitten numerous times, and in several very vital areas. His throat and chest had been punctured, the deadly venom undoubtedly going straight to his tiny, madly pumping heart.

Andy died in his mother's arms a few minutes later. Jack Landford, his father, returned from the hunting expedition to the sorrowful news of his son's terrible death. The baby was buried the following morning. Distraught with grief and guilt, Peg had sat rocking Andy's stiffened body the night through, and it was all Jack could do to pry the tiny, blanket-clad form from her unwilling arms and place it in the small, forlorn grave.

The sight of these two mourning parents putting their beloved babe to his final rest brought tears to many an eye and pain to many a heart. They left Piney Fort woefully, each of them praying that they would make it to Oregon without having to share such sorrow too many times more along the route.

Three days later, Jack Landford approached Jade and Matt with an earnest request. "I'd like to adopt your baby boy."

Jade's heart gave an awful twinge. "Zach?"

Jack nodded, his eyes, ringed with dark circles, mute testament to his anguish.

"Have you thought this through carefully?" Matt questioned. "I wouldn't want you to rush into anything only to regret it later, once you've had time for your grief to ease and your mind to clear."

Tears swam in Jack's eyes. "If you could see the way Peg clutches Andy's toys, how she endlessly strokes his clothes, how she sobs even in her sleep, you wouldn't need to ask, Reverend. She needs a babe to fill her empty arms."

"You're both young. There's plenty of time ahead for you to have more children of your own," Matt told him kindly.

"Yes, but Peg needs one now, or I'm afraid she won't get through this."

"What about Zach?" Jade put in quietly. "I wouldn't want ye or yer wife to resent him for takin' yer son's place. He means too much to us, and it would break me heart to see that happen."

Jack turned his sorrowful gaze toward her. "I swear to you, on my son's grave, that I'll treat that child with all the care and affection I would have given to Andy. So will Peg. She adores children, and it's tearing her soul apart not to have her baby to love. I . . . I'm afraid she'll come unhinged soon if she doesn't have another to fill the gaping hole his death has left in our lives."

Matt understood the man's reasoning, though he, too, hated to part with Zach. Zach was about the same age as Andy, and if Peg was willing to accept him, the baby might ease her terrible loss and the pain she was feeling.

"Have you talked with your wife about adopting Zach?" he asked.

Jack shook his head. "No. I wanted to discuss it with you first, but I'm sure she'll agree."

Matt sighed, reaching for Jade's hand, offering his strength to her. "Why don't we take Zach to Peg and see how she reacts to him?"

Reluctantly, her own heart aching, Jade rose to fetch the infant boy who had become like her own son in these past months. Parting with him would be one of the most difficult things she'd ever had to do, and she was being asked to do it voluntarily. Every stride that took Jade toward the Landford wagon seemed like a step toward the gallows. She wanted to turn tail and run. Had it not been for Matt gently urging her along, supporting her with his love, she might have done just that.

But when she saw Peg Landford sitting listlessly inside her tent, her eyes dull and heavy with grief, her hair lying lank about her slumped shoulders, pity welled up in Jade. This poor, helpless woman had offered her own sympathy when Skeeter was lost, and now Jade was being given the opportunity to return the kindness, if only she could.

Silently, gently, blinking back her own tears, Jade knelt and placed Zach into the other woman's arms. For a moment Peg just sat there, her arms limp and unresponsive. Then, slowly, her hold tightened about the warm, wriggling bundle. Her red-rimmed gaze lowered to the small face below hers, to the dark head nestled at her bosom. Tears rolled down her cheeks, and she bent to brush trembling lips against the baby's soft, downy hair.

An anguished sigh escaped. "Oh, God! How I've missed this!" she sobbed.

"His name is Zach," Jade said in a quivering voice. "He's yers, if ye want him . . . if ye promise to love him always."

A shaky smile etched Peg's mouth. "Yes," she breathed in hopeful disbelief. "Oh, yes! I'll thank God and you every day for him." Her yearning gaze finally rose to meet Jade's. "Please . . . please let me keep him."

Jade nodded, a sob caught in her throat. She swallowed hard. "Can I come visit him now and then?" she managed to choke out. "I'm gonna miss him so much. Even knowin' ye'll take good care o' him, 'tis hard givin' him up like this."

As the men watched, the two women shared a look of mutual need and understanding. "I know," Peg whispered, nodding. "I know."

That night, Jade cried herself to sleep in Matt's comforting embrace. His big hand stroked her hair, offering solace. His lips caressed her troubled brow.

"I wish I could promise that it will get easier to let them go," he told her, "but I'm afraid that's not going to be the way it works. We're bound to become attached to them and to ache when they leave us."

"I don't know how many more times I can go through this," she sniffed. "Why couldn't ye be a blacksmith, or a horse trader, or a farmer? Anything else."

"I can only be what God wills, sweetheart."

"Ye're a preacher. Ain't that enough?"

He sighed, pulling her nearer. "Evidently not. He keeps bringing these orphans to my door, and as long as He does I have to take them in and try to find homes for them. I can't turn my back on them, or the task God has set before me."

"Well, He didn't have to rope me into yer bargain, did He?" she complained irritably.

Matt chuckled and kissed her red nose. "I'm afraid so, darling," he commiserated, his tone sympathetic. "He brought you to my attention, too, and made you so tempting, so irresistible, that I could do nothing less than lose my heart to you."

"All part o' His grand plan for the two o' us?" she asked skeptically.

"Yes, and I'll be eternally grateful."

Jade snuggled close, her long wet lashes brushing his broad chest with her salty tears. "I love ye, Matt, with all me heart, but bein' yer wife sure hurts somethin' fierce sometimes."

❧❧❧ *Chapter 34* ❧❧❧

*T*he rugged mountains, the rocky canyons, the thick stands of timber, and the lush meadows with their swiftly singing streams were beautiful beyond description. More than one emigrant sighed wistfully in passing, wishing the area was not quite so uninhabited, for it would have been a wondrous place to homestead if only a fort, or a town, or some sort of civilization were nearby. As it was now, the nearest supply point or trading post was, regrettably, too far to make settling here feasible.

Their next major stop after Fort Piney was a place called Soda Springs. The area was liberally sprinkled with numerous natural hot mineral springs, some bearing appropriate names. Naturally, there was Soda Spring, where the bubbling water was strong enough to bring bread dough to an amazingly rapid rise. And Beer Spring, where the sulfur-laced water tasted similar to beer. Old mountaineers had claimed one could literally get drunk on the water. Of course, since men of this ilk were given to grand exaggeration, this statement had to be taken with a grain of salt—or soda, in this case, perhaps.

Hooper Spring was large enough to swim in, and many of the trail-smudged emigrants took full advantage of this opportunity to submerge their aching bodies in the warm mineral water. A few declined, preferring their own stench to that of the water. No one even suggested washing their clothing here.

Last, but not least, there was Steamboat Spring, with its fascinating geyser that sprang up recurrently. Each time it erupted, a nearby hole emitted a loud sound, like that of a steamboat whistle. An oft-repeated tale told of a group of pioneers who had stopped there in 1852. One man among them had made a sporting wager with his fun-loving fellows that he could stop the geyser by sitting on it. Though he gave it his best effort, with the aid of his friends, who tried heartily to help hold him down, the chap was bounced about like a cork until he finally had to give up the attempt. The geyser was simply too strong to suppress, though it had certainly afforded them much amusement to try.

It was at this juncture that the emigrants connected with the Hudspeth Cutoff, which headed west to the Raft River. A hard day's travel along this alternate route, which saved them twenty-five miles compared to the older trail, brought them to yet another mineral spring.

Before being discovered by passing pioneers, Lava Hot Springs, which seemed to spew out of the lava rocks at the base of an immense cliff on the Portneuf River, had long been a favored campsite of the Bannock and Shoshone Indians. These local tribes, though often peaceful when approached with a friendly attitude, were unpredictable, and had been known to attack without provocation. Thus, it was with extreme caution that the emigrants now stopped for the night, posting twice the number of sentries around the camp.

Lava Hot Springs offered waters much warmer than those at Soda Springs. Here, the water temperature was more that of a hot bathtub. It was so inviting that even the possibility of Indians in the area was not enough to deter these weary wayfarers, none of whom had soaked in a steaming tub since the outset of this long, exhausting journey. Luckily for Matt, their arrival coincided with the date the Mormon doctor had said he could finally remove his splints and bandages. He did so eagerly, able to submerge fully in water for the first time in weeks and take advantage of the spring's therapeutic effects.

The ladies were particularly thrilled at the prospect of relaxing in the hot mineral waters. With little delay, they gathered soap, towels, and children, and headed, en masse, to the springs. Recalling her embarrassment at Alcove Spring, so many weeks past, Jade was now more modest in her behavior. She entered the water still clad in her chemise, while Bliss and Lizette shucked down to their bare skin again, mocking Jade for bowing to protocol.

"If God had meant for us to bathe in our clothes, He would have created us with fur or feathers or somethin'," Bliss announced.

"Besides, just see how well zat chemise covers you, *cherie*." Lizette pointed out. "Once wet, it hides notzing."

Her friends were right. Jade's chemise was clinging to her like a second skin, outlining her petite form so faithfully that her erect nipples were clearly visible, as was the triangular patch at the juncture of her thighs. Still, she shook her head and told them, "As ridiculous as it seems, I'll do it if it means savin' Matt shame on me behalf. These ladies are just startin' to accept me, and I don't want to ruin everything now."

"If they had half the brains God gave a goose, they'd realize that it's not what you're wearin', or not wearin', that makes you a good person. It's what's inside that counts. Your compassion. Your quick mind. And your givin' nature."

Jade shrugged. "Not everyone is as discernin' as you are, Bliss. Or you, Lizette. It takes some a mite longer to look to the heart of things."

"And some never see," Bliss reminded her.

"While ozers perceive only what zey want to," Lizette added.

"Well, today they'll be viewin' me chemise—and whatever else shows through," Jade insisted. "At least this time Ike and Skeeter won't be spyin' through the bushes at us, catchin' us buck naked."

At her mention of Skeeter, Jade's joy abruptly ebbed. Two fat tears crept down her cheeks. "Lord, am I ever gonna stop missin' that wee lad?" she wondered on a sorrowful sigh.

* * *

It felt as if she'd just gotten to sleep, and now Matt was shaking her shoulder, telling her to wake up. Jade gave a sleepy groan and slowly raised one eyelid. The tent was still pitch-black, so dark that she could barely see Matt as he leaned over her. There wasn't even a hint of coming daylight around the edges of the canvas shelter.

"What . . ." She yawned. "What do ye want? What time is it?"

"Shhh!" Matt placed a finger over her lips in warning. "Don't wake the girls." Emily and Beth were snoring softly on the other side of the blanket.

He yanked the quilt down to Jade's feet, grabbed for her hand, and tugged. "Come with me."

"Where?"

"You'll see. You can bring the quilt if you want. Wrap it around you, but be careful not to trip on the ends."

"Dang it all, Matt," she grumbled, stumbling to her feet and tucking the blanket around her. She followed him out of the tent into the cool night air. "I was sleepin' so sound. This had better be real important."

Under the bright stars, she saw the quick flash of his smile. "I don't know how important it is, but it will definitely be worth your while. Now hush. We don't want to rouse the rest of the camp."

"Yeah," she muttered, "I noticed they're all still abed, which is exactly where we should be at this asinine hour."

As they wound their way past the wagons and tents, Matt pulled her along behind him, his long strides now unhindered by bandages and splints, with scarcely even a limp to remind him of his injury. At the north end of the camp, Jordan appeared so suddenly before them that Jade let loose a choked yelp of surprise, quickly stifled as Matt's hand closed over her mouth.

"All clear," Jordan told his brother. "I'll stand guard, as we'd planned. One hour. Then you have to relieve me."

Matt nodded. "Give a whistle if anyone happens by."

Jordan chuckled. "Better yet, I'll give them a rap on the head with the butt of my rifle, and they'll be none the wiser till morning."

Thoroughly confused, and more than a little miffed, Jade yanked Matt's hand from her mouth. "What sort o' shenanigans are the two o' ye schemin'?"

"The best sort," Matt answered cryptically as he strode forward, towing her with him.

A minute or two later, he stopped. Only then did Jade realize that he had halted at the edge of the hot spring. Before she could ask what he intended, he was tugging the blanket away and swiftly drawing her gown up over her head. In the next second she was stark naked, draped only in starlight.

With a gentle nudge, he aimed her toward the pool. "Climb in. I'm right behind you, as soon as I can rid myself of my own clothes."

"I . . . I already had me bath," she stammered stupidly.

"So did I. We're not here to get clean, sweetheart," he informed her with a soft laugh.

"What are we here for, then?"

"To play, love. Like a pair of frisky otters."

He slid into the steaming water at her side and promptly pulled her to him. "Can you swim?" he asked, grinning.

"No. That's why I hate makin' those river crossin's when the water's so high."

He shrugged. "No matter. I'll have hold of you."

Without warning, he began backing deeper into the pool. Jade sucked in a fearful breath. "Matt? Stop. Ye're scarin' me."

"Just relax, love. Put your arms around my neck. No, don't squeeze the life out of me, darling. Just hang on lightly and float along with me. Trust me. I won't let you drown."

As frightened as she was, it took an extreme act of faith, but once she had placed herself in his capable hands and allowed herself to relax a bit, Jade had to admit that the water felt wonderful as it skimmed along her naked flesh.

"This is like . . . like flyin' maybe, only in the water. I feel so light. So free," she marveled.

He twirled her in a slow circle, and she laughed with delight, her long, drenched tresses fanning out around her shoulders like the unfolding feathers of a peacock.

They frolicked for a short while. Then Matt led her toward the shallows, stopping when the water lapped at the upper slopes of her breasts.

"Wrap your legs around me, Aggie girl," he told her, the twinkle in his eyes rivaling that of the stars overhead. As she did, he hoisted her higher, until her legs twined about his waist, her feet locking at the small of his back. His air-cooled mouth sought her breast through the heavy satin veil of her hair. At the first touch of his lips, a delicious tingle arrowed through her. With the night breeze teasing at one damp, dimpled crest, and Matt suckling at the other, her pleasure was quickly doubled, the desire twofold as it sizzled a molten path from her breasts to her womb.

His mouth left her breast, his tongue painting intricate patterns across her chest, over her shoulder, up the slender column of her neck. "Wet as you are, with your hair streaming down about you, you remind me of a sleek, graceful swan," he murmured.

Then his lips claimed hers in a kiss so full of love and yearning that Jade lost all sense of time and place. All she could feel, all she could want, was him. His mouth on hers. His tongue tangling with her own. His hands, warm and caressing on her bare back. She melted into him, abandoning herself completely to the web of enchantment he was swiftly weaving about them both. Matching his intense desire. Building upon it. Adding her own sensual magic to his.

Her slippery limbs slid along his, and she wriggled to regain her grasp on him. Something smooth and warm grazed her thigh. With a gasp, she tightened her hold, her eyes popping wide. "Matt? Are there fish in here?" she asked anxiously.

His curious gaze met hers. "Not unless they're cooked. Why?"

"Something just brushed me leg," she whispered, swallowing hard. On a shiver, she added, "I hope it wasn't a snake."

He threw back his head and laughed. "Not the sort of snake you're worried about, I assure you." Shifting her in his arms, he rubbed against her, and she felt the sensation again. "That's me you're feeling, sweetheart. I'm the only serpent seeking a taste of your sweet, delicate flesh."

She heaved a fervent sigh of relief. "I'm glad."

Again he chuckled. "You should be. You're going to be. So am I."

Ever so easily, he let her slip downward, his hands guiding her descent. His body sought entry. Hers yielded. Inch by tantalizing inch, she felt herself become impaled upon his rigid staff, until she had taken all he had to give.

"What do you think of snakes now, my dear?" he teased, his voice deepened with his growing desire.

"I adore yers," she admitted on a silken purr.

"I thought you might, especially when he demonstrates his finest talents."

"And what might those be, sir?" she bantered back, batting her long water-spiked lashes at him.

His smile was pure, proud male. "Pleasing you. Filling you. Writhing within your tight, slick chamber. Stroking until you melt with passion and shower him with your hot, sweet essence."

Matt's words were having the most erotic effect on her. Then he began to move, lifting her, shifting his hips, driving into her with his pulsing power. The heavens seemed to tilt above her, the stars to swirl faster and faster, her blood to pound heavier and harder. The first wave of rapture swept over her, dragging her under, only to toss her upward once more, to be swamped again and again in an overwhelming tide of ecstasy. And all the while, Matt was riding the churning swells with her, his passion feeding on hers, hers on his, until both were joyously drowning in a whirlpool of splendor. Gradually they drifted to the edge of the eddy, clinging limply, breathless with bliss.

A while later, as they were lazily donning their clothing, Jade asked inquisitively, "How many different ways are there to make love, I wonder?"

Matt shook his head and grinned. "I have no idea, sweetheart, but we have the rest of our lives to find out."

❧❧❧ *Chapter 35* ❧❧❧

On the fourth day out of Lava Hot Springs, the wagon train arrived at the Raft River, and a final parting of the ways. Here, the California-bound emigrants would break off, heading southwest. The remaining group would take a northwestern track, up to the Snake River and on into Oregon Territory.

Once more, they were parting with friends and fellow travelers. Again, Jade was losing someone dear to her. Lizette had decided to go to San Francisco with John Halin. She was also trying to convince Bliss to go along.

If Jade was upset, Bliss was in an absolute quandary. The young woman was torn, her loyalties pulling her both ways at once. Going with Lizette meant sticking to at least part of their original plan. In San Francisco they would start up a gambling and dance hall, much as they had previously decided. However, if she chose Oregon, Bliss would be on her own if she wanted to initiate a similar establishment. That, or throw in with a pleasure palace already run by someone else, which she did not particularly want to do. Vera had been a rare jewel, and the chances of working for another madam who was just as generous were next to nil.

Yet another cause, more powerful and twice as risky, drew Bliss toward Oregon. Jordan. If only she knew the extent of his feelings toward her, it might help decide her course. Her own emotions were not in question in this area. Without a doubt, Bliss knew that she was irrevocably in love with the handsome gunslinger. If he but said the word, she would gladly follow him to the ends of the earth. But, thus far, Jordan had remained mute on matters of the heart. What was she to do? Certainly, she couldn't just march up to him and ask him point-blank what his intentions were toward her!

Bliss couldn't. But Jade could—and did. Without Bliss's knowledge or consent, or Matt's, Jade managed to corner Jordan alone. "I need to speak with ye," she announced in a firm, no-nonsense tone. " 'Tis about Bliss."

One dark brow rose, amusement lurking in those blue eyes, which were so like Matt's. "Oh?" he drawled. "What about her?"

"I need to know if ye're just toyin' with her affections or if ye might be harborin' some sincere feelin's toward her," she told him bluntly.

A slight smile curved his lips as he stared down at her. "Being married to my brother does not give you license to pry into my private affairs, Jade."

She countered swiftly. "Bein' related to me husband didn't give you cause to stick yer nose into mine and Matt's, either. But I seem to recall a mornin' back on the Platte when I stepped from me tent to find ye lurkin' at me campfire like a vulture about to pounce if I didn't measure up to yer likin'," she reminded him, her very stance, with her hands resting on her hips, issuing a bold challenge.

Jordan laughed and doffed his hat in acknowledgment of her assessment. "*Touché*, madam," he intoned with a smirk.

"Well?" she dared. "Are ye gonna answer me question or not? Ye do know that Lizette is tryin' to talk Bliss into goin' to California with her, don't ye? And poor Bliss doesn't know which way to turn."

"Did she send you to conduct this inquisition?" Jordan asked, frowning.

"No, and she'd likely rip a strip off me hide if she knew I was doin' it. But she's me best friend, and I want to help her in any way I can. If comin' to Oregon with us is only gonna bring her heartbreak, I'd rather see her go with Lizette and stand some chance o' happiness, though it'll nigh break me heart to see her leave. Now, I've made me own opinions clear enough. The question is, how do you feel?"

Jordan shook his head, one hand rising to rub at the back of his neck. "I honestly don't know, Jade. Certainly, I don't want to hurt Bliss, but I'm just not sure what I feel for her right now. Or what the future might hold in store for me." He shrugged again. "Who knows but that I might get to Oregon and decide I hate the place?"

"I'm not talkin' about Oregon. I'm talkin' about Bliss."

"I realize that, but it's not all that simple. My life's sort of up in the air right now. I have no idea what I'll be doing six months or a year from now, or where I might be. Given that, how can I assess a prospective relationship with any woman?"

Jade leveled her keen green eyes at him. "Tell me this, Jordan. How would ye react if Bliss took off for San Francisco and ye never saw her again?"

"I'd miss her. I suspect she'd linger in my mind for a long time, and I'd think of her often. Fondly. With warm memories of our time together."

Jade resisted the urge to roll her eyes at his typically male response. Lord save the world from men who either didn't know how to, or didn't want to, express their feelings openly for fear of ridicule. "Would it bother ye at all to think of her with other men?" she persisted.

His frown deepened, his eyes darkening to a stormy hue. He was silent for a long moment, then finally he said, "Yeah. I reckon it would. While I'd want her to be happy, I wouldn't want to imagine her bestowing her affections on someone else."

"Then go tell her that, ye big galoot!" Jade insisted. She poked a finger into his chest. "Give the lass some notion o' what's goin' on in there!"

"How can I, when I'm not sure myself how deeply my feelings for her run? I don't want to build false hope, only to disappoint her later."

"Then ye'd best go kiss her good-bye," Jade told him firmly. "If ye can't grant her somethin' to hang on to, some wee reason to stay with ye, then let her go find someone else who can. And if ye do let her slip through yer fingers, don't say I didn't warn ye when ye discover ye've made the worst mistake o' yer life."

Jade never did find out what Jordan said to Bliss, but when the train split to take separate paths, Bliss chose to remain with those bound for Oregon. When Jade hesitantly asked her friend why she had decided as she had, Bliss's wistful gaze strayed toward Jordan. "Stupidity, most likely," she retorted wryly. Then she shrugged. "Well, if things don't work out like I want, I suppose I can always go into the bakery business with Tilda." She laughed. "Buns are buns, any way you care to butter them, I reckon."

The Snake River was unlike any they had encountered thus far. The trail itself lay along the southern rim of a high slope, while the turbulent river ran through the deep gorge below. In many places the water was totally inaccessible. In those spots where the descent was less perilous, the emigrants clambered down the steep, rocky banks, gathered what they could, and labored back up the sharp grade with their precious burden. Often, by the time they reached the top, a good deal of the water had been spilled in the effort, but in this dry, sun-baked region both man and beast needed every ounce of this life-sustaining fluid they could obtain.

The oxen had a hard time of it along this section, for the trail rode overtop an ancient lava bed. Not only was it difficult for the animals to pull the wagons over the rigid, rough surface, but the lava tore mercilessly at their hooves. Having been forewarned, the emigrants had stored extra rawhide in their supplies. This they tore into squares which they wrapped around the beasts' hooves to cushion them against the rocky terrain. If a hoof was split, ointment was applied inside the rawhide, and with luck, in a few days the rift healed.

The wagons fared little better than the animals. Under the continual jarring, wheels and axles, tongues and reaches snapped like dry kindling. By now repairs were nothing new to the roadwise wayfarers, but it sometimes seemed they spent more time mending their broken equipment than they did traveling toward their destination.

The Richards party was now reduced to two wagons, since Lizette had taken one with her. Once more the girls had divided their dwindling possessions, each taking those furnishings she wanted most. The remainder, the heavier and most frivolous items, had been discarded along the way. The extra oxen, those used as replacements and for double-teaming when necessary, were separated into three lots, the end result gaining Matt and Jordan two additional draft animals each.

In this final allotment, Bliss had acquired, at Jordan's request, one full case of whiskey, while Lizette took the rest on to California. Jade and Matt gained another bed for their orphanage, but it was the big copper bathtub that Jade had insisted upon keeping for herself.

"I know 'tis a luxury, and a right heavy one at that, but I'll carry the blasted thing meself, like a tortoise, b'fore I leave it b'hind for some Indian to use for boilin' his dratted moccasins."

The men finally gave up trying to dissuade her and set about evenly distributing the weight of their combined goods between their two wagons, the better to save wear and tear on the wagons and the teams.

"That's one stubborn woman you have there," Jordan grumbled. "When she sets her mind to something, there's no getting around her."

Matt just grinned. "You have to use the right persuasion, brother. Haven't you learned that yet?"

"If you're so damned smart, then why the hell are we still stuck hauling that tub with us?" Jordan retorted.

"Because I've taken a fancy to the thing myself," Matt replied with a wink. "It looks big enough for two, wouldn't you say?"

Matt couldn't pinpoint exactly when he first became aware that their wagon train had gained an unwanted escort, but just about the same time, others became alert to the fact as well.

"We've got company," Jordan commented with a tight-lipped look, his eyes scanning the sparse treeline perhaps half a mile to the left of the long line of wagons. He'd left Bliss in charge of the lead wagon and walked back to speak with his brother.

Matt nodded grimly. "I know. How long do you figure they've been following us?"

"I'd reckon it's been some time before we took note of it. Those Indians can be mighty sneaky when they want to be."

"Why do you suppose they haven't charged us?"

Jordan shook his head. "That's anybody's guess. Maybe they want to barter with us and aren't sure how receptive we'd be to the notion. Or perhaps they simply want to watch and make sure we're only passing through their territory with peaceful intent and no designs on settling here."

Matt glanced around at the barren land and grimaced. "Who in his right mind would want to live in this desolate place?"

"Those Bannock and Shoshone warriors and their families, evidently," Jordan replied. "And I rather suspect they don't want us for neighbors."

For two endless days the Indians continued their surveillance from a distance. It was worrisome to lumber along, feeling their eyes following every movement, and not being able to surmise their intentions. Nerves drew taut. Tempers grew short. And still the savages made no move to attack. At times they would seem to disappear, and the fretful emigrants would hope that they had gone. But in the next mile or so they would again appear, sitting on a rise, mounted on a bluff. Waiting—watching—like silent, malevolent ghosts.

Toward the middle of the third morning, over the ever-present creak of the wagon wheels, shots suddenly rang out toward the rear of the column. Almost immediately, they were followed by a chorus of war whoops that raised the hair on the back of Jade's neck.

With more haste than care, Jade scooped Emily into her arms and tossed her into the back of the wagon. She and Beth tumbled in after her as Matt whipped the oxen to a shuffling trot, the fastest pace they seemed to know. Slowly, too slowly for ease of mind, the wagons formed a wide corral, everyone angling for space and scrambling frantically for their weapons.

The last emigrants, those at the tail end of the train, had the most difficulty joining the protective ring, for they were already under attack. One wagon stood stranded some yards away. Another lost a wheel in the mad dash for safety and toppled onto its side, perilously close to the rim of the canyon. A third crashed headlong through the linking ends of the circle, nearly tipping the wagons on either side as it squeezed into the small gap between them.

As the stunned emigrants took up defensive positions, they watched in horror as the people in the stranded wagons ran for safety. Those farthest from the circle met with immediate disaster. The riled savages swooped down upon them like a pack of ravaging wolves, letting loose a flurry of arrows. Within seconds, the entire family— husband, wife, and two half-grown sons—fell beneath the terrible onslaught.

From the second wagon, a lone, pregnant woman loped awkwardly forward, her arms wrapped across her bulging stomach, a pistol clutched tightly in one hand. Those watching from the relative safety of the corralled wagons tried their best to cover her flight by offering heavy fire at those warriors closest to her. One brave made it through the barrage of bullets. As his horse came even with her, the lady never broke her stumbling stride. She simply aimed her gun at him, fired, and kept running. Miraculously, she staggered through the protective barrier just ahead of two more advancing warriors, her escape aided as fellow emigrants dashed out to grab hold of her while others promptly dispatched her attackers.

Jordan half dragged, half carried Gwen O'Neall into

the shelter of the inner circle. There, he quickly turned his pregnant burden over to Jade and Bliss and hurried back to his post and the ongoing battle. For some minutes, Gwen was unaware of the identities of those who were ministering to her. Finally, as her shocked mind began to function once more, she reared back and nearly knocked the cup of water from Jade's hands.

"Get away from me, you hussy!" she hissed, though it cost her precious breath she was only now beginning to regain after her frantic sprint from her overturned wagon.

"Well, if that ain't a fine way to talk to someone who's tryin' to help you!" Bliss declared in exasperation. As Gwen began to cough, Bliss administered a sound whack to the woman's back.

"Bliss! Have a bit o' care, will ye?" Jade objected. "The lady's trying to get her air, and ye're knockin' it out o' her again."

Bliss smirked. "Sorry."

The spasm passed, and Jade again offered Gwen the water. "Have a wee sip to clear yer throat."

"What makes you think I'd accept help from the woman who was my husband's whore?" Gwen spat out hatefully.

As Jade knelt there, at a loss for words, Bliss again took up her defense. "Now look here, you spiteful bitch! Jade fell for that Irish bastard's line o' bullshit much the same as you did. From what I hear, he's damned good at spreadin' it on so thick and smooth that you're mired in it up to your neck before you know what's hit you. Jade believed him when he claimed he wanted to marry her, and she paid for his deceit with her innocence. And after he got what he wanted from her, he stole every cent she had and left her to starve on the streets of Richmond while he ran off to search for a rich American wife. That's what sort of low-down, belly-crawlin' vermin you're married to, and if you didn't know that by now, it's high time you learned it!"

Gwen's face contorted into a grimace. Slowly, her

trembling hands came up to cover her face. "I know full well what Sean is like, and what foul deeds he's capable of. Haven't I lived with him for months now, taking his abuse each and every day of this hellish trip?" she sobbed.

"Then believe me when I tell ye that I wouldn't have that jackal on a silver platter," Jade told her. "I've got me own husband, and a right good one, and I'm not out to steal yers."

Gwen nodded, wiped at her tears, and raised her tormented gaze to meet Jade's. "Maybe not, but Sean has made it abundantly obvious that he still lusts after you. That's not an easy thing to live with."

"Well, with any luck, you might not have to put up with it anymore," Bliss put in. "So far, you're the only one who's made it to safety. That bein' the case, maybe those Indians have solved your problems for you."

Gwen gave a hysterical laugh. "God forgive me, but I hope so! It would only be what Sean deserves, especially since he was the fool who fired that first shot which started this attack today."

Chapter 36

For the moment, the Indians had called a retreat, however brief it might be. They were currently amusing themselves by plundering the two lone wagons while the remaining emigrants watched helplessly from too far away to prevent the looting. During the lull in the fight, the wary pioneers bolstered their makeshift bulwarks, readied their arms and ammunition, and braced for another assault.

It was the waiting that was so wearing on frayed nerves. It was watching powerlessly as the savages set fire to the abandoned wagons and raced their ponies after the half dozen steers that hadn't made it safely into the enclosure of wagons with the rest of the herd. It was listening to their wild whooping and shouting as they celebrated their initial victory.

As time dragged on, tension continued to mount. The adults' anxieties soon transferred themselves to the children, who became more fretful. In an effort to soothe the frightened girls and keep them better occupied, Jade climbed into the wagon and retrieved their dolls for them. Beth simply nodded her thanks and remained silent. Emily clutched her cloth baby and whined, "Gertie's scared, too!"

Reaching into her pocket, Jade withdrew her flute. She blew a few soft notes, demonstrating how it was done, and handed the instrument to Emily. "Here, pumpkin. Play a song for yer baby. Maybe it'll make her feel better."

Emily's efforts were pathetic at best, mere wet whistles that produced little sound. Still, the girls' attention was momentarily diverted from the Indians, and for that Jade was glad.

At length, Emily gave up the effort and handed the flute back to Jade. "You do it, Mama," she requested sweetly. "I can't do it right. The music won't come out."

Jade brought the flute to her lips. Just as she began to play, three notes into the tune, someone shouted "Here they come!"

She was so startled that the next trill of notes emerged from Jade's flute in a piping screech that rivaled the whoops of the approaching Indians.

At that exact moment, the warriors drew their ponies to an abrupt halt midway into their intended strike. For no apparent reason, they began to mill about in confusion, some pointing at the wagons, others gesturing excitedly toward the sky.

"What the heck?" Matt wondered aloud. He called to Jordan who was stationed beneath the next wagon. "What are they doing? Why did they call off the charge?"

"Beats me," Jordan yelled back. "But something sure has them in an uproar. It looks like they're arguing with each other."

Once more, the emigrants waited apprehensively while the natives appeared to conduct a lengthy and lively debate. Emily began to whimper in renewed fright. At his wit's end, Matt grumbled, "Jade, if there is any way possible, please calm that child."

Not knowing what else to do, Jade retrieved her flute. As she did so, the Indians began to advance, more cautiously this time and much more quietly, as if watching for some unknown sign. As the first high, clear notes of Jade's music issued forth, echoing off the canyon walls with eerie resonance, the approaching warriors again reined in their horses so hastily that the ponies reared and shied and stumbled crazily. More excited discussion ensued.

"It's Jade!" Bliss exclaimed in amazement. "It's that blessed flute!"

"Son of a gun!" Jordan shouted. "I think Bliss is right! Whenever Jade starts playing that thing, those Indians stop as if they felt the Devil blowing his hot breath down their necks!"

Matt turned to Jade. "If they come at us again, commence blowing on that flute for all you're worth. And don't stop until I tell you."

Jade nodded, her tongue sweeping out to wet her dry lips, praying that her throat wouldn't close up on her at the crucial moment. Long minutes later, Matt barked. "Now, Jade! Play!"

For one heart-stopping second, she could not recall a single note, let alone a selection worth dying to. Then her mind unlocked and she launched into a rousing rendition of "Yankee Doodle." So fast and furiously did she play that the notes seemed to tumble over each other in rapid succession. The resulting echo from the canyon was absolutely unearthly, sending the warriors into a full-fledged panic.

As the astounded emigrants looked on in disbelief, the Indians spun about and fled as if all the hounds of Hell were snapping at their heels. This time they didn't stop to regroup but kept on going as fast as their befuddled ponies would carry them. In short order, they were out of sight with nothing but a plume of dust left drifting in their wake.

More astonishing perhaps than the swift departure of the superstitious-natured Indians was the sudden reappearance of Sean O'Neall a few minutes later. After having been presumed dead these past hours, he emerged from the rocky gulch as hale and hearty as ever, with only a bit of dirt and a torn sleeve to show for his travail.

Poor Gwen stared at him in dumbfounded dismay. "My God!" she murmured at last. "I seem to be destined to spend eternity bound to that man!"

"He certainly has the luck of the Irish, doesn't he?" Matt observed.

"Hmph! He's charmed a'right!" Jade sniffed. "Like some bad penny that keeps poppin' up when ye least expect it."

Sean had either been thrown clear when his wagon overturned or had climbed into the gorge to escape detection. Jade, and Gwen as well, heartily suspected he had deliberately taken the cowardly route and left his pregnant wife to her own devices. He didn't seem particularly pleased to find Gwen alive when he reached camp, but then, neither was she overjoyed to see him. His primary delight was that he'd been carrying all his money on his person and was still in possession of his ill-gotten wealth.

Of course, the O'Nealls were now destitute of a wagon, as well as all of their belongings and provisions. Had it not been for the fact that Sean would have pestered her mercilessly, and likely driven Matt to murder in the process, Jade would have offered Gwen a place in her own wagon. When she admitted as much, Gwen agreed that it was best to find temporary lodging with one of the other families until they arrived at Boise, where she and Sean could replace most of their lost goods.

"I am grateful for the kind thought, though," she told Jade. Her smile was self-derisive as she added, "Under the circumstances, you are being much more gracious than I could be, and more so than I probably deserve. You're a good person, Jade Richards."

Following that harrowing episode with the Indians, the emigrants had only mild appreciation for the wonders of the river falls they passed along the next few miles. They had too long a trip ahead of them to be spellbound by the same natural forces that were currently plaguing them with lame oxen, broken wagons and worries of Indian attacks.

Along a particularly rough stretch, the rear axle on Matt's and Jade's wagon broke. The cylindrical support simply snapped in the center like a dry fall twig, though it was several inches in diameter, hewn of solid oak, and reinforced with iron at both ends. The accident might not have been so disastrous, except for the fact that they had already used their only remaining spare axle to repair

Jordan's wagon the previous week. There was nothing to do but try to tie it up and hope it held as far as Boise, where they could get a new one made.

After several failed attempts, Matt was ready to give up. "I've tried lashing it with rope as thick as my arm, and splinting it with slats from the tail guard. I even tried using rawhide, and Jade's long-handled skillet as a brace. Nothing seems to work."

Jordan cast a disgruntled look at the offending axle. "I suppose we still have a couple of options left. If we remove the rear wheels, reverse the wagon, and rig the tongue to the rear, perhaps the team can pull it backwards, like a two-wheeled cart. That, or we can load everything into one wagon and leave this one behind. Of course, if it comes to that, Jade will have to abandon her copper tub and we'll probably never hear the end of it."

When Jade learned this, she was determined to find a way to save the wagon and her precious tub. Dragging Bliss beneath the wagon with her, the two women surveyed the problem from every possible angle.

"Ye know, there's a solution naggin' at the back o' me mind, but I just can't get a firm grip on it," Jade mumbled in dire exasperation.

Bliss agreed readily. "I know. It's like an itch you can almost, but not quite, reach."

"Horse feathers!" Jade grumped. "If ye can splint a man's leg, ye'd think ye could do the same with an axle!"

"Sure, but how do ye bind a broken . . . middle?" Bliss asked quizzically.

"With a stiff corset?" Jade suggested with dry irony.

Both girls stared at each other in mute wonder, until both exclaimed at once. "With a corset!"

"Of course!"

"That's it! Why didn't we think of it sooner?"

Naturally, the men thought they'd both lost their minds. "I've never heard of such an absurd idea," Jordan proclaimed.

Matt concurred. "It'll never work."

"Just try it," Jade implored.

Bliss added with a smirk, "Yeah. What have you got to lose but your dignity?"

To the amazement of one and all—and the vast amusement of most of the men of their group—the corset seemed to provide just the extra support they needed. With the axle heavily splinted, and wrapped with rope and leather, the corset was laced tightly over the lot, both stiff and pliant enough to endure the bumps of the trail.

However well it performed, it was ridiculous to behold. The rigid bust section of the corset made the axle resemble a thin, long-necked woman suspended facedown from wheel to wheel and clad in the most risqué garment of scarlet satin trimmed in black lace. It became a sport for the men to ride past, give a long, low whistle, and make some ribald jest about the "buxom beauty beneath the wagon."

Ludicrous. Embarrassing. Disgraceful. Nonetheless, that corset got them to Boise.

Boise offered a long-awaited and badly needed opportunity to stock up on dwindling supplies, repair wagons, replace worn parts, and exchange exhausted teams for fresh draft animals. Timber was plentiful, as was salmon, a particular pleasure to taste buds grown weary of antelope, beef, bacon, and the occasional rabbit or wild bird.

Here, too, were shops where Jade bought new boots for herself, Matt, and the girls. Their old shoes were almost worn through from treading the volcanic rock along the Snake River, and the mountains of Oregon still lay ahead. She also stocked up on bacon and beans, sugar and flour, and other staples. Then she treated Beth and Emily to a small sack of candy each. Their joyous faces were well worth the few cents extra on her bill.

On a whim, she added several sticks of butterscotch and cinnamon candy to her own bag. She left the store humming a merry tune, her smile one of pure delight. If Matt had thought licking ice cream from her body was delicious, he was sure to relish his two favorite flavors even more.

*   *   *

With no regrets, the travelers left the Snake River behind at a place called Farewell Bend. The terrain grew steadily more hilly. Three days later, they rounded Flagstaff Hill and looked down upon Baker City and the valley in which it was nestled. This was their first real glimpse of the Oregon they'd long imagined. Rolling hills, lush green grasslands, great stands of timber, and the Blue Mountains standing guard in the distance, the highest peaks still bearing the previous winter's snow as the emigrants sweltered in the late August heat of the lower valley.

"Glory be! That's a beautiful sight!" Matt declared.

Jade sighed wistfully. "I haven't seen that shade o' green since I left Ireland." She blinked back a tear. "Guess I didn't realize how much I'd missed it 'til now."

"I hope Oregon City is as pretty as this," Bliss added. "But even if it's not, it'll be nice to settle down in one spot again."

Everyone agreed wholehcartedly.

The Blue Mountains wore a verdant cloak of dense forests, and the first pioneers, some twenty years before, had been forced to hack their own route through the tall timber and thick undergrowth. Fortunately, these latter-day travelers found the trail well worn, though still extremely arduous. No sooner did they crest one mountain than half a dozen more loomed ahead, until there seemed no end to them. Teams and emigrants alike were being tested to the limits of their endurance, so weary that many dropped in their tracks, unable to go on until they had rested and regained a portion of their waning strength.

After that long, arid trek along the Snake River, it was strange to have a canopy of trees overhead—such heavy shade, in fact, that it was actually chilly at times, even in midday. Of course, the higher elevation also contributed to the lower temperature, and the wayfarers were glad that they were not trying to traverse this stretch in late fall, when the chance of snow would have been a real threat to their lives. Despite everything, they were making excellent time, and barring any major calamities, anticipated arriving in Oregon City sometime in early October, six or seven weeks from now. However, at the moment, their main concern was to survive this part of their journey, and it was a backbreaking mission, netting them few miles per day and requiring numerous rests.

During one of these many stops, Jade decided to take her mare for a short run. For the past few days, she had been so busy helping Matt coax and prod the oxen over the steep, circuitous terrain that Marvel had received little attention, and what exercise she got was not the right sort. What the little horse needed at this point was a good run, to work out the kinks and stretch her leg muscles.

Jade had just mounted and was riding along the perimeter of a small clearing when a party of ladies appeared before her, exiting from the bordering treeline. No doubt, they had been attending to private needs in the bushes, away from prying eyes. Among them were Nell Jansen, Charlotte Cleaver, and Gwen O'Neall. When Jade gave a jaunty salute, all but one woman waved or called out a friendly greeting.

Charlotte was less pleasantly disposed. Wrinkling her nose at the approaching rider, she exclaimed in a strident, perturbed tone, "Oh! Do get that animal out of our way! Unlike you, we don't have time to waste with frivolous amusements." She suddenly began to flap her apron. "Shoo! Move, you dumb beast!" she screeched.

Taken by surprise, Jade was unprepared when her usually docile mare gave an abrupt start of fright and shied away from the menacing white cloth. "Charlotte! Stop!" Jade cautioned nervously, trying in vain to calm her spooked mount while Charlotte continued waving her apron.

Nell added her own plea. "Charlotte, please! Have you no sense? It's dangerous to scare an animal that way."

This seemed to amuse Charlotte mightily, because she gave a shrill laugh, which only further agitated Marvel. The mare reared once, almost unseating her rider then and there—then bolted for the trees with Jade hanging on for dear life.

The next few minutes went by in a blur. Jade clung to the saddle, leaning far forward over Marvel's neck as the fleet little mare crashed through the thick underbrush. Low-lying branches clawed at Jade's hair and clothes, threatening to unseat her time and again.

One second Marvel's hoofs were thundering along the forest floor, and the next they were flailing for solid ground where none was to be found. Without warning, Jade found herself sailing over the mare's head, both she and her mount careening headlong down a steep, rocky slope.

❧❧❧ *Chapter 37* ❧❧❧

Trees flashed by at an alarming rate as Jade tumbled helplessly, instinctively grasping for anything that might slow her fall. Finally, she managed to clasp hold of a small pine, its trunk no thicker than her arm. She lurched to a halt, her arms feeling as if they were about to be torn from their sockets as they strained under the sudden jolt.

Breathless and frightened, she lay gasping for breath, her heart pounding as if to escape her chest. It was some moments before she was calm enough to begin to assess her situation. Slowly raising her head, she peered cautiously about. What she saw was not encouraging.

She was lying about twenty yards from the upper rim of a deep ravine. Though a number of trees dotted the slope, the grade was very steep, and layered with loose rocks and stones that would make climbing back up very hazardous. Some thirty feet below her, the gully seemed to run over another abrupt ridge—and how far it dropped off Jade could not tell. She only knew that she didn't care to find out by sliding off the edge.

She also knew that, scared or not, she was going to have to attempt to move into a more secure position. Immediately. Already her fingers were growing stiff, and beginning to lose their grip on the tree trunk, the only thing that was keeping her from tumbling farther down the treacherous bank. Slowly, carefully, she pulled herself upward, her boots scrabbling for purchase on the shifting pebbles. Her scraped elbows smarted as they incurred more abuse, but Jade ignored the pain. It was insignificant compared to what might happen with one false move.

With effort, she hauled herself to the upper side of the tiny pine and dragged herself into a sitting position, such that she could lean upon the tree and still maintain her hold on it. When her heart ceased drumming so deafeningly in her ears, she became aware of another sound, some distance below her. Her breath caught in her throat as she identified the agonized screams of a horse in pain. In her mind's eye, she could almost see the poor mare lying broken and bleeding somewhere on the lower slope. Tears blurred her vision, and she hastily blinked to clear them, not daring to free a hand from the tree to do so.

Then she heard another sound, faint at first but coming nearer. Miracle of miracles! It was Matt! Calling her name!

Jade's throat was so dry with fright that her first attempt to answer him came out as a hoarse squeal, little louder than the squeak of a mouse. She swallowed hard and tried again. This time her shout rang out strong and clear. Again and again she called his name, until at last he appeared at the rim of the ravine. Almost immediately, several other men joined him.

"Jade! Jade! Where are you?"

"Here!" she screamed. "I'm here! Matt, help me!"

His anxious gaze found her. "How seriously are you hurt, sweetheart?"

"Not badly, but I'm scared to move for fear I'll fall again!"

"Don't budge! Don't even blink! I'm coming down after you!"

"Be careful! These rocks just slide out from beneath yer feet."

He disappeared momentarily, then emerged again, this time with a rope tied around his waist. She heard him call to someone else out of sight, "I'm ready. Lower me slowly."

She watched worriedly as he worked his way toward her one slippery step at a time. It seemed an eternity before he reached her. Squatting cautiously beside her, he loosened the rope at his waist.

"All right, love," he crooned. "I want you to grab hold of me, let go of the tree, and ease yourself into the rope, in front of me."

"I can't! I'm afraid!"

"Come on, Aggie," he cajoled. "You can do it. I've got you. I won't let you fall."

It took every ounce of courage she possessed to let loose of the little tree that had been her sole lifeline. Somehow, with Matt's steadfast encouragement, she managed it, though her pulse skipped several beats in the process. In a matter of seconds, he had her placed before him, sheltered within his arms and the confines of the rope.

"Hang on now, and try to brace yourself with your feet if you can," he instructed. To those assisting them, he called out, "Haul away! Slow and easy!"

They had just started inching upward when a terrifying snarl grabbed their attention. Their heads swiveled as one to find a huge cougar just a dozen paces above and off to their right. It was glaring at them with bright golden eyes, its tail switching back and forth in agitation.

"Oh, dear Lord!" Jade gasped.

"Hush, darlin'," Matt whispered soothingly. "Just keep going, nice and steady."

"Matt!" she whimpered. "Can ye reach yer pistol if he decides to pounce?"

"I removed my holster so the rope wouldn't get caught on it. But don't you fret. That big cat is going to stay right where he is."

Her voice wavered precariously. "What makes ye so certain?"

"Remember the story of Daniel and the lions? Well, God is going to protect us just the way he did Daniel," he assured her.

"I'm not sure me faith's that firm," she murmured, her horrified gaze still trained on the crouching cougar.

"Don't worry. Mine is strong enough for the both of us."

To Jade's amazement, the cougar maintained its distance and let them pass unharmed. "If prayer works that well, ye might have tried it on the Indians."

"I did, honey. God just chose to resolve that problem in a different way."

With her few scrapes and bruises, Jade fared much better than her unfortunate mare. Jordan volunteered to descend the slope and put the poor animal out of its misery, but even as he was preparing to climb down, there rose an angry scream, an awful squeal, followed by the most dreadful silence. The hungry cougar, deprived of its human meal, had attacked the injured horse instead. By bullet or cat, the result was the same. Marvel was mercifully past her pain.

Nell Jansen was genuinely relieved that Jade had survived what could very well have been a fatal accident so much relieved, in fact, that she appeared at their campfire later that evening with supper in hand. "I thought perhaps you wouldn't feel up to cooking tonight," she told Jade.

She and Carl joined the Richards family for the meal, though Nell spent more time chattering nervously than she did eating. "I could throttle Charlotte for pulling such an idiotic stunt! My word, Jade! You might have been killed! I just can't stop thinking about it, or how horrible it would have been for Matt to lose another wife in much the same manner as he did Cynthia. Of course, Cynthia was expecting at the time, so that made her death doubly hard to bear."

"So is Jade," Bliss put in with a droll smile.

"Excuse me?"

"Jade's gonna have a baby, too."

Jade looked no less stunned at Bliss's pronouncement than Matt did. "Bliss, where did ye come up with such a fool notion?"

Her friend shook her head and grinned. "Don't tell me I'm the first to figure it out. You've been losin' your breakfast every morning for a week now. What did you think was causing it?"

Jade shrugged. "The mountain water? Those berries I ate a while back? A bad batch o' bacon?"

"No one else got sick," Bliss pointed out smugly. "And speakin' o' bacon, I've noticed you turn rather green while it's cookin'."

"The smell upsets me stomach lately, that's all."

Bliss shared a look with Nell, and both women nodded. "Honey, I'd start knitting booties if I were you," Nell suggested sagely. She blushed slightly, uncomfortable with speaking so bluntly in mixed company, but added, "Particularly if your monthly miseries haven't visited you in a while."

It was Jade's turn to feel color rising to her cheeks, a telltale sign that Nell's remark had struck a chord of truth.

"Well, I'll be darned!" Jordan exclaimed, clapping his stunned brother on the back. "I'd say this calls for a celebration!"

A silly, wondrous grin curved Matt's mouth. "Oh, Aggie!" he breathed. "This is marvelous news! You can't know how long I've wished for a child of my own. I love the other children dearly, but it will mean so much to me to have one of my own flesh and blood. And yours."

"I . . . I . . . I'm . . ."

"Flabbergasted?" Bliss supplied helpfully.

Jade laughed. "And delighted, and surprised, and just a wee bit scared all at once."

"You'll make a fantastic mother," Matt predicted. "Children adore you. And look at the way you've taken the orphans under your wing. Like a duck to water."

"Just the way Cynthia did," Nell piped up with a sorrowful sigh. "She was so loving and gentle, I just know she must have been thrilled at the prospect of granting Matt his first child, if she even suspected her condition." She turned her inquiry to Matt. "Did she say anything to you? Did either of you know before the accident?"

Matt's face stiffened noticeably. "Yes," he replied shortly. "In fact, she told me the same day she died."

"Oh, Matt! How awful for yc," Jade commiserated.

"Yes, but he has you now, and a new baby on the way," Carl stated on a more cheerful note.

Nell agreed readily, adding, "I'm happy for both of you, though I just can't get over wondering how Matt could go from someone like Cynthia to a woman like you." As several glares aimed her way, she amended hastily, "Oh, I certainly don't mean any offense, folks. It's just that Jade and Cynthia are so totally opposite in every way."

"Thank the good Lord for that," Matt muttered darkly.

Ignoring his interruption, Nell prattled on, enthusing about her favorite topic. "Cynthia was so proper, so modest, and so lovely it was almost a sin. I don't believe there was anything she couldn't do well, and everyone adored her."

Matt cast a glance at Jade's crestfallen face, looked back at Nell, and asked quietly, "How long has this been going on?"

"I beg your pardon?"

"How long have you, and others, been subjecting Jade to tales of Cynthia's perfection, offering comparisons and making her feel inferior in the process—while I remained blind to it all?"

Nell was taken aback. Bliss answered for her, glowering at the older woman. "Practically from the moment we left Missouri."

"Matt, I must apologize if I've hurt you or Jade, but I've said nothing that wasn't true."

Matt shook his head. "No, Nell, you never knew the truth, but maybe it's time you, and everyone else, heard it at last. I've held my silence too long, though I wouldn't speak up even now if Jade hadn't been made to suffer for your misconceptions."

Nell stared at him. "What on earth are you implying?"

Carl reached out and clasped his wife's arm. "Let the man talk, Nell. Listen and learn," he instructed her firmly. His sympathetic gaze met Matt's. "Go on, Matt. Enlighten her. I have a feeling I already know what you're about to say."

Matt took a bolstering breath and launched into his grim explanation. "Cynthia was not the paragon of virtue that you have made her out to be. Far from it. Oh, she put on a wonderful act, which fooled almost everyone she met into believing that she was the sweetest, most gracious lady they had ever met. The truth is quite a different matter. On the outside, she was, indeed, beautiful to behold; but on the inside she was cold, scheming, spoiled, and selfish beyond redemption.

"When I suggested starting a family, she protested. She didn't want to ruin her perfect figure. When I decided to take in orphans, she threatened to divorce me. Only her father's ire stopped her. Still, from that day forward, she moved into one of the guest rooms and refused to share a bed with me. When the orphans arrived, she shunned them as well, and if not for the servants who helped me, those homeless children would have gone hungry and in rags, with no affection afforded them."

"Matthew Richards, that's a bald-faced lie!" Nell exclaimed, unable to hold her tongue a moment longer. "With my own eyes, I saw Cynthia lead those youngsters into church, smiling tenderly at them, straightening their new clothes, sitting beside them in the pew, helping them find the songs in the hymnal. She couldn't have been more loving toward them."

"All for show," Matt assured her somberly.

"I think not," Nell argued. "Moreover, at the risk of further exposing your false claims, if Cynthia did not share your bed, how, pray tell, did you manage to get her with child?" she asked with a superior huff.

"I didn't," Matt stated flatly. "The child she was carrying when she died was not mine. She admitted it to me quite brazenly, just before she rode off to see her lover and tell him the glad tidings of his impending father-hood."

"Oh, my stars!" Nell gasped. "Oh, dear me! I just can't fathom it! It can't be so!"

"Believe it, Nell," Carl said. "Until this moment, I've never told a living soul, but Cynthia once attempted to entice me with her wiles, and got extremely nasty when I rebuffed her advances. So you see, I know full well that Matt is telling the God-awful truth about her."

Jordan let out a low whistle. "Little brother, I hate to speak ill of the dead, but it sounds to me as if you are well rid of your first wife."

"Oh, Matt! I'm so sorry!" Jade declared softly, her hand reaching out to gently enfold his.

His eyes became tender, the torment leaving them, as he turned his gaze toward her. "My dearest heart, you have nothing whatever for which to be sorry. Your love is the most precious gift I have ever received, and it has more than made up for any unhappiness that came before-hand. My purpose tonight was not to gain your sympathy, or anyone else's. Rather, it was to bring you comfort, sweetheart. Don't ever let anyone berate you again, for you are a thousand times the lady Cynthia professed to be. Generous, honest, loving, everything I could ever want in a mate. Every day of our lives, I'll thank God for you."

At last, after nearly a month's toil, the Blue Mountains were behind them, and the emigrants gratefully head-ed their wagons toward the southern banks of the great Columbia River. It took them three more days to reach the river and an additional three, following its winding course westward, to arrive at the The Dalles. The name of both a fort and a tiny town on the Columbia River, The Dalles came from the French word that meant "the trough." Since this was a point in the river where the water narrowed between two huge boulders and spilled over a series of rapids, the name was appropriate.

This was also the juncture of the Barlow Road, the overland route through the Cascade Range and around the base of Mount Hood to Oregon City. Before the road's construction in 1845, pioneers had had little recourse but to sell their oxen, barter for or build rafts, and continue down the dangerous Columbia River by boat, since there was no passable road along the riverbank at this stretch. Many a life had been lost traversing the rapids between The Dalles and Portland in those earlier years. Sam Barlow's route offered a safer, if much slower, alternative, though portions of it were considered to be the worst, most arduous sections of the entire Oregon Trail—made all the more difficult because by that point both teams and humans were nearly robbed of their last measure of strength.

In this early fall of 1867, the weary westward travelers had the same choice, though by now the rapids were regularly navigated by adventurous steamboat captains. These dauntless pilots had been daring their luck for nearly a decade, with astounding success and surprisingly few mishaps. Thus it was that Jade's three dearest companions set out to convince her that they should take the river route, which would get them to Oregon City in a mere two days, rather than take the longer roadway, which would add another two to three weeks to their journey.

"Think of it, Jade. Two days, instead of two long weeks or more, and we could be in Oregon City!" Bliss exclaimed.

"I'm not settin' one foot aboard a boat," Jade said firmly. "Ye don't know how sick I get."

"Oh, come on, Jade," Jordan cajoled, adding his own voice to the argument. "A couple of days isn't going to kill you. And it sure beats battling our way through those mountains."

"No. If I'd wanted to sail to Oregon, I'd have taken a boat in the first place."

"A ship, honey," Matt corrected mildly. "Boats on the rivers, ships on the seas."

She glared at him. "Ye know what I meant. Ye also know how much I hate crossin' rivers, let alone floatin' down one. With rapids, no less!"

"Sweetheart, it's perfectly safe. These steamboat pilots have been doing it for years."

"Not with me aboard, they haven't. B'sides, what would we do with our wagons and oxen and all our belongings?"

"We'll have to abandon the wagons, or try to sell them to someone taking the land route who needs one. We can trade or sell the oxen, and even my horse and Jordan's, if necessary. Once we reach Oregon City we won't need the wagon anyway, and we can always purchase new animals there, if we want. If there's enough room to store all our possessions, we'll portage them around to the boat dock and load them aboard. If not, we'll take what's most important and replace the rest when we get there."

She offered him a wary sneer. "I see ye've got it all worked out, as if I was gonna agree to this preposterous plan. Well, think again, Matt Richards. I'm not about to do it. We can either take the Barlow Road, like the more sensible members of our wagon train, or we can stay right here 'til we rot, for all I care."

Chapter 38

*E*arly the next morning, Jade was still harping on the same string, for all the good it did her. Even as Matt was gently urging her up the boarding plank she was loudly voicing her objections. "I don't like this one bit, ye know. I'm gonna be as sick as a dog, and it'll be all yer doin'. Yers and yer foolhardy brother's, and me fickle, brainless friend's."

"And we'll be with you all the way," he pledged. "Holding your hand."

"Ye'll more likely be holdin' me head," she predicted.

"Two days, darling, and I promise you'll never have to set foot aboard any sort of floating craft again. Besides, you even get to bring your copper tub with you. Doesn't that count for something? It was no easy chore, lugging that monstrosity along that slippery footpath to the docks, you know."

"A fat lot o' good it's gonna do me when I'm dead! I swear, Matt Richards, if anything happens and I drown, I'll haunt ye for the rest o' yer days."

He had the temerity to laugh at her. "And I'll treasure every minute of your ghostly company," he declared theatrically.

True to her word, the boat had no sooner launched from the dock than Jade turned seven shades of green and lurched for the tin pail that some kind soul had placed conveniently close at hand.

"Good grief!" Jordan grimaced. "If she's this bad now, what's she gonna be like when we hit the rapids?"

"We'll find out soon enough, I suppose," Matt said. "I imagine motherhood has something to do with her touchy stomach as well, which makes it twice as hard on her. But that is also one of the primary reasons I want to get to Oregon City as soon as possible, with the least amount of strain. I don't want Jade to lose this child trying to cross the Cascades. It's frightening enough to think what that tumble in the Blues could have cost."

While Jade lay miserably on her bunk, Bliss took charge of the two girls. "Ye're the one who should be a mother, Bliss," Jade told her friend. "Ye're so good with the children."

Bliss's smile was wistful. "Someday, maybe, but I'd sort of like to be a wife first."

As Matt had promised, someone was constantly attending to Jade. Either he or Bliss, even Jordan and the little girls, took their turns watching over her.

Bliss breezed in midway through the first day to announce, "If you feel up to seeing a new face hovering over you, Gwen O'Neall offered to sit with you for a spell."

Jade groaned. "Merciful saints! Are they aboard, too? I'm beginnin' to think I've grown a second shadow and his name is Sean O'Neall! Why couldn't they have gone to California?"

"I asked Gwen that same question, though not in quite that way. She said Sean chose Oregon because the land was good, the price right, and it sounded more like Ireland, from all he'd been told."

"Well, I can't fault him there. It is every bit as lush and green, and I hear the climate near the coast is similar." She sighed wearily. "If we're lucky, maybe he'll get so homesick he'll want to go back home. It'd be a blessin' to have half the world separatin' him from me."

Those periods when they were "shooting the rapids" were the worst. The boat would pitch and rock and shake as if in the throes of an epileptic fit—and Jade's stomach tended to lurch in rhythm with the plunge and roll of the deck. By the end of the first day, she felt like a wrung-out mop and knew she looked little better. Dark circles ringed her eyes, and weak tears dripped steadily down her pale cheeks. She was pathetically grateful when the boat tied up to the shore for the night, awaiting daylight to negotiate the final miles of their river trip the next day.

The following morning, Jordan was so jolly that Jade could have thrown him overboard. "Are you sure you don't want to go out on deck?" he asked her. "It's a glorious day. We've hit a calm patch, and the sun is dancing on the water until it resembles an avenue of sparkling jewels. The air is so fresh and clean, it makes you feel like singing."

"Please, spare me that at least," she begged. "Matt, hie yer brother out o' here, will ye? I don't know how much longer I can stand his good cheer."

Matt laughingly obliged. Not long afterward, Jade suggested that Bliss take the girls out for a walk. "They need to get out o' this stuffy room and work off some o' their energy," she told her.

"Will you be all right by yourself?"

"As long as I've got me bucket, I'll manage. B'sides, I could use a bit o' privacy while I'm about it."

"If you're sure. At any rate, we won't be long. Once you've seen one deck, you've seen them all."

"I know. It was a long way from Ireland to Richmond."

Soon Jade's stomach settled, and in the warm, quiet room, drowsiness overtook her. She was nearly asleep when she heard the door to the cabin creak open. Too tired to raise her head to see which of her caretakers had returned, she ignored the slight noise—until Sean O'Neall's soft brogue assaulted her ears.

"I thought I'd find ye in such pitiful straits," he said, chuckling. "Ye'll never make a sailor, Jade Donovan."

Jade's eyes popped open, and she struggled up on one elbow. "Me name's Richards now, and ye can leave just the way ye came, thank ye, or I'll start yellin' me head off. If Matt catches ye in here pesterin' me, he'd be more than willin' to break yer nose again."

The grin he offered was purely evil. "Go ahead and holler, darlin'. Yer protectors are all outside, where the wind is blowin' and the water's splashin' over the wheel loud enough to drown out any puny objections ye might have. Not to mention all the noise the engine is makin'. Ye can screech 'til ye turn blue and they'll never hear ye."

Like most of the men traveling the trail, Sean had taken to wearing a pistol on his hip. Now he calmly began to loosen the gun belt from his waist. He tossed it carelessly to the floor, his hands returning to work at the buckle of the belt to his britches.

"Get out!" she shrieked, scooting as far away from him as she could manage on the tiny bunk.

"Not until I get what I came after. I've been cravin' a piece o' yer sweet tail for too long now, and this might be the last chance I get for a while, though I imagine, livin' in the same town, the opportunity's bound to crop up from time to time in the future."

"I don't want ye, Sean. When are ye gonna get that through yer thick Irish head?"

He laughed. "It doesn't bother me if ye want it or not, luv. 'Tis what I'm needin' that matters here and now."

"Spoken like the selfish swine ye are and always will be," Jade spat out more bravely than she felt. Her narrowed gaze swept the tiny room. It was so small that she stood no chance of making it past him to the door. He had her successfully trapped, and his malicious smile told her he knew it full well.

Aside from Sean's gun, which was out of reach, there was nothing she could use for a weapon. Except her slop pail. Jade lunged for it at the same moment Sean pounced at her. The bucket skittered harmlessly across the floor.

As Sean came down upon her, Jade let loose a mighty scream. He was lying over her, his hands grabbing at her skirts, his mouth groping for hers as she strained to push him away. She wriggled one arm free and brought her nails up to rake viciously at his face. They gouged deep into his cheek, near his right eye.

With an enraged howl, he reared back, one hand rising to rub the bleeding wound. "Ye bloody bitch!" he roared. "Scar me face, will ye?"

In the next instant, his fist pounded into her jaw. Sparks of bright lights danced before her eyes, the pain so intense that Jade feared she would faint. Her ears were ringing so loudly she scarcely heard him say "If ye'd stop fighting me, I wouldn't have to be so rough with ye. After havin' that prudish preacher plow ye all this time, ye should be grateful to have a real man b'tween yer legs."

Neither of them heard the door fly open. It wasn't until Bliss threw herself at Sean's back, screeching like a mad-woman, that they were aware of anyone else's presence. Sean rounded on his attacker, fists swinging. Bliss placed one well-aimed kick at Sean's crotch, just as he gave her a forceful shove that sent her flying across the room. Her head hit the opposite wall with a sickening thud, and she slid silently to the floor.

Jade saw her chance and took it. While Sean was hunched over, moaning and grabbing at his throbbing male appendage, she slid from the bed and scrambled for his gun.

She had it half out of the holster. Sean now had his arms outstretched, reaching for her and the gun belt. This was the portrait they made as Gwen spoke from the open doorway, her voice eerily calm. "Don't bother, Jade. Let me have that pleasure. Lord knows, I've earned it."

Before either of them could move, Gwen's little derringer spat out a single missile. The bullet hit Sean square in the forehead, making one small, obscene hole just above the bridge of his nose. For a moment he simply stood there, staring at his wife in stunned disbelief. Slowly, his knees buckled beneath him and he crashed onto his face at Jade's feet.

Jade was quivering so violently that her teeth were chattering. "Is . . . is he dead?"

"If he's not, I've still got one more shot left in this thing," Gwen replied, sounding dazed now that the deed was done.

Abruptly, her legs gave out and she sank to the floor next to Jade, the two of them huddling together in trembling reaction.

That was how Matt and Jordan found them when they came dashing into the cabin. Jordan rushed immediately to Bliss's side, while Matt hunkered down next to Jade and Gwen. "Are you two all right?" he asked anxiously.

"We're a darned sight better than he is," Gwen stated shakily, waving her tiny gun toward her fallen husband.

"Jade?" Matt questioned, his eyes searching her ashen face. "Honey? Talk to me."

Jade felt as if her brain were swimming in mush. Slowly she turned toward Matt. "I'm fine. Just dizzy. And my face hurts. How is Bliss?"

Though his main concern at this moment was his wife's condition, Matt spared a glance toward the other side of the room where Jordan cradled Bliss in his arms, his face grim. The woman was moaning pitifully, just starting to regain consciousness. As she realized that she was not lying on the floor, that she was now held firmly in a strong embrace, Bliss panicked. In those first hazy seconds, she thrashed feebly, trying to fight her way free of his arms, mistakenly believing it was Sean O'Neall holding her fast.

"Hush, honey," Jordan crooned. "It's all right. I've got you. You're safe."

Bliss quieted at once. "Damn, my head hurts!" she groaned. "It feels like it's split open."

"That's understandable, considering the size of the lump on the back of it," Jordan told her.

Bliss squinted up at him. "Where's O'Neall? And Jade?"

"She's sitting right here, and she's just fine," Jordan said, praying that he was correct in his assumption. "O'Neall's dead."

"How?"

"His wife shot him, and it's a damn good thing she did, or I would have." Jordan cuddled Bliss close to his heart. "Lord, woman! You gave me quite a fright! When I stepped into the room and saw you sprawled on the floor, as still as a corpse, I thought I was going to die! Don't you ever scare me like that again!"

Bliss started to smile, but the result emerged as a pained grimace. "It's not like I did it on purpose, you know. I didn't exactly set out to get my brains rattled."

"I can see I'm gonna have my hands full trying to keep you out of trouble for the next fifty years or so," Jordan said with a crooked grin.

"You gonna be around that long?" Bliss countered breathlessly.

"You bet your sweet buns I am. Are you ready to settle down to one man for the rest of your life?"

"I was just waitin' for you to ask me, sugar."

"I'm asking. Will you marry me?"

Bliss sighed joyously, her arms curling around his neck, her lips seeking his. "Try stoppin' me."

Jade blinked back tears, her gaze locking with Matt's. "At least somethin' good has come o' this mess," she murmured. She rested her head on his shoulder for a moment, then gathered her strength and pushed herself free of his arms. "See to Gwen, darlin'. The poor woman looks as if she's about to expire."

"As soon as I get you back to bed and properly settled," Matt agreed. He drew a deep breath and again asked the question he feared most. "Did he hurt you, sweetheart?"

Jade knew what he was asking. She shook her head. "No. Bliss came in time," she assured him gently. "And Gwen. But if ye could send the girls to fetch a cool cloth for me face, I'd sure appreciate it. And me slop pail. And get me off this dadburned boat!"

Never was there a sweeter sight to behold than their first glimpse of Oregon City. Others might not have thought it so inviting, but to these travel-weary emigrants it rivaled the gates of Heaven. Because Oregon City was built on the terraces of a basalt bluff, the bustling town consisted of two separate levels. On the lower section, adjacent to the river, was a thriving business district abounding with shops, factories, mills, offices, hotels, and a few homes. The bulk of the residential area claimed space on the plateau a hundred feet above, accessible by steep streets that seemed to go straight up and long flights of wooden stairs for foot traffic. From their lofty perch, homeowners had a bird's-eye view of the Williamette River and its fifty-foot falls on one side, and depending on how they were situated, many could behold majestic snow-capped Mount Hood, which stood like a sentinel to the east.

On the dock, near which stood several mills—all utilizing the falls for power—they hired wagons from the livery stable to transport them and their belongings to one of the local hotels. In addition to various other stores and shops, as they rode through town they noticed a post office, half a dozen churches of various denominations, a printing company, a newspaper office, a photographer's studio, a schoolhouse, a library, even a furniture factory. And a jailhouse.

One of the first orders of business, after getting themselves installed in the hotel, would be to contact the local authorities and see about getting Gwen cleared of any charges that might result from killing Sean. Then they could get on about the job of finding a permanent place to live.

Bliss glanced around and commented, "Compared to Richmond or Savannah, I reckon Oregon City leaves somethin' to be desired, but for my money it'll do just fine."

"It's a little rough around the edges yet, but I imagine this town will meet our needs," Jordan agreed. "And if I decide being a farmer is not the ticket, I can always try my hand at something else. Should I find myself longing for more adventure, maybe I'll apprentice as a steamboat pilot, get my license, and ply the river. Shooting those rapids really got my blood up."

Jade gave a shudder. "I've had all of that brand of excitement I can stand, thank ye. At this point, I wouldn't care if I had to live in a hut in the midst of a pigsty as long as it was on firm, dry land."

"I doubt it will come to that," Matt said. "And don't forget. If we hadn't taken the steamboat, we'd still be hacking our way through the Cascades, like the rest of our fellows who decided to take the land route. They won't arrive for another two weeks or more, and will be lucky to secure winter quarters before the fall rains start. Some of them will have to live in their wagons and tents while they build their homes."

"What about us?" Jade asked worriedly. "We don't even have our wagons anymore, and it's too costly to stay in a hotel for very long."

Matt gave her one of those serene smiles she was coming to know too well, though his blue eyes twinkled with tender, mocking amusement. "Faith, sweetheart. The Lord will provide."

As usual, Matt was right. Within a week and a half, an elderly widow contacted them at the hotel. Bertha Brown had a big old farmhouse with six hundred and forty acres at the northeast edge of town, and she was willing to sell it for a reasonable price. She and her husband had farmsteaded there when Oregon was still a territory. Having outlived her spouse and two sons, Bertha could no longer manage the place on her own. She was ready to cut her losses, buy a smaller house in town, and try to make the proceeds stretch through whatever years remained to her.

Matt had a better idea, one more ideally suited to everyone. "If you will reduce your price, we'd be willing to let you stay on at the farm for the rest of your life. The only thing I would ask is that you help Jade run the house for as long as you are able."

Bertha was more than pleased with the bargain, as was Jade, for the widow claimed to be an excellent cook and had no qualms about sharing her lodgings with a houseful of noisy orphans. Within a week, they were installed in their new home, with plenty of space for all and room to spare for more homeless children. Jordan and Bliss also moved to the farm, and were already planning to build their own house on the property, just a short distance from Matt and Jade. Most of Bertha's furnishings remained in place and were heartily appreciated. The additional items they needed were purchased from local merchants or ordered from the furniture factory in town.

That first evening, the new residents gathered on the porch to survey their new property. The sun was setting to the west, turning the river to rippling shades of red and gold. To the east, the vibrant rays reflected off Mount Hood, transforming its snowy crest into a gleaming copper dome. All about them, they watched as twilight began to settle peacefully on the fields and orchards surrounding the house.

Matt cuddled Jade close to his side. Drawing a deep breath, he said softly, "It's a good place to set down roots, deep in this fertile soil. A good place to raise our children."

Jade sighed contentedly. "Home, sweet home. At long last."

A chorus of voices echoed a fervent "Amen!"

Chapter 39

*I*t was Christmas week. Jade could scarcely believe it. How these last three months had flown! And what changes they'd wrought in their passing.

Jade pulled the pan of butterscotch cinnamon rolls from the oven, sniffing in appreciation as she noted that they were done to perfection—and by her own hand, at that! Tilda could not have done better, even in her newly opened bakery. Certainly, Matt would applaud his wife's most recent culinary accomplishment. She could almost picture his delight.

The hall clock rang out the half hour, and Jade pulled herself from her musings. Matt would be returning any minute now from the docks with their houseguests, and she could hardly wait. They had received an unexpected telegram from Peaches just last week. She and Will Sutton were coming to Oregon City to spend the holidays with them.

Jade dusted her hands on her apron, wondering if she had time to dash upstairs and run a brush through her flyaway curls. Through the kitchen window she caught a glimpse of Jordan as he wandered through the orchard, undoubtedly trying to decide which trees he should prune next spring and which he wanted to graft in his efforts to produce different and more succulent varieties of fruit. He was becoming quite the botanist these days, and Jade had a notion that the "call of the river" would never lure him away from his current interest as a gentleman farmer and fruit grower.

As childish laughter echoed down the hall from the

386

front parlor, Jade smiled. Bertha and Bliss were helping the youngsters put the finishing touches on the Christmas tree Matt and Jordan had cut the day before. Their small family had grown by leaps and bounds in the past few weeks. They now had a total of seven orphans residing with them, and half a dozen other children whose parents boarded them with the Richardses while they worked. Matt had his hands full these days, running both the farm and the orphanage and its school.

Jade was no less busy. From morning till night, and often later, her days were filled with the varied demands of a wife and mother. She'd long since lost count of the number of knees she bandaged, noses she wiped, diapers she changed, and stories she told. This on top of the laundry, cooking, cleaning, and heading up the new church choir. There was never a dull moment, and she didn't know how she would have managed without Bliss, Bertha, and Beth, who was still her best little helper.

Jade shuddered as she realized how close she'd come to losing Beth a short time back. A farmer and his wife from farther down the valley had stopped by the orphanage and had taken a shine to Beth. They'd seriously discussed adopting the girl, and Jade and Matt had nearly agreed. Until Jade had witnessed the lascivious gleam in the man's eyes as they rested on Beth's body. In rare form, Jade had nearly tossed the man out on his ear, while Matt looked on in confused astonishment.

"What's gotten into you, Aggie?" he'd asked when the offended couple had gone off in a huff.

"Didn't ye see how that fellow kept starin' at Beth, like he was undressin' her with his eyes?" she railed. "I've seen that look too many times not to recognize it. 'Tis the same one me uncle Tobias used to give me while he was contemplatin' how to get me trapped in the pantry without me aunt knowin'."

Matt blinked in surprise. "No, I didn't notice that Mr. Tate was regarding Beth in such a manner. But I'm certainly glad you detected it before we let her go off with them. Lord, I'd never forgive myself if I placed one of these children into the wrong hands and some harm came of it. And all because of my lack of perception."

"Don't fash yerself, Matt. I probably wouldn't have known it, either, but for havin' to outwit Tobias all those years. We'll just have to be more careful about those folks who want to take the youngsters in the future."

Beth had stayed, and Matt and Jade had since adopted her themselves. Cute little Emily would have left them long ago but for the fact that Bliss and Jordan couldn't bear to part with her. They'd taken her for their own, and the child would be moving with them when their new home was finished. Jade was overjoyed that Emily would not be going far, that she would always be a part of their family.

Of the other orphans they'd gained, one other was very special. He was Gwen O'Neall's son, delivered nearly a month early, and born blind. Eli was two and a half months old now, and the doctor held little hope that the infant would ever see. He told them he highly suspected it was Gwen's bout with the measles that had caused the handicap.

Poor Gwen hadn't been able to cope with Eli's impairment. As soon as the baby's blindness had been diagnosed, she'd brought him to Jade and Matt. Tearfully, she had begged them to take him.

"I realize this is a lot to ask of you both, especially considering that he is Sean's son. But I simply cannot keep him." She dashed a tear from her eye. "I've decided to go back east and live with my parents, to make a fresh start, perhaps to marry again. As awful as it sounds, I don't want to take Eli with me. To be perfectly frank, I'm not certain I could deal with his problem for the rest of my life, especially in light of the fact that I detested his father so much that I killed him. Eli would be a constant reminder of Sean, and I'm afraid I'd come to resent him. I'd much rather see him in a loving home, with people to care for him."

Despite herself, and the way she'd felt about Sean, Jade

had quickly come to adore Eli. So had Matt. They doubted they would ever find anyone to adopt him, but that didn't seem to matter now. For however long Eli was with them, he would never lack for affection or attention.

Jade's thoughts naturally veered to her own babe, due in just four months. Instinctively, her hand went to her burgeoning stomach. With Jade carrying so high, Bertha swore the child was bound to be a boy. The widow also claimed she was rarely wrong in her predictions. Jade hoped Bertha was right, for she dearly wished to bear Matt a son.

Once again Jade's mind had wandered. This time it was Bliss's joyous exclamation from the next room that brought her back to the present. "Jade, they're here! The carriage just pulled up front. Oh, my stars! Is that who I think it is? Jade! Jade! Come quick!"

Jade dashed into the hall just in time to see Bliss throw the door wide in welcome. Matt was ushering their guests inside, out of the rain. Confusion reigned as Bliss and Peaches hugged and kissed in a lively reunion.

Then Peaches spotted Jade. "Well, look at you! All fat and sassy!" she declared delightedly, throwing her arms around her pregnant friend. Jade's protruding stomach made the embrace somewhat awkward, and they came apart laughing.

Peaches reached behind her, grasping for something hidden behind her skirts. "I brought you a little Christmas present," she said mysteriously. "One I'm sure you're just gonna love."

Peaches shifted aside, and the sight that met Jade's eyes set her heart expanding in her chest and tears welling in her disbelieving eyes. She dropped to her knees, her arms outstretched. "Skeeter! Oh, Skeeter!"

The little lad bounded into her embrace like an exuberant pup. For long minutes, Jade held him tightly to her breast, her tears wetting the top of his head, rocking him and crooning to him. Finally he wriggled free and excitedly began to make odd gestures with his hands and fingers.

Jade glanced up in confusion. "What does he want? What's he doin'?"

"He's talkin' to you, sugar," Peaches explained with a wide smile. "With his hands. Makin' words and letters and such."

"Well . . . what's he sayin'?"

Peaches turned to Will. "You tell her, darlin'. The kid's movin' too fast for me to follow."

"He says how much he loves you. How much he missed you, and how glad he is to be back," Will interpreted.

Matt was astounded. "How did you know?"

"Sign language," Will explained, grinning. "The Indians use it all the time, and over the years I've caught on to most of it."

"But how did Skeeter learn it? Did ye teach him?" Jade asked curiously.

Will shook his head. "He learned it from the Cheyenne. That's where he's been all this time, or most of it, until this past week."

Peaches took up the tale. "As near as we can figure from what Skeeter told us, he was wandering around lost. Then he fell into the river, just like Will thought he had, and was carried downstream. He must have been nigh on to drownin' when an Indian brave happened along, fished Skeeter out of the current, and took him back to his village."

Jade's eyes widened in horror. "Begorrah! I can't stand to think what they must have done to him!"

Will quickly sought to calm her fears. "He wasn't abused, Jade. Not in the least. Cheyenne, like most other tribes, adore children. Theirs or anyone else's. It didn't matter to them that Skeeter was white. And rather than look upon his affliction with revulsion or pity, as many of our race might, they'd consider him a very special child, one touched by the spirits."

"Will's tellin' you the truth, Jade. They fed him and clothed him and taught him how to talk with his hands, and brought him back to us without a mark on him."

"The Indians brought him back?" Jordan asked in

amazement. "Don't they usually keep any children they find?"

Will nodded. "Yes, but apparently Skeeter convinced them that he wanted to be with his 'real' family, as he puts it. And he had some help persuading them, didn't he, Peaches?" Will cast a reproving glance at his wife.

Peaches grinned, not in the least chastened by his harmless glower. "He sure did. Jade, Bliss, you're not gonna believe who brought Skeeter practically to the gates of the fort!" Not waiting for them to guess, she blurted out, "Fancy! And her warrior! God, I couldn't believe my eyes!"

"Fancy?" the two friends echoed.

"She's alive?"

"And well?"

"What did she say? Why didn't she come with you?"

Peaches held up her hands for quiet. "She's not here because she's still livin' with her Indian, I reckon. I didn't get a chance to talk to her." She went on to explain, "You see, I got into this habit of ridin' outside the fort, which just about drives old Will here crazy, for fear of my safety. That day, I was riding along when out o' nowhere I saw this kid runnin' toward me. The closer he got, the more sure I was it was Skeeter. Well, just about the time he reached me, I looked up and saw this pair of Indians on the hill, watching us. Only one of them wasn't an Indian at all. It was Fancy, dressed in buckskin, with her blond hair done up in long braids. I waved and called to her, and she waved back, but when I started up the hill toward them, they wheeled their ponies around and galloped off, leavin' Skeeter here behind."

"Are you sure it was her?" Jade asked skeptically.

Peaches nodded and slid a locket from around her neck. "Skeeter was wearin' this."

Both girls recognized the gold heart-shaped locket with their friend's name inscribed upon it.

"Did she look all right to you? Could you tell at all from that distance?" Bliss questioned in concern.

"She was smilin', if that says anything. And from what

Will managed to drag out of Skeeter, she's happy enough where she's at. She's livin' in her man's tipi, so Skeeter tells us, but we don't know if that means they're married or just sharin' a blanket, and Skeeter's too young to decipher the difference."

"He's also too young to guide us back to their camp," Will put in with mild exasperation. "A fact which pleased Peaches considerably. She also took her good sweet time returning to the fort with Skeeter. Long enough for Fancy and her warrior to escape undetected. Naturally, we never did find them. They'd covered their tracks too well for us to follow."

"I'm glad," Bliss announced bluntly.

"So am I," Jade added softly. She reached down to gently brush the hair from Skeeter's forehead. "I just wish I could thank her for helpin' to bring this wee lad back to us."

It was a happy, thankful group that crowded around the big oak trestle table that evening. Everyone was chattering gaily, including Skeeter, who was so busy signing with his hands that he almost knocked his cup of milk into Matt's lap.

"Where can we learn sign language?" Matt inquired of Will.

"If you're willing to put up with us, I've got a month's leave, and I'd be glad to teach anyone who wants to learn."

"Can we learn it in that short a time?" Jade wondered.

Will nodded. "Enough for you to start communicating fairly well with Skeeter. After that, he'll be able to teach you."

Peaches was bursting with more news. "We rode to Salt Lake City to catch the southbound stage, and I got to visit with Mavis. She said to say hello and to wish you a Merry Christmas, in case her letter arrives too late. She mailed it two days before we got there or I'd have brought it along with me."

"It came yesterday," Jade told her. "She sounds very

content, even with the twins runnin' her ragged."

Peaches laughed. "They're rascals all right, and growin' like weeds."

"I suppose, this time of year, you came the southern route and on up the California coast. Did you put in at San Francisco?" Bliss asked.

"That we did, and you'd better make up a spare room, if you still have one with this mob of yours. Lizette and John are about two days behind us, which means they should pop in here sometime Christmas Eve."

"Oh, dear!" Jade muttered, sliding a glance toward Matt.

Peaches arched an eyebrow. "Is that a problem?"

Matt shrugged. "It could be, if Lizette and John intend to share a bedroom under this roof. What you girls did on the trail was one thing, and entirely your own business, but this is my home, and I have a houseful of children to consider."

Peaches grinned back at him cheekily. "That's where you come into this, Reverend. Lizette and her gambler thought it would be nice to have you marry them on Christmas Day. 'Course, if you want to keep 'em honest, it looks like you'll have to stay up until midnight Christmas Eve to do it. Then you'd best marry 'em right quick, before they can head off to bed."

"And I'd lock the barn door until the 'I do's' are said," Bliss suggested with a chuckle.

Jade shared an intimate look with Matt. "Locked from the inside or out?" she questioned impishly.

Later that night, Jade and Matt lay snuggled in their bed, whispering to each other in the dark. "I can't believe how well everything has worked out for all o' us," Jade marveled. "And Skeeter! Oh, Matt! I thought we'd never see him again, and now here he is, safe and sound with us once more. 'Tis like a miracle!"

"A Christmas miracle," he agreed. His hand caressed her rounded tummy. "And this little one will be our Easter miracle."

His lips sought hers as he murmured, "Have I told you today how much I adore you, my irresistible green-eyed sprite?"

"Show me," she coaxed on a throaty sigh. "And I'll answer ye with all the love in me heart."